FRACTURED STATE

ALSO BY STEVEN KONKOLY

THE PERSEID COLLAPSE SERIES

The Jakarta Pandemic

The Perseid Collapse

Event Horizon

Point of Crisis

Dispatches

THE BLACK FLAGGED SERIES

Black Flagged Alpha

Black Flagged Redux

Black Flagged Apex

Black Flagged Vector

WAYWARD PINES KINDLE WORLD

GENESIS SERIES

First Contact

Last Betrayal

Sanctuary

FRACTURED STATE

STEVEN KONKOLY

THOMAS & MERCER

Text copyright © 2016 by Steven Konkoly
All rights reserved.

Published by Thomas & Mercer, Seattle

www.apub.com

Amazon, the Amazon logo, and Thomas & Mercer are trademarks of Amazon.com, Inc., or its affiliates.

ISBN-13: 9781503935587
ISBN-10: 1503935582

Cover design by Marc Cohen

Printed in the United States of America

To the heart and soul of my writing:
Kosia, Matthew, and Sophia.

PART I

PART I

Chapter 1

Elissa Almeda closed her eyes, wishing she could keep them shut for the rest of the short ride back to her townhouse. After spending the entire day in an increasingly hostile Capitol building, followed by a painfully long dinner with two of her least favorite colleagues in the House of Representatives, the last thing she wanted to do was field another round of questions. But she could feel him glaring from the dark shadows of the seat behind her.

"Don't you ever take a break?" she asked.

"Not while you're in DC," he replied.

She shook her head imperceptibly, opening her eyes to the well-lit, ornate facades of Embassy Row passing her window. As the SUV slowed to enter Dupont Circle, Almeda tapped the glass twice with her index finger, replacing the scene with a muted, dark-green image. The security agent seated across from her in the driver's-side captain's chair tapped his window moments later, dimming the rest of the backseat area.

"Thank you," she said, pausing awkwardly while she struggled to remember his name. No use. "The lights were giving me a headache," she added.

"Yes, ma'am," he said, flipping the compact optics attached to his communications headset in place against his face.

She assumed that the binocular-shaped device interacted with the window's digital tinting technology, restoring his view of the streets surrounding the SUV. Almeda still wasn't sure what to think of her new security team. They were slick, professional—and no doubt expensive. California was paying a fortune to protect her, and she wasn't about to protest or ask too many questions. Not with the secession issue raging across the state again.

"So, what prompts my chief of staff to stalk me while I'm having dinner?" asked the congresswoman.

"I just happened to be walking by Sonoma when your security team offered me a ride," said Jacob Preston.

"Uh-huh. Mr. Leeds, can we keep my schedule and whereabouts secret from Mr. Preston after hours?" she asked, smiling back at Preston. "I could use a few minutes to myself while I'm in DC."

Her new security chief looked back between the front seats to address her. "Do you want us to remove him from the vehicle right now? This is a stable part of town," he said dryly.

"I can't tell if he's serious," said Preston.

"He's not serious, and neither am I. Just making a point," she said, catching the faintest trace of a grin from Nick Leeds.

His name she remembered. She imagined not many women forgot it. His ruggedly handsome but weathered face suggested someone more comfortable out of the tailored suit that barely contained his muscular frame.

"Sorry I have to resort to hitching rides in armored SUVs to secure an uninterrupted conversation with you these days," said Preston.

"It's been busy. What's up?" she asked, turning her body as far as she could within the confines of her seatbelt.

"I don't think we can hold off taking sides much longer."

"I don't control the state legislature," said Almeda. "I told them that."

"You're a senior congressional representative with a nuclear triad plant and a nuclear desalination plant in your district," he said, "along with eight hundred thousand voters that have reelected you by a very wide margin for eleven terms. You have considerable sway with the state legislature."

"It's not that simple."

"We've run the polls over and over again. The Forty-Ninth District is not interested in cutting economic ties to the federal government. We're letting a vocal minority hold court, and if we're not careful, the sentiment might catch fire," he said. "Look at what Sean Jarvis is dealing with in his district."

"His district's demographic is a little more susceptible to secession fever."

"Fiftieth District's demographic is strikingly similar to ours."

"I meant economically," she added.

"Point taken, but he has two gigawatts in solar farms near the Anza Borrego Desert, which is enough to power most of the homes in his district," said Preston.

"Which they share with the state grid. We have twice that capacity with San Onofre alone, not to mention the runoff electricity created by the Del Mar plant."

Preston didn't respond immediately, which meant he was letting her reflect on her own statement. It was one of many annoying quirks that came with the thirty-nine-year-old political genius she'd hired in the wake of the ever-unpopular California Resources Protection Act. Preston had reinvented Almeda's platform leading up to the 2030 elections, single-handedly guaranteeing her return to Congress. She'd learned to live with his quirks.

"People can do the math," said Preston, "and they start to ask questions when the answers don't add up. That's what Jarvis is facing."

"The numbers add up. The state isn't energy independent, or water independent. California has a ways to go before we can start to seriously consider independence."

"That's not what people are hearing from the California Liberation Movement crowd," said Preston. "You don't want to play catch-up like Jarvis. I think it's better to get out ahead of this one. Send a strong signal to the state and surrounding districts. Ease some of our pressure here in DC. No point in making more enemies than necessary. How was your dinner?"

"The water is still free," said Almeda. "Ironic for a restaurant named after a county in California."

"Did you have the avocado salad?"

"Of course," she answered.

"That must have cost a pretty penny."

"I wasn't picking up the bill," she said.

Five years earlier, California had cut avocado and almond yields by half in response to the federal government's continued refusal to deal with the Colorado River issue. States upriver from California had been siphoning off far more than their share of water from the withering river for the better part of two decades. The US Department of the Interior's Bureau of Reclamation turned a blind eye to the water pipelines diverting water to the growing number of fracking fields expanding across the parched Great Plains. The cuts had been presented as a protest, but they were mostly a necessity. Almonds and avocados were two of California's most water-intensive agricultural products, outside of beef and other livestock.

"I hope that wasn't the extent of your protest tonight," he said.

"It was about all I could manage with those two. I liked it better when the lobbyists were open about their manipulation—not hiding behind my colleagues at five-hundred-dollar dinners," said Almeda.

A few moments of silence passed before Preston responded.

"One Nation Coalition's financial backers are getting really nervous about the secession issue. California's already an inhospitable business climate for a number of major industries."

"Nobody is losing money. They make it sound like they're destined for the poorhouse," she replied.

"It's not just the money. They stand to lose even more control over the regulatory environment in the state," said Preston. "It sets a difficult precedent, reducing their leverage in other markets."

"Which makes it harder to squeeze every dry penny out of those markets," said Almeda. "It's always about the money. At least they're consistent."

"And relentless. I'm pretty sure most of my appointments tomorrow will revolve around the topic."

"The session ends Friday," she said. "We'll test the waters when we get back to California. I don't see any good coming out of the California Liberation Movement's renewed activity either."

"None at all," said Preston. "I'll start working some angles."

As the car slowed for the final turn onto Thirty-Fourth Street, Nick Leeds's angular face reappeared between the front seats.

"Ma'am, a second team cleared your townhouse a few minutes ago. We'll escort you to the door and take Mr. Preston to his residence, unless you'd prefer one of my agents to conduct a walk-through with you."

"That won't be necessary," said Almeda.

She suspected her new security arrangement included twenty-four-hour coverage, though she had never seen a second car on the street. She had to admit that the recent increase in death threats made her a little wary. She'd lived with threats like these since she first ran for the California State Senate, nearly thirty-one years ago. They had become a routine part of her life as a public figure, a part she had mostly ignored—until this serious upgrade to her security detail.

"I'll be fine, too, Mr. Leeds," said Preston. "I'm just a few blocks away. I could use the fresh air."

"Understood," said Leeds, before quietly issuing orders through his headset.

The SUV straightened on Thirty-Fourth Street, maintaining a steady speed down the cramped one-way street. The driver abruptly stopped the vehicle when they reached the streetlight across from Almeda's townhouse. She tapped her window, revealing a redbrick facade with black shutters. There was a small concrete stoop with black cast-iron railings guarding each side of the short stairway.

The agent next to Almeda whispered, "Ready," prompting Leeds to open the front passenger door and step outside. Through her window, Almeda watched Leeds glance up and down the sidewalk, speaking into a microphone she assumed was embedded in his collar. The second security officer slipped out of the driver's-side rear door, closing it behind him before stepping back to assume a protective stance behind the SUV. A few moments later, Leeds opened Almeda's door, offering his hand to help her down. She caught a glimpse of a gun barrel protruding from the bottom right of his suit jacket.

"I got it. Thank you," she said, taking an exaggerated step onto the uneven brick walkway beyond the curb.

Preston followed her into the humid night air, meeting her at the bottom of the townhouse steps.

"Coffee at Saxbys?" he said.

"Six a.m. sharp," she answered. "Leeds, can you have a vehicle pick up Mr. Preston at five fifty-five?"

Leeds didn't immediately respond, which was odd. This man had a knack for anticipating her questions.

"Nick, do you think—" she started, freezing at the sight of her security chief in a combat stance, staring over the illuminated scope attached to his short-barreled rifle.

"Back in the vehicle," he hissed.

Almeda stared past Leeds, searching the shadows. "Is there a problem?" she asked, instinctively taking a step toward the safety of her townhouse.

A strong hand pressed down on her shoulder from behind, pulling her off balance, as a sudden snap fired past her head. A deafening fusillade from Leeds's weapon illuminated the tree trunk and red cobblestones next to the SUV. She tried to turn around to find Preston, but a firm shove knocked her to the ground behind the SUV's open passenger door. Almeda's protest was masked by a discordance of hollow thumps and cracks striking the other side of the bullet-resistant door.

A burst of gunfire erupted directly above her, showering her with red-hot shell casings. She flipped onto her back, screaming—just in time to see part of the second security agent's head splatter against the spider-cracked passenger-door window. Almeda pressed against the SUV as the agent's body crumpled to the cobblestone walkway in front of her.

Beyond the dead agent's twisted corpse, Jacob Preston lay in a motionless heap next to Almeda's townhouse stoop, one of his arms hanging limply through the bars of the metal railing. Her eyes darted from Preston to the front door, craving the perceived safety of the posh Georgetown home.

Almeda gripped the SUV's blood-slicked elbow rest and started to lift herself off the pavement when Leeds materialized. He stepped over the dead agent and jerked her to her feet with one hand, tossing her into the armored Suburban by her suit-jacket collar.

"We're leaving!" he yelled, firing a quick burst down the street.

"What about Preston?" she yelled, reaching for the door.

"He's gone," said Leeds, slamming it shut in her face.

Her fingers clawed at the leather interior, seeking the door handle. Muted thumps and sharp cracks filled the SUV's interior, seeming to come from every direction. The door didn't budge when she located the handle. *I'm locked inside,* she thought, raising her fists to pound on the sticky window.

A blast rocked the SUV, spraying her with warm chunks. Almeda whipped her head toward the front of the vehicle, glimpsing a three-inch hole in the supposedly bulletproof windshield. The door beside her opened, and she spilled onto the pavement at Leeds's feet, still processing the ghastly front-seat image. The driver's headrest and most of his head had been missing.

"Change of plans," said Leeds, grabbing at her free hand.

When she shook her head and buried her hands under her armpits, Leeds grabbed her shoulder-length hair and was using it to drag her toward the townhouse when the car door shattered from another explosive impact. She screamed and clawed at the ground to keep up, looking back at the mangled door she had moments ago assumed was safe cover.

Finally reaching her feet, Almeda stumbled over Preston's body, glancing down long enough to see his glazed-over eyes and a small bullet hole to the right of his nose. The grip on her hair eased, replaced by an insistent tug on her arm. Leeds pulled her into the front hallway and kicked the door shut, turning to a severe-looking female agent who had somehow materialized in the townhouse.

"There's a fifty-cal rifle to the south, covering the street," Leeds said, pausing to catch his breath. "At least three shooters in covered positions at street level. Two south. One north. Place a Claymore at the front door. How does the back look?"

"No good. Night-vision sweep picked up IR beams. They'll cut us down as soon as we step outside," the agent answered.

"We need a new exit," said Leeds.

"Already working on that. Downstairs," she said, removing a paperback-size, olive-drab object from a pouch attached to her tactical vest.

The female agent brushed past them, dragging one of the antique wooden chairs from Almeda's sitting room into the middle of the foyer. In one motion, she stepped up onto the ornately carved chair and jammed the olive-drab object into the plaster ceiling with two barbed spikes. On her way down, she flipped a switch, which momentarily bathed the hallway beyond the device in a faint green light. The woman pushed the chair against the wall and jogged away from the front door as Leeds yanked Almeda deeper into the townhouse.

"Stop it. You're hurting me!" yelled the congresswoman, reluctantly following him to the basement staircase.

"My job is to keep you alive. You can fire me when this is over," said Leeds, tightening his grip and pulling her down the staircase. "Watch your step."

"The basement is a dead end," she stated, before the smell of dust and smoke hit her nose.

"Not anymore," he said, triggering his weapon's attached flashlight.

The flashlight struggled to penetrate a thick layer of suspended dust at the bottom of the stairwell. A thunderous explosion rocked the townhouse above and behind her, showering them in wood and plaster fragments. A hand shoved her forcefully from behind.

"Let's go, ma'am," ordered a female voice.

Leeds pulled Almeda into the dust-choked darkness, moving them rapidly toward a flickering light on the other side of the narrow space. As they approached the light, Almeda realized the source of illumination couldn't possibly come from her basement. A deeper-sounding explosion rumbled, dropping lines of dust from the ceiling in front of Leeds's flashlight.

"What the hell was that?" asked Almeda. "Where the hell are we going?"

"My team is working on a new exit," said Leeds.

"We should wait here until the police arrive," said Almeda, pulling against his grip.

"DC Metro police scanners are quiet," said Leeds, ducking through a jagged hole in the basement wall. "Nobody is coming for us."

"How can they be quiet?" asked Almeda, hesitating. "Where the hell are we going?"

"Townhouse next to yours. Watch your head."

She stumbled into the adjoining basement, tripping over broken bricks and wooden debris.

"Why aren't the police responding? What happened to the Capitol police security detachment assigned to watch my residence?"

"Ma'am. We don't have time for this," said Leeds. "My backup vehicles are a few seconds away."

None of this made sense. Who would want her dead badly enough to launch a high-profile attack in front of her house? Her colleagues in the House? The industries pulling their strings? Or were they all the same thing? The timing of the attack couldn't be a coincidence. She'd just left a tense dinner meeting, no doubt sponsored by the same industries.

"How dare they?" she muttered. "Maybe it's time to cut our losses."

"Cut whose losses, ma'am?" asked Leeds, glancing furtively up the stairs leading into the adjoining townhouse.

"California's," said Almeda. "They just fucked with the wrong congresswoman."

Leeds stared at her for a few seconds, for the first time seeming unsure how to proceed. "If you discover One Nation is behind this attack," he asked, "will you support the liberation movement agenda?"

"What?" she responded, puzzled by his oddly timed question.

"If the One Nation Coalition is responsible for Mr. Preston's murder, will you side with the secessionists?"

They didn't have time for a drawn-out political discussion, so she answered bluntly.

"Mr. Leeds, if we uncover any connection between the ONC and this attack, I'll personally barge onto the statehouse floor in Pasadena and demand that California cut ties with the federal government—and seize every industry asset within the state."

"I really wish you hadn't said that," he stated, pointing his menacing weapon at her face.

She instantly understood the mistake she'd made with her brutally candid response.

"I should have known," she said, spitting in his face before he pulled the trigger.

_____

CHAPTER 2

Deep-scarlet ribbons of scattered clouds layered the horizon, dissolving into a dark-blue sky. Mason Flagg sipped Canadian spring water from a tall glass, admiring the day's quiet transition from his cliffside terrace. Occasionally, his glance dropped to the vanishing expanse of rippled ocean converging on the shoreline far beneath the balcony. He'd miss the view but not the state.

Nothing could save this place. Not the billions pumped into renewable energy projects by the state. Certainly not the untraceable millions transferred to Cerberus Group's bank accounts to fund Flagg's operations. None of it would make a shred of difference in the end. California faced a Malthusian-grade dilemma, solvable only by genocide—and the last time he checked, Cerberus didn't accept that kind of work. Not on US soil, anyway.

The satphone lying on the table next to him rattled the smooth glass top, turning his head toward the indigo-blue hologram hovering an inch over the phone's surface: "LEEDS."

"Answer call," he said.

The miniaturized earpiece fitted snuggly inside his right ear acknowledged the request, and the holograph changed to "ENCRYPTED CALL IN PROGRESS."

"I assume our friend has retired for the evening?" asked Flagg.

"That's one way to say it," replied Leeds, pausing for a moment. "We need to have a very private conversation."

Flagg stared at the softening colors in the distance, placing a half-empty glass of water on the white-marble tabletop. He took a deep breath before grabbing the phone and retreating to the home's main-level safe room.

"I'm inside," said Flagg, shutting the door to the eavesdropping-protected sanctuary.

"Almeda's dead," said Leeds. "Successful assassination attempt at ten forty-five eastern standard time."

"I'm not in the mood for games, Leeds," said Flagg.

"That makes two of us. We were ambushed in front of her townhouse. Preston and three of my agents are dead, in addition to Almeda."

Flagg's mind processed the implications. His continually updated feed of comprehensive—and extremely expensive—field intelligence reports didn't support the possibility of a California Liberation Movement–sponsored assassination attempt. One of the patrons funding Cerberus's operation got nervous about Almeda.

"I need to make a few calls," said Flagg. "Are you set for now?"

"We're not sticking around, if that's what you're asking. We took some pretty extreme measures to protect Almeda. Claymore mines aren't on DC Metro's approved list of personal protective gear, not to mention breaching explosives and armor-piercing ammunition."

Something didn't make sense. If the team used Claymores and breaching charges, Almeda must have made it into the house alive.

"You used Claymores? What really happened to Almeda?" asked Flagg.

"We only used one," said Leeds.

"You didn't answer my question."

"Someone fucked up big-time."

"I'm well aware of that," said Flagg. "I just want to make sure it wasn't you."

"Thanks for the vote of confidence," said Leeds, pausing before he continued. "Preston came through as predicted—and one of our patrons killed him right in front of her. Next stop would have been an impromptu press conference at the airport, declaring her support for the CLM. No way I could let her walk out of that house alive."

Flagg took a deep breath and exhaled. "That's why I assigned you to babysit Almeda. I never have to second-guess your decisions. What are we looking at in terms of forensics? Any way this traces back to the protective detail?"

"She took an unlucky bullet to the head when we tried to move her to the backup vehicle."

"Witnesses?"

"Negative," said Leeds. "Strickland was killed in the same gun battle. She was the only other agent in sight of the congresswoman."

"Two lucky shots?"

"Would you have preferred a different outcome?" asked Leeds.

"No. We can't afford any loose ends," said Flagg. "And I didn't just order you to deep-six the rest of the team."

"The rest of her team was out of sight, clearing a path to the backup vehicle."

"What did you do with Almeda's body?"

"The backup team just delivered it to the George Washington University ER," said Leeds. "They'll stay behind to answer questions. As far as they're concerned, I wasn't here."

"Perfect. A Cerberus cleanup team can handle the rest. I need you back in California immediately. I'm accelerating the timeline."

"I'm headed to Hyde Field. Should be airborne in forty-five minutes."

"I'll call you with instructions when I have them," said Flagg. "I expect you to hit the ground running."

"How much of an acceleration are we talking about?"

"I expect you to be here for the recovery phase of the Del Mar mission," said Flagg.

"Please tell me you're not talking about tonight?"

"California needs to wake up to a more pressing distraction than Almeda's assassination. See you in roughly eight hours."

Flagg disconnected the call and sat on the edge of the mahogany desk dominating the center of the room. He had a long night ahead of him. Leeds had extinguished the most immediate fire, buying them a day or so before the separatist propaganda machine kicked into full gear.

"Dial Raymond Olmos," he said.

"Dialing Raymond Olmos," his cell responded. "Encrypted call in progress. Connected."

"Good evening, Mr. Flagg," said Olmos.

"Ray, I need to move up the timeline for the Del Mar mission," said Flagg, pausing. "Is there any reason your team can't execute the mission tonight?"

Olmos paused a little longer than Flagg had anticipated. "Is there a problem, Ray?"

"Negative," said the operative. "We'll make it happen. Everything is pre-staged."

"Good. I'll meet you in Point Loma. What's your estimated time of departure?"

"Twenty-three hundred hours," said Olmos. "We'll make up the time on the water."

"I'll see you then. Call me immediately if you run into a problem."

"There won't be any problems, Mr. Flagg."

The call ended, leaving Flagg with a distinctly unpleasant task: he had to call his executive handler at Cerberus and explain the mess One Nation Coalition had just created.

CHAPTER 3

Mason Flagg checked the illuminated dial on his watch again. So much for the boats making up time on the water. They had already been pushing mission parameters with an eleven o'clock start. He walked up to Raymond Olmos, who was inspecting one of his divers' MK27 rebreather rigs.

"How much longer, Ray?" he said.

Olmos, a squat, muscular ex–Navy SEAL answered without turning around. "This is the last rig."

"I feel like I've already heard that a few times tonight."

"Well," said Olmos, "I didn't anticipate my equipment tech getting pinched at a police checkpoint."

"He shouldn't have been carrying a firearm under his front seat. We have specialized containers and procedures for that."

"He shouldn't have been pulled over in the first place. His car was supposed to be off-limits," said Olmos, still without looking up. "Shit like that makes the team nervous. It's not like we're in town for a yoga retreat."

Flagg stifled a laugh. "The last thing I'd want to do is make your team of hardened operators nervous. I'll see what I can do about preventing a repeat. Until then, make sure your team transports firearms in approved containers. Checkpoint detection systems are too sophisticated for the Ziploc-bag-under-the-seat trick."

Olmos slapped the dry suit–encased diver on the shoulder and turned to face Flagg. "We're ready to roll, sir."

"We need to make up some time," said Flagg.

"I'll take us over the horizon to throw off any of the Coast Guard radars that pick us up on the way out."

"Just stay out of obvious visual range from the coast. Even the navy's newest radars have a hard time detecting these," said Flagg, patting the grayscale-painted hull of the sleek, shallow-angled craft next to him.

The Mark X SDP (Stealth Delivery Platform) had been designed to bring SEALs ashore undetected in the most radar-infested maritime environments imaginable. The Department of Defense put the program on indefinite hold two years ago—leaving General Dynamics Marine Systems with a sizable, and unrecoverable, research-and-development loss. Eager to plug the financial holes in their rapidly declining maritime portfolio, General Dynamics sold the program to Sentinel Group, Cerberus International's parent corporation.

Mason Flagg had taken possession of two experimental craft several weeks ago, in an unobserved nighttime delivery to the beach outside of the building. The radar-invisible boats were instrumental to Cerberus's plan to turn the tide against the separatists.

"We'll scan for thermal signatures on the beach and in the structures," said Olmos. "That's the only time we're vulnerable to a beach sighting. Even then, we're barely visible."

"All it takes is one self-styled vigilante with a night-vision scope to cast some serious doubt on the accident," said Flagg, taking a step back. "Move your team out."

"Roger that," said Olmos, turning to face the team that had assembled in front of the boats. "Power up the winches! Open the doors! It's go time!"

The squad dispersed, each team member tending to a different launch task. Within seconds, the harsh, fluorescent overhead lighting switched to a deep-red glow, releasing a monochromatic cascade of crimson-and-maroon shadows. A briny ocean smell instantly filled the two-story structure, carried under the doors by a brisk sea breeze. The boats started to move forward before the doors had cleared the halfway point, causing Flagg to glance at Olmos.

"It's all synchronized to minimize the amount of time the doors are open. Never know who's watching—and from where. Can't be too careful, right?" asked Olmos, barely concealing a smirk.

The boats slid toward the rolling bay doors, their bows disappearing under the steadily rising hatches. A few seconds later, both of the MK X's vanished into the darkness, barely discernible to Flagg as dark, receding shapes.

"This is where I say *adios*," said Olmos, slapping Flagg on the shoulder before jogging into the night.

He hated when Olmos did that. There was no reason for the man to touch him, under any circumstances. It was a purposeful act of disrespect. Almost enough to have him replaced—which meant far more than just a handshake and "Good luck with your next job" at this point in the operation. Fortunately for Olmos, he was the best in the business—one of Cerberus's most effective operators. Replacing him was not an option at this point, unless he severely compromised one of their missions.

Recruiting morally ambiguous top-tier Special Operations types had become nearly impossible over the past decade. With Joint Special Operations Command's footprint shrinking every year, turnover within the elite units had come to a standstill. Technology was rapidly replacing the elite soldier, making Flagg's job difficult. Operations conducted by Cerberus simultaneously required the best warriors and the worst human beings. A rare combination in today's market.

A deep rumble joined the sound of crashing waves, drawing Flagg through the open bay doors into the crisp surf-side air. His shoes crunched the thin layer of fine sand blown over the expanse of asphalt extending to the water, as a second rumble interrupted the night on the western side of Point Loma. The rhythmic thrum of the boat's sound-damped engines faded into the pounding surf less than a hundred feet away.

To the untrained ear, the boats would draw little attention from the shore. The expanse of beach selected as their primary insertion and extraction point was located just outside the surf zone, in front of a hundred-yard stretch of nature conservation land. The nearest building or home was easily more than two hundred feet away. His only worry at this point was the timing.

Olmos's team was working on a highly compressed timeline, which left him uneasy. Once they started working on the seawater-cooling intake pumps, there was no turning back. The schematics and firsthand intelligence provided to the team made that abundantly clear. Even under optimal time constraints, they could not reverse any work they had begun. The divers had to complete the work, and they were already two hours behind the originally planned timeline.

The winches inside the building whirred to life, signaling a successful launch. Peering over the crashing surf, Flagg caught a shrouded glimpse of the boats speeding away. It was out of his hands now.

Flagg took a deep breath of the ocean air, shaking his head. He'd trade the smell of decaying sea life any day for clean, pine-scented mountain air. He really didn't get what people saw in this state.

CHAPTER 4

Nathan Fisher inhaled the scent of brewing coffee and rubbed his face, turning his head toward the fifty-inch flat-screen television mounted to the bedroom wall. The unit displayed the time in a muted-green color barely distinguishable from the rest of the screen. Three minutes before his alarm. *Shit.* He could have used the extra three minutes.

A problem with the desalination system had kept him up long past his normal bedtime hour. Four hours of sleep. Four hours short of what he typically needed to feel human. Careful not to wake his wife, Nathan slid out of the blankets, placing his bare feet on the cool laminate floor and rising to his feet.

"Be careful out there," Keira whispered, poking her head out of the covers.

He leaned over his side of the bed and softly kissed her lips. "Every time is the same," he said. "A few cars on the road. A checkpoint after the interstate exit in Del Mar. The same dogs barking near the beach. There and back in ninety-three minutes, if I don't stop for coffee."

"I already smell coffee," she grumbled.

"I thought I'd treat us to Starbucks," said Nathan. "Always tastes better on the outside. The stuff in the kitchen should hold you over until I get back."

"Sounds wonderful. Did you get the pump working?"

"Yeah, but the entire setup is showing signs of age. I don't know how many more times I can take the pump apart and put it back together without breaking something I can't fix. Some of the parts look rough."

"It's been more of a luxury than a necessity. We'll be fine. We've never relied on it. Make sure to grab us something sweet at the coffee shop," she said, pulling the blanket up to her eyes. "And be careful."

"Yes, ma'am," he said, kissing her forehead.

In the hallway outside of their bedroom, he paused at his son's open doorway. The room was pitch-black beyond the softly illuminated walls triggered by his presence. He concentrated on the room's silence, listening for the nearly imperceptible sounds of his son's breath—a habit Nathan had never broken since Matt was an infant. A parent's baseless paranoia that a child might fall asleep and never wake up.

The light vanished, his fleeting moment of stillness deactivating the glow. Ridiculous. At this rate, he wouldn't be surprised if they were a year or two away from seeing battery-operated light bulbs—100 percent grid-energy efficient! That was the mentality now. Keep it off the grid, no matter how ridiculous the idea, and there was no shortage of asinine ideas.

The night-light was just one of several hundred daily reminders showcasing the unintended, overreaching effects of the California Resources Protection Act. What started out as a well-intentioned effort to regulate and enforce the efficient use of key natural resources quickly devolved into a quasi–Big Brother state for residents. Nearly every aspect of modern life required the use of the state's natural resources in some way. A stark wakeup call for a population with a long history of ignoring Mother Nature's perils. Massive cities built on active fault lines. New developments constructed around hills and canyons hit year after year by wildfires. Houses built at the bottom of mudslide-prone slopes. A water-distribution infrastructure designed around century-old population figures.

But who was he to point a finger? Nathan was one of the more than forty-seven million people who continued to cling to the California dream—twenty years into the worst drought in recorded history. Even worse, he chose to move here knowing exactly what he was getting into. On the surface, it was a logical move for a water-reclamation engineer schooled at the University of California–Davis in the art of turning toilet water into drinking water, but in reality, it was a practical, well-calculated move, based on several years of observations across the United States.

While most of the country poked fun at the thought of Californians swiping their California Resource (CALRES) cards to buy groceries, gasoline, and lattes, or laughed at the notion that nearly every Californian drank recycled toilet water, they tended to conveniently forget a few sobering statistics that Nathan had made it his business to watch closely.

Like the fact that while more than half the population of the New Dust Bowl region had relocated to the nation's largest cities outside California, the state's domestic immigration reform and strict border-closure policies had prevented the overwhelming population flood experienced by the rest of the country. Close to eleven million domestic refugees had fled the states hit hardest by the drought and sandstorms, mostly migrating east to compete with several million displaced illegal immigrants for the few jobs the nation's struggling economy could support.

Meanwhile, California's gross state product topped $5.9 trillion, growing in the double digits for more than a decade, while most states saw a decline. Despite the drought, California thrived economically, an observation that wasn't lost on Nathan when he received multiple job offers after resigning from the Tucson Water Authority. Things were under control in California. Swiping a state-issued card to buy food and gas for the rest of your life seemed like a small trade-off for the security California seemed capable of providing.

Seemed. He had a contingency plan in case the situation imploded, which was part of why he was up at four in the morning.

He turned into the bathroom, the lights activating upon entry, and relieved himself. He closed the self-sealing toilet-seat lid when he was finished, pressing the "Liquid Recycle" button and eliciting a high-pressure hissing sound. Success. His fluids, along with a modest amount of water, had been evacuated into a small tank, the odor neutralized with an eco-friendly chemical agent. The liquid would be held for the next flush, eventually accumulating sufficiently in the recycle tank to handle one of life's more solid bathroom moments. A green light on top of the toilet announced its readiness to receive.

Nathan turned to the sink embedded in a marble countertop and waved his hands under the brushed-silver faucet. Cold water mixed with an undetectable quantity of antimicrobial soap sprayed onto his hands, filling the bottom of the sink before stopping. As he held his hands in place, the water instantly drained from the sink and was sprayed over his hands. The cycle could repeat endlessly if the manufacturers hadn't programmed a four-cycle limit to save electricity. Newer models offered three cycles of reused water. Reminder number three, and he hadn't walked more than twenty feet. Time to stop counting.

Lights followed him through the house, into the kitchen, where he pressed a button to override the motion sensors. Coffee was ready. The car was loaded. And he was three minutes ahead of schedule, giving him plenty of time to enjoy his coffee and catch some news before shuffling out. He swiped his phone from the kitchen island and selected the home-control application.

"Kitchen television. On," he said softly.

The monitor mounted above a low row of cabinets came to life, displaying a local news feed, which he ignored while fixing his coffee. He took a long sip of smooth espresso roast and turned to take a seat, his eyes catching the news banner at the bottom of the screen.

"Holy shit," he muttered, processing the banner.

Breaking News: California Congresswoman Elisa Almeda (R) assassinated in front of Georgetown residence.

"Volume. Medium," he spoke, slowly taking a seat while the broadcast came to life.

"*. . . amid rampant speculation that the attack was sponsored by anti-secessionist interests in Washington, DC. The attack, which occurred at ten forty-three eastern standard time, came on the heels of a high-stakes dinner meeting with Allen Rushby and Candice Montgomery, House representatives from Kansas with close ties to the One Nation Coalition. Anonymous sources claim that Congresswoman Almeda had been under constant pressure to support the ONC's stance upon her return to California. Officials from both congressional offices were unavailable for comment.*"

"Kitchen television. Off," he said, placing the coffee mug on the island.

Ten forty-five eastern standard time? Major news outlets probably had the story within the hour, which meant every Californian watching television or surfing the Internet last night knew about Almeda's assassination. The entire state could have descended into chaos while Nathan tinkered with a positive displacement pump in his garage. He thought about stepping out of his front door to see if downtown Mira Mesa was burning, but dismissed the idea. The early morning was quiet. No sirens. No angry voices. No different from when he stepped onto the patio last night to breathe in the crisp ocean air before going to bed. Not like the last time the secession debate gained momentum. They'd spent three long days waiting for the fires and riots to subside, wishing they'd moved to Michigan.

Still, Almeda's murder was bad news all around. She'd straddled the fence far too long, giving hope to the California Liberation Movement and scaring the shit out of the big-money folks who stood to lose a ton of money if California divorced the United States. Someone obviously got tired of waiting for her to take sides—setting a very dangerous precedent. Without a doubt, this wouldn't be the last desperate act to emerge from this political conflict.

The CLM had grown bolder over the past few years, attracting attention and gaining momentum through savvy media campaigns, attention-grabbing protests, and effective political lobbying. Like the One Nation Coalition, they appeared to have deep pockets, which some had suggested might be filled by foreign investors. Mexico's president had openly suggested that she would welcome a trade alliance, free of Washington interference.

Nathan sniffed at his coffee, no longer interested in drinking it. The whole issue soured him. He'd grown so tired of the endless ebb and tide of political arguing that he wasn't convinced California would be better off either way. One thing was for certain, though—if the conflict between the two factions intensified, living in California would become increasingly difficult, possibly dangerous. If he could cast the deciding vote today, he'd keep the status quo. The last thing he wanted for his family was the fear and uncertainty of a civil war, regardless of what either side promised.

Nathan glanced at the blank television screen, considering the immediate implications of Almeda's murder. Maybe today wasn't the best time to be hanging out too close to the Del Mar desalination center in the early-morning hours. They might be on alert and have extra security patrols combing the nearby neighborhoods.

Now he was just being paranoid. He'd never seen that before, even when the facility was overtly threatened by eco-terrorists.

Letting go of the warm mug, he stood on hesitant legs and considered waking Keira. No. She'd talk him out of making the trip, and he needed to go now, before Californians took the secession debate to the streets. If things got ugly, the San Diego County PD wouldn't hesitate to impose stricter restrictions on travel outside of approved residential zones. He wanted to top off their water supply before that happened.

CHAPTER 5

Nathan drove across Vista Sorrento Parkway, steering his car through an empty, unlit intersection onto the northbound ramp for Interstate 805. The moment his vehicle crossed the four-lane parkway, a soothing female voice filled the passenger cabin, accompanied by a visual alert on his windshield Heads-Up Display (HUD).

"You have exited Residential District Forty-Two."

"Thank you," he said flatly, continuing down the on-ramp.

"You're welcome," said the voice. "I noticed you are not taking one of several authorized routes to your work address of record. Is this trip official San Diego County Water Authority business?"

"No," he replied.

"Very well. The time spent out of your residential district will be recorded. Thank you."

"Yeah, you do that," said Nathan, merging onto the empty interstate.

In the distance, thinly spaced high mast lights activated sequentially, illuminating the northbound highway lanes as far as he could see. In his rearview mirror, darkness chased his car, as the interstate's digital processors raced to optimize the lighting needs of the highway based on a single automobile. From the road, it was both impressive and intimidating to think that a fixed interval of light followed your car. From above, in the sparsely traveled morning hours, it was nothing less than spectacular. Each car a beam of light threading the California highway system like electrical impulses. Each car tracked by GPS.

San Diego County was one of the first in the state to implement EcoTrak, a mandatory, vehicle-based "position management" system designed to encourage fuel conservation and support local business growth. Each family, based on the number of drivers, was given a fixed amount of time to spend out of their residential zone, with travel related to employment exempted.

In reality, the time limits were far less restrictive than they sounded, allowing citizens to enjoy a full day out of their zone every two weeks. With carryover hours permitted each month, it was easy to register and schedule an overnight trip within fuel ranges, or you could pay an exorbitant fee to add gasoline to your allotment. Modest fines were issued as an enforcement mechanism, and the incessant reminders helped modify the behavior of citizens.

"Merging onto Interstate 5. Three hundred and thirty-seven out-of-zone minutes remaining," he said out loud, beating the onboard computer system to the announcement.

"Correct. Thank you, Mr. Fisher," said the very polite voice.

Of course, EcoTrak had more insidious applications. With all its data managed by the county's Mobile Tracking Division, the police department had real-time access to nearly every citizen's movement. Like any system, there were loopholes—none of which you wanted to get caught exploiting. EcoTrak implementation was not optional. The typical price for noncompliance was a loss of civic privileges, which could result in being exiled from the state, unless the offender was willing to become a laborer in one of the agricultural zones. There was no shortage of those jobs. Mass deportations of Mexican migrant workers in the wake of the California Immigration Initiative ensured that these jobs went to American migrants seeking seasonal work from other states.

The Del Mar Heights exit appeared shortly after the I-5 merge, depositing Nathan's vehicle in front of a San Diego County PD checkpoint. Figured. As he eased the car down the ramp, powerful pole-mounted LED lights blazed to life, illuminating the mobile barriers placed to funnel traffic toward the police officers. His windshield adjusted, deeply tinting the interactive glass to a point where he could barely see.

"Disable window tinting. Safety override seven three nine nine," he said, giving the code that would prevent the car's onboard artificial intelligence processors from trying to talk him out of the decision.

The windows cleared, causing Nathan to squint and turn his head as he rolled up to three body armor–encased police officers. A fourth officer peered around the back corner of a tactical vehicle positioned at the bottom of the ramp, the outline of the officer's helmet-mounted night-vision goggles visible behind the black SUV.

His car spoke. "Your vehicle's camera feed has been temporarily disabled. Recording an ongoing public safety operation is not permitted by San Diego County—"

"Silent mode, please," Nathan said, uninterested in hearing the police department's broadcasted propaganda.

Police checkpoints typically utilized a selective proximity jammer to hijack a vehicle's wirelessly transmitted, 360-degree camera coverage, and force their own messages through the system. The police had even legally "tapped" people's car cameras, using a loose interpretation of surveillance warrant verbiage. All part of the surveillance state, which, in this case, state consumers had imposed upon themselves. Camera systems came as standard equipment on most vehicles sold in major California markets, by popular demand. *Careful what you ask for.*

Nathan nodded rapidly when the lead officer held out a gloved hand, motioning for him to stop. Once Nathan shifted the transmission into park and placed his hands at the ten and two o'clock positions on the steering wheel, the two additional officers crossed in front of his vehicle. They approached the passenger side, probing the interior of his car with excessively bright handheld flashlights. He restrained himself from covering his eyes when the beams crossed his face, not wanting to make any sudden moves.

The lead officer approached, shining a flashlight into the rear driver's-side seat before tapping on his window. Nathan obliged by fully lowering the window, a prerequisite for the stop.

"Good evening, Officer," said Nathan, making deliberate eye contact.

"Good morning," corrected the officer, continuing to search beyond him. "Do you mind popping the trunk?"

With three heavily armed officers surrounding his vehicle at four in the morning on a deserted off-ramp, he decided the better course of action was to acquiesce to the Fourth Amendment violation. He had nothing to hide.

"Sure," he said, slowly moving his left hand to trigger the trunk release.

"Thank you," said the officer, imperceptibly nodding over the car at one of his checkpoint partners, then turning back to Nathan. "Kind of early for a personal trip, Mr. Fisher."

His identity had been confirmed within milliseconds of arriving at the checkpoint. Cameras attached to the mobile light poles had scanned his face, matching the image to vehicle-registration information transmitted by the radio frequency identification system embedded in his car. A quick search of the database for authorized drivers instantly determined if officers needed to make a deeper inquiry about the person driving the vehicle.

"Trust me, I don't relish getting up this early. I collect seawater samples at the beach," said Nathan, not intending to expand the description of his weekly morning trips.

"Is this related to your job at the water authority?"

"Negative," said Nathan, purposely changing his vernacular. The police department actively recruited Marines from Camp Pendleton to boost their ranks. The chance of interacting with a former Marine was high, and speaking the lingo often eased the pain of a checkpoint stop.

"Former service?" asked the officer, taking the bait.

"Negative. My father retired as a sergeant major. Regiment level. I grew up on Camp Pendleton," said Nathan, all of which was true.

The officer nodded. "Got out as a staff sergeant in '28, right when the county was looking to expand. Couldn't have timed it better. They cut my battalion next year. Fuckers."

"Sounds like you landed in the right place," said Nathan.

"The Special Activities Group is a shit ton better than the regular patrol division, that's for sure," said the officer. "How long will you be at the beach?"

"I usually don't take more than thirty minutes."

"All right. You're good to go," he said, patting the top of the car. "Make sure you don't cross the San Dieguito Lagoon. Security is tighter around the plant because of the assassination."

"I would hope so. Unbelievable waking up to that tragedy this morning."

"It was only a matter of time before someone crossed the line," the officer said, stepping back from the vehicle and speaking into his helmet microphone.

The checkpoint lights darkened as Nathan pulled into the empty Del Mar Heights Road intersection and took a left toward the beach. A few minutes later, he nestled his car into a rare, vacant beach parking spot on Ocean Front Road, directly in front of the San Dieguito River beach preserve.

CHAPTER 6

Nick Leeds stepped on the brightly lit tarmac at Montgomery Field Airport, taking a moment to test his legs. Flagg's insistent calls had kept him awake for most of the flight, adding another eight hours to a severe sleep deficit. Personally managing Almeda's security needs had required him to work consistent eighteen-hour days in DC. He felt borderline combat ineffective standing next to the whining luxury jet.

His earpiece sounded before he could take a step forward. "Encrypted call from Mason Flagg."

"Mother fu—" he began before remembering that Flagg could simply cut into his wireless feed.

"I hope that wasn't directed at me," said Flagg. "Did you manage to grab a nap?"

"Very funny, and that was definitely directed at you," said Leeds, spotting one of his men waiting just outside one of the open hangar-bay doors. Looked like his entourage would bypass the airport arrival building for a far more private exit.

"I sent coffee with your team," said Flagg. "I need you in Del Mar ten minutes ago."

"Del Mar? Don't we have people working up there right now?"

"That's the problem. They're still working, and Olmos hasn't received the signal to pick them up."

Leeds looked past the sleek jet behind him and examined the eastern horizon. A faint ribbon of blue peaked over the pitch-black hills. "They have about twenty minutes before some asshole decides to go for a sunrise stroll," he said, starting to jog toward the hangar.

"Precisely," said Flagg. "I need you up there running interference."

"I presume that means no witnesses?"

"People drown at the beach, especially after they witness one of my operations. You can access the precise diver pickup coordinates on the Cerebrus server, under current operations. There's a police checkpoint at the Del Mar Heights exit, so use Carmel Valley Road."

Carmel Valley added time to their trip, if he obeyed the speed limits. "ETA?" requested Leeds, picking up the pace.

"Twenty-eight minutes, and watch your speed. I know Carmel Valley is slower, but it beats rolling the dice at a checkpoint," said Flagg. "I can replace a dive equipment specialist. You, on the other hand . . ."

"Is that a compliment?" asked Leeds, breathing heavy.

"Depends on how I finish the sentence. Call me when you've reached Del Mar."

The call disconnected, leaving Leeds in a dead sprint to reach the idling SUV that no doubt waited for him on the other side of the hangar.

CHAPTER 7

Nathan's eyes fluttered, opening slowly to focus on milky bands of star clusters above him. He raised his wrist over his face and squinted at his watch. Shit. He'd fallen asleep in a patch of soft sand behind a thick row of beach scrub. He knew better than to lie down, but the soothing rhythm of the crashing surf provided an all-too-tempting backdrop for stargazing after he'd stowed the water bottles in the car. San Diego County's strict light-pollution laws had restored vast swaths of the night sky to coastal viewers.

A low rumbling drew his attention away from the celestial panorama. He turned on his side and had started to push his body off the soft ground when the sound of distant voices froze him in place. Nathan remained still, straining to determine the direction of the new sounds over the steady plunge of Pacific waves. After listening for several seconds, he rose high enough to see through the windblown scrub.

He didn't see anything at first. The obsidian canvas beyond the wavering bushes yielded little more than a series of fading gray lines where the continuous onslaught of surf plunged into the water, but he continued to stare into the blackness, convinced that the sounds had come from the ocean. Noise tended to travel much farther over water. His peripheral vision caught movement beyond the breakers.

Rising a little higher, he spotted the suspected source—too far away to identify details with the naked eye. Nathan opened his backpack and removed a pair of compact binoculars, training them on the early-morning interlopers. Two shadowy, military-style boats bobbed in the water, holding station just beyond the surf zone. He adjusted the focus and searched for markings. Nothing. One of the boats twisted rapidly, pointing its stern toward the beach.

Behind the boat, a cluster of dark objects emerged, floating in the choppy water. He watched as four heavily laden divers climbed onto the deck of the craft and disappeared through unlit hatches on the starboard side of the low-profile, angular superstructure. A deeper rumbling floated across the beach, indicating a throttle change. By the time Nathan processed this information, the boats had receded into the distance—swallowed by the darkness.

He lowered his body to the cool sand and lay on his back, contemplating the bizarre scene. What the hell had he just witnessed? Nothing good. There was little doubt about that. Two stealth boats retrieving a covert diving team less than a mile from the Del Mar nuclear desalination plant. Without a doubt, nothing good. He should have trusted his first instinct and stayed home.

Or, maybe he was being paranoid, and the whole thing was one of dozens of regular exercises conducted by the Marine reconnaissance units or SEALs stationed on the Southern California coast. Camp Pendleton was less than five miles north, and all of the West Coast's SEAL teams operated out of the Naval Amphibious Base on Coronado Island—twenty miles to the south. A military exercise was well within the realm of possibilities. Right?

Nathan wasn't altogether convinced as he took in the fading light show above him—shades of lighter blue from the west creeping into the periphery of his vision. Time to get moving. He liked to get home before his neighbors woke up. The fewer questions he had to field about his trips, the better.

Nathan shouldered his backpack and took a moment to brush the bulk of the sand from his cold, clammy pants. Keira was going to be pissed about the sand he'd drag through the house—and the time. He should have been home by now with her coffee.

Three-quarters of the way across the shrub-covered nature preserve, Nathan paused, detecting the sound of an approaching vehicle. Unable to resist his paranoia, he kneeled below the tops of the bushes, peering through the thin wisps. The moment his knees touched the sandy trail, headlights illuminated a pair of expansive palm plants surrounding a white garage door on the corner of Ocean Front Road. The palms' shadows grew on the street as a black Suburban crept into view between the tightly spaced homes at the edge of the preserve.

Nathan's eyes darted to his sedan parked thirty feet away, and he grimaced as the SUV's headlights bathed the silver Toyota. *Shit.* What were the chances this was unconnected? He lowered his body further, placing the palms of his hands on the sand and crawling into the dense brush. The SUV idled at the corner, giving him second thoughts about staying in place.

A powerful spotlight swept the tops of the bushes, passing over his head and stopping at the seaward edge of the preserve. The light probed the bushes along the beach and disappeared. Moments later, the SUV's engine roared, and Nathan heard the oversize tires crackling over the street. He risked a peek through the shrubs, catching the red glow of the SUV's taillights. It had turned on Twenty-First Street, heading away from the beach. He rose a little higher and watched the SUV turn right onto Coast Boulevard.

Nathan counted to thirty, watching and listening for the SUV before sprinting the rest of the distance to his car. At the edge of the small public parking lot, he paused in the bushes and scanned the neighborhood, praying the SUV hadn't returned. Ocean Front Road was deserted as far as he could see, along with the rest of the tight roads leading to the preserve.

He walked down the passenger side of his car and paused behind the trunk, calculating the angle from the back of his car to the corner.

Based on a quick estimate, he didn't think the occupants of the SUV could have read his license plate from where they stopped. They could have read it on the way out, using a magnified night-vision device, but he doubted they'd bothered. The SUV had departed in a hurry. Thank God he'd loaded the bottles in the trunk before he took a nap. He was in the same hurry to get the hell out of there.

As Nathan drove away from the beach, he wondered if he should mention the strange encounter to Keira. She had a far more active imagination, not to mention a touch of the conspiracy bug. No. He'd keep it to himself. News of the assassination would be more than enough for her today. Black-ops boats, covert diving teams and suspicious, black Suburban SUVs would push her over the top. The last thing he needed was a full-blown panic at the Fisher household. He felt edgy enough cruising through the abandoned streets—on the constant lookout for a black SUV.

CHAPTER 8

Gary Reynolds massaged his temples as he focused on the reactor's digital seawater-cooling display. He didn't like the vibrational sensor readings from the primary circulating pump's housing unit. They were well within normal ranges but had twice strayed beyond baseline readings in the past minute. The system hadn't registered a vibration out of baseline parameters since they'd started the reactor 849 hours ago. Little things like this drew his attention.

As the plant's senior reactor operator, he'd overseen every aspect of the plant's operational life cycle, from initial testing to commissioning. For the past thirty-five days, he'd spent most of his life in this reactor control room, teasing out irregularities and establishing best practices from the reactor control teams assigned to the plant. He knew more about this system's behavior than his own children's. Like any well-designed, newly constructed reactor, Unit One was flawlessly predictable, unlike his preteen son and teenage daughter. An irregularity detected this soon in the life cycle was a sign of trouble.

"This has happened twice in the past forty-five minutes?" Reynolds asked James MacDonald, the shift's duty reactor operator.

"Two series of spikes out of baseline. Uneven spacing. Progressively intensifying."

"But still far inside acceptable operating parameters."

"Correct, but that pump has purred from the start," said MacDonald.

"Yes, it has," mumbled Reynolds, eyes fixed on the display.

Before he could air his thoughts, another vibrational spike appeared, registered by several sensors throughout the pump housing. Instead of quickly dropping back under the baseline threshold and remaining there, the vibrations tapered off at a new level.

"This is not good. Have we seen any unusual vibrations near the seawater filter screens? Maybe an impact that damaged one of the screens?" he asked, knowing the answer.

Any impact large enough to breach one of those screens would register one hell of a vibration, triggering alarms throughout the control center. The screens were designed to filter ocean debris or any fish unfortunate enough to be snagged by the plant's intake conduit. Located more than two thousand feet offshore, the submerged conduit employed a velocity cap to discourage fish entrainment, but no system was 100 percent effective. The screens were constantly rotated and power-washed to remove impinged fish and debris.

"I ran a system check. Nothing unusual," said MacDonald.

Reynolds glanced over his shoulder, finding what he expected: the rest of the shift's reactor control team staring at the main display. He turned back to the screen in time to see the beginning of the end. Pump One registered a vibration at the edge of safe operational parameters, immediately trailed by a persistent reading outside the safe zone. Red lights flashed on multiple panels in his peripheral vision, quickly followed by a high-pitched alarm. Reynolds gave the situation a few more seconds to unfold—for little reason beyond sheer disbelief. Pump One was in the process of tearing itself apart. Worse yet, Pump One was the plant's only direct seawater-cooling intake pump, a concession made by the San Diego County Water

Authority to ease opposition to the plant by California's vocal eco-lobbyists.

"Shit," muttered Reynolds, seeing only one viable option moving forward. "Initiate emergency shutdown procedures. Mr. Macdonald, stop Pump One, and stop the reactor when you have a green light to drop the control rods. Transfer full cooling responsibility for the deactivated reactor to the wet cooling system, and monitor the temperature levels closely. I'll notify the shift supervisor. We're in for a long day."

"That's an understatement," said Macdonald. "Shutting down a few months into operations is unprecedented. State and federal regulatory teams will descend on us within the hour."

"Good. They can revisit their decision to approve the accelerated construction timeline of the Del Mar plant, while they help us monitor the yet-unproved emergency cooling system. Should be a grand day for us all."

Reynolds considered the implications of running the wet cooling system as the sole source of reactor coolant. When the control rods are inserted during emergency shutdown procedures, reactor power drops immediately but does not completely cease. A small percentage of the reactor's steady state power remains, thanks to a continuing, low-grade fission decay of neutrons. In other words, the reactor will continue to produce heat that needs to be cooled—for a long time.

According to the plant's designers, the wet cooling system could handle it. Reynolds wasn't one 100 percent convinced, but what did his thirty-plus years of experience in the field matter? Not much, apparently. He just worked here.

"Ready to SCRAM the reactor," said Macdonald.

"Do it," said Reynolds, after quickly examining the digital displays for any less obvious signs that Macdonald may have missed.

While reactor power levels plummeted, he took a deep breath and inhaled. Thirty-five days and they already had a key equipment failure. The vast majority of reactor units in service today had gone thirty years without a critical failure. This morning's pump fiasco didn't bode well for California's sustainability efforts. He wouldn't be surprised if they shut down all the recently built nuclear plants to inspect the pumps. All this on top of Congresswoman Almeda's assassination? California had hit its first real rough patch in a decade, and he hoped the state didn't unravel too far.

CHAPTER 9

Nathan eased the car onto the Mira Mesa Boulevard exit ramp, slowing for the sharp curve that would deposit him in his authorized district. The moment his car turned east on Mira Mesa, the heads-up display announced his return, projecting basic details of his trip in a light-blue digital readout in the center of the windshield.

"ENTERING RESIDENTIAL DISTRICT 42. TIME OUT OF AUTHORIZED ZONE: 83 MINUTES. TIME REMAINING FOR OUT-OF-ZONE TRAVEL: 254 MINUTES."

A whole four hours left to enjoy with his family on the weekend. Looked like they'd be staying local. Keira wouldn't be happy to hear this. Eighty-three minutes was a record for him. He'd closed his eyes on the beach before, but never for that long. His Bluetooth system announced a call with a muted klaxon, the customized ringtone he'd jokingly set for Keira. He suspected she would live up to the joke this morning, especially if she'd checked the news before starting her morning routine.

"Accept call," he said, pausing until the HUD displayed "CONNECTED." "I'm about to stop for coffee, honey. I should be home in about ten minutes."

"Don't worry about the coffee. Did you see the news?" she said, clearly too worked up to piece together his extended absence.

"I caught it right before I left."

"Why didn't you wake me?"

"I didn't want to stress you out at four in the morning."

She paused before responding. "Please tell me you didn't go to your usual spot."

"'You didn't go to your usual spot,'" he said quickly.

Unsurprisingly, his wife didn't laugh. "Jesus. You actually went to Del Mar—ground zero for the next attack?"

He'd definitely hold off mentioning the black-ops boats.

"Nobody is going to attack a desalination plant. It's not in either side's best interest. Plus, it's a heavily guarded site," said Nathan. "It's business as usual out here for ninety-nine point nine nine percent of the population."

"California was attacked. Nothing will be business as usual today. Remember what happened last time. That's why we have that room," said his wife. "We need to be ready for a quick departure."

He didn't respond immediately, letting her words and tone sink in. She was agitated, and in full conspiracy mode. There was no point fighting against this tide. "I can't imagine any scenario requiring us to flee, but I'll get our bug-out gear ready," he said. "After work."

"I'd feel better if you took some time this morning to pre-stage everything."

Nathan hesitated, choosing his words carefully. "That's fine. I'll make sure everything is where it needs to be—just in case. I'm still getting coffee, by the way."

"Thank you, Nate," Keira said, sounding less troubled.

"I promised you I would get you coffee."

"I meant for putting up with me," she said.

"It's all good, honey. It can't hurt to take a few precautions. That's why I insisted on going to the beach this morning. Just in case."

"I just have a bad feeling about the assassination. Someone has taken the secession issue to the next level. I'm worried it won't stop there."

"Either way, we're in good shape. We can pack up and be on the road in an hour. We'll be out of the populated areas a few hours after that."

"I love you," she said.

"I love you more," he replied. "See you in about eight minutes."

"See you then."

He turned into the second of four Starbucks shops lining the five-mile stretch of Mira Mesa Boulevard, settling into the drive-through line behind three early-morning commuters. After ordering two grande cappuccinos, he swiped his California Resource Card (CRC) over the self-pay scanner, followed by his debit. The CRC recorded everything a California resident purchased and was mandatory for every transaction, no matter how trivial. All retailers, from flea market vendors at Kobey's Swap Meet to high-end art dealers in Hillcrest, were required to sell through CRC-connected, point-of-purchase devices—including cash purchases. Online transactions required a valid CRC number, regardless of the transaction's fulfillment location.

The CRC program had met with considerable protest when it was implemented in 2030, solidifying the California Resource Protection Act's nickname as the "Anti-Hoarding Act." With every Californian's detailed purchase history in the state's closely held possession, citizens waited for the hammer to drop on overconsumption. Instead of black helicopters dropping Resource Card SWAT teams into backyards to seize excess food and consumables, the hammer came in the form of an individualized grade sheet. Each household received a CRC-generated sustainability statement, analyzing consumption habits and comparing them to neighborhood, city, and county averages.

No late-night door kicking, flash bangs, and reeducation camps in the desert like many had suggested. Just good old-fashioned behavioral modification, pitting neighbor against neighbor, neighborhood against neighborhood, city district against city district—with small perks for the winners. Extended water-use hours. Added time out of residential districts. District-wide discounts on consumable purchases. Small things that everyone mocked at first, but not anymore. The California

Resources people knew exactly what they were doing when they started mailing statements.

The program had achieved a 32 percent reduction in consumption averaged across all categories. They even managed to squeeze a 5 percent reduction in the water-use category—a small miracle, given the fact that most families were living close to their "water breaking points," an artificially determined level of water use, beyond which a family might experience "water hardship." That's what state water officials liked to call dehydration.

The barista handed him two piping-hot to-go cups, forgetting the insulated sleeves he'd splurged on. Tops and sleeves were extra, and from what he could tell by the weight of each drink, getting a full cup of coffee was extra, too. Served him right for ordering cappuccinos. The barista had opted for the drier version. Now his sustainability statement would reflect thirty-two ounces of "liquid consumables," when the drinks couldn't possibly contain more than twenty between the two of them. He stifled a laugh as he lowered the coffees into the center-console cup holders. That was the kind of nonsense rattling around every Californian's head, every minute of every day, thanks to the monthly sustainability statement.

His house was less than five minutes away from the Starbucks, buried in a maze of bungalow-style homes valued between $1.2 and $1.5 million, depending on upgrades. On average, $950 per square foot, nearly five times the national median price per square foot—not that anyone was selling. Property was passed down from family to family these days. Nobody got rid of California real estate anymore.

Few could afford to buy it, and even fewer could afford to sell it. Most Californians had exhausted the equity in their homes to refit them with solar panels, solar batteries, water-reclamation upgrades, and hundreds of sleek, eco-friendly options required to survive. Families were stuck in place, unable to move up, and unwilling to move down. Only people leaving the state sold their homes—to highly paid tech-industry immigrants. The concept of upward housing mobility had dried up along with the reservoirs and rivers.

Nathan turned north onto Camino Ruiz, a perpetually busy six-lane thoroughfare, and cruised through a crowded block of strip malls and apartment complexes. Beyond the business district, tall sand-colored stucco walls lined the broad street, marking the start of the residential neighborhoods. Built and maintained by the town, the walls provide a modicum of privacy and sound reduction to the residents backed up against the road. He and Keira had considered a few homes along busy roads when they'd first arrived in California, but had passed on the lower price. During rush hour, Camino Ruiz sounded like a Grand Prix speedway at their current home, more than two blocks away. He couldn't imagine how it sounded directly behind one of these walls.

Nathan eased right onto Hydra Lane and navigated a few turns to arrive on Pallux Way, a street indistinguishable from the hundreds of streets crammed in the one-by-two-mile residential area. Most of the homes on his block were tidy, well-maintained one-story structures jammed onto lots barely ten feet wider than the house itself. With backyards featuring less square footage than the homes, you could watch and listen to your neighbors' TVs if they left the shades open. Only in California.

With the sun still lingering a few degrees under the horizon, the ugly zero-scaping remained shaded, and mercifully invisible. Crushed rock. Hardened dirt. Red-and-brown mulch. Pieces of driftwood. Decorative fieldstone boulders. Antique wheelbarrows. The occasional zero-water cactus. Everything carefully arranged in the front yard to resemble the kind of perfect high-desert scene you'd expect to find in a natural history museum display—minus the rattlesnakes and scorpions.

The Fishers hadn't bothered with the faux panorama. Hardened dirt was the order of the day, much to the dismay of a few neighbors. Nathan wasn't sure why any of them cared. The yards looked like shit, regardless of how much they spent at Home Depot, and the packed dirt didn't absorb as much rain—resulting in a higher neighborhood water-reclamation score. Nathan was taking one for the team.

The zero-scape effect was bad enough observed at street level. From the air, on approach to San Diego International Airport, the sight made you wonder why anyone would choose to live here. The city and its surrounding communities looked dead, compounded by dried-up canyons and browned-out parks that seamlessly morphed into the dull gray asphalt jungle. Golf courses resembled tan Rorschach scars. Even Mission Valley, once prominently recognizable from the air, barely registered to the casual window-seat observer. The Golden State was more on the light-brown side these days.

"Open garage door," Nathan said, receiving a courteous, affirmative reply from the car.

A double bay door two houses down on the left started to rise, signaling his imminent arrival to anyone watching. He pulled the car next to his wife's jeep and stopped the engine, turning off the vehicle's headlights.

"Close garage door, please," said Nathan, grabbing the two coffee drinks.

He made his way to a door in the right corner of the garage, which led into the laundry room adjacent to the kitchen. A second door, located in the middle of the garage's back wall, was hidden from street view by a row of steel-backed industrial shelves placed several feet forward of the wall. The concealed door led to an unused bedroom he and Keira had converted into their readiness workshop. After he delivered the coffee, he'd head there with the full water bottles to start the desalination process and ready their mobile supplies for Keira's benefit.

CHAPTER 10

Waiting patiently for Nathan to get home required every ounce of restraint Keira Fisher could muster. Gut instinct told her it was time to pack up the cars and take a long trip out of the state—a permanent trip. The assassination had changed everything.

She'd closely monitored the secession issue since they'd moved from Tucson, watching it grow from the Northern California fringe movement she'd remembered as a teenager in the Bay Area to a strongly supported statewide campaign. The rhetoric on both sides had intensified as California's Twenty-Year Self-Reliance plan entered its final years and the idea of an independent California started to look more viable—and more appealing—to a growing number of Californians. A scary thought for supporters of the One Nation Campaign. Scary enough to brazenly murder an influential public official.

Almeda had been instrumental in the construction of the Del Mar desalination plant and the reactivation of the San Onofre nuclear power plant. She must have been on the cusp of unveiling a new project, or possibly pledging her support for California's independence. Whatever the reason behind the desperately violent move, California Liberation Movement activists were sure to retaliate, possibly igniting a civil war within the state.

As much as she supported the concept of an independent California, Keira had no intention of letting the situation deteriorate around them.

They'd been through that once, and once was enough. She just needed to convince Nathan. Easier said than done. He'd watched the news and left to collect seawater—like it was no big deal. Like the police wouldn't be out in force, questioning anyone headed toward the desalination plant at four in the morning. What was he thinking? Unfortunately, she knew exactly what he was thinking. Nothing. Nathan didn't believe the secession issue was serious.

A low, distant rumble from the laundry room drew her eyes to the door leading into the garage. Finally. She muted the television and waited for her husband to open the door. When he appeared with a smile and her cappuccino, she wasn't happy to see either. Just for once, she wished he'd look concerned. Just slightly worried. Seeing him standing in the doorway with coffees like it was any other day bothered her. It shouldn't, but it did—which caused her to pick a fight.

"What took you so long?" she said, shaking her head.

"I had three cars ahead of me in line," said Nathan, placing her coffee on the island in front of her and kissing her temple. "Careful. They steamed the milk long enough to blister your skin."

"I meant your trip to the beach. When I saw the time, I got worried. I figured you got pulled over trying to reach the water."

Nathan sat on the stool next to her, glancing upward at the television before answering. "I hit a routine checkpoint at the Del Mar exit. The officers told me the county had added a few checkpoints closer to the Del Mar plant."

Keira glanced at her wristwatch for dramatic effect, raising an eyebrow.

"I kind of fell asleep on the beach," said Nathan, half grinning.

"That sounds safe," she said. California might be on the brink of a civil war, and her husband was napping on the beach without a care in the world.

"I was up in the beach scrub," he said. "Out of sight."

She shook her head. He still didn't get it. Time to play a card she never would have considered before this morning.

"Anyway," she said, swiveling her stool to face him, "I think we should consider taking a road trip to visit your parents."

"Really?" he said, halting the coffee cup a few inches in front of his face. "You're voluntarily suggesting we visit my parents. In Idaho. By automobile."

Hearing the plan spelled out gave her pause. She liked it far better when Nathan's parents came to California to visit. His father, a retired Marine sergeant major, had somehow convinced Nathan's mother to abandon civilized life for an Idaho homestead. An hour from the nearest semblance of a town, they lived in complete isolation more than a mile off State Highway 75 on a road that required Nathan to rent a four-wheel-drive SUV whenever they flew into Boise for a visit.

She didn't see Sergeant Major Fisher's mountain stronghold lasting too much longer. Jon and Leah Fisher were still spry enough to hike the trails, paddle the rivers, and shovel heavy snow off the deck, but they were in their late fifties—about to embark on that long, often problematic journey through the golden years. She'd seen it firsthand. Keira's parents were older than Nathan's, and had already hit some rough patches.

"A few weeks of pristine mountain air and endless green fields wouldn't be a bad thing for any of us," said Keira. "We haven't been on a real vacation since Owen was five."

"Since we left Tucson," said Nathan, appearing to take her suggestion seriously. "Six years without a family vacation." He shook his head.

None of them had even left the state since they'd arrived in '29. Even with Nathan's generous, state-sponsored relocation bonus, mortgage payments stretched the monthly budget uncomfortably thin. Even worse, the constantly increasing California Resource Protection Act–related fees and taxes guaranteed they never closed the budget gap. Any increase in pay at either of their jobs was swallowed by the rising cost of living.

Fortunately, both of them worked for the county in critical, high-demand jobs. While Nathan figured out new and inventive ways to recycle a community's wastewater, Keira tackled the growing autism epidemic. Of course, they didn't call it autism anymore. Pervasive Developmental Disorder—or, even better, PDD—had replaced the term *autism* several years ago.

All variations of the word *autism* were perceived on the same pejorative level as the term *retarded*. She couldn't remember a time when anyone used the word *retarded* regularly, but she'd finished her master's degree in cognitive disability therapy with a focus on autism spectrum disorder. Keira had to be careful. One slip of the tongue in front of a parent at the therapy center could abruptly end their California dream.

Sometimes, she wished it would happen. They could ditch everything and move pretty much anywhere they wanted—outside of the United States. Nathan's job experience alone could get the family a permanent residency visa in most countries, regardless of the debt they'd left behind. One of her husband's colleagues had vanished without a trace last year. Skipped out on a million-dollar mortgage and a six-figure credit-card balance. She resurfaced a few months later in Buenos Aires, making twice her salary helping the Argentinians stay ahead of the water crisis. That transition didn't sound so bad, especially when Keira learned that the company in Argentina had paid to ship all their household goods and two cars. The only thing standing in their way was Nathan.

"Owen is done with school on Friday," she said. "I don't think taking him out a few days early will be a problem. He said they're just watching movies and wasting time at this point."

"I can't drop everything at work and leave on the same day," said Nathan. "And who knows what will come down from the top in response to the assassination. I wouldn't be surprised if they fast-tracked the facilities security review due at the end of the summer."

"If one of your parents passed away, they'd let you leave on the first flight available," she said. "And I'm not suggesting you make up a story. Just pointing out that it's possible for the office to survive without you."

"I'll look into it."

She stared at him. "I'll look into it" was his version of "We can think about that."

"Seriously," he said. "I'll ask."

Keira cocked her head slightly.

"Really ask," he said, leaning over to kiss her. "Promise."

"I'm probably being paranoid, but I get the sense that this could spiral out of control quickly. Let's put a little distance between the Fishers and California for a few weeks. If I'm wrong, which I hope I am," she said, lying, "we'll recharge ourselves with clean air and fresh water."

"I hope you're not impugning the quality of San Diego County's water supply," said Nathan, grabbing her wrists playfully. "Our tap water is far cleaner than any of that freshwater swill you might get in the mountains—even if it leaves a *slight* chlorine aftertaste."

"Slight?" she said, pulling his arms around her.

"We're working on that." He nuzzled against her. "Different department."

"Feels like you're working on something else," she said, pressing against him.

"Do we have time?" he asked, kissing her lips.

The sound of feet shuffling in the bedroom hallway answered the question. Keira eased back onto her stool at the kitchen island.

"Apparently not," she said as the bathroom door closed.

"Tonight," said Nathan, stroking her inner thigh.

She smiled. "I was hoping to be on the road by then."

"We'll see." He checked his watch. "I need to get moving."

"You weren't in a big hurry a few seconds ago."

"I'm easily corrupted by the woman I love," said Nathan, kissing her.

"That's what I love about you. And the fact that you don't mind splurging on coffee," Keira said, taking her cup from the island.

"I have a few redeeming qualities," he said, grabbing his own cup and disappearing into the garage.

She still wasn't convinced that he'd give the vacation idea his best effort. He was infamously nonconfrontational, likely to back down if his boss gave him shit about leaving on short notice. She'd have to be all over him today. Holographic messages. E-mails. Phone calls. Virtual reminders. Anything and everything. She might even contact his boss if prospects looked grim. She could find Scott Warren's e-mail and phone number on the San Diego County website, or raid Nathan's phone— which he'd conveniently left on the counter. She eyed the device, shaking her head.

Chapter 11

Nathan pressed the oversize garage-door button and walked between his car and Keira's mini-SUV, waiting for the bay door to close before he opened his car's trunk. The less his neighbors saw, the better. Thanks to government programs encouraging neighbors to be nosy, he was paranoid. Nine reports had been filed against his address, online or through the California Resource Waste Hotline, since they'd moved in six years ago. All bogus "trolling" claims related to water use. Each one easily refuted by his household's water-reclamation percentage, the highest in the neighborhood, and one of the highest within a square mile—unsurprisingly.

As a water-reclamation engineer for the county, he'd taken extra steps to maintain a pristine water-use record. Leadership by example was a priority in his line of work, along with keeping San Diego County Water Reclamation Authority investigators out of his house.

Once the garage door closed, Nathan ran his fingertips under the trunk latch, triggering the biometric scanner. The hatch popped, rising slowly to a fully opened position. Inside, three light-blue, five-gallon water bottles lay side by side, filled to capacity with seawater. He heaved one of the forty-pound bottles out of the trunk and tucked it under his right arm, squeezing carefully between the two cars.

Stepping behind the packed industrial shelving toward the rear of the garage, Nathan lowered the bottle to the floor next to a locked steel door, took a moment to disable the biometric sensor lock and turn the deadbolt, then dragged the bottle through the doorway.

Overhead lighting automatically illuminated the room, exposing a ten-foot-by-ten-foot windowless square surrounded on three sides by three-tier plastic shelving units. The "bunker" held the emergency supplies he and Keira had collected over the past few years, along with Nathan's pièce de résistance: a refitted, portable, electric desalinator and water maker.

He removed the bottle's lid and emptied the raw seawater into a deep-blue thirty-gallon rain barrel perched on a sturdy wood platform. A briny smell filled the room as the water splashed into the barrel. After the barrel emptied, he placed it on top of a stacked pair of long plastic bins next to the door and took a step back to examine the water-making rig.

A clear plastic tube protruded from the bottom of the elevated barrel, connecting the food-grade plastic container to the desalinator stowed beneath the wood platform. A second clear hose rose from the output valve on the other end, climbing the wall and disappearing into the top of a second rain barrel that occupied the other half of the table.

The system was simple. He poured the seawater into the open-top container, powered the desalinator, and waited ten hours for fifteen gallons of fresh water to fill the second barrel. Fifteen extra gallons per week may not sound like a bounty, but in the context of California's draconian water-preservation efforts, the added water made a big impact on their daily lives. Sometimes he wondered if Keira had forgotten that, especially when she called the water a *luxury*. It was far from a luxury in his mind.

Californians fell into three main categories when it came to water consumption. Those who couldn't afford to exceed their allowance and didn't; those who incurred inescapable debt to exceed the allowance, even if just marginally; and the smaller group, who could pay the exorbitant, escalating fees for overconsumption.

The standard water allowance for each Californian provided a bare minimum for consumption and basic hygiene. The allowance was based on age, assuming average height and weight. Each household received the combined allowance for all verified occupants of the dwelling, which inevitably led to a host of fraudulent occupancy claims. Water Resource Authority analysts estimated a 9 to 12 percent difference between the reported number of San Diego County water users and the actual number at any given time. WRA investigators, outnumbering emergency services personnel three to one, spent most of their time chasing fraudulent occupancy leads.

They dedicated the rest of their time to checking requests for larger allowances. Variations from the county-assigned water allowance were granted based on drastic departures from human growth averages, medical conditions, or state-approved employment-based waivers for strenuous job-mandated activities. Variations didn't come easy, and they were subject to frequent review.

The Fishers had created their own version of the variance program, with Nathan taking weekly trips to the ocean to collect enough seawater to keep them from second-guessing every single water-use decision. The fifteen gallons granted the Fishers a small respite from the water-obsessed madness that consumed most Californians. It also provided them with viable, atypical options in the unlikely event of a system-wide man-made or natural catastrophe—which was the whole purpose of the bunker.

Anchored around forty-five gallons of stored water split into fifteen, three-gallon plastic containers, the bunker contained enough supplies to successfully weather a short-term local crisis or evacuate the state by car. A quick glance at the shelves demonstrated that the Fishers had focused most of their energy and resources on the latter scenario. He had Keira to thank for that.

One critical year—2031—had been a bad tremor year for Southern and Central California, reigniting fears of the revised thirty-year, 8.0-magnitude scare initiated by the National Geological Survey in late 2018. The chances of California experiencing an 8.0 quake by the middle of the century more than doubled from 2015 estimates—hitting an unprecedented 20 percent likelihood. The next decade or so had been relatively quiet for California, burying those fears. That year brought them back to the surface, with a tripling in the number of micro-tremors along multiple critical fault lines. That was the year the Fishers started preparing for the possibility of a sudden exodus. Keira had insisted, backed by Nathan's father, who had converted to "prepperdom" after he retired from the Marine Corps.

Now Nathan had a room filled with survival gear, dehydrated food, MREs, water containers, medical supplies, spare gasoline, and "bug-out bags," all of it waiting to be thrown into his wife's mini-SUV at the first sign of trouble—and much of it waiting to get them thrown out of California, should it be discovered. The gasoline alone would get them deported without a hearing—or shot in the head by criminals. Fifteen gallons of untraceable gasoline was worth a mint on the black market.

Despite the constant low-grade anxiety generated by the bunker, its contents gave Nathan some peace of mind. Unlike the vast majority of Californians, the Fisher family could head east into the wastelands with enough fuel and supplies to link up with his father in Idaho.

Nathan turned the blue switch on the desalinator's plastic housing unit to the "On" position and watched the dirty seawater climb down the tube. He listened to the desalinator for several seconds. It sounded fine. Not the smoothest hum it had ever produced, but not the worst. By the time he finished hauling the remaining two bottles into the room, a column of clear water crept toward the top of the freshwater storage barrel.

"As long as it works, I don't care what it sounds like," he mumbled.

CHAPTER 12

"Atten—hut!" growled Major Kane, Second Battalion's executive officer.

Captain David Quinn pushed his chair back and stood at attention amid a cacophony of metal scraping linoleum. Most of the battalion's officers and senior staff noncommissioned officers were present. Close to eighty Marines packed into a classroom designed to accommodate forty. Under normal circumstances, the colonel would assemble a group this large in the parking lot, but Quinn sensed that nothing the colonel had to say to them this morning fell under the "normal" category.

The space fell silent moments before Lieutenant Colonel Smith plunged through the door and headed straight for the dark faux-wood podium next to the wall-mounted digital screen at the front of the room. Smith, "two-four's" battalion commander, was a bulldog—short and barrel-chested, with ripped arms bulging against his rolled-up combat uniform sleeves. He was followed closely by the battalion sergeant major, a hulk of a Marine, who stood at attention next to the stand holding an olive-drab digital tablet.

"As you were," said Smith, gripping the sides of the lectern and turning to Major Kane. "Secure the door."

A faint murmur rippled through the room as the major turned the latch above the door handle and tested the door. The Marines settled back into their seats or standing positions along the walls of the classroom.

"All field exercises scheduled for June have been canceled," said Smith. "Regiment, ergo division, wants to keep all units close to the vest for the time being. As of right now, every Marine and sailor in the battalion falls under a two-hour recall, and we will most definitely test this recall at the most inopportune time, like zero dark thirty on Friday or Saturday night."

A restrained grumbling erupted, as Quinn made eye contact with his company first sergeant. The recall order would not be well received by Fox Company Marines, who'd recently returned from a month-long joint exercise at the National Training Center in Fort Irwin, California. Being on two-hour standby placed a lot of restrictions on them.

"It's better than an indefinite division-wide confinement to Camp Pendleton, which is exactly what will happen if our Marines fuck this up," said Smith. "It's up to each and every one of you to impress the importance of following this order. With that said, all leave commencing in June is canceled. No exceptions. Marines currently out of the state on leave are fine, but there will be no extensions. If they're in-state, you're to make every effort to get their asses back. Any questions?"

Echo company commander stood up in the front row. "Sir, what can we tell the Marines? I assume this is related to the secession issue?"

"Leave your assumptions out of it for now. Issue and enforce the order. I don't need Camp Mateo transforming into a liberal arts college campus, with seven hundred brand-new political science majors," said Smith, eliciting some laughter.

"This is for the Marines' very own safety and security. Division doesn't want any of our Marines left flopping in the breeze if the political climate goes south. Frankly, I don't know any more than you do about the situation, but at the risk of making an assumption, I think the assassination rattled a few cages in the Pentagon—probably the White House, too."

A wiry master sergeant from headquarters and support stood next. "What about families living off base, sir? Will we have a contingency plan for their evacuation?"

"I never said anything about an evacuation, Top," said Smith.

"I just—" started the master sergeant.

"Assumed? Let's take this one step at a time. General Nichols considers our families to be just as important as our rifles, so I feel confident that his plan will soon include families. Right now, he's concerned with basics, which is taking several thousand federally sworn killing machines out of the state political equation on short notice. Any more assumptions?" asked Smith, suppressing a devilish grin.

Nobody stirred as Smith surveyed the group.

"Very well. Sergeant Major Harmon will answer any specific questions related to the restrictions and expectations surrounding the two-hour recall," said Smith, stepping around the podium and taking the digital tablet from Harmon. "Major Kestler. Captain Quinn. Follow me."

Shit. Had he done something wrong? Had he rolled his eyes? It couldn't be that. Smith had tapped the operations officer, too, and Kestler was poker-faced, 24-7. The guy even wore the same dour expression at command picnics or officer socials.

No, this was something bigger. Maybe a lateral-to-weapons company commander? Fox Company was running smoothly, but Weapons Company still struggled after the tragic DUI-related death of Captain Lee. He glanced at his first sergeant and nodded, before sliding past several chairs to catch up with Lieutenant Colonel Smith.

Without speaking, Smith led the two officers into an adjacent classroom and closed the door.

"This is for your eyes and ears only," said Smith, activating the tablet. "Division is exploring a long-dormant plan to move the bulk of our Pendleton-based force to Marine Corps Air Station Yuma. They're just looking at the plan, making a candid assessment of its feasibility."

"Jesus," muttered Quinn, instantly processing the far-reaching consequences of a full division-level evacuation from Camp Pendleton.

"This is an ancient plan drawn up in the wake of the 1992 Landers earthquake. Marine Corps planners in Quantico wanted a contingency plan to evacuate Camp Pendleton on short notice if geological trends suggested an imminent 8.0-or-greater earthquake in Southern California."

Major Kestler's eyes narrowed—the first show of emotion Quinn ever recalled seeing from the Marine many called "the cyborg."

"Sir," said Kestler, "I didn't think Camp Pendleton was situated on an active or inactive fault line."

"It isn't," said Smith. "I think they were looking for an excuse to come up with this plan."

The screen illuminated, showing two digital thumbprint scanners.

"Two-person integrity. A right thumb from each of you opens the tablet, which contains the plan. If one of you walks more than twenty feet away from tablet, it shuts down and requires two thumbs again. Or my thumb. Study this plan and report to me by sixteen hundred. I want to know exactly what might be required of the battalion if California goes to shit," said Smith. "And David?"

"Yes, sir?" asked Quinn.

"I'm appointing you as my liaison to division. They know you're approved for every level of the planning phase. Don't lose that thumb," said Smith, cracking a smile.

"Copy that, sir," said Quinn. "Who should I contact at division?"

"I haven't figured that out yet, but I'll let you know shortly," said Smith. "I do know that they are planning a site visit to MCAS Yuma within the week, and I expect the *bastards* to be well represented on that visit. One of you will make the trip with a squad of Marines. You can draw straws."

"I'll take care of it," said Kestler.

Better you than me, David thought. MCAS Yuma was a desert dumping ground.

"It probably goes without saying, but I'll say it anyway. Keep this under wraps. If anyone asks about the trip, we say the battalion got tagged to escort one of Pendleton's regular resupply runs to Yuma."

"Yes, sir," said Kestler.

"I'll leave you to this mess," said Smith, glaring at Kestler. "Sixteen hundred hours in my office."

When the door closed behind Smith, Kestler unveiled a thin smile. "This is going to be a grade-A cluster fuck," he said, shaking his head.

"That's an understatement, sir."

"Call me Harry," said the major. "Looks like you and I will be joined at the hip for a while."

"Won't your assistant operations officer be jealous?" asked Quinn.

"He won't have time for emotions, if my guess is correct," said Kestler. "This plan is going to require his full attention, if implemented."

"Let's hope it isn't," said Quinn, suddenly worrying about his wife.

CHAPTER 13

Nathan Fisher lowered his window and poked his head out of the car, pushing on the center-console armrest for leverage. The eight-story, mirror-windowed building containing his office loomed in the distance, shining through the thick shield of tall palm trees lining the San Diego County Water Authority's main access road. He was accustomed to hitting traffic outside the facility, but nothing like this. The snarl of automobiles extended from the Poway Road turnoff to the security gate—nearly half a mile. It had taken him nearly twenty minutes to go half that distance. Creeping along at this rate, he was undoubtedly going to be late.

"Dial Robert Taff's phone," he said, lightly pounding on the steering wheel.

"Dialing Robert Taft at the San Diego County Water Reclamation Authority. Mobile number," said his car.

A few moments later, the car informed him that the call was connected.

"Morning, Nathan," said his supervisor. "I bet I know where you are."

"Breathing carbon monoxide fumes in front of the main gate," said Nathan, rolling up his window. "Looks like I'm about forty minutes out, unless this speeds up."

"I'm about ten minutes behind you," said Taff.

"All of this because of the assassination?"

"No," said Taff. "The seawater-cooling pump at the Del Mar plant failed this morning. State authorities raised the critical infrastructure protective posture, the CIPPR, about thirty minutes ago. That's confidential information for now. Del Mar hasn't hit the news yet."

Shit. The plant looked fine from the beach when he left. Those boats. Jesus. They had to be connected. Right?

"Nathan, you there?"

"Sorry. I thought the car in front of me stalled," he said, steering his mind back to the conversation. "Do they suspect a terrorist attack?"

"I don't think they're ruling it out, especially on the heels of Almeda's murder. Did you catch the details of that mess? Someone really wanted her dead. The scene looked like a war zone."

"Yeah, it was unbelievable," said Nathan. "Looked like they used high explosives to blow up her townhouse."

Should he report the stealth boats he'd spotted off the beach? He was positive they had retrieved divers. The seawater-cooling pump station was located on the banks of the San Dieguito Lagoon, directly accessible to the ocean. Could a diver team travel that far? Military divers could. *Fuck*. A trip to visit his parents wasn't sounding so bad.

"On-scene police investigators said something about antipersonnel mines," said Taff. "The front hallway in Almeda's townhouse was riddled with Teflon bearings."

"Like a Claymore?"

Nathan was uncomfortably familiar with military weaponry, thanks to dozens of trips to the "office" with his dad. Sergeant Major Fisher loved to showcase the lethal tools of his trade when Nathan was a child, arranging to bring his young son to Camp Pendleton whenever possible to witness "the sheer joy of firepower." He'd even bent the rules to put his son behind the standard service-issue weapons. The deafening blasts, sharp cracks, and deep percussions had scared the hell out of him then and, truth be told, still did today, but he never let it show. In fact, he excelled at marksmanship in the company of his father, continuing the deception that would eventually crush Sergeant Major Fisher.

Nathan never took to the joy of weapons and the glory of the Corps as his father had hoped. He talked the Marine Corps talk throughout high school and even joined the NROTC college program at UC Davis as a Marine option, but when it came to signing on the dotted line, Nathan surprised everyone except himself. He quit the program at the end of his sophomore year. That was one long-ass summer in Oceanside, with his dad barely speaking to him.

"Something like that," said Taff. "Hey, I better give Susan a call and let her know I'm not going to make it to her eight o'clock. Block off time around eleven for me. Say, two hours? I wouldn't be surprised if they bumped up the Critical Infrastructure Systems review timeline. Bureaucrats have to do something, so we might as well get ahead of them."

"No problem. I'll see you on the inside," said Nathan, disconnecting the call.

The car in front of him surged forward, giving Nathan a fleeting moment of hope. False alarm. The small red sedan shuddered to a stop, forcing him to plant his foot on the brake. Were they searching cars at the gate? What could be taking this long? He'd find out soon enough.

"Tune radio to NPR," said Nathan.

"Tuning to KPBS-FM," replied the car.

If anyone had figured it out by now, it would be KPBS. He was convinced that station reporters watched the facility 24-7, all year round. KPBS had been all over the Del Mar project, from start to finish, with a decidedly antinuclear slant.

Environmental concerns. Cost overrun fears. Property value impact. Fraudulent bidding processes. Every negative imaginable was exhaustively aired, leaving out one important aspect of the triad plant discussion—the fact that it endlessly produced three resources critical to California's survival: fuel, electricity, and freshwater.

Nobody got excited about having a nuclear power plant in his or her backyard, but without the added nuclear sites, California stood little chance of surviving, as an independent economic zone or a full-fledged state of the union. People had lost sight of that, but Nathan lived this fragile reality day in and day out at his job. When you spent your entire day trying to squeeze a few more fractions of a percent out of the population's wastewater just so they had enough to stay minimally hydrated, you gained an entirely new appreciation for the scope of the problem.

The car's surround-sound speakers brought KPBS to life inside the car. Before Nathan could process what the voices said, he knew they were talking about the Del Mar plant. The audio had a wide-open outdoor quality, far from the studios.

". . . Department of Energy just confirmed that the reactor powering the Del Mar Triad Station was taken offline earlier this morning, explaining early morning brownout reports from San Diego Gas and Electric customers. KPBS has requested detailed information from California's Nuclear Commission and the California Department of Energy, along with plant officials. Just thirty-five days into the reactor's life, the emergency shutdown represents a significant setback for the controversial plant, and California's plan to open additional nuclear reactors . . ."

Nathan pressed the "Mute" button on his steering wheel. Maybe it was time to consider a more permanent trip out of town. He could take his magic water-making skills where they could make a real difference. A place trying to get ahead of the water crisis—or, even better, trying to prevent it. He'd bring it up with Keira later tonight and see where the conversation landed. At the very least, the discussion would soften the bad news that he couldn't imagine any scenario leading to a sudden two-week vacation. Today and tonight were going to be miserable.

CHAPTER 14

A double-stacked, parabolic array of flat-screen televisions faced Mason Flagg and Nick Leeds inside the Point Loma operations center. When Leeds returned from his scouting trip to the beach rendezvous site, they started scanning dozens of major news channels between the two coasts, analyzing the impact of the Del Mar operation on the secessionist-fueled media frenzy surrounding Almeda's assassination.

Initial coverage of the desalination plant's reactor shutdown had managed to nudge the congresswoman's murder out of the spotlight—in California. Throughout the rest of the country, where the state was viewed through more of a *schadenfreudian* lens, Almeda's spectacular demise dominated news feeds and lead segments. Before the end of the day, national mainstream media pressure would bleed into California, pushing Del Mar aside even here.

They needed a murder on par with Almeda's—one they could easily blame on the California Liberation Movement. One that might, given the right push from behind the scenes, cast doubt on the media's initial suggestion that One Nation Coalition supporters were behind Almeda's assassination.

Flagg finished a glass of fresh-squeezed orange juice and turned to Leeds, who was drifting asleep in his seat. He snapped his fingers. "You can take a beauty nap later."

Leeds didn't startle in his chair. He remained still, his eyes opening slowly to regard Flagg.

"Not enough?" asked Leeds, nodding at the news feeds.

"Unfortunately, trashing a nuclear reactor isn't enough to grab people's attention these days."

"It's hard to compete with a gun battle on the streets of Georgetown," said Leeds. "Though I'm sure Olmos and his crew had some fun in the water last night."

"Too much fun," said Flagg. "They were nearly two hours behind schedule. I'm still not convinced the boats went unnoticed."

"Our contact in the department is on it. Nothing called in, texted, or e-reported so far. She'll comb through the investigative-branch records throughout the day looking for anything related to the incident."

"These idiots like to walk on their beaches. I'd be surprised if nobody heard or saw the boats."

Leeds stifled a laugh. "You really hate California, don't you?"

Flagg stared at him, slowly shaking his head. "I'd nuke the place if that was on the menu."

Leeds grinned. "Give it time and you might get your wish. We have some trigger-happy clients."

"Don't remind me," muttered Flagg, pouring a glass of ice-cold water from a sweating glass pitcher.

He took a long drink and stared at the screens, his eyes darting between them.

"If anything pops up at county, I want to know about it instantly. If Olmos's crew did the job right, the reactor shutdown will be attributed to the unusual, but not impossible, failure of a critical part in the seawater-cooling pump. If anyone saw the boats, we might have a problem," said Flagg. "And get some rest. I have something in mind for tonight that will require your direct supervision."

"Local?" asked Leeds, pushing up from the chair.

"Sacramento area," said Flagg. "I think I know how to turn the media tide, and clean up a few loose ends in the process."

PART II

PART II

CHAPTER 15

Nathan sensed movement and looked up from his computer screen. Robert Taff stood in the doorway, looking grim. He glanced at the time on his computer. It was 9:52 a.m. Odd.

"I'm finishing up an e-mail," said Nathan. "I'll be right there."

"E-mail can wait," said Taff, holding the serious face. "I need you in Ortiz's office immediately."

Odd, indeed. He could count on one thumb the number of times he'd been summoned to the division director's office before—and Taff never called Susan by her last name. This was either a promotion or a termination.

"What's up?" asked Nathan, slowly standing.

"I'm not sure," said Taff, betraying no sign of the friendliness or familiarity he'd oozed for the past six years.

Terminated. Or maybe Susan planned on giving him Taff's job. Whatever it was had to be serious. Taff looked stiff, like someone was holding a gun to his head. Nathan reached for the keyboard to lock his workstation.

"Don't worry about that," Taff said tersely. "They're waiting."

"They?"

Instead of responding verbally, Taff raised a probing eyebrow.

"Okayyyy," added Nathan, stepping through the door and heading toward Susan Ortiz's office.

He arrived at her closed door ahead of Taff, and stepped aside. Avoiding eye contact with Nathan, his supervisor rapped on the door and opened it a sliver.

"It's Robert Taff," he said, pausing. "With Fisher."

He was Fisher now? This couldn't be good.

"Come in," said Ortiz.

As soon as Nathan caught sight of the division's lawyer, he knew the day was about to go even further sideways than he had suspected. When he saw the pair of suited police-detective types seated at Ortiz's mini-conference table, he steeled himself for a day flipped entirely upside down. Next to them, Ortiz managed a purse-lipped smile from the head of the table.

His face suddenly felt warm, despite the near refrigerator-level atmosphere in the office. While his skin flashed from the sudden adrenaline rush, his brain ran through every possible scenario imaginable that might have landed the police in his path. Only one situation stood out: his trip to Del Mar. *Damn it!* He should have listened to Keira. The door closed, and he turned his head, unsurprised to find Taff gone. This all looked several levels above Taff's pay grade.

"Mr. Fisher, please take a seat," said Ortiz.

He nodded and did as he was told, scanning the two faces seated in front of him. They looked bored, which he suspected was quite the opposite of how they felt. The dark-haired detective on the right slid her badge holder forward, flipping it open.

"Supervisory Detective Anna Reeves, San Diego County Police Department," she said, watching him impassively.

"Inspector John Ramirez," said the angular-faced man seated next to her. "County Energy Commission."

Nathan pretended to examine their credentials while Ortiz perfunctorily introduced Alan McDermott as the division's chief counsel. He looked up from the badges, watching Ortiz's face closely as she cast a nervous glance at the lawyer, leaving Nathan nagging doubts regarding the legitimacy of this meeting. He waited several moments before shrugging.

"I guess I'll go first," said Nathan. "How can I help the San Diego County PD?"

Detective Reeves forced a tight smile. "We'd like to ask you a few questions about your travel habits, specifically your weekly trips to the beach in front of the San Dieguito River beach preserve. I believe you paid the coastline a visit this morning?"

He nodded hesitantly, unsure whether he should answer the question. Alan McDermott certainly wasn't here to represent Nathan's best interest. Ortiz was in full cover-the-county's-ass mode.

"Is that a yes or no?" asked Reeves.

"Do I need legal representation?" asked Nathan. "No offense, Alan."

"None taken," said the lawyer. "I represent the Water Reclamation Authority. Though I'd be remiss if I didn't suggest you only speak to these detectives in the presence of a retained attorney."

Ortiz's face twitched at his mention of retaining an attorney.

"We're not there yet," said Detective Reeves. "But by all means, we can continue this conversation downtown in the presence of your attorney—all morning and afternoon—or you can answer some simple questions for us now."

The chief counsel raised his hands, palms out. "It's your show, detective."

Nathan wasn't sure how to interpret McDermott's last statement, but his warning rang true, along with the detective's not-so-veiled threat. He had nothing to hide—well, that wasn't exactly true. Nothing criminal to hide. A few violations of the California Resources Protection Act, for sure, but that didn't concern the police, unless he made this harder for them than necessary. He'd heard the stories about "blanket warrant" searches related to state security matters, and there was little doubt that these investigators were digging around for a domestic-terrorism angle related to the Del Mar station. Why else would they question him?

He faced a difficult decision. Admitting why he visited the ocean in front of Ortiz could cost him his job, but it would also likely take him off the county's list of terror suspects. If he lawyered up and played the role of aggrieved civil libertarian, the police would undoubtedly search his house, sharing information about his supplies with the omnipresent California Resource investigators. Without fail, he'd receive the infamous one-week deportation packet, complete with a list of Realtors or investment groups ready to purchase his home—slightly below market value, of course.

Nathan decided to take a gamble.

"I'll be glad to answer all of your questions," he said. "But not in front of these two." He nodded at Ortiz and McDermott. "I don't see why they're here, frankly."

"Excuse me?" asked Ortiz, exaggerating a quizzical look.

Reeves turned to her. "Both you and Mr. McDermott are excused."

"This is my office," said Ortiz.

"And this is my investigation," said Reeves. "Which I could expand to everyone in Mr. Fisher's division. You know, just to be thorough. Give us a few minutes and we'll be out of your way shortly. Or we can spend the entire day here."

"This is bullshit, detective," said Ortiz. "No way to treat a fellow county employee. We're all on the same side."

"Exactly, which is why I'm asking you politely to stop interfering in our business."

"What?" asked Ortiz, shaking her head in disbelief. "Interfering? Alan?"

The lawyer shook his head quickly. "We're not interfering, but why don't we leave the police alone to conduct their business. Easier that way."

"I'm worried about the liability," said Ortiz, holding her seat.

"Don't worry, Susan," Nathan said, winking at her. "I won't hold you responsible if the detectives beat me to a pulp after you leave the room."

"That's not what I was going to say, Mr. Fisher," she said.

"You can call me Nathan," he said. "Like you have for the past six years."

"Don't get cocky," she said. "I'm still your boss's boss. We'll talk about this later."

"This isn't a big deal," said Nathan. "Trust me."

"I'll be the judge of that," said Ortiz.

When the door shut behind them, Reeves leaned forward. "Tell us about your visits to the beach."

"And don't leave anything out," said Inspector Ramirez.

"There's really not much to it, honestly," said Nathan. "I collect and desalinate seawater every week. Almost every week. I fill three five-gallon bottles and leave."

The two investigators stared at him without changing facial expressions.

"I own a small desalinator," said Nathan. "I like the beach in front of the San Dieguito preserve because it's close and I can park in the lot without a permit. I occasionally go to Torrey Pines or La Jolla Shores Park, but those tend to be a little more crowded in the morning. I don't like hauling bottles in front of people. I've had a few run-ins with local idiots."

"That's it?" asked Reeves.

"Sorry to disappoint you, but I didn't sabotage the seawater-cooling pump," said Nathan.

"Who said anything about sabotage?" asked Ramirez.

Nathan held his breath. He'd temporarily forgotten about the stealth boats until Ramirez repeated the word *sabotage*, or so he'd thought. His subconscious clearly hadn't discarded the memory. He went with the first train of thought available, hoping to avoid a telling pause.

"Why else would you be here? Neighborhood complaint?" asked Nathan. "The media pundits are already suggesting the possibility."

"I'm no expert in filling up water bottles," said Reeves, "but it would seem to me that you spent more time than necessary at the beach this morning."

"I fell asleep in the tall grasses beyond the high-tide mark. I sometimes can't resist taking a few minutes to stargaze and listen to the surf. I'd been up till midnight working on the desalinator," said Nathan. "And drifted off for a few minutes."

"Close to an hour," said Ramirez. "The seawater-cooling pump failed exactly thirteen minutes after your departure."

Nathan shook his head. *Now that's a shitty coincidence.*

"Look. I've done the same thing pretty much every week, with little variation, for the past three years. I'm sure you've analyzed the patterns. I occasionally linger to enjoy a quiet moment at the beach. I've only fallen asleep a few times, once at Torrey Pines and the rest in Del Mar."

Reeves glanced at Ramirez and nodded subtly, probably confirming Nathan's information. The California Department of Energy investigator acknowledged her body language and leaned back in his seat, appearing to be satisfied with his story—for now.

"Did you see anyone or anything at the beach?" asked Reeves.

He felt instantly warm again, like he could break into a sweat. Should he mention the SUV? They already knew about the truck because of the county tracking system. Right? Why didn't they mention it? *Shit.* The time between the question and his answer felt like an eternity.

"I didn't see anybody on the way in or out. It was completely quiet—like usual."

If they brought up the SUV, he'd say he was asleep.

Reeves leaned forward, propping her elbows on the table and lacing her fingers together. "So if I were to stop by your house, all I'm going to find is a tub full of seawater?"

"At this point," he said, glancing at his watch, "you'll see two barrels. One filled with about ten gallons of seawater, the other filled with about five of fresh. I can convert about 1.5 gallons an hour with my rig, which is in desperate need of repair. I do this so we don't have to watch every drop of water that comes out of the faucet. My kid can run cross-country. My wife can break a sweat practicing yoga and make an extra pot of tea every night. We can raise a few tomatoes and peppers in the backyard—hidden from the neighbors, of course."

"There's nothing illegal about a desalinator," said Reeves. "Why the secrecy?"

"It's a gray-area activity here. Upper management frowns on any real or perceived water-allowance advantage by Water Reclamation Authority employees. Bad for the water authority's public image, or some bullshit like that."

Reeves stared at him for several uncomfortable seconds before breaking eye contact and turning to the inspector. "Any questions?"

"I don't think so," said Ramirez, shaking his head.

"A few more questions for me," said Reeves.

Nathan nodded.

"Are you affiliated with the California Liberation Movement?"

"What? No. No. I haven't donated money, signed any petitions, or any of that. That's not my thing." Nathan shrugged.

"Because of water-department policy?" asked Reeves.

"No. I don't have any interest in getting involved, which fits nicely with the county's preference that we keep our opinions on the issue private. We live a comfortable life here. I see no reason to rock the boat, so to speak."

"So you'd support a campaign against the CLM? To keep things the same," said Reeves.

"I didn't say that," said Nathan. "I don't get involved either way."

Reeves produced a tan document-size envelope and slid it across the conference table toward Nathan. He stared at the envelope, noting thick block letters forming the words *CLASSIFIED: INTERNAL US BUREAU OF RECLAMATION USE ONLY*. Nathan couldn't suppress a smile. *They'd done their homework.*

"Can I assume you know what's in this envelope?" asked Reeves.

"If it's my master's thesis, you can correctly assume I know what's in the envelope. I'm surprised you have access to this," he said, patting the envelope. "I wasn't allowed to keep a copy."

"You don't exactly take a neutral stance about California's water crisis in the paper."

"Did you read the paper?" asked Nathan.

"I read the Bureau of Reclamation's executive summary."

Nathan was tempted to engage Reeves in a blatantly "over her head" conversation about the paper's topic, to demonstrate the perils of relying on a jaded bureaucracy's executive summary of an eighty-page, meticulously documented academic paper, but decided it wouldn't be in his best interest.

"I guess you can attribute the tone of the paper to my more idealistic college years. I'm quite happy working on the more practical and lucrative side of the problem now. The ongoing theft of 1.6 trillion gallons of water per year from the lower Colorado River basin keeps my expertise in demand."

Reeves kept a neutral expression. "And your wife?"

"What about her?"

"Does she support the CLM?" asked Reeves.

"Do you think she drove my car to the beach this morning? County can confirm that I was the only one in the car. I was stopped at one of their checkpoints on the way to the beach. Northbound exit ramp at Del Mar Heights."

"We know," said Reeves. "I'm required to ask the question."

Did they actually suspect that the CLM was behind the sabotage of a project they spent millions lobbying to support? Everyone was losing their minds over this.

"All right. I'm good to go," Reeves said, pulling the envelope to her side of the table.

"Thank you," said Nathan, wishing he could read the bureau's executive summary.

"I wasn't finished," she said. "I'm good to go with a temporary geographic restraint. I want you close to home until someone figures out what happened in Del Mar. I'm going to submit a request to restrict your movement to San Diego County."

Shit. Keira was going to kill him. Even if he lost his job today, he was stuck in San Diego County. Better than having the police dig around his house. Maybe.

"I can live with that," Nathan said weakly.

Reeves cracked a short-lived laugh and handed him a card. "Bet your ass you can live with that. Log into the website on this card with your California ID number to access the court paperwork. And don't even think about leaving the county."

CHAPTER 16

Detective Emma Peck typed a string of sixteen keys into her system, triggering the "blind spot" virus provided by her handler. Until she retyped the sequence backward, her activity on the San Diego County Police Department's Virtual Investigative Division's server would remain invisible and unrecorded. She'd have free rein on the department's most classified and powerful data network, with zero limitations.

Total insider access, which is exactly what her clients wanted—badly enough to pay an exorbitant, untraceable monthly fee. She'd been on their payroll for two and a half years, amassing enough money in a confidential overseas account to comfortably retire anywhere in the world. She planned on sticking around another year or so before resigning—and putting as much distance between herself and California as possible.

She glanced over her shoulder more out of nervous habit than necessity. Due to the sensitive nature of her team's work, which frequently involved Internal Affairs requests, her cubicle walls extended to the ceiling, and she could lock the door. Inside her eight-foot-by-eight-foot haven, she could examine the police commissioner's expense account or view the chief of Internal Affairs' e-mails without anyone knowing.

As usual, the information request she'd received through an encrypted, self-erasing message packet on her phone seemed mundane:

an hourly sweep for all San Diego County Police Department data related to the Del Mar Triad Station. She'd scour every investigative case file and e-mail in the county system, along with 911 and online reporting sources. Overall, an easy search to execute, since the parameters were narrow and the keyword layers had been predefined by her clients. They'd obviously done their homework—whoever *they* might be.

Peck entered the keywords, in a system application exclusive to the Virtual Investigative Division, and waited for the results. The program returned eighty-three hits in the first layer, seven in the second, and nothing in the final filter. She typed an eight-digit code into the keyboard, which packaged the data in a file and sent it to her phone. The wireless transfer took less than a second, her cell vibrating briefly. Now all she had to do was take a short break in the detectives' lounge on the second floor—the only room in the building designed to permit communication outside of the VID network. She'd walk in, buy a cup of coffee from the vending machine, and the program installed on her phone would do the rest when it connected with the room's wireless signal. Easy retirement.

CHAPTER 17

Mason Flagg checked his watch, wondering if Leeds had slipped and killed himself in the bathroom. He'd woken him seven minutes earlier, with assurances that he'd be there shortly. "Shortly" had been five minutes ago, and time was ticking in front him on the computer screen. He scrolled through the police report, frustrated by its lack of detail. His gut told him something was missing, but he couldn't put his finger on it.

Nathan Fisher, a San Diego County Water Department engineer, had been at the beach when Olmos retrieved the dive team. There was little to no doubt about that. The time-stamped vehicle track data attached to the investigating detective's report confirmed that Fisher's vehicle had been at the San Dieguito River beach preserve at the same time, further backed by Leeds's report of a matching silver Toyota sedan parked alone in the small lot on Ocean Front Road. Strangely enough, Leeds didn't record the car's license plate or investigate the beach on foot.

Flagg read the text of the police report again, trying to figure out what bothered him. In this morning's interview, Fisher had made no mention of the boats, or any activity at the beach, which was consistent with the claim that he'd fallen asleep in the beach grasses above the high-tide line, but—but what? That was the question.

The door behind Flagg buzzed, drawing his attention to the left-most screen on the parabolic array beyond his computer station. Leeds's face filled the screen, his head positioned too close to the security camera embedded in the door. *Finally.* Flagg touched the security icon on the bottom right-hand corner of his computer monitor and selected "GRANT ENTRY-FULL CLEARANCE" from several choices.

When Leeds opened the door, the other screens retained their images, which would not be the case following the entry of most of the Cerebrus team assigned to the operation. Like all larger-scale Cerebrus operations, information was compartmentalized, with teams operating independently of one another, with no concept of the bigger picture. The current California operation utilized eighty-three operatives divided between several groups. Of these, only Flagg and Leeds knew the full scope of the operation, though Flagg was quite sure a few more had put together enough of the pieces to figure out why Cerebrus was here. When the operation ended, Flagg would make sure those pieces didn't come together in a meaningful, public way—even if it meant *terminating* a few employment contracts.

Leeds closed the door and walked straight for the coffeemaker.

"I figured you'd already grabbed a coffee—and breakfast—down the street, perhaps," said Flagg over his shoulder.

"You didn't stock the bunkroom with adult diapers, so I took the liberty of using the toilet—and, God forbid, brushing my teeth."

"I'm not sure how the two are related, and I don't want to know," said Flagg. "Take a look at this. We might have a problem, thanks to you."

Leeds abandoned his coffee-making efforts, instead sliding a chair next to Flagg. "Thanks to me?" he said. "I'm sorry, was I even on the ground in San Diego when Olmos ran behind schedule?"

"Why didn't you conduct a detailed sweep of the beach preserve area?"

The operative squinted at the center computer screen, absorbing as much as possible before answering. "Thermal surveillance from the boats indicated no observers," said Leeds, his eyes never leaving the monitor.

"But you reported a car in the parking lot."

"I scanned the area with a spotlight. The beachside area was empty," said Leeds. "It's not uncommon to find cars parked overnight at the beaches."

"According to the report you've been scrambling to read since you sat down, somebody was at or near the preserve when the boats picked up the divers," said Flagg. "In fact, this somebody may have been less than a hundred and fifty yards away from the pickup."

"Why did Olmos pick them up so goddamn close to the beach?"

"Because they were behind schedule, and dawn was breaking," said Flagg. "That's why I sent you over to sanitize the area, which you apparently failed to do."

Leeds seemed to ignore him, focusing on the screen for a few seconds before responding. "He didn't see the boats or the SUV."

Flagg thought about his comment for a moment, suddenly realizing what he'd missed. He'd been so focused on the boats, he'd forgotten about the vehicle. His fingers worked the keyboard furiously, adding the GPS track for Leeds's SUV to the geographic overlay. When it hit the screen, he didn't like what it suggested. Maybe Fisher's omission had been intentional.

"He left in a hurry, less than a minute after you drove away," said Flagg. "That's too quick for someone shaking off a nap. He had to be awake when you stopped at the intersection."

"Maybe I spooked him with the light. He might have thought I was a cop and bolted as soon as I left."

"The police stopped him at the Del Mar Heights exit on the way to the beach and let him proceed," said Flagg. "He wouldn't be worried about CPD."

"Everyone is worried about CPD," said Leeds, continuing to read the screen. "It's odd that he didn't report the SUV. He had nothing to lose by mentioning it."

"Or, he felt that he had more to lose by mentioning it—especially after discovering that the nuclear reactor shut down," Flagg said. "Suspicious boats in the water. Black Suburbans combing the neighborhoods. Sudden reactor shutdown. I might be a little cautious about what I disclosed to the authorities."

"Or was he asleep?"

"I propose finding the answers to a different question: How long was he awake?"

"I'll work up a surveillance package," said Leeds.

"I want full electronic access to his devices, a neighborhood-based stakeout, and a team following him, twenty-four seven."

Leeds stood up, staying in place for a moment. "I should have taken the team through the scrub at the beach."

"It worked out better this way," said Flagg. "If this Fisher character still managed to elude you, he might have become overly suspicious and reported the boats to the police. We can contain this. A little watch-and-wait to determine what Mr. Fisher knows—and make sure the police are none the wiser."

Chapter 18

Nathan pushed his food around, forcing a polite smile that betrayed his desire to be left alone when his son or wife looked up from their dinners. He felt anxious and distant, his mind far away from the fish tacos, seasoned pinto beans, and spicy coleslaw on his plate.

He knew they felt it, too, caught them trading nervous glances while efficiently finishing the food on their plates. Everyone wanted dinner to end, especially Nathan. He had no appetite at all. His presence at the table was a ruse to feign normality—and not a very successful one. In fact, he'd probably made matters worse by coming to dinner. Now his family knew for a fact that something was wrong. Maybe he could turn this around.

"Sorry I'm so tense," said Nathan, placing his fork on the plate. "Everyone at work was in a panic over the reactor shutdown. County is looking at our division to make up for a significant portion of the difference in lost drinking water, and nobody has any idea how to do that. We're squeezing just about every drop possible out of our—"

"Don't say it," said Keira, finally cracking a smile.

"—suburbs," said Nathan, shrugging.

"That's not what you were going to say," she insisted.

"What do you think?" asked Nathan, nodding at his son.

"I think it was going to rhyme with scoop," said Owen, grinning.

"More like a combination of ship and fit," said Nathan, causing his son to break into a laugh.

"Honey!" said Keira, shaking her head. "He repeats that stuff at school, you know."

"Good," said Nathan. "Just don't tell them you heard it from me. How was school today?"

"Fine."

"Just fine?" asked Nathan, raising an eyebrow. "This is your last week of school. You should be excited."

"We're barely doing anything. And I hate going to camp. Do I have to go to camp this summer?"

"Yes," Nathan and Keira said in unison, his wife continuing to answer.

"Both of us have to work," she said, "and you can't stay home by yourself."

"I know a lot of kids that stay home, and they're the same age."

Keira beat him to one of their signature parent lines: "Well, that's not how we roll. You're eleven."

"I'll be twelve in July."

"If you'd said fourteen, you might have had a chance, buddy," said Nathan. "I don't think it's legal to leave you home by yourself."

"It's legal when I'm twelve," said Owen. "I'll be twelve in forty-two days."

"We'll consider it next year," said Keira. "Anyway, we're planning a trip to visit Nana and Pops. You won't be in camp all summer."

"In Idaho?" asked Owen, clearly excited by the prospect.

"In Idaho," said Keira.

"Awesome! When are we going?"

Nathan barely heard the question. Keira's unsubtle reminder of her plan to flee California prompted a cascade of concerns and questions; he was also saddled with a county command to stay local. He dreaded the prospect of bringing this up with Keira.

"Did you hear Owen's question, honey?" asked Keira.

"Yeah," he said, picking up on of his tacos. "Uh . . . I'm not exactly sure when we're going."

Keira's smile waned a little.

"It might be a little tight with work stuff," he said. "Why don't we talk about it after dinner? Settle on a date and figure out how long we can be gone. I know they'll be super excited to see Owen. It's been two years. We'll get you swimming in a real lake."

"Grandpa said the lakes were freezing up there," said Owen.

"They're cold, but the water is crystal clear, and you can drink right out of the lakes and rivers. The second you see it, you'll want to jump right in. There's nothing like it."

"Is it colder than the ocean?"

"It's like the beach here in the winter," said Nathan. "Cold, but once you get in, you're fine. And it's freshwater, so it doesn't burn your eyes. You'll love it."

"I hope we can go," said his son. "Maybe I could stay up there after you leave and come back later in the summer. Nana said that was okay."

"You really don't want to go to summer camp, do you?" asked Keira.

"Him staying on there isn't a bad idea," said Nathan.

Keira appeared to be considering the proposal, which underscored her fear of the situation in California. She had politely entertained the idea whenever his parents brought it up in person, dodging the question and eventually declining the offer based on a host of flimsy excuses. Nathan knew better than to broach the subject himself. She'd made her feelings much clearer to him in private.

"I don't know about staying up there alone, sweetie," she said, unconvincingly.

"Please!" said Owen.

"We'd have to drive back to pick you up, which would be extremely expensive."

"Nana said they'd pay for me to fly," said Owen, looking at his plate.

"We've already gone over this," said Keira, flashing Nathan a dirty look. "They don't have a direct flight, and you're not old enough to be in an airport by yourself."

"I don't even know if we'll be taking a trip, buddy," said Nathan. "Things are going to be crazy at work for a little while. Once we figure that out, we'll see about letting you stay for part of the summer."

His son took a few moments to respond, placing his fork on the plate and looking up with a disappointed face. "It'll never happen," he said at last. "Can I be excused?"

Nathan glanced at Keira, who nodded. "That's fine, buddy," he said. "Finish your water first."

Nathan forced a few more bites of a taco into his nervous stomach, watching his son guzzle the water he'd retrieved from the Pacific Ocean this morning. He understood Owen's frustration. Southern California sucked for kids.

Years of drought had radically transformed Southern California's adolescent experience. Once marked by daily trips to the community pool with friends, year-round weekend and evening trips to the beach, plus a whole host of outdoor fun just a short bike or car ride away, the California Resource Protection Act had put an end to all that.

All the pools were drained, either left empty and cracked, or filled with sand. Most parks had turned into dry, brittle pockets of suburban tinder, long ago bulldozed and treated semiannually with weed killer. Only the seaside parks, desperately sucking moisture from damp coastal air, retained a semblance of the glory that used to attract thousands to picnic and lounge in the grassy shade.

Then you had the beaches.

Little remained of the original beach culture beyond decayed concrete boardwalks, long stretches of the finest sand beaches in the country, and the same unexpectedly chilly water that always took tourists by surprise. California's lively but run-down beach communities had been completely transformed by 2030. Rapid gentrification occurred in the early '20s, when lawmakers lifted statewide property tax limits to pay for early infrastructure projects mandated by the California Self Reliance Act's "Twenty-Year Plan."

Slapped with significantly higher tax bills overnight, longtime residents of famed tourist meccas like Pacific Beach were forced to move inland within a few months. Leases were broken by landlords, as the new tax burdens forced building owners to sell their property to real estate conglomerates. As tenants and residents vanished, the bars, gift shops, restaurants, and tattoo parlors evaporated with them. Within a few years, the bungalows and dilapidated apartment buildings gave way to new construction, giving birth to upscale communities on par with La Jolla, Del Mar, and Encinitas.

With the new communities came town-implemented police checkpoints, elimination of public parking, and an unwritten municipal code promoting the harassment of outsiders. The beaches remained public, but few families were willing to sacrifice precious out-of-district time to sit in beach traffic, fight for outrageously expensive parking, and subject themselves to an undertone of disapproval.

"Inlanders" mostly steered clear of the immediate coast, making only the traditional pilgrimage when the rare out-of-town guest visited, or on public holidays, when the powers that be eased up on their harassment policies.

"We'll figure something out, sweetie," said his wife, as Owen skulked away toward the bedroom hallway.

When Owen had closed his bedroom door, Keira pushed her chair back and turned it toward him. "What's really going on, Nathan? I've seen you stressed from work before. This is something different."

He hesitated, still unsure how much to tell her.

"Nathan," she hissed, keeping her voice low, "what's going on?"

"Not here," he said, nodding toward the hallway.

Nathan led his wife onto the backyard patio, closing the glass slider behind her. They sat across from each other at a rectangular wrought iron table situated under a worn, double-slatted pergola attached to the house. Beyond the six-foot-tall stucco wall bordering the western side of their tiny backyard, the horizon glowed deep-orange, fading into a deep-blue sky. Long shadows from their neighbor's dwarf palm trees reached across the yard, touching the edges of the patio.

Keira raised both eyebrows. "Well?" she said, leaning forward in her chair.

"The police talked to me this morning."

"At the off-ramp checkpoint," said Keira. "You already—"

"No," he interrupted. "At my office."

"What?" she said, slapping her hands on the table. "When were you planning on telling me this?"

"I got home late, and Owen was in the kitchen with you," he said, tripping over his own words. "I didn't want him to—"

"You should have called me," she said, sounding angrier. "You know, like as soon as the police left! I don't like being kept in the dark like this."

"Sorry. I just didn't want you to worry about it all day—and it's not a big deal," he said, immediately wishing he hadn't added that last part.

"Not a big deal?" she said, sitting back. "The police don't visit you at work unless it's a big deal." Keira rubbed her face, sighing through her hands. "What did they want?"

"They had questions about my weekly trips to the beach, especially my extended visit this morning. All easily explainable."

"You told them about the desalinator?"

"I had to," said Nathan. "They didn't seem to care."

His wife took a few moments to process what he'd said.

"They think the reactor was sabotaged?" she said.

"They're certainly not discounting the possibility," said Nathan. "Though they didn't come out and say it."

"This is serious, Nate," she said. "How did they leave things with you?"

Nathan dreaded telling her.

"I can't leave San Diego County," he said, wincing.

"For how long?"

"Until someone figures out why the cooling pump failed."

"We really need to leave before that happens," said Keira. "If the station was sabotaged, the secession issue will go critical. Staying here could become extremely dangerous."

"We—I can't go anywhere," said Nathan. "They filed a geographic restraint with the county. If I leave, they'll issue a warrant for my arrest."

"No state outside of California honors that crap," she stated. "Plenty of counties in Northern California don't either. A few hours of driving and that won't be a problem anymore."

"Except we can't come back to the county without me being arrested and detained as a permanent flight risk," said Nathan. "Then I'm fucked."

"Maybe we don't come back," she said quietly, turning to face the sunset.

"The thought crossed my mind, but skipping out on a geographic restraint can seriously backfire. I looked into it as soon as the police left the office. I can be charged on a felony level for violating a court order. And regardless of what other states think about the constitutional legalities of the geographic restraint system, municipalities and corporations tend to frown on employing felons. And if the county wanted to get really pissy, they could file a petition with the feds to have my passport revoked."

She considered his assessment, and her lips formed a grimace, barely visible in the fading light.

"I hear what you're saying," Keira said, "but I'm more worried about what might happen if we stay."

"The state won't descend into outright civil war overnight, even if the reactor was deliberately sabotaged."

"No, but the police might round up everyone on their list and drop them off at one of those new detention centers on the border, in the name of state security," she said. "You're on that list."

"That's not going to happen."

"Are you willing to bet our family's survival on that hunch?" asked Keira, lowering her voice. "We sure as shit can't live here on my income alone. Not even for a month."

She had a point, but the thought of driving off tonight or tomorrow, never to return, felt reckless and impulsive. Life outside California wouldn't be easy. When the county classified him as a permanent fugitive, they'd face immediate foreclosure on their home, which would destroy their credit rating. Within a few weeks of fleeing the state, they'd lose access to the rental market. Not the entire market—just the areas without sky-high crime rates, crippling unemployment and bottom-tier schools. California had its flaws, but at least it was safe.

"I think we need to give it more time," he said. "A few days, at least. We'll have everything ready to go, and if the situation is the same on Friday, we'll take off over the weekend."

"A lot can change in two days."

"We'll keep the plan flexible," said Nathan. "We can be on the road in an hour."

"I don't know."

Nathan got out of his seat and nestled behind his wife, wrapping both arms around her waist. He kissed her neck, before placing his forehead on her shoulder. "We'll be fine," he whispered. "If anything weird happens in the next few days, we'll take off. Promise."

She leaned her head into his. "I do love you . . ."

"But?" he said, filling the pause.

"I sometimes worry about your everything-is-going-to-be-all-right attitude," she said. "This would be one hell of a time to be wrong."

"Wrong or right, we have a good plan. We can be out of the state in two and a half hours if we head east on I-8."

"The wastelands?" she said, pulling her head away. "I'd rather take our chances with a longer trip north."

"We won't have to go anywhere," he said, holding her tight. "They rushed the construction of that place. All of the new triad facilities, actually. We'll wake up to news of an improperly calibrated electrical part, or some kind of design flaw. Everything will be back to normal."

She shook her head. "Does Mr. Optimistic ever take a break?"

"No. It's bad for family morale," he said, his thoughts drifting to the mysterious boats and the black SUV at the beach. Probably new security measures implemented in light of Almeda's assassination. Nothing to get worked up about, and certainly not something he was going to bring up with Keira right now. She was one conspiracy theory away from booking three airline tickets to Argentina.

CHAPTER 19

Nick Leeds watched the target through a powerful digital spotting scope, hoping that nothing had been omitted from his intelligence packet. They had zero margin of error tonight; a failure here could unravel the entire California operation.

"Target stationary in great room," he whispered, his throat microphone transmitting the message to the rest of the team. "On my mark, initiate the sequence."

"Copy that," murmured Raymond Olmos, loud enough for Leeds to hear without the help of his earpiece.

Olmos lay a foot away to Leeds's right, his full attention focused on the illumination-adaptable scope attached to the latest-generation 50-caliber sniper rifle. The XM-850 was a semiautomatic, recoil-compensated killing machine, capable of reaching out and touching targets over a mile away. At the current distance, a little more than a half mile, an experienced sniper like Olmos could hit a target center-mass with two successive shots—virtually ensuring a kill.

Unfortunately, tonight's mission wouldn't be that simple. Gareth McDaid, lieutenant governor of California and staunch antisecessionist supporter, was one of the most heavily guarded public officials in the nation. In addition to an ever-present California State Police special operations detail, McDaid privately bankrolled robust security at his Sacramento foothills mansion.

Leeds had quickly dismissed the possibility of a direct raid against the house. McDaid kept a platoon-size contingent of hired guns on the property, and Flagg wasn't keen for the kind of bad exposure a full-scale ground assault might generate—especially if the state police detail got in the way or one of McDaid's family members took a stray bullet.

He settled on the sniper option, which carried less risk to his team and bystanders, but still presented its own unique challenges. First, a dizzying and exhaustive array of active and passive security measures prevented his team from approaching closer than eight hundred yards. Covered by thermal protective blankets and dressed in military-prototype, heat-signature reduction suits, they had cautiously inched into position, well within the detection range of the thermal sensors surveying the foothills. Computer simulation models and practical experience—not to mention his nerves—kept them from moving any closer.

Then there was the small matter of locating and shooting the lieutenant governor, a task made both easy and difficult by the vast sheets of floor-to-ceiling glass facing the foothills. With the exception of a single trip to the bathroom, McDaid had been under direct observation since the teams moved into position a few hours ago. Olmos could have taken the shot already, if that same glass hadn't been designed to withstand 50-caliber, armor-piercing rifle fire. Fortunately for Leeds, the intelligence packet provided by Cerberus had suggested a work-around—which he was moments from initiating.

"Stand by. Three. Two. One. Mark," said Leeds, triggering the laser designator on his spotting scope.

The soft, hollow thumping of four tripod-mounted 25mm smart grenade launchers broke the high-desert silence, as he centered the laser designator's targeting reticle at the nape of the lieutenant governor's neck. His attention split between the reticle and the scope's built-in digital timer, he vaguely noticed the basketball game playing on the screen beyond McDaid. A few seconds later, the green digital counter in the bottom of the spotting scope's display read "2.5 seconds."

"Fire," he said, his command answered by the repeated, thunderous bark of the 50-caliber rifle.

While the 50-caliber, laser-guided bullets raced toward the lieutenant governor at three thousand feet per second, sixteen 25mm high explosive grenades finished their lazy, coordinated arcs toward the fifteen-foot-high sheet of ballistic glass. The grenades struck within milliseconds of each other, creating a ripple of compact explosive flashes that cleared the way for Olmos's bullets.

Through the falling cascade of shattered blue-white glass pieces, Leeds caught a splash of crimson-red against the wall-mounted flat-screen television. An instant later, after the glass had fallen, he watched with grim satisfaction as the final two 50-caliber projectiles tore through the lieutenant governor's headless torso, propelling the bloodied corpse halfway across the room.

"Confirmed kill. Move to extract," said Leeds. "Teams Alpha and Delta cover the withdrawal. Be advised. Do not engage state police assets without my permission. I repeat. Do not engage state police assets without my permission. All teams acknowledge."

While the teams acknowledged his explicit order over the radio net, Leeds expanded the scope's field of vision to view the entire property. A bedside lamp on the far side of the house suddenly illuminated the master bedroom, exposing McDaid's confused wife to outside observation. Two men carrying compact rifles burst through her bedroom door, one of them smashing the lamp to conceal their movements.

Despite the absolute darkness in the room, his scope's image sensors maintained a near perfect color picture as the men dragged her out of the room. While taking in the scene, his eyes registered a small flash from the center of the home's rooftop—triggering an instantaneous survival instinct.

Leeds straight-armed Olmos, using the momentum from the shove to roll in the opposite direction under the thermal blanket. A sharp crack exploded next to his head, ripping the thick blanket away. He scrambled backward along the rocky ground until the rooftop's dark outline disappeared. Somewhere to his right, he heard Olmos hiss obscenities in the thick darkness as the sniper's boots struggled for purchase against the rocky fold.

"Delta engaging sniper nest," Leeds's earpiece announced. Still half-dazed by the near miss, he squinted at the shadow moving next to him. "You good?"

"Oh yeah," said Olmos, breathing heavily. "Saved thirty bucks on a haircut. How the fuck did our intel people miss that?"

"I have no idea," said Leeds, hoping they didn't miss anything else.

A short burst of distant explosions snapped him back into focus.

"Rooftop sniper neutralized," said the Delta team gunner. "I have two groups of four working their way past the pool, firing in our direction."

The sound of automatic gunfire drifted through the hills, followed by overhead snaps and ricochets off nearby boulders. With more than eight hundred meters of rocky, uphill terrain to negotiate, the security teams didn't present a serious danger to their escape. Still, there was no reason to risk any casualties at this point.

"Can you identify any state police officers among the responding teams?" Leeds asked the gunner.

"Looks clear to me. No police in the mix."

"Copy. Alpha and Delta, engage and eliminate the two groups. Everyone else pack up," he said, crawling back into position on the ridge.

He raised the spotting scope in time to witness a tight cluster of explosive flashes tear into the rocks beyond the far right side of the glowing pool. Half of a severed leg skipped along the smooth deck, tumbling into the pool trailed by more body parts. A nearly identical horror show unfolded on the opposite side of the pool.

The sharp explosive concussion of the grenades reached his ears a few seconds later, followed by a stark silence. He carefully surveyed the property for several seconds. A few random heads peeked through door frames deep inside the house. A small group cautiously edged its way toward the lieutenant governor's body. Infrared flashlight beams stabbed into the night on the unobserved side of the house.

Unsurprisingly, little else stirred inside or outside of the former lieutenant governor's house. The 25mm smart grenade launcher was a devastatingly evil weapon to use against soft targets, and it apparently deterred whoever was still alive.

"All teams withdraw to the primary rally point," said Leeds, continuing his vigil over the house.

Olmos reloaded his rifle before jamming the torn thermal blanket into his rucksack. "Ready when you're ready," he said, lifting the sniper rifle off the ground.

Leeds grabbed the spotting scope and folded its mini-tripod before swinging his assault rifle into the ready position. He lowered the night-vision goggles attached to his head mount and tapped a button on his wrist tablet. The muted infrared screen gave him four easily accessible preset options. He pressed his gloved index finger against "EXTRACT NAV," activating the internal navigation Heads-Up Display in his night-vision device. He could now follow the icons displayed in his goggles to navigate toward the team's extract point.

He headed northeast, pressing the "Banshee" button a few minutes later. The display indicated a connection moments later.

"Banshee, this is Wraith," said Leeds. "Two has been flushed. I say again. Two has been flushed. ETA primary extract point in one-eight minutes."

"This is Banshee, copy your transmission," replied Flagg's voice. "Spectre en route to primary extract point. Contact Spectre on separate channel to coordinate pickup."

"Copy. Wraith out."

Twenty minutes later, Leeds and his team of nine Cerberus special operators sat crammed together inside the sparse cabin of a first-generation military stealth helicopter. Flying nap-of-earth to ensure radar invisibility, the helicopter headed due west for the California coast, a forty-minute flight taking them over the sparsely populated areas just north of California's wine country. Once over the Pacific Ocean, the helicopter would turn south, seeking its launch pad on a Sentinel Corporation–owned offshore oil platform outside of Morrow Bay. The two-hour trip would give Leeds a much-needed rest. Flagg had him running on fumes for the past twenty-four hours.

He leaned his head back against the vibrating metal interior. Just after he'd closed his eyes, an annoying earpiece chirp alerted him to an incoming satellite call. His night-vision HUD confirmed what he already knew: Flagg had no intention of letting him sleep tonight. He accepted the call with his wrist tablet, increasing the volume so he could hear over the helicopter engine's perpetual whine.

"Leeds," he said.

"I hope I didn't wake you," said Flagg.

Leeds broke into a laugh. "I wouldn't dream of taking a nap on the job."

"Good. I pay you too much as it is," said Flagg. "Any problems tonight?"

"Not really. Either the first or second bullet removed the target's head. The rest just amplified the message," said Leeds. "Approximately eight private security contractors engaged from the pool area. I doubt any of them survived. No apparent casualties in the house beyond what I just reported."

"You said 'not really' any problems. I assume you're not feeling guilty about the security contractors? Am I missing something?"

"They had a concealed sniper on the roof. Gave us a close shave," said Leeds. "Satellite pictures should have picked that up. Unless the intelligence team used outdated imagery."

"Correct," said Flagg. "I'll address that with our people shortly. Anything else?"

"Negative. It was a clean operation—if you consider the use of high-explosive projectiles clean."

"I consider the use of high explosives a bonus," replied Flagg. "Tonight's operation will guarantee that all eyes remain focused on California—and the brutal tactics the California Liberation Movement will employ to get what they want."

"I wouldn't get in that group's way," said Leeds, hoping Flagg was done.

"Speaking of getting in the way," said Flagg, pausing. "I've been thinking about our beach witness."

"That doesn't sound good for his health."

"I don't suspect it will be," said Flagg. "Surveillance suggests he might flee California in the next few days. I believe tonight's news might expedite his departure."

"Accidents are fairly common on the high-desert roads leading out of California. The sooner he gets on the road, the better, I say."

"I think Mr. Fisher will better serve our needs here in Southern California," said Flagg. "I have something special in mind for him."

"And you'd like to work out the details right now?" asked Leeds, his interest oddly piqued despite his state of exhaustion.

"Not unless you have more important plans."

"You have my undivided attention—as always."

A half hour later, Flagg disconnected the call and Leeds closed his eyes, replaying the conversation. Flagg's latest plan was devilishly depraved, giving Leeds a rare glimpse into the man's deepest thought processes. He could see with full clarity why Cerberus had put Flagg in charge of the group's most important operations. The man gave zero fucks about anything but getting the job done. Leeds needed to remember that when he woke up, because Flagg wouldn't hesitate to burn him if it benefited one of Cerberus's clients.

CHAPTER 20

Nathan tried to pretend he was dead asleep—a nearly impossible ruse with his wife's hands throttling his upturned shoulder. What time was it? He peered beneath one of his eyelids, glimpsing the wall-mounted screen, which read 6:05 a.m. Why was she doing this? It was still early.

"I can see you looking at the clock," she said, hitting him harder. "I need you awake. Now. We're leaving."

"What the ffffuh?" he grumbled.

"You want to know what the fuck is going on? Try this," she said, letting go of his arm. "TV activate. Lieutenant Governor McDaid assassination. Replay latest broadcast."

McDaid's assassination? The monitor flashed, displaying the smart cable logo. A female digitized voice replied to his wife's request. "Replaying KGTV broadcast. Six o'clock a.m., pacific standard time."

"You better be watching," said Keira.

"Can't I have my coffee first?" he said, meekly testing the waters.

"You won't need coffee after this," she said, just as the broadcast started.

"This is KGTV anchor Natalie Ruiz broadcasting live from our studios with the latest update in this unbelievable overnight development. For the viewers just waking up to the news, Lieutenant Governor Gareth McDaid was assassinated last night at his Sacramento residence, in what

the governor's office calls the most brazen and deplorable act of violence ever perpetrated against a public official in the United States."

"Jesus," Nathan muttered, squeezing his wife's hand.

"Details of the attack are still unconfirmed, but we do know that Sacramento County Police dispatchers received a frantic call from a state trooper assigned to the lieutenant governor's security detail at 11:35 p.m., reporting that the residence was under heavy attack and requesting armed drone support. With the investigation ongoing, neither the police nor the governor's office have provided additional details, but neighbors confirmed the sound of multiple explosions and automatic gunfire coming from the direction of the lieutenant governor's vast property on the northern edge of the exclusive Sacramento foothills community.

"Let's go to Brett Abrahams, who is on the scene outside of El Dorado Ranch Estates. Brett, what can you tell us?"

"Natalie, the scene has been surreal, with armed police drones buzzing overhead and tactical vehicles roaming the streets inside the gated community. The few residents willing to speak with us painted a grim picture of the evening's attack.

"Explosions rocked the tranquil community just after eleven, setting off home alarms and waking residents to what one neighbor described as a 'Fourth of July light show.' Whatever happened at the lieutenant governor's mansion was short-lived, according to residents; the streets quieting again a few minutes later."

"Has anyone seen the lieutenant governor's house?" asked Ruiz. "Do we have any idea what happened?"

"The lieutenant governor's property is a private twenty-acre estate at the northern tip of the community. The house can't be seen from streets, or viewed from any of the neighbors' properties, and all efforts to bring a media helicopter or drone into the foothills have been thwarted by authorities. We do know that the lieutenant governor was pronounced dead on the scene by the Sacramento County Coroner's Office, a fact confirmed by the governor's press secretary."

"Brett, has there been any on-scene speculation about who might have been behind the attack?"

"Here we go," said Nathan.

"Official sources have been surprisingly quiet, including the governor's office, but it's no secret that Gareth McDaid was a tireless supporter of the One Nation Coalition, publicly opposing the secessionist efforts," said Abrahams.

"With recent rumors about Congresswoman Almeda's connection to One Nation racing across social media, is it too early to link the two assassinations?" asked Ruiz.

"It's too early to tell, but McDaid clearly stood in One Nation's corner. Almeda's position on the secession issue remained unclear up until and after her death, though she had just left a dinner meeting with congressmen linked to the ONC."

"Two high-profile assassinations of public officials linked to the One Nation Coalition within a twenty-four-hour period will undoubtedly raise a lot of questions," said Ruiz.

"Mute the television," said Keira, deactivating the broadcast's sound. "Unless you need to hear more."

"No," said Nathan. "We leave tonight. Late. Everything is staged and ready to be loaded. We'll have dinner—"

"We need to leave now," she insisted.

"I'm probably under police surveillance," he said. "And I'm definitely subject to a court-mandated geographic restriction. I need to show up to work, like they expect."

"Until they escort you to one of those camps on the border," said Keira. "Where you'll disappear."

"That's not going to happen," said Nathan, his thoughts flashing to the black boats and SUV.

"Are you sure?" she said. "We can be in Arizona by nine o'clock in the morning."

"Arizona is not a viable option, for a lot of reasons. We'll head north on Interstate 15 tonight. It's four and a half hours to the Nevada border. It's a safer route."

She ran a hand through her sandy-blonde hair. "We leave no later than nine tonight."

"All right," he muttered.

"Really?" she insisted.

"Really," he said, still trying to wrap his uncaffeinated brain around the big picture.

It all felt disturbingly connected now. Two brazen assassinations. Stealth boats retrieving divers near the Del Mar Triad Station minutes before the reactor cooling pump fails. A black heavy-duty SUV scanning the beach for witnesses. Jesus. Why hadn't he put that together earlier?

But the police didn't mention the SUV. Why? Something was off.

Nathan lowered his head to the pillow and stared at the popcorn ceiling.

Keira was right. The sooner they left, the better—but they had to do it smartly, though he wasn't sure what that meant anymore. He had absolutely no idea how closely the police might be watching him, especially in light of the lieutenant governor's murder. Had he already missed his window of opportunity by not listening to Keira last night and leaving immediately?

If the San Diego County PD had him under tight surveillance, the police would likely stop them at the county border. Even worse, they could claim Keira had helped him violate a court order, and throw both of them in a detention center and toss their son into the Child Protective Services system. Nathan's parents would have to fight to extract Owen from that mess. Maybe they should leave separately and rendezvous outside of California, in case the police nabbed him along the way.

"You all right?" she said, kissing him on the forehead.

"Yeah," he said, rubbing his face. "I'll . . . uh . . . call my dad a little later. Give him a heads-up that we're heading his way. Maybe I can convince him to grab a few of his survivalist friends and meet us halfway. The stretch between Las Vegas and Salt Lake City can get a little rough."

"I thought the I-15 was safe."

"It is, between here and Vegas. Nevada does everything it can to keep the route safe," said Nathan, getting out of bed. "Beyond that . . . things go to shit again until Salt Lake City."

"Worse than Arizona and New Mexico?"

"Probably not," he said, stretching his arms and yawning.

She nodded, smiling nervously before glancing in the direction of Owen's room. "We could go north and head for Reno if you think it won't be safe," she said. "I haven't heard of any problems that far north in Nevada or Utah. Your dad wouldn't have to drive as far."

"It'll take us another five hours to get out of California that way," said Nathan. "I think our best bet is to get out of the state as fast as possible. If we really feel unsafe about driving past Vegas, I wouldn't be opposed to hopping on a flight at that point."

"I wonder if we should fly out of San Diego," said Keira. "On the next available flight."

"We'll be fine driving," said Nathan, not entirely convinced he was right.

CHAPTER 21

Mason Flagg removed a pair of wireless headphones and placed them on the table next to his keyboard, waiting for Leeds to do the same before speaking.

"That conversation between Fisher and his wife was recorded about thirty minutes ago," said Flagg. "We'll obviously have to bump up the timeline. I've already spoken with our technical support about creating a custom-upload file for Detective Peck at the Virtual Investigative Division. She'll dump that into the system late this afternoon. All of the electronic crumbs will be in place for your grand finale tonight."

"It's an ambitious plan. I'll give you that," said Leeds, taking a sip of steaming coffee from a Styrofoam cup.

Flagg glared at him for a moment, dismissing the skeptical, borderline-insolent comment as a function of the man's exhaustion level. Leeds hadn't slept more than five or six hours in the past two days, a recipe for testiness. Still, Flagg didn't like it.

"As long as the pieces of this puzzle somewhat fit together," Flagg said, "the bigger picture will be inescapable—the conclusion inevitable. Public support will sway so far away from the California Liberation Movement, its founders will need a telescope to find it again."

"What do we know about Fisher?" asked Leeds.

"I presume you have a reason for asking a question easily answered by reading his file."

"Fisher is too much of a Boy Scout on the surface. Comes from a career Marine family. Engineering type. Family guy. No criminal record. Clean credit. No bank-account anomalies—"

"Not yet," said Flagg. "We can always dump money into an overseas account and point investigators in the right direction."

"Killing Fisher and his family effectively ends the story," said Leeds. "I can't see the upside to letting them live. If he saw the boats and somehow managed to describe them accurately, there's no way we can blame the reactor sabotage on the CLM. Someone will poke around and make the connection between the scrapped General Dynamics program and Sentinel's purchase—which leads to One Nation. Fisher has to go, sooner than later."

Flagg examined him, shaking his head. "I think you need more sleep. This will be the biggest story of the year. A midlevel county-employed water engineer in up to his neck with known CLM contacts, and a corrupt detective. Recently questioned by police about his bizarre early-morning trips to the beach next to a recently failed nuclear reactor. Found slain with his family a day later, along with the detective and a power-plant engineer, who happens to have access to the cooling-pump unit at the Del Mar station. I'm not exactly sure how I can improve that story," said Flagg. "You don't even have to pack Mr. Fisher's car to make it look like he was preparing to flee. He's very conveniently taking care of that for us."

"Why Fisher, though?" asked Leeds. "The engineer and detective make sense. Why would the CLM use Fisher?"

"Let the police and feds rack their brains trying to figure it out. The damage will be done."

Leeds sipped his coffee.

"I hate when you do this," said Flagg. "What do you suggest?"

"We pin Detective Peck's murder on Fisher," said Leeds. "Cop killer shoots corrupt cop. Nobody will dig too deep into Fisher's connection with the California Liberation Movement. Everybody hates a cop killer."

Flagg slowly grinned. "An interesting twist."

"What about the father?" asked Leeds.

"You want to get rid of him, too?"

"No," said Leeds. "But a former senior enlisted Marine with a combination of infantry and counterintelligence experience shouldn't be dismissed. Depending on how much Fisher shares with his father, the man could pose a problem. Especially if he gets vocal—and still has friends within the intelligence community."

"Tech support is working on that, too," said Flagg. "Expedited surveillance package."

"Should I position one of our Northern California teams in Idaho?"

"I don't think that's necessary at this point," said Flagg. "We'll have plenty of time to deal with him."

"We can't be too careful with his type."

"And we can't disappear him on the eve of his son's murder. We'll have to use some discretion handling Jon Fisher."

Chapter 22

Jon Fisher raised a pair of olive-drab binoculars and searched the tree line directly behind the house. Something had moved out there while he took a sip of coffee. He was sure of it. The wide-angle, magnified image yielded nothing, but he wasn't convinced. He'd seen it from a distance a few times on hikes through the dense woods. He lowered the binoculars and let his eyes settle on a young fir tree nestled into a sea of mature giants populating the rising slope on the southern side of his property.

He stared at the sapling, letting his peripheral vision do the work— a trick he'd learned as a young Marine. Densely packed rod cells on the periphery of the retina were far more light- and movement-sensitive than the cone cells located in the center. In Iraq and Afghanistan, when the sun had just set, Marines at observation posts stared at fixed points in the distance, spotting movement for the unit's dedicated snipers or mortar teams.

His patience was rewarded a few minutes later. He trained the binoculars on a thick stand of pine trunks twenty yards to the right of the sapling, finding a shaggy six-point bull elk partially concealed behind the thick trunks.

"There you are," he whispered, as it emerged from the tree line.

The bull was on the big side of what he'd come to expect from mature elk, probably pushing eight hundred pounds. The antlers still had a fuzzy, velvety covering common to early-summer antlers. Elk shed their rack in the spring, quickly growing a new pair. From what he could see, this bull's antlers would have a five-foot spread between main antlers—one of the biggest spreads he'd seen in person since they'd built the house.

He could only hope this big guy returned in the fall, after the rack's velvety skin had peeled away to expose solid bone antlers. Actually, anytime after October 10—the start of B-tag rifle hunting season—would be nice. Of course, Leah would just as soon heave him over the deck's railing than let him shoot from the deck. He'd have to pack a rucksack and hike his Remington 783 a few miles southwest. Out of sight and out of mind for his wife, who'd never taken to hunting—especially in her backyard.

The screen door behind him banged open, and he nearly dropped the binoculars onto the stone patio thirty feet below. Like a boot lieutenant, he'd neglected to secure a critical piece of gear with its conveniently attached strap. How many times had he yanked a young officer's binoculars out of his hands by the neck strap to teach him just this valuable lesson? Too many to count by the end of a thirty-year career. After getting the binoculars back under control, he tried to the find the elk, catching a flash of its lightly colored hindquarters fur before it vanished into the forest.

"You scared him away," he said matter-of-factly.

"Good. I hope he stays away," his wife said, stepping onto the deck with their satphone. "Nate's on the line. He doesn't sound like himself."

Jon stepped away from the railing and let the binoculars hang around his neck. "What's going on?"

"He didn't say." Leah shrugged. "He was pretty insistent on talking to you."

"I'll bring the phone in when I'm done," he said, accepting the device. "I'm sure he'll have time to talk to his favorite mother."

She kissed him on the cheek and whispered, "Be nice."

He rolled his eyes before putting the phone to his ear. "Nate," he said. "What's going on?"

"I'm not exactly sure," said his son. "But we're heading your way for a visit."

"Okay," he said, hesitating. "Sure. Absolutely. We'll be here. When can we expect you, and how long do you want to stay?"

"Sometime tomorrow. I don't know how long we'll stay."

His son had always been cryptic with his answers, a habit that drove him crazy. "Are we talking one week, two weeks, three days?"

"Probably a lot longer than that," said Nathan. "We're packing up both cars this afternoon and driving out tonight."

This didn't sound good at all.

"Is this related to all of the craziness down there?" asked Jon. "Looks like the California Liberation Movement reared its ugly head again. Whatever happened in Sacramento was serious business."

Nathan didn't answer immediately, which Jon found unusual. His son wasn't shy about sharing his opinions about the secession brouhaha.

"Nathan. Is everything all right?"

"Not really." said Nathan, after once again hesitating to answer. "I don't know how to explain it without sounding crazy, but the San Diego County Police have me under surveillance."

"What? Nathan, you're not making a lot of sense. Why would the police be watching you? Are you—wait. First things first. Can you borrow a phone in another office, or maybe one of your work colleague's phones? Preferably someone in a different division."

"I don't—probably. Why?" asked his son, who then paused. "Oh shit."

"Exactly," said Jon. "And leave your phone in your office for now. They can listen to you using your own device."

"All right. I'll call you back as soon as I can," said Nathan. "Thanks, Dad."

"No problem, Nate," said Jon. "We'll get this sorted out. Find another phone, and whatever you do, don't bring it back into your office. You'd be better off talking to me on a landline if possible, anyway. Some of the phone-intercept technology is scary."

"Got it," said his son, disconnecting the call.

Leah stood in the open doorway, concealing a worried face, a habit she'd perfected sending Jon Fisher on a dozen or so wartime deployments.

"Sounds serious," she said.

He grimaced, wishing he could disagree. "Sounds like he got himself wrapped up in something big enough to leave the state—without looking back. I'm going to grab the encrypted satphone."

She cocked her head, raising an eyebrow slightly.

"Yeah, I have a gut feeling it's that serious."

A few minutes later, the satphone in his hand buzzed, displaying a 619 area code prefix.

"Nate?" he answered.

"Yeah. I'm on an office phone."

"Perfect. I want you to call me back at a different number," said Jon. "Can you copy a number down?"

"Send it."

He passed the encrypted number. "Give me about thirty seconds to get that phone operational."

Jon opened a metal ammunition can on the workbench in his ready bunker and removed the satphone, pressing the "Power" button. When the phone illuminated, indicating a full charge, he dashed through the finished walk-out basement. Once outside, he jogged several yards into the backyard, extending the phone's antennae. Within seconds, the device locked onto two low earth satellites hooked into the Department of Defense's Distributed Tactical Communications System (DTCS). Shortly after that, the satphone rang, its display showing the same 619 number.

"All right," said Jon. "Let's keep this short. They shouldn't be able to tap into this satphone, but I'm not sure what they can do on your end."

"I'm on an office phone. I think it's a cable line."

"The police shouldn't have access to that," said Jon. "But we are talking about California. Are Owen and Leah safe?"

"Yeah. They're fine. I'm probably overreacting, but we thought it would be a good idea to get out of the state."

"Let's back up a bit. Why do you think the police are watching you?"

"I went out yesterday morning to collect seawater for the desalinator," said Nathan. "One of my favorite spots is a stretch of beach very close to the Del Mar Triad Station."

"I see where this is going."

"Yeah, they stopped by my office to ask some questions," said Nathan. "I think my explanation made sense to them."

"You're lucky they didn't drag you in and hold you."

"They slapped a GEO restriction on me."

"Shit," said Jon, giving his son's revelation some thought. "You're not going back."

"No. Once we cross the San Diego County border, there's no going back."

In a way, Jon was relieved. California was hurtling headlong into a wall—on nearly every front. He'd left tire tracks driving out of there after his retirement ceremony. Even Leah, a California native, couldn't wait to put the state behind her. When Nate announced he was leaving Tucson, they were overjoyed—for the three seconds it took him to tell them they were headed to San Diego. Only Tijuana could have been a worse choice, and that was debatable. Your money went a lot further in Mexico, if you remained alive long enough to spend it.

He was happy to hear they'd be staying in Idaho for a while. He missed spending time with his son and grandson. Keira wasn't bad either, even if she was a bit of a liberal. He'd just have to watch his scotch consumption. He tended to shoot off his mouth after a few belts of the good stuff, but he was getting ahead of himself.

"That's fine. You guys are welcome to stay here as long as you like. Your mom and I would love to have you, even if you are sort of an outlaw."

"Good news."

"That GEO stuff is a bunch of unconstitutional bullshit, anyway," Jon assured him. "Nobody outside of California gives a shit about it. When are you leaving?"

"Tonight. Probably around ten or so. Figured we'd keep our usual schedule today to minimize attention. I haven't decided if we'll head north to Vegas or drive due east to Arizona. Arizona would get us out of the state the quickest."

"Head to Reno. It's a longer stretch through California, but it'll put a few counties and a bunch of bureaucracy between you and San Diego County. Heading due east dumps you into Imperial, which is more or less an extension of San Diego nowadays. Plus, the whole route is far safer. Arizona isn't called the wasteland for nothing."

"I'm tempted to book us on the next flight out of here."

"If the police haven't grabbed you yet, they're probably in no hurry. Booking flights might trigger some kind of alert and expedite the process. They could grab you on the pretext of intending to flee, or some crap like that. Unless you have some compelling reason to take off right now, I think leaving at night is a smart call. You'll probably set off a few alarms in the system when your car crosses the county border, but I doubt it'll be flagged for immediate action."

"Unless they're following me around right now." Nathan's voice had tightened.

"If you're under that kind of surveillance, you're screwed. Sorry," said Jon, "but they won't let you leave. In fact, they'll probably grab you as soon as the garage door opens."

"That's what I'm worried about," said Nathan. "I have no idea what the police are doing."

"It sounds like your explanation for being at the beach would be easy to confirm. You've been doing this for almost two years, right?"

"Three."

"Then you have nothing to worry about. You were making regular early-morning visits to that beach long before they started building the station. Frankly, you could probably just wait this out in San Diego. They'll get to the bottom of the reactor issue in a few days. Even if it was somehow sabotaged, there's no link between you and the reactor, aside from easily explained visits to the beach."

His son was silent for a few seconds, seeming to give the idea some serious thought. Fleeing California right now would land him in legal hot water, which could give him problems moving forward. He'd heard the song and dance about Nathan being able to find work anywhere in the world, even if they walked away from their mortgage and lost all creditworthiness. His daughter-in-law never failed to sing that tune, making it abundantly clear she wanted to leave California. And he didn't blame her. In fact, he'd actively encouraged them to leave since the day they arrived, but this was different. There was no telling what might come of Nathan's fugitive run, especially if the secession violence escalated.

"I don't want to stay here. I saw something weird at the beach. I'm not sure how it fits into this, but I can't stop thinking it might be connected to the reactor problem."

"What? What are you talking about?"

"I could have sworn I saw two black boats pick up some divers just outside the surf zone," Nathan said, lowering his voice. "Then a black SUV showed up and searched the beach area with a spotlight."

This didn't make any sense. What the hell was his son talking about? "Don't take this the wrong way, Nathan, but are you sure you saw boats and divers? Could it have just been a fishing boat or something?"

"I've never seen a fishing boat on one of my trips. I'm not a hundred percent sure what I saw, but it looked military."

"What does an SUV have to do with it?"

"That's the strangest part," said Nathan. "Right after the boats left, an SUV crept into the area, sweeping the beach preserve area with a spotlight."

"Where were you during this?"

"In the beach preserve—hiding."

"Jesus," said Jon. "Though it's probably nothing. Might have been security for the station conducting a routine sweep of the area, or maybe an added security measure because of the congresswoman's assassination."

"The police never mentioned the boats or the SUV," said Nathan. "I thought that was odd. I mean, they'd have the same GPS data on the SUV, right?"

"Why didn't you tell the police? Either it's a privately registered vehicle or it's registered to an official state agency. Either way, the police would know you crossed paths with the SUV at the beach. They know you're lying, Nate."

"Unless it's something else."

"Like what?" asked Jon, exasperated.

"I did a little Internet digging at work before I called. Have you ever heard of the Sentinel Group? I saw a few theories—"

"I wouldn't put too much stock in what you read on the Internet. Especially those conspiracy sites."

"I know, but I kept coming across references to this Sentinel Group. It's heavily invested in the industrial and energy sectors. Agribusiness, too—"

"According to the websites?" Now Jon was wondering if his son was blowing this entire situation out of proportion.

"Sentinel Group exists," said Nathan, "but it's a privately held, international company, so there's not a ton of public data out there.

The information about their holdings and business affiliations came from an internal leak."

"Right," said Jon. "I don't suppose the sites posted any actual documents? Or is this all word-of-mouth?"

"I don't know, Dad. It's just a theory. The sites speculate that Sentinel is deeply vested in the success of the One Nation Coalition. Bad things happen when Sentinel's interests are threatened. You should check it out. A lot of the hot spots you deployed to with the Marines have links to Sentinel."

This crazy-ass Sentinel thing had his son genuinely spooked.

"Let me ask you a pointed question, sergeant-major style," said Jon. "Shoot."

"Do you no shit think you'll be better off leaving it all behind and getting out of Dodge?"

"If you'd asked me the same question yesterday, I would have said no. But I'm not so sure anymore. The more I think about the beach, the less it adds up."

"Then get out of there," said Jon. "Consider your tour of duty finished."

"Do you still think I should wait until tonight?"

"I don't think there's anything to this Sentinel business. This may sound harsh, but you wouldn't be trading on the world oxygen exchange right now if an organization like that existed."

"Why doesn't that make me feel better?"

"Your biggest worry is the police, and it doesn't sound like they're paying much attention to you right now," said Jon. "Tidy things up around the house, gather all of your important documents, pack up what you need—and drive out tonight. Call me when you get on the road, but don't say anything over the phone about your intentions."

"Shouldn't I buy some prepaid phones or something?"

"What are you, a covert operative?" asked Jon, laughing. "There's no such thing as a burner device anymore, unless you have an active fake license and matching credit card. One of the Homeland Security acts closed the burner-phone loophole to pretty much everyone but the real criminals. From what I understand, if the police have a standing surveillance warrant, you'll get about a minute of unrecorded airtime, if you're lucky."

"All right, Dad," his son said, taking a deep breath. "I'll call you to let you know we're on the road. We'll probably take separate cars and travel apart until we get out of California. I don't want them grabbing Leah on some BS aiding-and-abetting charge. Owen would end up in Child Protective Services."

"And Sergeant Major Fisher would form a one-man hostage rescue team to get his grandson back. Not to mention your mother—that would be more like a hunter-killer team."

They both laughed.

"Don't split up, Nate," said Jon. "You want to keep the team together for this one. Marines that fight together, survive together."

"I'll call you around ten, Dad. We're looking forward to spending time with you and Mom."

"Jesus, Keira must be really worried," said Jon, causing them both to laugh again.

"That's the first thing I said," said Nathan, still chuckling.

"I bet. We'll talk to you later, Nate."

The call disconnected. Six minutes and twenty-two seconds. Jon lowered the phone and stared into the trees where he'd seen the elk.

"Sounds like Nate might be in trouble," said his wife, startling him.

"Damn it," he muttered. "Don't you ever announce yourself?"

"I like to keep you on your toes," she said, leaning over the railing above him.

"Trying to give me a heart attack is more like it."

"I need you to cut and stack the firewood," she said. "It's not in my best interest to get rid of you. What's going on with Nate?"

"Bunch of California nonsense," said Jon. "He's heading our way—indefinitely, from what I understand."

"Are they in any danger?"

"What do you mean?" he said, staring up at her.

"I eavesdropped," said his wife. "What's Sentinel?"

"Nothing. An Internet bogeyman used by conspiracy nuts to blame everything that goes wrong in the world of big business or the government."

"Should you check into it?"

"Check into what?" asked Jon. "Sentinel? Nate's biggest problem is the San Diego County PD. He picked the wrong morning to collect seawater in Del Mar."

She glared at him with *that* look.

"What?" he said, shrugging.

Leah continued to stare at him, slowly shaking her head.

"All right. Jesus!" said Jon. "I'll do a little digging if it makes you feel better. Outside of the almighty Internet."

"It would," she said, smirking. "Isn't Quinn's son at Pendleton?"

"Are you a mind reader, too?" asked Jon. "Never mind. Don't answer that."

"I'll keep your breakfast warm," she said, winking at him before walking away.

Holding his breakfast hostage again. No surprise there.

Jon walked deeper into the yard, sitting on one of the crude granite benches he'd constructed with the man he needed to call. The five-foot-long, blue-gray granite faced Galena Peak—one of the biggest selling points of the property. They had spectacular views of the nine-thousand-foot peak year round, a point reinforced by several benches strategically situated throughout the twenty-acre plot.

He scrolled through the satphone's three preset numbers, pressing "Send" as he sat down. The call connected after three rings.

"I assume this isn't a recipe-trading call?" asked a familiar voice.

"Affirmative," said Jon. "It's probably nothing, but better safe than sorry,"

"'Better safe than sorry' means Leah's standing somewhere close by, giving you the stink eye."

"You guessed it."

"Let me call you right back from a secure line."

"I'll be here," said Jon, ending the call.

Jon stared at the display, forming a thin smile. Stuart Quinn, retired colonel, had parlayed a twenty-two-year career as a Marine Corps intelligence officer into a successful decade-long run on the national intelligence circuit. Now a beltway insider, Quinn would be in a position to defuse Nathan's baseless conspiracy concerns.

He hated to bother his friend with this, but Leah wouldn't give him a moment's peace until he did his due diligence. More important, she wouldn't serve him breakfast. And, it couldn't hurt to ask if Stu's son might be willing to deliver a few throwaway phones to Nathan before they left tonight, just in case Big Brother was listening.

CHAPTER 23

Flagg stood up and grabbed his headset—ready to rip them off. Nine minutes had passed. Eight minutes too long. Young Nathan sounded despondent, and big daddy Fisher was about to solve his problem. He would have been back on a phone within minutes.

"Where's the damn feed?" asked Flagg.

The surveillance technician on the other end of the speakerphone conversation immediately replied. "He's not in audible range of any phone in the building," said the tech. "I guarantee that. He probably found a conference room with an intra-office phone."

The dad had been clever suggesting that.

"And why can't I listen to that?" asked Flagg.

"We're working on it," said the tech. "I need a few more minutes."

"No. I want to know why I can't already listen to it."

"The surveillance package didn't specify intra-office landlines."

"And it didn't occur to you to be tapped into that system?"

"The package request was very specific," said the tech, his voice echoing through the operations center. "We'll have it shortly."

"What about the new satphone number?"

"It's either an unregistered satphone, or the call hasn't gone through yet."

"I guaran-fucking-tee the call went through. It's probably done at this point," said Flagg, pounding his fist on the computer station and turning to Leeds. "And don't say a fucking word, Leeds. This is your fault."

Leeds raised his hands in a defensive pose.

"You have to do all of the thinking for the tech-support group," spat Flagg, pausing to catch his breath. Then, again to the tech: "Patch the feeds through to me as soon as you acquire them."

"Yes, sir."

Flagg disconnected the call, glaring at Leeds—who shrugged his shoulders.

"It doesn't matter," said Leeds. "One way or the other, Fisher is out of the picture."

"And if he talks to his father about the boats and the SUV?"

"We can take care of that, too—very quickly and very quietly," said Leeds. "The parents live in the middle of nowhere."

Flagg shook his head and grimaced. "How soon can you have a team in place?"

"A few hours."

"All right," said Flagg. "Let's hope we don't have to use the team. Killing the parents will raise questions."

"Nobody will figure out what happened. They'll be there one day, gone the next," said Leeds. "Disappeared."

The computer screen in front of Flagg indicated an incoming call from Cerberus technical support. He clicked the mouse, transferring it to the operations center's speaker system.

"Do you have my feed?" asked Flagg, not feeling the least bit hopeful.

"We're tapped into Nathan Fisher's office building, but—"

"Let me guess," said Flagg. "The call is finished."

"Voice-recognition software doesn't have a match for any of the ongoing calls," said the technician. "I apologize for this, sir."

"A lot of good that does me. I suppose you didn't have any luck with the satphone either?"

"Correct," answered the tech. "But for a different reason. The number Jon Fisher gave to his son connects to a National Security Agency satellite-redirect node. It's a ghost phone. Untraceable and virtually impossible to tap—outside of Fort Meade. The only way we can listen to Jon Fisher is if he calls a line we've tapped."

"Then I want every conceivable method of communication available to Nathan Fisher monitored. Understood?" asked Flagg. "If he buys a prepaid device, I want access the second he activates the phone. If he buys matching pink Barbie walkie-talkies, I want your people listening in on a frequency-hopping radio. I don't care if he walks out of a store with two tin cans and a spool of string, one of you fuckers better be listening in on the other end. You get the picture?"

"Yes, sir."

Flagg ended the call and turned to Leeds.

"Deploy the team immediately," said Flagg. "And dig deeper into Jon Fisher's background. I want to know everything there is to know about the supposedly retired Marine sergeant major with access to a ghost phone. He either knows somebody or he *is* somebody. I'd like to know which before we make a move against him."

PART III

CHAPTER 24

Nick Leeds strolled under the wide palm canopies covering the sidewalk along Third Avenue, casually examining the Villa Camino apartments. In the fading light of early evening, the four-story building's chipped yellow-stucco facade had absorbed darker shades of the sunset's deep red-orange hue. He studied the ground floor for access points, noting a gated entrance to a small parking garage under the first floor. Not his first choice, for obvious reasons. He walked beyond the garage entrance, making room for the two young men approaching him on the sidewalk. Walking arm in arm, they passed him with a cordial smile, which he returned with a noncommittal nod.

He slowed his pace and gave the couple time to cover some distance on the sidewalk before briskly turning between the two square-cut, shoulder-height hedges that flanked the apartment building's front entrance. The front door was a solid black-metal slab fixed with an institutional-looking vertical handle. It resembled the kind of uninviting back entrance one might find in a trash-strewn alley. A worn card reader stood next to the door, partially illuminated in the shadow of the worn alcove. The Villa Camino apartments had seen better days.

A quick swipe with a specially designed keycard turned the reader's LED indicator green. He pretended to check his phone, giving the decryption program embedded in the card's chip time to break through the reader's simple electronic cipher. The door buzzed moments later, admitting him to the building.

Torn maroon carpeting held down by three off-white lawn chairs greeted him in the lobby, competing for his attention with dank, musty air. For what they paid her, he hadn't expected the place to be a complete shithole. Then again, the housing situation matched her official paycheck, so maybe a smart move on her part. Nothing drew more attention to a moderately paid civil servant than that exquisitely furnished apartment in a trendy neighborhood, or the sudden appearance of a six-figure luxury car.

Judging by the appearance of the building, Leeds opted for the staircase. Given the choice between maintaining mandatory California Resource Protection Act upgrades or handicapped-accessible elevators, most landlords would rather take their chances with the Americans with Disabilities Act. ADA violations didn't get you deported from California.

The concrete stairwell held most of the building's heat and humidity, leaving him with a thin film of perspiration by the time he reached the third floor. He opened the door, strangely relieved to breathe the stale air circulating through the hallways. The hallway was empty, and he found apartment 3C a few doors away from the stairwell on the right side. Convenient enough. Leeds examined the door, opting against using the decryption keycard.

The building's landlord hadn't upgraded the security system in more than a decade, a fact only the most security-clueless tenant might overlook. He could expect a minimum of two physical security measures holding 3C's door in place. A deadbolt for sure, backed up by either a chain lock or some type of heavy-duty door jam. The chain-links could be snapped quickly and quietly. The doorjamb was a different story.

He reached into his left pocket and removed a black thumb-size rectangular device, fixing it in place against the peephole. With the object snuggly in place, Leeds flicked a small switch with his finger and waited for the signal light on the back of the item to flash green. Then he unzipped his windbreaker and drew a suppressed compact pistol from a concealed, nylon shoulder holster.

Leeds knocked on the door and waited a few seconds before knocking again. The floor creaked inside the room, betraying her presence before a shadow appeared under the door. He tensed, aiming the pistol directly in front of him.

"How can I help you?" asked a muffled voice from the other side of the door.

Damn. He'd hoped she might open the door without any questions. The digital video feed playing through her peephole showed her two uniformed San Diego County Police Department patrol officers, but they wouldn't appear to respond to her questions. He might have to force his way in.

"Detective Peck?" asked Leeds. "Officers Hopper and Santiago. The Virtual Investigative Division has received a credible threat to your department. Something to do with the Sinaloa Cartel. Captain Volk wants all VID detectives back at headquarters for a security briefing."

"We have phones for this kind of shit," she said, turning the deadbolt.

"They suspect a device hack within the division," said Leeds.

"Hold on," she grumbled.

A clunking sound came from the bottom of the door, confirming his suspicion of a doorjamb-type security bar. He could have kicked this door all day and never broken inside. When the door went quiet, he edged closer, holding the pistol in a stable two-hand grip. The door opened to a few muttered obscenities, followed by a confused look.

"What the fuck is—" she started, a bullet hole appearing between her trimmed eyebrows.

Leeds slid inside the room and grabbed the collar of her gray San Diego State Aztecs sweatshirt with his left hand, lowering her limp body to the carpet without a sound. He retrieved the peephole device and checked the hallway, confirming that it was still empty before closing the door and sliding the deadbolt in place. Tucking the pistol into the shoulder holster, he headed to the kitchen table, eyeing her phone.

He removed a thin wallet-size digital tablet from the inside pocket of his windbreaker and set it next to her phone, activating its screen and entering a six-digit code. The tablet immediately recognized her phone and automatically transferred a self-erasing virus designed to scrub any deeply hidden evidence that she spied on the San Diego County Police Department.

While it sanitized her phone and all peripheral devices with any possible link to Cerberus, the program rewrote her digital life, adding fake geographic tracks, bank transactions, text messages, calls, and web-browsing history to match the data profile she had unwittingly uploaded to the heavily encrypted Virtual Investigative Division portal earlier today.

Peck's VID colleagues would have a field day piecing together her connection to the California Liberation Movement and other shady characters implicated in the sabotage of the Del Mar Triad Station.

Satisfied that the tablet was doing its job, Leeds withdrew a two-inch-thick, rubber-banded roll of fifty-dollar bills from his jacket and approached Peck's corpse, careful not to step on the bloodstained carpet. He opened her right hand and closed it around the money wad a few times, spreading her fingerprints evenly—a small detail meant to boost the murder investigation's confirmation bias. Finding ten grand in relatively inconspicuous fifty-dollar bills was a recipe for jealousy and foregone conclusions.

Leeds stepped into Peck's tidy, modestly appointed bedroom and headed for the closet. He slid the mirrored door open and examined her tightly jammed wardrobe, selecting a ski jacket pressed against the inside wall. The coat displayed a few tattered ski tags from Snow Summit, and plenty of inside pockets. He slipped the money into a zippered phone holder on the left waist, and tucked the jacket back into place.

Back in the kitchen, the tablet screen told him the digital transfer was complete, with no errors. He pocketed the device and left the apartment, walking briskly down the dingy hallway to the stairs. Less than thirty seconds later, he was back on the sidewalk, headed north on Third Avenue toward the car he parked just out of sight on Robinson Ave. Approaching the intersection of the two streets, he spied the nondescript silver sedan to the right, partially obscured by a line of brown-tipped dwarf palmetto palm plants lining the corner lot.

He removed the skin-colored latex gloves after turning onto Robinson Avenue, checking his watch when he peeled one of the gloves away. He still had two hours to get the teams situated for phase two of the evening's operation.

Chapter 25

Jon Fisher heaved an olive-green, five-gallon plastic jerrican into the 4Runner's cargo compartment, pushing it against the back of the seat bench, next to a second water can. He loaded two black milk crates filled with packets of dehydrated survival food, MREs, first-aid supplies, and tools next to the water cans, barely leaving enough space on the other side to fit two five-gallon cans of gasoline.

The red fuel containers, similar in shape and size to the water cans, filled the void, leaving little side-to-side wiggle room. After several dozen camping trips, he'd developed a system that fit all their gear in the rear compartment—leaving the second row of seats open for Leah's last-minute surprises. Without fail she always had a few up her sleeve that somehow took up most of the back seat. On cue, Leah appeared next to him, carrying a camouflage-patterned backpack over one shoulder and dragging an oversize duffel bag along the garage floor. He smiled and shook his head.

"Aren't you supposed to spring a few extra suitcases on me a little later?" asked Jon. "Those are part of my planned loadout."

"I'll throw something together a few minutes before we leave," she said, dropping the backpack next to the SUV. "Thought I'd help out."

"Spying, is more like it."

"Can't a man's wife of thirty-six years spend a little time with him without raising suspicions?"

"Thirty-six years has left the man paranoid," he said, lifting the backpack into the 4Runner and turning to her. "I'll be fine, honey."

"I'd feel better if you took one of your buddies along for the ride."

"I can take care of myself," he said. "And I might need the extra room if they have car trouble, or if Owen wants to drive with his grandpa."

He wrapped his arms around her waist and pulled her in, gently kissing her neck. "I'll give them a proper escort through Nevada. Things aren't exactly safe and sound there, especially for someone like Nathan."

"I don't think you give him enough credit," she said. "He's a smart kid. Very capable."

"He doesn't own a gun," said Jon, stepping back to push the backpack deeper into the SUV. "Smart and capable will only get you so far in the high-desert wastelands."

"Guns don't solve every problem."

"They're a good start," he said, lifting the duffel bag filled with guns, ammunition, and optics gear and sliding it into the open backseat.

She'd started to respond, when his satphone rang. He'd synched the phone with his home satcom system, allowing him to receive a notification when a call was inbound.

"Hold that thought," he said, pulling the phone out of a cargo pocket and rushing onto the driveway, where he could acquire a signal.

"I thought I might hear from you earlier," said Jon. "It's pretty late there, right? Did you find something?"

"Are you done?" asked Stuart Quinn.

"Sorry," said Jon. "Just a little jumpy. I'm about to head south."

"You might want to reconsider that."

"You found something."

"It may be nothing. It may be everything," said Quinn. "First things first. Pack up and get out of your house immediately. Five minutes and gone. Go dark, except for this satphone."

"That bad?"

"I'm already on the road, if that answers your question," said Quinn. "I did a little classified-level digging into Sentinel Group and didn't like what I found. First, they're without a doubt bankrolling the One Nation Coalition. They're heavily invested in every major business sector that stands to lose significant revenues if California splits, and like your son suggested, bad shit happens when Sentinel Group faces big losses. Think small wars, coup d'états, genocides, terror attacks, infrastructure damage, and targeted assassinations. Starting to sound familiar?"

"Remarkably," said Jon, whispering a few obscenities.

"Here's the real kicker. They're connected to a nasty group few people know about called Cerberus International—essentially Sentinel's private black-ops army. We don't know a lot about Cerberus, but extrapolating from the list of misfortunes I recited earlier, they'll stop at nothing to guarantee Sentinel's profits. You know: Kill a congresswoman here, a lieutenant governor there. Maybe wreck a nuclear reactor or two along the way."

"I thought they determined that the reactor shutdown was a mechanical issue," said Jon, somehow knowing that Stuart had an answer waiting.

"That's a preliminary assessment," said Quinn. "Your son saw two low-profile boats at the beach by the Del Mar station?"

"That's what he says, but I don't think Nathan would know a Boston whaler from a submarine," said Jon, glancing at his wife—who glared at him disapprovingly.

"Hmm. Guess who recently purchased the Mark X Stealth Delivery Platform program?"

"I thought that program was scrapped by General Dynamics."

"So did I, until about twenty minutes ago," said Quinn. "Turns out they found a buyer."

"Let me guess," said Jon. "Cerberus International?"

"Actually, Sentinel Group bought the program, but from what I can tell, that's like parents putting their name on the dealer paperwork for their teenager's first car. The program included two Mark X SDPs."

Nathan was in serious danger.

"Jesus," whispered Jon. "I need to go. I have to get in touch with Nathan. Did your son ever bring him the phones? Shit. Sorry. I don't want to involve your son. I'll figure this out."

"Jon," said Quinn forcefully, "this may be nothing at all."

"Or everything," said Jon. "Like you said."

"Right, which is why we'll treat this like the worst-case scenario until proven otherwise," said Quinn. "David is on his way with the phones. There was no stopping him—*especially* after I explained the situation. The Fishers are in good hands; however, I suggested that David execute a radically different plan. With Cerberus involved, I don't think driving long stretches of empty desert highway is a healthy idea. They can hide at Camp Pendleton until we figure out how to proceed. The base isn't exactly airtight, but it's a shit ton safer than anywhere else I can think of."

"I can't thank you enough, Stu. Or your son," said Jon. "Shouldn't I wait here until I hear from Nathan, or David?"

"Nathan's phone will be tapped, at the very least," said Quinn. "I wouldn't be surprised if Cerberus was tracking his car through the California Resource system. David will take them back to Pendleton in his car. They'll call you with one of the throwaway phones once they're on the road. Right now, I highly suggest you get out of there. Once Nathan disappears, they'll start turning over stones. You don't want to be under one."

"All right," said Jon, turning to a very concerned-looking wife. "We're out of here in the next few minutes. I appreciate you sticking your neck out like this for me."

His wife gave him a knowing look, quickly leaving the garage.

"Anything for the illustrious Sergeant Major Fisher. Say hi to Leah for me, and tell her everything will be fine."

"I'll pass that along," said Jon, fighting the reflex to reciprocate the sentiment. Stuart's wife had passed away two years earlier, after a short, unexpected battle with ovarian cancer, but Jon still thought of them as a couple. As did Stuart, he was sure. The call disconnected without a response.

Jon walked into the garage, slightly dazed by the conversation.

"The only thing we're missing are my last-minute bags," said Leah. "I can have those ready in a few minutes."

He forced himself to smile at her joke. "We'll head a few hours north to the Montana border," said Jon, conflicted about driving away from his son. "I have a Marine friend in one of the survival groups up there."

"How bad is it?"

"It might be nothing," he said, looking into her eyes.

"Or it might be everything?" his wife whispered.

He nodded, his mind more than nine hundred miles away, in Mira Mesa.

CHAPTER 26

David Quinn waited at a stoplight on Camino Ruiz, anxiously thrumming his fingers on the steering wheel. What the hell was he getting himself into here? This had gone from delivering a few untraceable phones—a sketchy proposition in itself—to whisking away a family and hiding them on base. He still didn't know exactly why the Fisher family was on the run, only that they might be in the crosshairs of a notoriously ruthless military contractor—and that this *favor* might be dangerous.

It still sounded a little far-fetched, though he had to admit that his dad sounded serious. He had repeatedly insisted that David take precautions, which gave him pause. He'd thrown a few precautionary items in the jeep before taking off, just in case. Now he was glad he'd listened to his dad. For some odd reason, the closer he got to the Fishers' neighborhood, the more uneasy he felt.

"Typical pre-mission jitters," he told himself.

When the light turned green, he cruised south on Camino Ruiz, passing a rundown strip mall on the left. A liquor store, hair and nail salon, Mexican taco shop, chain pizza counter, Laundromat, and dental office—the usual collection of fluorescent storefronts standing guard over a mostly empty parking lot. The place looked like every other strip mall in the state. Unappealing and dingy in every aspect, except for the lure of finding the perfect taco. Some of the best Mexican food was concealed in the most hideous strip malls in Southern California.

His jeep's Heads-Up Navigator displayed a left arrow and a distance on the windshield above the dashboard. One thousand feet until Camino Morelos. He squeezed the wheel, telling himself he was relieving tension. *Damn it!* His dad had done a number on him. "Shadowy black-ops group working on US soil. Be careful. Watch your surroundings. Don't trust anybody. Don't make any assumptions. This group will not hesitate to flick you out of the way." *Thanks, Dad. Thanks for turning a simple favor into mission impossible with your new brand of conspiracy melodrama.* David eased his grip on the wheel and forced a grin.

He turned onto Camino Morelos and drove a short distance to Virgo Place, the first street that connected with his destination. The streets darkened significantly after turning onto Virgo. San Diego City ordinances prohibited the use of streetlights or outdoor home lighting along secondary suburban roads. His fingers started tapping the wheel again.

Deciding to indulge one of his father's more paranoid suggestions, he stopped the car and unzipped the backpack lying on the front passenger seat. Reaching inside, he produced the thermal riflescope given to him by his father a few years ago. Many of his dad's retired Marine Corps friends took lucrative jobs in the defense-contracting sector, and every time his dad visited, he brought some kind of high-tech gadget provided by one of his buddies. The thermal scope was one of David's favorites, though he rarely had an occasion to use it. He'd spotted a few coyotes camping with Alison and had dragged it out to impress his nieces and nephews a few times. Tonight he'd put it to better use, more to ease his fears than anything else.

He rolled down the jeep's windows and activated the scope, letting it adjust to the cabin's ambient temperature. A few minutes later, he pulled onto the street and continued his journey with the scope in his left hand, scanning the road ahead of him for heat signatures appearing through parked car windows. Then he'd search the roads parallel to Pallux Way, driving a loop through the neighborhood. Once he cleared the streets, he'd relax and embrace babysitting duty.

Two blocks from Pallux Way, he raised the scope to his left eye for a few seconds, which was as long as he dared on a dark, narrow street with parked cars. *Huh.* He could have sworn he'd picked up a sizable white spot in one of the cars on the left side of the road just past Pallux. Probably a warm engine. The cars on that side faced him, exposing their engine hoods to the scope. He slowed the car and raised the scope again, keeping it leveled for several seconds. The digital image came into sharp focus.

His grip on the wheel tightened. Three people sat in the vehicle, their heads and shoulders visible through the windshield. No engine thermals. They'd been there awhile. The image was distant, but there was no mistaking the obvious human shapes. He lowered the scope, taking in the road ahead. Completely dark beyond his headlights. Maybe they'd just gotten in the car.

The jeep's navigation system indicated he was about to pass Summerdale Street, one block away from Pallux Way. He turned the scope down Summerdale as he cruised through the intersection. *Fuck!* Two more people in a vehicle halfway down the street. Engine cold. He lowered the scope and kept on toward Pallux Way, wondering once again what the hell he'd gotten mixed up in. His pulse had quickened, his skin suddenly clammy. He wiped his forehead, feeling a light sheen of perspiration.

As the turn onto Pallux approached, David debated how to proceed. He couldn't just pick up the Fisher family and drive away. That much was clear now. This would take a decidedly different approach. First, he needed to make a better assessment of what he was up against. A plan had started to form based on what he'd seen so far, but he needed more tactical intelligence. Instead of turning onto Pallux, he kept driving on Virgo, toward the first set of thermal signatures he'd spotted.

His headlights probed the street ahead, illuminating cars on each side of the street and shining right through the windows. When the lights reached an oversize black SUV on the left, the windshield remained dark—impervious to the human eye. He kept his eyes forward as he passed the ominous hulk, worried what the occupants might do if he looked in the window. If any of what his dad had told him was true, someone in the SUV had a rifle pointed at his head while the jeep rolled by.

Clearing the SUV with his head still intact, he rapidly approached Westmore Road, where he planned to turn left and approach Pallux from the other side of the neighborhood. He was very interested to see if Fisher had additional admirers. After making the turn, he lifted the scope to scan the road, immediately dropping it in his lap. Three cars away, fully illuminated by his headlights, a black cargo van towered over the street's collection of vehicles, its tinted windows denying any hint of who or what might be inside. A second dark-colored van, sporting a serious antennae array, sat directly behind it.

He could only hope they hadn't seen his scope. If they had, there was little doubt in his mind that his car would never reach the end of the street. Sweating profusely, he drove the speed limit past the two blatantly out-of-place vehicles and continued down Westmore. The situation had drastically changed, calling for new rules of engagement. Four vehicles indicated more than surveillance, especially since they were parked well out of sight.

The vans worried him most. One clearly contained a highly sophisticated surveillance and communications suite—overkill for a stakeout involving anything less than a terrorist cell. The other van? He only needed to know one thing about the other van. Keep Nathan Fisher and his family out of it.

By the time his jeep reached the end of Westmore Road, his heartbeat was back to normal. He'd come to terms with what had to be done.

Chapter 27

Nick Leeds watched the jeep cruise by from the passenger seat of his command-and-control vehicle. The team assigned to the SUV on Virgo had reported the car a few minutes ago, indicating that it had briefly stopped at the top of the street before continuing on its way. The driver, a buzz-cut male in his early thirties, hadn't paid any attention to the SUV—and it didn't appear that he'd taken an interest in either van. Leeds scrutinized the man's face through the one-way tinted windshield, detecting nothing unusual about the man's mannerisms.

"What do we have on this vehicle?" he asked once the jeep had passed.

"Car is registered to Alison Quinn. Current address one-four-six-six-two Camino Alto, Oceanside," said one of the technicians in the back of the van.

"Alison isn't driving her car tonight," said Leeds. "Check her associations for a white male, late twenties or early thirties. Possibly a Marine stationed at Camp Pendleton."

The high and tight haircut, age, and Oceanside address made this a distinct possibility.

"Copy that," said the tech. "Running associations now."

Leeds checked his watch. Eight fifty-two. About an hour to go until showtime, if Fisher didn't take off early. Leeds had decided to grab the family a few blocks away, before they reached Camino Morelos.

Three-dimension pulse-burst Doppler radar, cross-referenced with real-time thermal imaging, suggested that the Fishers had packed one car for their midnight run to Nevada.

"Jeep's turning left onto Giraldo," said one of the techs.

The guy had already come from that direction. Was he backtracking? Lost?

"Left?" asked Leeds. "How are we doing on those associations?"

"I found him," said the tech. "David Quinn. Same address. Checking Department of Defense database now. Give me a second."

"I want access to all of his personal devices."

"Already working on that," said the tech. "Here we go. Captain David Quinn, United States Marine Corps. Infantry officer assigned to Second Battalion, Fourth Marines. Camp Pendleton."

"Anything else jumping out at you?"

"Regular infantry career according to his quick profile. I'm not seeing anything—wait," said the tech. "Attended the counterinsurgency course in Quantico after Expeditionary Warfare School."

"Abbreviated or full course?"

"I can't tell."

"Transfer the screen to monitor three," said Leeds, trying his best not to sound annoyed.

His rightmost dash-mounted monitor changed from a digital map of the neighborhood to David Quinn's DOD profile page. "Counterinsurgency Course 8/0380." He'd attended the specialized eight-week course, which gave him a secondary Marine occupational specialty as a counterinsurgency officer. In all likelihood, David Quinn commanded Second Battalion's counterinsurgency company. Not a group of Marines Leeds would want to meet in a dark alley—or a dark neighborhood in Mira Mesa. He hoped Quinn's presence in the neighborhood was just a coincidence. If not, they might have a problem.

Leeds opened his communications channel to the other teams. "All units, keep an eye on the black four-door Jeep Wrangler headed north on Giraldo. I want to know if it stops again."

"This is Hudson," said a voice through his wireless earpiece. "I have a Jeep Wrangler turning onto Pallux from Giraldo. Came from your direction."

"I want you watching that vehicle and its driver closely," said Leeds.

"Streaming video and audio to the van," said Hudson.

John Hudson led a small team of field-surveillance operatives stationed in the house diagonally across the street from the Fishers. They had maintained the direct surveillance gear used to spy on the family and watched the neighborhood for the past two days.

"Copy," said Leeds. "All units stand by to move. We might have to do this right at the house."

Once all the units responded, he ordered the tech in his van to activate the full surveillance display. The three monitors arranged side by side in a slight curve on the passenger side of the dashboard changed to various displays of the surrounding area. He had a three-dimensional, thermal, see-through-the-wall image of the house, which showed the Fishers as indistinct orange-red masses. Another screen showed a two-dimensional, green-scale schematic of the house, with blue icons indicating the real-time locations of the family members. The burst pulse Doppler through-wall radar penetrated the entire house, detecting movement and mapping whatever was inside. The Doppler image was by far his favorite. The third screen displayed a full-color, near-daylight image of the front of the house.

"What do you want on the HUD?" asked the tech.

"Whatever Hudson is transmitting on the jeep."

The windshield directly in front of him transformed into a semi-transparent screen, featuring a live image of the jeep driving down Pallux Way and a green audio-wave readout. The audio wave looked active.

"Patch audio to my left ear," said Leeds.

"I don't recommend that," said the tech. "Loud music."

"Hudson, can you see what he's doing in the car?"

The HUD image zoomed in on the jeep, clearly showing Quinn talking into a phone.

"Talking on a phone," said Hudson. "It'll take me a while to separate his voice from the music track. I need to upload the track."

"Do it," said Leeds, watching as the jeep pulled into the Fishers' driveway.

A voice deep down inside told Leeds to take Fisher and the Marine now, but Flagg had been specific about how he wanted the events to unfold. Fisher's tortured, mangled corpse would be found by a California Border Division patrol near Mexico, alongside the bodies of his wife and son. One of the Fishers' vehicles, fully packed for a long trip, would be discovered parked outside a Mexican car-insurance storefront in a San Ysidro strip mall, not too far from the bodies. The implication would be unavoidable. The Fishers had tried to flee to Mexico.

Evidence planted in his house and uploaded through various digital sources would lead investigators to suspect Fisher had been murdered, along with Detective Peck and a nuclear reactor engineer, to conceal the California Liberation Movement's involvement in the sabotage of the Del Mar station. Grabbing Fisher at the house required the entire team, and exposed the kidnapping to a neighborhood full of witnesses. Still, it was better than losing control of the operation. If Fisher attempted to leave with Quinn, then Leeds would pounce.

CHAPTER 28

Loud, muffled music boomed from the other side of the garage bay door, causing Nathan to freeze in place behind his wife's mini-SUV. He held a five-gallon plastic can of gasoline in place against his chest, the forty-pound mass tugging at his arms. The music stopped abruptly, replaced by the low growl of a car engine. From inside the closed garage, he couldn't tell if the car had parked on the street or in his driveway. Either way, it was close, and he wasn't expecting visitors. He eased the gasoline can into the back of Keira's vehicle, careful not to make any noise, and tiptoed quickly into the house.

His wife stood in the kitchen with their largest kitchen knife in front of her face, peeking down the short hallway leading to the foyer. Nathan edged toward the opposite side of the hallway entrance and peeked around the corner. A shadow loomed behind the front door's frosted, shatterproof-glass panels. An insistent knock followed, startling both of them. Nathan mouthed, "I got it," followed by "Get Owen." She nodded and disappeared into the bedroom hallway, whispering for their son.

Nathan reached into his front pocket and withdrew a folding utility knife with his right hand, extending the blade with his thumb. He kept the serrated blade hidden behind his thigh as he walked toward the door. A second round of heavy knocking made him jump. He stood to the side of the door, worried that his visitor might kick it in and knock him down.

"No solicitors, please," said Nathan.

"I have a delivery from Sergeant Major Fisher," said a male voice. "Two phones."

"What's your name?"

"David Quinn," said the voice. "I'll hold up my ID card."

Nathan moved behind the door and touched a small black screen embedded between the frosted panels. A young man, with the same high and tight haircut Nathan's dad had worn apparently since the dawn of time, stared at the screen for a moment before raising the ID card. Nathan pressed the screen a few times to zoom in on the card. QUINN, DAVID S. CAPT/O3 US MARINE CORPS ACTIVE. The picture pretty much matched every white Marine at Camp Pendleton, and Nathan hadn't seen David Quinn since high school, when both of their fathers had served together in the First Radio Battalion. He opened the door, figuring it really didn't matter. If this wasn't David Quinn, a single reinforced door wasn't going to change the final outcome.

As soon as the man entered the house, he held an index finger to his lips and quickly reached up to Nathan's right ear with his other hand, removing the small wireless earpiece synched to Nathan's personal phone. The man took a new device out of his front jeans pocket and offered it to Nathan. Quinn leaned in close and whispered, "It's your dad. You listen only. I have it in retro mode—phone to ear," patting Nathan on the shoulder.

Nathan took the phone and put it to his ear, immediately hearing his dad's voice.

"Nate? Are you there? Nathan? If you can hear me, press a numeric key."

Nathan pressed 3.

"All right, Nate. Don't say a word. Just listen. I'm going to make this quick so David can do his thing. You were right about this Sentinel business. It's bad news, and there's a better-than-good chance they're operating in California. We don't know if you're in danger, but we're not taking any chances. The trip to Reno is canceled. David is going take you right to Camp Pendleton and hide you on base until we can come up with a plan. You have to trust David and do what he asks, no matter how dangerous or ridiculous it sounds. He's going to sneak you out of there, somehow. Press another key if you're good to go with this."

Nathan pressed *3* again.

"All right," said his dad. "Nod at Quinn and keep the phone to your ear. Let him lead the conversation."

He nodded at the Marine, who wasted no time launching into his performance.

"Sorry to barge in on you like this," said Quinn. "I wasn't sure if you left."

"It's no problem," said Nathan, pausing for a second to think of something else to say. "I really appreciate you dropping off these phones. They'll come in handy if the police hacked our other devices."

"Yeah, I'd leave those behind before you hit the road. They can track your position, too," said Quinn, walking into the kitchen. "Do you mind if I get a drink of water?"

Over the phone, Nathan's dad said, "He's going to dunk your other phones in case they've been turned into listening devices."

"Go ahead," said Nathan. "Glasses are to the right of the sink. There's a pitcher of water in the fridge."

"Nathan?" asked Keira from the back of the bedroom hallway. "Is everything all right?"

"Totally fine, honey," said Nathan. "One of dad's Marine friends dropped off a few untraceable phones."

"Our dads served together in the Fifth Marines," said Quinn, finding a glass in the cabinet. "Back in their sergeant days."

Keira entered the kitchen slowly, holding the knife like she was ready to use it. Nathan held a finger to his lips and removed her earpiece before offering her the phone.

"Keira," he said, handing her earpiece to the Marine, "this is David Quinn."

"Nice to meet you. Thank you for helping out," she said, silently mouthing an obscenity at Nathan before putting the phone to her ear.

"Marines do what they can for other Marines. *Semper fi*," said Quinn, opening the refrigerator and removing the pitcher.

Nathan could tell from Keira's expression that his father was speaking to her.

Quinn poured a glass of water and took a long drink, setting the glass on the counter. Without warning, he swiped Nathan and Keira's personal phones from the kitchen table and dropped them into the pitcher, holding a finger to his lips. He added the two wireless earpieces to the water before returning the pitcher to its refrigerator shelf and closing the door softly.

Keira looked at Nathan and shook her head angrily, handing the phone back. "I'll help Owen with the rest of his stuff," she said, keeping the knife in her hand as she left.

"Sounds good, honey," said Nathan. "I'd like to be on the road by ten, maybe a few minutes earlier."

"We'll be ready," she called out from the hallway.

Quinn pulled a message pad off the refrigerator and wrote while he talked.

"The phones come with two hundred minutes each, and unlimited messaging, which should be more than enough to get you out of the state. Avoid calling any in-state numbers you regularly call. The police might have a reciprocal trace activated that will lead right back to these phones. If you screw up and call a number you shouldn't, ditch the phone and use the backup. That's why I bought two."

While he continued droning on about the phones, Quinn slid the message pad across the table for him to read:

Gather family and get ready to leave. Plan on two mins max between my departure and a text telling you to leave. Take ladder from garage and climb wall directly behind backyard. Any dogs there?

Nathan looked up from the paper, not hearing a word that Quinn was saying, and whispered, "No dogs."

He continued to read:

Get to Summerdale and turn right. Do not stop for any reason. I will meet you on Summerdale, and we will take my jeep to Pendleton. Must be ready to go when I text. Understand everything? Good to go?

Nathan read the message again, his heart pounding. He wasn't sure he could do this. Maybe he should just call the police. Tell them someone was trying break into the house with a gun—anything to get them there fast. He could tell them about the boats in the water. Request some kind of witness-protection program. Anything but this. If Sentinel was out there watching, how could Quinn pull this off?

Quinn's finger pressed against the last question on the piece of paper, jarring him out of the self-induced trance. He looked up at Quinn, unable to give him an immediate answer. The Marine took the phone out of Nathan's hand and whispered, "He's having doubts" to his father, quickly handing it back to him.

"Nate. David spotted four very suspicious vehicles within a block of your house. Two cargo vans and two Suburban-style SUVs. That's overkill for surveillance. He thinks they plan to grab you tonight," said his dad. "I trust his judgment on this. You have to get out of there. Press a number twice and hang up if you can do this."

Nathan's chest tightened, and he suddenly felt nauseated. He took a few long breaths before pushing his index finger against the question on the paper and nodding. Quinn put a strong hand on his shoulder and nodded back with a grimly determined look. Nathan pressed two numbers on the screen's pad, followed by "End Call."

"I should get out of your hair. Sounds like you have a long night ahead of you," said Quinn. "Good luck, man. Grab some energy drinks or something on the way out. I remember a few midnight drives to Vegas that almost ended unexpectedly. Once you get past Barstow, the drive becomes more of an endurance event—day or night."

"We're going to fill a thermos with coffee," said Nathan, barely squeaking the words past his lips.

Nathan started his watch's chronograph time as soon as he slid the deadbolt on the front door. Two minutes would go fast.

CHAPTER 29

Leeds studied the screens as David Quinn walked out of the house. All surveillance feeds indicated that he'd left alone. Thermal and Doppler showed the Fisher family inside the house, continuing to prepare for their imminent departure. Nathan Fisher returned to the garage while his wife and son continued to pack for the trip in the bedrooms. Electro-physio scans further confirmed that he wasn't watching sophisticated thermal decoys. Hudson assured him that his team was tracking three live heartbeats.

On the surface, the phone drop didn't raise any significant alarms. Conversation inside the house was a little stilted, but it didn't surprise Leeds. Nathan Fisher and David Quinn had no direct connection, and they were both nervous—Fisher for obvious reasons, Quinn because it didn't take a rocket scientist to understand the implications of delivering untraceable phones to someone about to leave the state. Still, he didn't like the timing. Quinn showing up an hour before Fisher was supposed to leave bothered him.

"The jeep is clean?" asked Leeds.

"We hit it with every sensor," answered Hudson. "Nobody hiding in the back, and we didn't detect any signal emissions. Just a dude and his jeep from what I can tell."

"All right. Watch the house like a fucking hawk. I need to know if you detect anything unusual."

"Funny you say that. I have a sound-quality degradation inside the house. The laser microphones are still picking up sound, but . . ."

"But what?" asked Leeds.

"We lost the phone feeds exactly three minutes and forty-three seconds ago."

"The batteries are internal," said Leeds, stating the obvious. "Any way he can shut the phones down?"

"I'd still have control," said Hudson. "I think he deep-sixed them somehow."

"He didn't leave the kitchen," said Leeds.

"Sir?" It was one of the techs in the van. "The phones are still transmitting, but all we're getting is a low-frequency hum. Barely that. Actually, only one phone is transmitting. We're trying to separate the signals."

Hudson and Leeds spoke at the same time: "Refrigerator?"

There was no other explanation. At some point during Quinn's brief visit to the house, Nathan and Keira Fisher's phones had been surreptitiously placed in the refrigerator. They could have done this in the open, and it wouldn't have raised any suspicion. Both of them had openly discussed the burners with the other phones still operational, so why the secrecy about disabling the phones? And how did they pull this off so quietly? Something was off.

"Where is the jeep?" asked Leeds, searching for it on the windshield HUD.

"Just turned left on Giraldo," reported Hudson.

"Backdoor," said Leeds, addressing the team in the SUV behind Fisher's house, "make sure the jeep keeps going north on Giraldo."

"This is Backdoor. Do you want us to follow him out?"

"Negative," said Leeds. "Just visually confirm, from your position, that the jeep continues north." He didn't want to pull them away. If anything else appeared out of place, he'd hit the house immediately.

"I have the jeep passing Summerdale, headed south," reported an operative in the SUV on the same street. "It's gone."

Leeds stared at the various displays in front of him, searching for an excuse to launch the raid. Nathan Fisher returned to the kitchen for a moment, then checked on his wife and son in the bedrooms. Several seconds later, he headed to the garage and lingered behind one of the cars like before. He'd probably just carried a few suitcases or bags from the bedrooms that needed to be packed. Leeds wasn't finding the excuse he needed on the screens.

"Anything on Quinn's personal phone?" asked Leeds, turning to face his team of surveillance technicians.

The back of the van resembled a naval ship's combat information center—dark except for deep-blue lighting and the subdued glows of several dimmed screens. The technicians sat back-to-back in harness-equipped seats bolted to the floor, facing side-by-side flat-screen displays fixed to the sides of the van. Beyond the techs, a thick blackout curtain blocked the surveillance hub from computers, servers, and electro-generators that powered the high-tech surveillance architecture. A small portion of the space beyond the curtain contained specialized equipment and additional weapons.

Dan Vega, his lead mobile-surveillance tech, shook his head. "I'm not getting any kind of response from Quinn's phone."

"He was using it when he pulled up," said Leeds.

"He wasn't using the phone registered to his name and address through Verizon," said Vega.

Or, Quinn strongly suspected Nathan Fisher was under direct surveillance. Surveillance he managed to identify on his wandering loop through the neighborhood. *Shit.* Anything could be in play right now, including a call to the police. Leeds and his team would have to depart immediately if the cops got involved. He couldn't risk that. If they moved now, they could be in and out of the house by the time any police units responded. Leeds pressed a button on his dashboard command tablet, dialing a number he'd hoped to avoid using until they'd successfully grabbed Fisher. His earphone crackled.

"I wasn't expecting to hear from you until later," said Flagg.

"Fisher just had a visitor. A Marine infantry captain with serious counterinsurgency training. I don't have time to explain, but something is off about the visit. I want to hit Fisher now."

"Then do it," said Flagg. "I'm not sure why you're bothering me with this."

"I'm going off a gut feeling."

"That's why I put you in charge of my most critical operations. You have good instincts. Don't lose Fisher or you'll be mopping the floors around here tomorrow," said Flagg, abruptly ending the call.

More like mopping the floor with my head.

He couldn't afford to take a chance on Quinn's visit. "All units. We roll on the house in thirty seconds," said Leeds. "Hudson. Start the cleanup process."

Chapter 30

Nathan eased the aluminum extension ladder through the door leading into the house from the garage, careful not to bump it against the door frame or one of the hallway walls. The ladder made a distinctive sound when jostled, and he didn't want to arouse any suspicion. He pointed the front end of the ladder toward the kitchen and walked slowly down the hallway, frequently checking the back end to make sure it stayed clear of the walls.

His family stood between the kitchen table and the open glass sliding door, shouldering the bug-out packs that had been stored with the family readiness gear in the room behind the garage. As soon as Quinn had departed, Nathan pulled Keira and Owen away from packing their suitcases and told them to grab the prepacked rucksacks. Each individually designed bug-out pack contained enough basic supplies, food, and extra clothing to last roughly forty-eight hours on foot. The packs would slow them down, but under the nebulous circumstances, he felt better knowing they had some measure of independence if something happened to Quinn.

He carried the ladder to the sliding door and cautiously lowered it to the tile floor. Keira stood next to Owen, holding the phone given to them by Quinn. She looked up from the device and whispered, "Nothing yet." He nodded and returned to the garage to lock the door leading into the house.

Back in the kitchen, Nathan grabbed his own light-brown bug-out pack from the table and slid his arms through the shoulder straps. He let the weight settle on his back before connecting the chest strap and securing the heavy pack tightly against his frame. When he looked up, he met his son's worried gaze. Owen clutched his pack's shoulder straps with both hands tightly enough to turn his knuckles white.

"Come here, buddy," Nathan whispered, beckoning him closer.

Eyes open wide, his son hurried to his side.

Nathan crouched beside him, putting a hand on his shoulder. "You've probably figured this out already," he whispered to Nathan, "but we're in danger right now. I don't have time to explain it, but I need you to do exactly what we say, when we say it."

"Are you in trouble with the police?" whispered Owen, his face grave.

"No. I promise you I'm not in trouble with the police. But it might be something more serious than that, even. We need to get out of the house immediately. The man who just visited us is going to help us get somewhere safe. We're going to meet him behind the house on Summerdale Drive."

"Grandpa's house?" asked Owen.

Nathan nodded. "Yes. Eventually. Are you good to go, buddy?"

"I'm scared."

He pulled his son close, hugging him tightly. "Everything's gonna be fine. We'll make sure of it."

A low rumbling sound drew his attention to the front of the house. The garage bay door?

"Do you hear that?" he said to Keira.

She nodded, putting a hand on Owen.

"It's the garage door," said his son.

"Go!" hissed Nathan. "Out the back. Run like crazy for the back wall. I'll be right behind you." He pushed Owen toward the patio and hooked the ladder with his right arm.

"He didn't text yet," Keira said, showing him the phone screen. "They're coming. Go!"

He lifted the ladder off the floor, clanging it against the tile. Keira and Owen dashed through the slider and across the patio with Nathan in close pursuit. The back of the ladder hit the metal edge of the door frame, and he glanced back at the house, expecting to see armed men rushing through the kitchen. The house was still empty, and for the briefest moment, Nathan thought he might have imagined the rumbling noise. Then, as he reached the edge of the patio, a loud crash inside the house erased any doubts about what he'd heard. Someone was smashing through one of the doors.

Nathan turned all his attention to navigating the shadowy backyard. He didn't have far to go to reach the privacy wall directly behind his house, but a crash-and-burn moment right now spelled disaster for his family. Their escape would come down to mere seconds. His hiking boots dug into the soft bed of river rock beyond the patio, propelling him toward Owen and Keira, who'd stopped at the seven-foot stucco back wall. He raised the front end of the ladder as he approached them and slammed it down on top of the thick wall, then grabbed his wife by one of her shoulder straps and pulled her to the foot of the ladder.

"You first. Then Owen. Wait on the other side. We don't know what's going on with Quinn."

Keira didn't hesitate. She was halfway up the ladder when Owen started climbing. Nathan kept his back to the ladder, watching the house for the first visible signs of the intruders. While the ladder clanged behind him from Owen's quick ascent, the house went dark. He turned then and started up the aluminum rungs just as his son's dark form disappeared over the wall above him.

CHAPTER 31

David Quinn sat in his jeep on Giraldo Avenue, steeling himself for what needed to be done. He waited a few more seconds, carefully checking his rearview mirror for any signs that they'd sent a car to follow him. Nothing. He'd been lucky with their stationary vehicle deployment. A quick scan through his thermal scope indicated he was alone on Giraldo Avenue—for now. Once he put his plan into action, he didn't expect to be alone for very long. He wasn't sure how he'd deal with extra company while escorting a panicked family back to his jeep—just another small detail to work out in the next minute or two, in the haziest scheme he'd ever concocted.

Making sure the jeep's overhead lights had been deactivated, he opened the car door and stepped onto the quiet street. Standing in the darkness with the door still open, he prepared a text message on his phone, making certain to use the correct number for Nathan's burner. He stuffed it in one of his front pant pockets, then reached across the driver's seat for the only two items in his backpack that might prove useful. *Might* being the operative term.

He tucked an expandable steel baton into one of his cargo pockets, making sure it was secure. Quinn had trained extensively with the baton for his last two deployments to Afghanistan, but had never used it against thinking and moving targets. He considered using it to smash open a window to get at the occupants, but just as quickly dismissed the idea. The metal baton generated significant force at its tip when swung like a club, but not enough to shatter bullet-resistant glass. Not even close.

He wasn't sure how he could use it in this situation, but he wanted to keep the option available. In hand-to-hand combat, the baton could be devastating, though he'd prefer to avoid any close-up scuffles with highly trained ex-military operators. For standoff distances, he packed a different weapon: the civilian authorized version of the military's CEW-19 (Conducted Electrical Weapon) pistol.

Firing projectiles capable of complete neuromuscular incapacitation for twenty seconds, the three-shot pistol accurately extended his fighting radius to seventy feet—against unarmored targets. The projectiles could not penetrate plate armor and had limited effectiveness against newer ceramic-scale flexible armor vests, drawbacks that would drastically reduce his engagement range. He'd have to aim for the unprotected parts of the body. Not an easy or desirable feat when your targets carried powerful, compact firearms.

Staring briefly at the orange pistol-like device in his hand, he wished he'd gone back to base to retrieve a personal firearm from the base armory. He was going up against heavily armed special-operator types with a metal baton and a Taser—and a three-inch foldable knife. Quinn had almost forgotten about the knife in his pocket. Unfortunately, it didn't make him feel any better. He closed the car door and sprinted across the street, nestling against the corner of the first house on the northern side of Summerdale.

A quick glance around the corner told him he should have little trouble reaching the back of the SUV undetected. A line of dwarf palmettos in the next yard down extended to the sidewalk, blocking the occupants' line of sight if he crawled. Tucking the gun into his waistband, he dropped to the dusty, rock-covered ground and low-crawled across the yard. By the time he reached the edge of the palmettos, his forearms and elbows were bleeding from the jagged terrain.

He peeked over the thick palm fronds at the sedan parked in the driveway two yards away. Slipping onto the sidewalk, he crawled around the edge of the palmettos and headed diagonally for the car. When the sedan blocked his view of the back of the SUV, he rose to a low crouch and sprinted the rest of the way. He arrived at the sedan and stopped, listening for a reaction. Nothing. Now for the riskiest part of his trip.

A tall palm stood next to the sidewalk, about ten feet behind the SUV. If he could reach it undetected, he should be able to slither along the curb, arriving behind the vehicle. Unfortunately, he needed to cross an open yard to get there, and there was no way to determine if the operative in the front passenger seat was paying close enough attention to the side mirror. Even in the darkness, he couldn't miss Quinn sprinting from the car to the tree if he was looking in the mirror. There was only one way to find out.

He burst into the open, headed directly for the street. If he could put the tree between himself and the mirror, he stood a lower chance of being detected. Halfway across the barren yard, the SUV's motor roared to life. *Shit.* That could only mean one thing. They were making a move against Fisher.

Quinn took a chance and ran directly for the SUV—hoping its occupants would be too preoccupied by their imminent business with Fisher to notice his approach. He barreled past the thick palm trunk and ran diagonally for the back of the black Suburban. Crouched behind the bumper, he struggled to get his breath under control, while deciding the best course of action to neutralize the SUV. After a few seconds of deliberation, he concluded there was no best course of action—only the least shitty one.

He grabbed his phone and activated the screen, pressing "SEND." There was no going back now.

"This is fucking crazy," he muttered, burying the phone in his pocket and crawling under the bumper.

He scraped along the pavement until he felt the rear right tire. Sliding his right hand back, he dug the knife out of his pocket and flicked it open. He pushed the tip into the right rear tire's sidewall, invoking a loud hiss. Still breathing heavily, Quinn shoved it a little farther, working the blade back and forth to create a bigger opening. The SUV would be equipped with run-flat tires, so his goal was to activate the tire-pressure monitoring system and draw one of the occupants out of the vehicle.

Before he could pull the knife out of the tire, one of the car doors opened. He peered through the darkness, watching the ground on each side of the vehicle with his peripheral vision. A pair of boots hit the sidewalk on the passenger side, pausing momentarily before starting toward the back of the SUV. Quinn scrambled backward along the pavement, until he cleared the bumper. Rising slowly, he pressed against the left side of the bumper, holding the gun in his left hand—and the baton in his right.

"Here we go," he whispered, sliding toward the opposite side of the Suburban's tailgate.

Quinn extended his left hand and the side of his face beyond the edge of the SUV and searched for his target. In the blackness, he saw a human's shadow walking along the curb in his direction. Unable to immediately determine if his target wore heavy body armor, he aimed for the man's face and pressed the trigger. A crack broke the silence as the projectile left the barrel at subsonic speed and spanned the distance in a fraction of a second—dropping the man to his knees.

Without pausing, Quinn extended the baton and stepped into the open. Three sharp baton strikes to his target's unprotected head rendered the man twitching on the sidewalk. Quinn paused long enough to pocket the baton and retrieve the disabled operative's weapon, a Heckler and Koch MP-20, fitted with an integral suppressor.

The MP-20 was HK's latest model of compact assault weapon, chambered for body-armor-piercing, caseless ammunition. This wasn't a simple surveillance team by any stretch of the imagination. He slid the MP-20s over his right shoulder and leveled the CEW at the door, staying below the windows.

"Ragan," hissed the driver, "we need to get moving."

Quinn leaned into the open door and fired, striking the driver's night-vision goggles a half inch above his exposed face. The projectile ricocheted off the device's frame, striking the windshield with a thunk. The driver reacted faster than he expected, slamming the CEW into the passenger seatback with his right hand. Quinn panicked and pressed the trigger, discharging his last projectile. He let go of the plastic pistol and pulled his arm back before the operative could grab it.

The driver cursed and thrust Quinn's left arm between the front seats. Quinn raised the MP-20 and disengaged the safety without thinking, pressing the trigger twice. The first shot passed through the driver's head, shattering the driver's-side window and splattering it with blood. The second 5.7mm projectile penetrated his neck, spraying the windshield.

Quinn stepped back and stared at the mess inside the SUV, questioning what he'd done. Could they be police? He'd just assumed they were some kind of assassination team. Watching the man bleed out onto the dashboard, he wasn't so sure anymore. A crashing sound drew his gaze from the pulsing arterial spray to the house across the street. *Shit.* Fisher and his family were making a racket in the backyard.

He opened the rear passenger door and searched for the driver's weapon, finding a loaded MP-20 in a horizontally mounted rack. A quick search of the incapacitated operative on the sidewalk yielded six additional thirty-round magazines for the MP-20s. He slung the extra rifle over his shoulder and closed the door, stepping toward the front of the SUV.

Three shadows emerged from the darkness between the two houses across the street moments after he peered over the hood. It was too soon to be the Fishers. He'd just sent the message. Quinn rested the MP-20 on the vibrating hood and found the first darkened figure in the rifle's light-intensifying sight. *What the fuck?* It actually was Fisher.

A snap passed over his head, a bullet thunking into the house behind him. Through the rifle sight, he searched beyond the stucco wall between the two houses. A man stood on the back wall of the property, tracking the family with a suppressed rifle. Quinn centered his sight's green dot on the man's face and pressed the trigger, knocking him off the wall. A flash erupted from another point on the wall, followed by loud thumps and cracks against the SUV. Time to go.

CHAPTER 32

Nathan Fisher stopped halfway across the front yard, spreading his arms in a futile attempt to shield his family. A shadowy figure, mostly concealed behind the SUV's hood, aimed a weapon at them. How careless. He'd tripped over a wheelbarrow in his neighbor's backyard and had stumbled right into their guns. He should have taken his chances with the police. A crack exploded above his head, spurring him to grab Keira and their son and pull them toward Giraldo Avenue. Toward Quinn—if he was still alive.

A second crack echoed between the houses, followed by a muffled grunt from the yard behind him. A burst of muffled gunfire followed, hitting the SUV. He couldn't process what was happening in the dark, so he kept pulling his family across the neighboring yard. It was the only thing he could do for them at this point. He glanced to the left and saw the shooter reappear behind the SUV.

"Nathan!" the man yelled.

"Get down and stay down," said Nathan, pushing Keira and his son behind a two-foot-high paver wall lining the home's driveway.

When he peeked over the top of the wall a second later, the man was running full speed in their direction—waving his arms like a lunatic.

"Nathan. It's Quinn!" the man said. "Keep your family moving. We don't have much time!"

"Quinn? How the hell?" He rose up slowly, motioning for his family to stay down.

"Let's go!" hissed the man, barely recognizable in the dark.

The guy took off for Giraldo Avenue, crossing the street before pausing in a crouch.

"Get the fuck moving! I promised your dad I'd get you out of here!"

It was Quinn. They still had a chance.

"It's really him," he said, pulling his son up. "We have to move fast, Owen. Can you keep up?"

"I can do it," said Owen, his voice trembling.

Nathan wasn't so sure. Owen had slowed them down crossing the neighbor's yard, the overstuffed backpack weighing him down.

"Go," said Nathan, spurring them into motion.

Owen climbed over the paver and started running toward Quinn, struggling with the pack. Keira deliberately slowed her pace to stay by his side.

"You can move faster than us," Nathan told her. "Catch up with Quinn."

"I'm not leaving you and Owen."

"At least get on the other side of me."

"I'm right where I want to be," she said, keeping herself between their son and the threat.

Halfway across the street, Nathan muttered a curse. Owen wasn't moving fast enough with close to thirty pounds on his back.

"Owen," he said, "drop your pack."

"Right now?" asked Owen, huffing from effort.

"Right now. Drop it and run."

Owen disconnected his chest strap and slid his arms under the shoulder straps, dropping the pack on the far side of the street and bursting ahead of Keira, no longer burdened by the weight. Nathan slowed to grab the dropped rucksack, but the sound of snapping bullets changed his mind. He followed his family to Quinn's position behind a thick palm trunk.

"Where are you parked?" asked Nathan, panting.

"On Giraldo. A few cars down," said Quinn, sliding next to him. "What the fuck happened back there?"

"The garage door opened by itself," said Fisher. "We got the hell out of there."

"Son of a bitch," said Quinn. "They were coming to kill you. Keep moving."

Nathan pounded the ground with his family, struggling to keep up with Quinn. Car tires squealed nearby, causing him to quicken the pace. Quinn sprinted ahead, dodging between two parked cars and racing across the street. He yanked open the rear driver's-side door of a jeep and turned back to meet Nathan and Keira halfway across Giraldo Ave.

"I want your wife and son in the backseat. Heads down," said Quinn, pulling him next to the jeep. "Keira, you stay in the jeep with your son. Do not get out for any reason."

Before Nathan could react, Quinn jammed one of the rifles into his chest, nearly knocking him off balance. His wife followed Owen into the jeep, slamming the door shut.

"I need you to use this," said Quinn, pressing the rifle into him.

"I'm not familiar with this—"

"It works like the rest," said Quinn, leaving the metal and polymer weapon in his hands. "Center the green dot on your target and pull the trigger. The safety is off."

"I haven't fired one of these in—"

Quinn yanked him off the street and dragged him between the back of the jeep and the steeply sloped hood of a mini-sedan. Two streets away to the south, a low, dark shape eased onto Giraldo Avenue. *Holy shit!*

"I saw a car," said Nathan. "Lights were off."

"I saw it, too," said Quinn, pulling him onto the sidewalk. "Stay low."

"What's the plan?"

Quinn stared at him in the darkness for a moment. "Point and shoot at the vehicle when I tell you. You remember how to use one of these, right?"

Nathan cradled the rifle in his arms, pressing it into his right shoulder. He'd fired several combat rifles with his father at Camp Pendleton, using a variety of magnified and unmagnified rail-mounted optics. This weapon was shorter, with the magazine protruding from the pistol grip. More like a submachine gun than a rifle. Regardless of the design, it would work just like Quinn said. Point and shoot. He could do this.

"I'm good," he said. "Are you sure these are enough?"

"They'll do for now," said Quinn. "You aim for the windshield; I'll work on the tires. We just need to stop them."

Quinn slipped between the back of the mini-sedan and a standard-size SUV, whispering to Nathan. "Use that tree trunk for cover," he said, pointing down the sidewalk. "You have twenty-seven rounds in the magazine. Fire methodically at the windshield. I'll do the rest."

Nathan crawled to the tree, careful not to discharge the rifle, and crouched at its base, waiting for some kind of signal. The deep rumble of the approaching vehicle's engine froze him in place. He tried to peer around the side of the tree trunk but couldn't bring himself to move. This was a bad idea.

"Quinn," he said, the word coming out as a whisper.

"What?" came Quinn's reply.

"When are we shooting?"

"Now," he heard, followed by three muted snaps.

Nathan leaned to the right and pressed the rifle's hand guard against the palm trunk, thinking about Keira and Owen as he centered the green dot on the driver's-side windshield and pressed the trigger evenly—like his father had taught him.

CHAPTER 33

Ray Olmos searched the street for three running targets, finding nothing in the daylight image displayed by his goggles. "You see anything?" he asked.

"No," grunted his driver.

They couldn't have gone far, and there was no way they'd escaped in a car. The road was empty when they turned onto Giraldo.

"Leeds, this is Olmos," he said, transmitting on the tactical network. "I don't see shit on Giraldo. You sure they bolted in this direction?"

"I'll ask Carrington when they piece his head back together," said Leeds. "Any vehicles on the road?"

"You mean driving?" asked Olmos, getting irritated with Leeds.

"Yes. Driving," said Leeds. "As in escaping."

"Negative. The roads are clear," said Olmos, wanting to add, *like I said.*

"Then they're on foot," said Leeds. "Get your team on the ground at the intersection of Summerdale, and be careful. We're still not sure what we're up against. Trenker's team is turning onto Summerdale from Virgo, so don't light them up."

"Copy that," he said, turning to his team in the back of the van. "Prepare to deploy when we reach Summerdale."

A loud smack resonated through the van. Olmos turned his head to see a softball-size, milky-green splotch on the windshield in front of the driver. A second splotch appeared next to the first, cracking a two-foot-diameter section of the windshield, followed by repeated bullet strikes against the rest of the bullet-resistant glass—obscuring his view of the street.

"Out the back!" he screamed, pulling himself through the opening between the front seats and pushing against the tight cluster of five operatives.

The smacking sound continued unabated, until he felt a warm spray hit the back of his neck.

"Get down!" he yelled, flattening himself against the hard rubber floor matting.

Bullets hissed through the compartment, one of them striking the operative next to him in the head, spraying the rear van door crimson-red. Glancing over his shoulder toward the front of the van, Olmos watched bullet holes stitch through the weakened glass windshield. The armor-piercing bullets passed through the front seats, striking flesh and metal behind him.

He was too preoccupied with the bullets passing inches above his head to realize the van had accelerated, until it struck the back of a parked vehicle, catapulting him against the dashboard's center console. He sank to the gore-encrusted foot well, battered and unable to move, fading unconscious before he could report what had happened.

CHAPTER 34

Leeds opened the bottom drawer of the dresser in the Fishers' master bedroom and tucked a worn box of 9mm ammunition against the back of the drawer with gloved hands. The box contained sixteen jacketed, hollow-point rounds, thirty-four rounds short of the fifty it had been designed to hold. Thirty-three of the missing rounds would be found split between two pistol magazines discovered in Fisher's car.

The final bullet would turn up in Detective Peck's head, pointing the finger at Fisher, a tragic figure who'd struggled with Internet-gambling-induced financial problems he thought could be solved by working for the California Liberation Movement. He closed the drawer and turned toward the bedroom door.

"Leeds, this is Trenker," his earpiece announced. "Backdoor has been neutralized. One KIA and one critically injured. Jesus—is Olmos engaging targets? I'm hearing a lot of suppressed gunfire from Giraldo."

"What?" asked Leeds. "Olmos just reported all clear."

A metal-on-metal crash reverberated through the house.

"What the fuck was that?" Leeds yelled, sprinting into the kitchen.

One of his operatives barreled through the open slider leading to the backyard, pausing long enough to answer. "Olmos isn't responding. I'm covering the front door."

The body armor–clad operative leveled his rifle toward the front hallway and disappeared into the house's shadows.

Leeds triggered the tactical communications net. "Olmos, this is Leeds. Report your status," he said, receiving no response.

"This is Kline," said an exasperated voice through his headset. "We took heavy fire from the north on Giraldo. Multiple shooters."

"Are you still engaged?"

"Negative. Shooters drove north on Giraldo," said Kline. "Pretty sure they turned right on Morelos."

"Roger. What's the status of the team?" asked Leeds, jogging toward the front door.

"Olmos is out cold, but he looks intact. Roscoe made it out of the van. The rest are injured or dead. The driver and Marco are definitely KIA. Headshots."

"What about the van?" asked Leeds, stopping next to Kline, hidden in the dark foyer. Bodies could be hauled away, but he couldn't exactly tow a disabled vehicle.

"It hit a parked car hard," said Kline. "But the engine's still revving."

Leeds peered through the open front door, scanning the neighborhood. Exterior house lights had begun to brighten the street as neighbors investigated the unusual level of noise. This would get way worse if he didn't get his teams off the streets immediately. He ran a quick mental count of his remaining assets and balanced them against the mission at hand. He barely had what he needed to evacuate his own team, let alone pursue Fisher. Fisher could wait. Getting his operation off the streets could not.

First things first. He needed to clean up the immediate vicinity. He turned to the operative standing behind him in the foyer.

"Maclean. I need you to remove Carrington's body from the backyard," said Leeds. "Bring him through the side gate, not the house, and drop him in the van."

"Got it," said the man, starting to move.

Leeds grabbed him by the sleeve before he left and fished two sets of keys out of his right cargo pocket.

"When you're done with that, I need you to return to the Fisher house," said Leeds. "Close all of the doors and turn out the lights, then pick one of the vehicles and drive it out south on Interstate 15. Someone will call you with more information in a few minutes. Close the garage door when you leave—and whatever you do, don't speed. We need that car."

"Why can't one of the surveillance guys drive the car?" replied Maclean. "This takes me out of the action."

"This isn't a job for a surveillance tech. Never was," said Leeds, letting go of his sleeve. "You'll get your payback for Carrington."

"I better," grumbled Maclean, disappearing into the house.

Leeds stepped through the front door, heading for the surveillance van parked two houses away. A porch light directly across the street illuminated more of Fisher's driveway than he preferred. He raised his sling-attached MP-20 and fired a single shot, dousing the light.

"All units," Leeds said into the net, "we have a situation requiring an immediate change of plans. Kline. Take Roscoe and get that van out of here. I don't care how you do it, but I want the van gone. I'll dispatch a cleanup team to meet you on the road."

"Copy. I think we can limp the van out of here," said Kline.

"Trenker, clean up the mess on Summerdale and split your team between the two SUVs. I need two chase vehicles to pursue our target. I'll send as many as Hudson can spare to fill seats."

"Roger. We'll pick up Hudson's crew at the corner of Virgo and Summerdale in fifteen seconds," said Trenker. "Where do you want us to go after that?"

"I want one vehicle headed east, toward Interstate 15, and the other west, for the 805. Fastest available routes. I'll pass instructions once we get out of here. Hudson, are you packed up?"

"I'm getting there. Moreno and Volk are headed in Trenker's direction."

"I want to be out of here in less than thirty seconds, Hudson," said Leeds, glancing across the street at the stakeout house. "Can you do that?"

"Thirty seconds works," said Hudson.

Leeds opened the front passenger door of the van and stepped onto the running board, leaning into the van to address his lead surveillance tech. "Here's what I need—"

"GPS track data is not available on the jeep," said Vega. "DOD registered. Category One. Exempt from state travel restrictions and tracking. I've started prepping both Ravens."

Leeds had forgotten about the active-duty military personnel exemption.

"I was going to ask for smoke grenades," said Leeds. "How long until the drones are ready?"

"I can have them assembled, spooled up, and ready to fly in—how long?" asked Vega, yelling into the back of the van.

"One minute," said a tech hidden behind the rear curtain. "Unless you want to zombie launch. I can set a cardinal direction and altitude. We can take over anytime after it reaches altitude."

"Do it," said Leeds. "Set northeast and northwest. Altitude one thousand feet."

"Both of them?" asked the tech, pulling the curtain open.

"Is that a problem?"

"Negative," he said. "But I'll need help."

"Vega, make it happen. Launch directly from the street," said Leeds, directing his next question at the driver. "Do we have any smoke grenades in the van?"

"Yep," the driver said, reaching behind the passenger seat and lifting a black duffel bag between the front seats.

When the duffel hit his seat, Leeds unzipped the top and pulled it open, finding several gray cylindrical canisters. "Start spreading these around," he said, grabbing one and pulling the metal pin. "We've drawn quite an audience."

He hopped onto the pavement and heaved the metal cylinder as far as he could throw it down the street. The grenade bounced in front of Fisher's house and skittered past a few parked cars before exploding in a thick, billowy cloud of grayish-white smoke. The clang of a second grenade rattled on the street somewhere behind the van. He met the driver at the vehicle, reaching for more grenades.

"Closer this time," said Leeds. "Put a few in the yards, too."

An underhand lob placed a smoke grenade in the middle of the street, directly in front of Fisher's driveway entrance, detonating moments before Maclean appeared next to the garage, shouldering Carrington's lifeless body. The smoke expanded rapidly, shielding Maclean's trip across the front yard from anyone across the street. Leeds deployed another grenade in the front yard directly across Pallux Way from the van, instructing his driver to do the same on the other side. By the time Maclean met Leeds at the back of the van, the street was enshrouded in thick, slowly drifting chemical fog.

Maclean lowered Carrington's body to the pavement behind the bumper and pounded on the rear hatch doors.

"I'll take care of Carrington," said Leeds. "You take care of the car."

The operative disappeared in the haze without saying a word, moments before one of the techs kicked open the van's rear barn doors and hopped out holding one of the dark-gray RQ-18 Night Raven drones. The tech landed on Carrington's legs, tripping face-first onto the pavement. Throughout the graceless fall, the tech kept his arm extended upward, preventing the delicate fiberglass machine from hitting the street. Leeds swiped the Night Raven out of the groaning tech's upright hand.

"Nice save," he said, taking several steps away from the van.

"I think I lost a tooth," said the tech.

"You just stepped on a guy who lost his head," said Leeds. "Is this thing ready to go?"

Vega jumped clear of the body with the second drone, landing to the side of the van.

"There's a selector switch on the bottom," said Vega. "Switch it to 'RUN,' three clicks to the right, and hold on tight. That little bitch will want to fly right out of your hands. Once the propeller is buzzing, turn the switch two more clicks to 'MODE A.' Get a little running start and throw it at a forty-five-degree angle. Don't throw it toward any trees."

Leeds couldn't see more than twenty feet in any direction through the smoke at this point—and he didn't remember the locations of the street's intermittently spaced palm trees. "You go first," he said. "Everyone else, in the van. We're out of here once these are airborne."

A few seconds later, Vega's drone buzzed like a weed trimmer in his hand, the rear-mounted propeller quickly building up speed. He fiddled with the selector switch again before cocking his arm back and taking a few steps forward. He aimed the drone down the middle of the street, behind the van, and threw it into the air. The thinning chemical cloud swallowed the Night Raven, leaving them with nothing but a persistent, high-pitched buzzing to prove it was still in flight. As the sound faded, Vega gave Leeds a thumbs-up.

"It's clear," said Vega. "Send it straight down the middle."

Leeds lifted the five-pound drone high enough to find the selector switch. He couldn't read the small print, so he turned it slowly, feeling three clicks. The propeller burst to life, tugging the drone in his hand. Vega had been right about the thing wanting to fly. He pinched his fingers tight and turned the switch two more clicks, though over the noise and vibration created by the propeller, it was hard to tell if it had clicked. He lined up between the cars materializing in the smoke behind the van, ran forward a few steps, and threw the drone. The Night Raven pulled away effortlessly, disappearing into the night.

"Leeds, this is Hudson," he heard in his earpiece. "I'm opening the garage door. We're ready to scoot."

"Perfect timing," said Leeds, passing the back of the van as the barn doors closed. "Give us about ten seconds before pulling onto the street. I don't need any more problems."

"Copy that," said Hudson.

Leeds hopped into the van's passenger seat and closed the door, spotting a set of taillights ahead of him through the smoke.

"Maclean?" Leeds asked his driver.

"Yeah. Just left the house."

"Get us out of here. Head to Morelos and take a right," said Leeds. "Vega. How are my drones looking?"

"Good to go. Strong signals," said Vega. "Give me a minute to take positive control. I'll patch the feeds to your HUD."

Less than a minute later, they reached Calle Morelos, rolling through the stop sign headed east. He'd fucked up by not stationing another vehicle on Giraldo. Quinn had pretended to drive away, instead parking on Giraldo and doubling back on foot to neutralize the team in the SUV. The Fishers had been ready to run when Olmos's team hit the house—that was the only way to explain the ladder found propped against the back wall of the property.

Leeds strained to think of anything they had forgotten that could unravel the plan to frame Fisher—other than the fact that they had failed to kidnap Fisher. That was the most obvious problem, but one he intended to fix. He didn't have the option of returning to Pallux Way. San Diego PD would be all over the neighborhood in a few minutes, trying to make sense of what the neighbors were saying. The police wouldn't find much. All the rifles used fired caseless ammunition, leaving no brass cartridges behind. Carrington left half of his head in Fisher's backyard, but they wouldn't find that right away. The most puzzling evidence left behind would be the smashed-up car on Giraldo and some broken glass from the van. Not the cleanest operation by any stretch of the imagination, but not an unmitigated disaster. Of course, Flagg would see it differently. He dreaded making that call.

"Vega, set us up with the quickest route to Black Mountain Road, and give me a map with all of our units' locations."

A digital map of Mira Mesa and its immediately surrounding communities filled the windshield HUD, instantly showing the location of every vehicle assigned to the Fisher operation. The two SUVs were headed in opposite directions, several blocks away. Kline had traveled half that distance in Olmos's van, traveling east on Mira Mesa Boulevard at just under twenty-five miles per hour. Kline needed to find a place to hide the van fast—and Mira Mesa Boulevard was not a good start. *Why the fuck did he pick the busiest road in Mira Mesa?*

"Vega, can you reroute Kline? He's driving a shot-up, mangled van down Mira Mesa Boulevard. Get him off the road and get a cleanup team to his location immediately."

"Got it," said Vega. "I'm putting together some surveillance parameters for the drones. I assume this is a handoff?"

"Actually, I just need to know which interstate he's using," said Leeds. "I can almost guarantee he's headed north to Pendleton."

"All right. I'll send the Ravens higher for a wider view," said Vega.

Leeds fiddled with the track pad on the keyboard in front of him, selecting Flagg's number and choosing to route the call through his headset. A moment later, Flagg answered, his irate voice coming through Leeds's left earpiece.

CHAPTER 35

Flagg took a moment to absorb the information presented on all his screens before answering the call. Judging by what he saw on the displays, something had gone definitively wrong during what should have been a relatively simple abduction. Leeds had vehicles driving in every direction conceivable—except for the one direction they should be headed! He clicked the icon connecting the phone call to his headset. Leeds spoke before he could say a word.

"Sir, we've had a little problem," said Leeds.

"A little problem?" asked Flagg. "I'm monitoring a half-dozen 911 calls originating from Pallux Way alone, reporting everything from car crashes to wildfires. Even a few mentions of guys running around with guns. Sound familiar?"

"We're still on track," said Leeds. "This'll add to the confusion and drama surrounding Fisher's disappearance, and his eventual discovery near the border."

Flagg stared at the digital navigation map, trying to figure out why Fisher's car was headed south, without the rest of Leeds's vehicles.

"Help me out with something," said Flagg. "If I didn't know better, I'd guess that Fisher had escaped and was driving south. But I know that's not possible. That would have been the first thing out of your mouth, right?"

When Leeds didn't answer him immediately, Flagg pressed down on the touch pad with enough force to warp the plastic.

"Maclean is driving the car south," said Leeds. "We're still looking for Fisher and his family."

"How the fuck do you consider that to be *still on track?*" yelled Flagg. "Wasn't he there when I talked to you? Where did he go?"

"He was tipped off by the Marine and escaped over the back wall of his yard."

"And evaded the team you had watching the back?"

"He neutralized the team. One KIA. One critically injured."

"Fisher did that?"

"No. The Marine did it," said Leeds. "David Quinn. Infantry captain stationed at Camp Pendleton. He killed Carrington with a single headshot in Fisher's backyard, and somehow lit up Olmos's van, taking out most of the team. I have two confirmed KIAs and an unknown number of wounded in the van. We're going to need—"

"Stop right there," said Flagg. "An infantry Marine does not *by himself* take out a Cerberus black-ops team. What the fuck are we up against, Nick?"

"Quinn arrived and left Fisher's house alone. All of our sensors confirmed this," said Leeds. "We saw the same vehicle leave the area after Olmos's van was hit. If he had help, they either squeezed into the jeep with Fisher and his family or melted back into the neighborhood."

"Or Fisher never left the neighborhood," said Flagg. "They could have stashed him in someone's backyard and lured you away."

"My money's on a different scenario," said Leeds. "Quinn is taking Fisher to Camp Pendleton, where he thinks they'll be safe."

"Your money!" screamed Flagg. "You don't have any money in this game! What are you doing to find Fisher? And don't tell me you're driving cars in every direction until you stumble across a black jeep!"

"I have two Ravens in the air. One headed for the 805. The other for the I-15. We can't track the jeep using state tracking data, because it's a DOD-registered vehicle."

"Of course it is."

"But we can take them up high enough to transmit a live stream, then overlay CALRES tracking screens over the drone feeds," said Leeds. "They won't match up perfectly, but we're looking at light traffic. We'll find the jeep."

"I'm glad to hear your brain damage was temporary," said Flagg. "When did you get the Ravens airborne? They have a limited range."

"I got them up less than sixty seconds after learning Fisher drove away," said Leeds. "They're flying northeast and northwest for their respective highways at forty miles per hour. Quinn is stopping, turning, waiting at stoplights, and generally obeying the speed limit to avoid attracting attention. My drones will beat him to the highway."

"But you won't."

"We don't have to," said Leeds. "I just need to find them with the Ravens. We won't be that far behind. Hold on, sir. I'm getting a report—shit, I just lost one of the SUVs."

"Another attack?"

"Hold on," said Leeds, requesting information. "Negative. Rear-tire blowout."

"The vehicles are equipped with run-flat tires."

"Just like they're supposed to stop armor-piercing bullets?" asked Leeds. "Cerberus might want to look into the vehicle supplier."

Flagg ignored Leeds's comment and expanded the digital map in the center of his array to include the southern edges of Camp Pendleton. He gauged the distances and made a few quick mental calculations. The math didn't add up.

"You're down to two vehicles, split between two interstates that are twelve miles apart," he said. "Camp Pendleton is less than thirty miles away along the coast. Add about ten miles to that total if they take I-15.

Whichever route Fisher and his new partner in crime chose, you'll never get the second vehicle across in time for a roadside takedown. You're in surveillance mode for the rest of this op."

"We can take care of this," said Leeds.

"I can't let Fisher reach Camp Pendleton, or wherever they're headed. Especially now. We don't know how Quinn fits into the picture, but he went through some trouble to sneak Fisher away," said Flagg. "I'm launching an armed drone from Ramona. We're done playing games with this guy. I need you to find the jeep, and mark it with a laser for the drone."

"You're going to blow him up on the freeway?"

"Exit 54 in Oceanside empties right into Camp Pendleton. You want to try to pull him over on the freeway with the surveillance van, in front of a hundred cameras? Or ambush him right in front of the base's main gate? I'd rather let the latest in Lockheed Martin guided-missile technology clean up this mess."

"I'm pretty sure detonating a twenty-pound high explosive charge on a federal highway will leave more of a mess," said Leeds.

"They won't have enough forensic evidence left to determine who was in the car, beyond Quinn," said Flagg. "And that'll be an educated guess."

"The car is registered to his wife."

"Hmm. Then perhaps we should pay her a visit once this is done," said Flagg. "Make it even harder for authorities to figure out what the hell happened tonight. Who knows? This might work out even better than the original plan."

CHAPTER 36

Nathan Fisher wanted to crawl into the backseat to be with his wife and son, but was worried he might cause an accident. Quinn was completely amped, teetering on the edge of barely functioning as a driver. The last thing he needed was Nathan jostling him as he squeezed between the front seats.

Quinn had blown through several stop signs bringing them to Black Mountain Road, narrowly escaping at least two potentially fatal accidents, yet somehow to this point avoiding law-enforcement interest. Quinn had eased up on the gas enough for Nathan to risk diverting his attention from the road. He twisted in his seat, finding Keira on her knees in the middle of the rear bench seat, watching the road behind them for pursuers. Owen clung to Keira's side but otherwise looked alert.

Nathan reached back and grabbed his son's shoulder. "You okay?"

Owen nodded, easing his grip on his mother. "I'm fine."

Nathan ruffled his hair. "I'm proud of you, buddy. You did good back there."

His compliment barely made a dent in his son's worried expression. Nathan gently touched the back of his wife's neck, drawing her attention away from the scene beyond the rear window.

"How is Mom doing?" Nathan asked.

She turned her head and forced a smile. "I've been better."

"Maybe you should turn around and buckle in."

Keira went back to scanning the road behind them between the headrests. She held Owen tight with one arm and used the other to grip the headrest support for balance.

"She needs to buckle in," said Quinn.

"Keira?" asked Nathan.

"How am I supposed to watch the road if I'm buckled in?" she demanded.

"We're safe for now," said Quinn.

"Yeah, I feel really safe," said Keira.

She faced the front and buckled in next to Owen. Nathan met her stare, which told him to leave her alone for now.

"What's the plan?" asked Nathan.

"The plan?" asked Quinn. "I'm taking you to Pendleton. My wife reserved a room for you at the Ward Lodge."

"Do you think that'll be safe?"

"Pendleton, or the lodge?"

"Either," said Nathan. "The lodge is one of the first places they'll look. They know who you are, where you're stationed. Everything, by this point."

Quinn looked deep in thought for a few moments. "I need to make a quick call."

"You want me to dial the number?"

"Why? So I don't crash?" asked Quinn, digging through the center console for his phone while watching the road. "I'm good to go now. Just a little postcombat adrenaline."

Nathan removed the phone from one of the cup holders under his elbow, at least a foot from where Quinn was searching, and thrust it in front of the steering wheel. "Yeah, you're good to go," he said, flinching when Quinn swiped the phone from his grip.

Quinn pressed the screen a few times and placed the device to his left ear. "Alison, I need you to listen. Things went very badly in Mira

Mesa," he said. "No. No. Hey! I'm not kidding. Don't worry about what phone I'm using. Where are you right now?"

Nathan could hear her muffled voice but couldn't tell what she said.

"Perfect. Do not leave Pendleton for any reason. Head to the Mainside Center and take as much cash as you can out of the ATM. Is anything open over there?"

Quinn paused to listen.

"Forget about the room at the lodge. We need to think off the grid. I really can't talk right now, Ally. Get the cash, and wait for me to call you."

He shook his head and sighed. "It doesn't matter where. Just don't leave the base. I'll call you when we get through the gate." He nodded sharply. "Yes, it's that bad. I love you," he said, disconnecting the call.

"I'm really sorry about this," said Nathan, glancing into the backseat.

Keira met his glance briefly before burying her forehead into the top of Owen's unruly mop of hair. Quinn just stared at the road ahead, slowing for a light that had been red for a while.

"And thank you," said Nathan. "I can't imagine what would have happened if you didn't show up."

Quinn glanced at him and nodded. "You can thank my dad—your dad, too. I was doing them both a favor."

"You could have driven home after dropping off the phones," said Nathan, pointing at the green light.

Quinn gunned the engine, launching them through the intersection and building up speed.

"I knew my dad was right when I saw what they had stacked outside of your house," said Quinn. "Life as I knew it ended the moment they read my license plate. This Cerberus group is serious business."

"Who are you, exactly?" asked his wife, suddenly talkative. "And what is this Cerberus?"

"David Quinn. Captain. United States Marine Corps," said Nathan.

Quinn turned his head to Nathan. "You remember me?"

"My dad was sergeant major for First Radio Battalion when your dad was CO," said Nathan. "You were a freshman at San Clemente High for the last year of that. I graduated that year."

"My dad spoke highly of your dad—and you," said Quinn. "He was really surprised when you left the Marine Option program at Davis."

"Apparently everyone was surprised, except for me," said Nathan.

"How about we catch up on old times a little later," Keira cut in. "What is this Cerberus group? Nathan's dad didn't say anything about them on the phone. Only that our lives were in danger. His included."

"David, this is Keira," said Nathan.

"Sorry if I come across unfriendly," she said. "But I wasn't expecting a gun battle in my neighborhood. Cerberus?"

"My dad didn't go into detail," Quinn said, "but it sounds like Cerberus International is the enforcement arm of a massive international conglomerate called the Sentinel Group. Bottom line? Sentinel uses Cerberus like a private army, to make sure Sentinel's best financial interests are protected worldwide." Quinn shot them each a glance. "They can be very proactive in their approach, as we all just witnessed."

"Hold on," demanded Keira. "What does this Cerberus have to do with the police investigation into the nuclear desalination plant?"

"What do you mean?" asked Quinn. "Cerberus is working independent of the police."

Nathan's skin tingled. He'd completely forgotten that he hadn't told Keira the full story about the boats and divers he'd seen at the beach. Given their imminent departure from California, he hadn't thought it would make a difference. In fact, he'd convinced himself that he was better off not telling her. She'd been anxious enough after the lieutenant governor's assassination. Now that a group linked to the boats had attacked them, she was likely to explode.

Nathan saw an opportunity to steer the conversation away from the beach. "Cerberus is very possibly linked to the assassinations," he said.

"And the group that tried to kill us is Cerberus?" asked Keira. "Are you sure that wasn't the police?"

"They weren't cops," said Quinn. "I saw them up close and personal behind your house."

"Why would this mystical black-ops group be interested in us?"

Nathan squirmed in his seat, barely meeting her gaze.

"Because of the boats," Quinn said matter-of-factly.

"What boats?" she said, looking directly into Nathan's eyes, confused.

"You didn't tell her about the boats?" asked Quinn.

"I saw some boats at the beach," said Nathan, holding her stare. "The same morning the reactor cooling pump failed."

"What kind of boats?"

"I don't know. Military-looking boats. Low-profile stealth stuff. They picked up a team of divers."

"And you kept this from me?" she said, not looking so confused anymore.

"I didn't think it would—" He shook his head. "I never thought something like this could happen. I'm sorry. I wasn't thinking."

Keira glared at him for a few seconds. "We don't have time for this right now." She looked away to the rearview mirror. "How far do we have until Camp Pendleton?"

"Thirty-five minutes or so," said Quinn. "We should have a reasonable head start on them. I'll go west on State Route 56 in a mile."

"Interstate 15 is closer," she said.

"They'll expect us to take Interstate 15," said Quinn. "And they're short at least one vehicle. Maybe two. I weakened a tire on the SUV behind your house."

"They might have more in the area," said Nathan.

"Possible, but not likely. They could have easily sealed the neighborhood with a few more vehicles, but they didn't. I think we saw everything they brought to the show—which is still more than enough to end our trip," said Quinn. "Can your wife work one of the MP-20s?"

"I grew up in a liberal, gun-fearing Bay Area household," said Keira. "I never saw a gun until I visited Nate's parents in Idaho. His dad carries one in a holster—in the house."

"It was an unforgettable moment," said Nathan, hoping to elicit a smile.

She ignored his comment. "I suppose I can make an exception in this case."

"Give her the one I was using," said Quinn. "It has a fresh mag. Check the safety again."

Nathan lifted the MP-20 by the hand guard, keeping the barrel pointed at the jeep's soft-top. He checked the selector switch, verifying that the safety was engaged.

"I know you're not talking to me right now, but here's how it works," he said, putting his thumb on the switch. "It's set to safe. If you need to fire the weapon, press down on this switch for one click. That puts it in semiautomatic, which means—"

"I know what it means. How does the sight work?" she asked, taking the weapon away from him.

"Integrated holographic sight," Quinn broke in. "Center the green dot on your target and pull the trigger. You won't see the green reticle unless you're looking directly into the back of the sight."

"Point and shoot," said Nathan. "Worked for me."

"It more than worked for you," Quinn said. "Half of my Marines don't shoot that well."

Keira glared at Nathan. Because of the blatant distaste for firearms she'd inherited from her family, he'd always downplayed his proficiency with the tools of his father's trade. "Any other secrets you want to confess?" she asked, laying the weapon on the seat next to the left passenger door.

"Is your son up for an important job?" asked Quinn.

Nathan glanced at Owen, whose eyes brightened. His wife looked skeptical.

"As long as you don't expect him to use the other machine gun," said Keira.

"I know how to use the MP-20," said Owen. "I use it all the time in CDV."

"CDV?" asked Keira.

"Call of Duty virtual online gaming," said Quinn. "All of my younger Marines play it."

"Where do you play this?" Keira demanded of Owen.

"At all of my friends' houses."

Keira shot Nathan a dark look. "His obsession with guns is all your dad's fault."

"Why don't the two of you sort that out later," said Quinn. "I was just thinking he could wear the night-vision goggles I found in the SUV behind your house."

"Wouldn't it make more sense for me to wear them?" asked Keira.

"We have plenty of light to see if someone's coming up behind us. I need him to continuously scan around us for infrared lasers. We can't see them with the naked eye, but they show up bright and shiny in the NVGs. It might be the first indication we get that we're being targeted for surveillance—or worse."

"Wonderful. Hand them over," she said.

"They're by your feet, Nathan," said Quinn.

He handed the NVGs to Keira, who tried to make sense of the gear.

"You can tighten the head strap once you have it in place on your son's head," said Quinn.

Less than a minute later, she had the NVGs firmly attached to Owen's head.

"Button on the left side toggles between modes," said Quinn.

Nathan knew his son had figured it out when he heard, "Whoa! This is so cool! Just like the game."

"Just like the game," muttered Keira, shooting Nathan a steely glare.

Keira had every right to be infuriated. He'd almost gotten them killed by keeping a secret, though he had to wonder what might have happened if they'd tried to leave this morning, or a day earlier. If Cerberus had been watching them all along, he suspected the three of them would have met with an unfortunate end in the desert. He would never say this to Keira, but the chain of events leading to Quinn's arrival tonight might've been the only scenario in which they survived.

Might've being the operative term. They still had a long journey ahead of them.

CHAPTER 37

Leeds felt a persistent tightening in his chest as he studied the two maps projected side by side on the windshield. The California Resource tracking data overlays almost perfectly matched the thermal imagery transmitted from the drones, allowing his techs to match registered car movements with real-time thermal signatures. More precisely, they were looking for thermal signatures without corresponding CALRES tracking icons, indicating vehicles exempt from CALRES tracking requirements. So far, they had eliminated five San Diego County Police Department vehicles and two unknown vehicles that didn't fit the right description. Leeds was starting to wonder if Quinn had decided to double back and head south. A clever move like that would complicate matters.

The Ravens could stay airborne for two hours, but every minute represented a wider search area, and longer distances. While the Ravens were controlled by satellite-relayed signals transmitted from the van, the data-intensive feeds generated by the drones' sensors were sent directly to the van by line-of-sight links. Those links were notorious for experiencing "data burps" at longer ranges, which would play havoc with the overlay process. They needed to find Quinn's jeep within the next few minutes, or risk a complete mission failure.

"What are we missing?" asked Leeds. "Did he park somewhere? Is he hiding in a car wash? Does he have a buddy with a garage in the area?"

"If he parked in a garage, we're fucked," said Vega. "Seriously. We need to cross our fingers and hope they're running like frightened mice."

"They're not behaving like frightened mice," said Leeds. "We have several casualties to confirm that."

"Even a cornered rat will stand and fight, before it runs like hell. We'll find them," said Vega. "I suggest we expand the search. Start scouring the roads north of Penasquitos Creek."

"Do it."

"We're almost to the 805," said the driver.

"Head north," Leeds said, wondering if it might be a better idea to stay put, in case Quinn doubled back.

The van turned right on Vista Sorrento Parkway, headed for the Carmel Mountain Road on-ramp a little more than a mile away. He was putting all of his eggs—all of Flagg's eggs—in one basket by focusing his surveillance efforts north. Once the van started driving toward Camp Pendleton, there was no going back, and if he lost the jeep, he wouldn't be surprised if Flagg used the drone to put Leeds out of his misery.

"Sir?" announced Vega. "I found him. Red icon on the left screen. He's approaching Interstate 5 from Del Mar Heights Road. He must have split the middle up Black Mountain Road."

Leeds watched the icon turn north and merge into traffic on the interstate. The screen next to the overlay map disappeared, reappearing as a thermal image.

"Hold on," said Vega. "Zooming in and adjusting to regular imagery."

The image changed to a synthetic daylight view, and magnified until the vehicle filled half of the display area. The black Jeep Wrangler's left rear signal flashed as the vehicle moved to the leftmost lane and accelerated.

"That's a bottle of Johnny Walker Blue for you," said Leeds, relieved beyond comprehension.

He dialed Flagg, who picked up instantly.

"Even a broken clock is right twice a day," stated Flagg.

Leeds wanted to say something irreverent, but decided against it. The drone Flagg was about to launch was equipped with two AGM-120 Strikefire missiles, and he didn't want to push his luck.

"We're 2.4 miles behind them," said Leeds. "I'm confident we can take them out."

"It's too risky. I don't doubt that you could disable the vehicle, but killing everyone inside isn't guaranteed."

"I can guarantee it."

"I can't have you pull the van over and fire bullets point-blank through their heads while dozens of cars drive by and traffic drones watch from above. Not to mention the cameras mounted everywhere on the highway," said Flagg. "The drone will be airborne in a few minutes. Follow the jeep and be ready to mark it with a laser. Once our Raptor identifies the marked target, I'll have you break off pursuit. It's out of our hands at that point."

"Copy that," said Leeds, swallowing his misgivings about using the drone.

"Cheer up, Nick. You're still my favorite tac-ops boss," said Flagg. "Speaking of which, I think it's time your team in Idaho paid Nathan Fisher's parents a visit. Capture and interrogate, if possible. I need to know how far this has spread, and where David Quinn fits into the picture."

"I'll issue the order. They're in Ketchum, less than forty miles from the parents' house."

"Tell them to be careful," said Flagg, ending the call.

A minute later, Leeds's van merged onto Interstate 5, accelerating to catch up with Quinn's jeep. Under normal circumstances, a two-mile highway separation would take forever to close without drawing law-enforcement attention. Fortunately for Leeds, his van was invisible to the highway's automated speed monitoring and ticketing system. He could expect to have eyes on the jeep in a few minutes.

CHAPTER 38

Lisa Fesko, former US Army captain, focused the night-vision spotting scope on the eastern edge of the airstrip and triggered the digital recording function. Three nights ago, a convoy of military-style vehicles had delivered a small garrison of armed guards and a shipment of heavy equipment to the previously abandoned hangar.

Armed men patrolled the hills and placed surveillance sensors in a wide, oval-shaped perimeter around the airstrip, while a pack of technicians off-loaded the contents of the heavy transport trucks. From her position nestled into the front of a hill overlooking the airstrip, just under a mile away, Fesko had a sweeping view of the facility, without the corresponding risk of detection.

Patrols out of the field remained confined to the first ring of lower hills forming a shallow bowl around the runway, reinforcing the tight string of motion sensors and thermal-detection cameras placed just beyond the hills. The security strategy served well to keep hikers or curious locals from getting too close, but did little to dissuade serious surveillance, especially when an interested party had ample warning.

Fesko had been sent into the hills with Landon King, a former recon Marine, eight days earlier, when her organization learned about an imminent two-day construction project to level and repack the neglected dirt runway. A contact at the Ramona-based construction outfit hired to do the work passed the information up the chain of command as soon as it had been announced. It had been a lucky break, considering the vast scope of recent and unusual shell-company-sponsored land purchases in Southern California—far too many to watch at any given time.

The construction tip-off turned out to be one of the California Liberation Movement's most important discoveries in months. They watched the men dolly sections of an SQ-17 Raptor drone into the hangar, along with enough communications and electrical equipment to run a small airport. Even more ominous, they off-loaded air-to-ground missiles from one of the trucks. Fesko couldn't positively identify the exact missile type from this distance, but she recognized the unmistakable quad-carrier dolly used to transport helicopter or drone armaments on military runways or aircraft-carrier decks.

She and King had cut their daily ration intake in half to extend their time at the observation post. An armed stealth drone represented a serious escalation in the One Nation Coalition's war against the secession movement, its significance underscored by the past two days' events. While they couldn't directly prove ONC was behind the reactor failure in Del Mar, the timing suggested their suspicions were well founded. The assassinations were undoubtedly the work of the industrialist-funded group, likely perpetrated to turn the tide of public opinion permanently against the CLM.

Personnel at the end of the runway scrambled in the darkness to ready the drone, which had appeared several minutes ago, when the supposedly decrepit hangar's bay door slid open way too smoothly to reveal a dark-red, dimly glowing interior. The Raptor carried a stubby missile on each side of the fuselage, attached to a pylon under its swept-back wings. Two missiles—each capable of destroying a house, obliterating an entire floor in an office building, or turning an armored vehicle into a twisted heap of melted, smoking scrap metal.

Base had insisted they send the raw flight data captured by night-vision and infrared scopes immediately. The flight profile imagery would be processed and integrated with a sophisticated search program designed to detect the Raptor drone. Fesko wasn't sure how the CLM planned to stop the Raptor once it took flight, but she suspected they had something ready. Base told her that a critical asset was in danger on the ground, and they suspected that the sudden drone launch was not a coincidence. Their languid mission in the rolling hills outside Ramona had suddenly become the organization's focus.

"Are we good?" she said.

King kept his face pressed into the thermal scope's eyepiece, giving her a thumbs-up. "Yep. I'll track and record until I lose visual contact, though I'm not sure what good it'll do them. That thing will be virtually invisible over San Diego County."

"We're doing our part," she said. "The rest is up to them."

"We could be doing more. Another twenty-five pounds of gear would solve this problem. Probably save some lives."

Fesko agreed. With her organization's recent acquisition of guided, rifle-fired projectiles, they could have put the drone out of business before it launched, but mission planners hadn't anticipated the sudden intensification of hostilities—and they certainly hadn't expected One Nation to field armed drones. Surveillance drones? Sure. Everyone used them. Only specific military units and the Federal Border Patrol operated armed stealth drones—legitimately.

A few highly questionable private military contractor outfits were rumored to use them overseas, but international investigations into the matter had proven fruitless. The launch of an armed Raptor drone from a strip of worthless land purchased by a "watch list" company raised some hard questions.

"You always want to shoot things," Fesko said.

"I hate shooting video of targets better served by steel," King said. "That thing is heading into the night to ruin lives."

She thought about what he'd just said, and found herself wondering about King's 0.308 chambered assault rifle. "Can you hit it from here with your rifle?"

He took his eyes off the scope and turned on his side in the tight, cocoon-shaped tent. "Are you tempting me?"

"Can you do it?"

"Only if I moved about a thousand feet closer."

"Yeah, but a hundred feet out from here, you'll lose your sight lines. You'd have to top one of the hills ringing the airstrip to reacquire, dodging sensors and patrols."

"What about the first observation post we scoped? It's closer," said King.

"That would work," she said. "But it's too far away from our current position, and you'd have to be careful on the approach. The Raptor will be long gone by the time you get there."

King turned his attention back to the airstrip. "It's a moot point. They're about to launch."

Fesko scoped the far end of the runway, watching the guards and personnel step back from the rolling drone. A muted buzzing sound reached the observation post, propagated through the hills by the drone's sound-dampened, rear-mounted propeller. A few seconds later, the unmanned aerial system rolled forward, picking up speed as it traversed the unlit, hard-packed gravel runway. She kept the scope's synthetic daylight image centered on the fast-moving drone, following the graceful machine into the sky until it passed the low-lying hills beyond the southern end of the runway, taking its persistent buzzing sound with it.

"I'll start transferring video," Fesko said, removing the scope from its tripod mount. "They need this ASAP."

She took her night-vision scope and backed out of the tent, which opened at the edge of a shallow boulder-strewn gully traveling down the back side of the hill. Behind the closest boulder, a satellite antenna pointed skyward. She plugged the night-vision scope into a military-style data terminal just outside the tent's rear hatch and followed the onscreen prompts to synchronize the two devices.

A pair of boots struck her in the side, nearly knocking her into the gully.

"Watch it!" she whispered, gripping the terminal so King didn't kick it over the side.

"We have a problem," he said, pulling his rifle and the thermal scope out of the tent. "The fucking drone returned."

"Returning to base?" she asked, reaching for the rifle she kept at the foot of the tent.

"I don't think so," he said, grabbing for her night-vision scope.

"It's transmitting," Fesko said.

"Shit," he said, shouldering his weapon and flipping open the rifle-scope's lens covers. He raised the rifle, aiming slightly above horizon, due east of their position. "Hell. We're being marked by a laser from the Raptor. How much have you transferred?"

She checked the screen. "Eighty percent."

"That's enough," he said, thrusting his thermal optics device into her chest. "Start sending the thermal data."

King jumped into the gully and started to move downhill.

"What are you doing?" she yelled.

"Buying you some time," he called back, pausing next to the satellite antenna. "Drag all of that shit into the tent and transmit the thermal imagery. It's about to start raining missiles."

Fesko gripped the briefcase-size terminal and pulled it into the tent with her, yanking the cable from her scope. Working feverishly, she connected King's thermal-imaging device to the terminal and started the synchronization process. While the gigabytes uploaded, she secured the tent flap, hoping the thermally insulated and chemically treated material would render her invisible long enough to send an adequate amount of data to her organization.

An ear-shattering detonation ripped through the hills, shaking the ground and shredding the tent with rocks and fragments. A sharp burning seized her right leg and the tent collapsed over her. A few moments passed before she realized she'd survived the explosion intact. Her leg responded sluggishly, but other than that, she was still in the fight. The tent hadn't taken a direct hit.

She dug through the loose tent material to find the communications terminal, pushing a torn layer away to see the display. It was still transmitting, but at a slower rate. Thirty percent complete. She wasn't sure if that would be enough. They probably wanted to see what the drone looked like under thermal observation while it was flying, which was at the end of the file. King had probably just given his life protecting the transmission source from the first missile; she'd do the same with the second missile.

As Fesko backed out of the collapsed tent, it occurred to her that they couldn't fire the second missile without jeopardizing the Raptor's original mission—the drone only carried two missiles, and refitting it with two more would take time. They'd come after her in vehicles, which gave her all the time she needed to send the data and prepare a defense that would cost them dearly.

She emerged from the tent to the acrid smell of high explosives and gritty taste of settling dust. If King had somehow survived that blast, he was in worse shape than she was. She'd look for him in a minute. A distant flash drew her attention to the airfield, where a small orange light arched skyward. She craned her neck, following the light until it disappeared high in the sky above her.

They didn't use the Raptor's missiles.

Fesko rolled into the gully, clutching the data terminal and the thermal scope to her chest as the missile fired from the airfield struck the ground where the tent had been assembled. While the lip of the gully protected her from the fragmentation effect of the twenty-pound warhead, the blast's devastating pressure wave killed her instantly.

Shielded by her partially jellified corpse, the two electronic devices continued to function, sending data through the intact cable to the still-functioning satellite antenna.

CHAPTER 39

Nathan watched Quinn examine the rearview mirror and both side mirrors, waiting for his verdict.

"I don't see anyone following us," said Quinn. "At least nobody obvious. What about you, Owen?"

"No lasers," said Nathan's son, craning around in his seat. "But I can't see straight up."

"Why would he need to see straight up?" asked Keira.

Quinn and Owen responded at the same time: "Drones."

"You've got to be kidding me," mumbled Keira.

"We're more than halfway there," said Nathan. "They would have caught up to us or done something by now."

"Maybe they don't want to machine-gun us on the highway, in front of the cameras. The entire highway is monitored," said Keira. "If they know where we're headed, they could hit us when we exit the highway."

"Possible, but unlikely," said Quinn. "The first exit for Pendleton dumps us right in front of the gate. The Marines keep a quick reaction force inside the gate in case of terrorist attacks, which they'll deploy if gunfire erupts too close to the base."

"Maybe we should remove the suppressors from these weapons," said Nathan. "So we can instigate a reaction."

"We can't. The suppressors are built right into the MP-20, which is why they're so quiet," said Quinn, checking the rearview mirror again. "If we're going to have a problem, it's going to happen on the highway, or they'll try to figure out a way to get to us on base."

"That's reassuring," said Keira.

"That's reality," said Quinn.

"It's pretty scary to think we're not safe on a military base," said Nathan.

"I wish I could say you'd be safe, but I get the distinct impression that Cerberus has the reach," said Quinn.

"If we can't stay at the lodge, what's the plan?" asked Nathan.

"We have a few options that I think will keep you safe. One, I convince a friend living on base to take you in."

"I don't want to endanger another family," said Nathan. "We've already screwed you over."

"I appreciate your concern. Seriously," said Quinn. "That would have been my last option, anyway. Another idea would be to split the two of you up."

"There's three of us," said Keira.

"You didn't let me finish," said Quinn. "I get both of you haircuts and uniforms, then stash you in the barracks with my Marines. Your son can stay with a family I know that lives in base housing."

"Too complicated," said Nathan. "And I'm not letting Owen or Keira out of my sight."

"That's what I thought," said Quinn. "Which leads us to door number three."

"I can't wait to hear this," said Keira.

"It's actually the easiest, and in my opinion, the best option," said Quinn. "I hide you deep inside one of the camp's training areas—they're enormous—and set you up for a family camping trip."

"I like that plan," announced Owen.

Nathan looked into the shadow-infested backseat, meeting his son's eyes.

"Then that's the plan, buddy," said Nathan, reaching back to give him a fist bump. "If your mom approves."

"A family camping trip it is," said Keira, grabbing Nathan's wrist and kissing his hand. "I'm still mad at you."

"I would expect nothing less," he said, turning to Quinn. "Do you have kids?"

"No," he said. "Or I would have told my dad to hire a courier to deliver those phones."

Nathan left the subject alone. Quinn had expressed a raw sentiment rarely broadcast by childless couples: kids changed everything. Nathan had thought the world had changed when he married Keira, but it had barely shifted under him. Even after they thought they were at their height of readiness and understanding during Keira's pregnancy, Owen's arrival had been a ten on the Richter scale, instantly reshuffling all their priorities. Nothing remained the same, but everything was better. Quinn somehow understood.

He stole a glance at Keira, catching a sympathetic smile aimed at Quinn. She interpreted his comment the same way.

CHAPTER 40

Leeds zoomed in on the back of the jeep, the video captured by a powerful camera mounted on the van's roof. At a distance of nearly eight football fields, the synthetic daylight image didn't provide enough clarity to identify the occupants, which was fine in this case. Much to his relief, the camera verified the presence of three adults, one of them female, confirming that Quinn had not hidden the Fisher family in a neighbor's yard and drawn Leeds's team away by fleeing north.

The HUD indicated an incoming call from Flagg, confirmed a moment later by a chirp in Leeds's headset. He reached for the touchpad to accept the call, but Flagg started talking before his finger pressed the screen.

"—drone just crossed Interstate 15, a few miles north of Escondido. It should be in position to intercept the target in five minutes. Barring any unforeseen difficulties, the target will not reach the first Carlsbad exit. I'll let you know when our drone pilots can see the interstate."

"Copy that," said Leeds. "We're trailing at about seven hundred meters. They're maintaining a constant sixty-five-miles-per-hour speed, so I don't think they've spotted us."

"We're lucky this didn't go down an hour later," said Flagg. "The highway switches over to on-demand lighting at ten-thirty."

"That would definitely present a challenge," agreed Leeds. "We need to figure out a way to drive the highways without triggering the lights. Not that it comes into play very often."

"The technology exists. I'll put in a request to equip a few of our vehicles with the system—for special occasions," said Flagg. "How will you mark the target?"

"Worried much?" asked Leeds, feeling confident enough again to joke with Flagg.

"Hell yes, I'm worried. You're heading into this with a van full of surveillance techs—"

"In a van with the team's backup gear," interrupted Leeds. "I have a few ACR-20s with rail-mounted dual-beam lasers at my disposal."

"Make sure that shit works," said Flagg. "Or I'll have you pull alongside the jeep flashing an infrared beacon."

"I've already op-tested the lasers."

"T-minus four minutes," said Flagg, disconnecting the call.

"Fucking prick," said Leeds, turning to face Vega in the rear compartment. "Let's make sure those lasers work."

CHAPTER 41

Mason Flagg watched the drone feed on the largest screen in the operations center with wary satisfaction. He wouldn't feel completely at ease until one of the drone's Strikefire missiles turned Quinn's jeep into a flaming wreck.

He'd never envisioned the need to use the Raptor drone to destroy a civilian vehicle on a major California highway, but the need and opportunity had presented itself—why not? The dramatic mid-interstate explosion would dominate headline news across the nation, no doubt immediately linked to the recently intensified secession conflict. When authorities managed to scrape together enough DNA to identify the jeep's occupants, the revelation would support Flagg's anti-California Liberation Movement agenda. In fact, erasing Fisher with a Strikefire missile might give the agenda a stronger push than his original scenario.

He liked the way the story was shaping up. Nathan Fisher and his cop-killer accomplice, a Marine counterinsurgency officer stationed nearby at Camp Pendleton, are brazenly killed in a missile attack on Interstate 5, while fleeing San Diego. One Nation's media machine, already primed to circulate Flagg's propaganda surrounding the evening's gruesome discoveries, strongly suggests the possibility that the California Liberation Movement is behind the interstate attack. The CLM is on a rampage, linked to two high-profile assassinations. A third, even more dramatic night of murder and mayhem was not out of the question for these secessionist lunatics, One Nation's bought-and-paid-for media pundits would propose. Once the deeper details emerged about Fisher's cozy-turned-lethal relationship with a corrupt detective and an engineer employed by the Del Mar station, combined with a secretive connection to radical CLM organizers, the conclusion would be unavoidable: the California Liberation Movement was cleaning house—systematically erasing the evidence tying it to the reactor sabotage.

Flagg could smell victory. He didn't expect a quick triumph, but the conditions would be ripe. If One Nation's state lobbyists, backed by the generous support of Sentinel Group and an enthusiastic recommendation by the governor, could convince the state legislature to declare the CLM a terrorist organization, victory was nearly guaranteed.

He felt the corners of his mouth tugging upward as the drone leveled off at one thousand feet above ground level and a long, illuminated stretch of Interstate 5 filled the screen. The room's speakers activated.

"Sir, the drone is on terminal approach, tracking the surveillance van. Three miles and closing. I see two potential targets—a dark-colored jeep approximately six hundred meters ahead of the surveillance van, and another jeep two hundred meters in front of that. Standing by for positive handoff of the target," said the drone operator.

"Copy. I'll pass along your request. Happy hunting," said Flagg, pressing a button to connect his headset with Leeds's van.

"Leeds, the drone is in position," said Flagg. "Paint the target."

"Stand by," said Leeds.

The audio feed hissed in Flagg's headset for a few seconds.

"Leeds! You're transmitting static," he said. "Report your status."

"I have my head and arms out of the window," said Leeds. "Painting your target—right now."

Flagg watched the screen as a green line connected the van with the closer jeep. He checked the digital map display on the desk array, noting the location of the next interstate exit.

"Leeds. When the Raptor acquires the target," said Flagg, "take the La Costa exit in 1.3 miles. Don't miss the exit or you'll be dodging a fireball."

"We're tracking the exit," said Leeds. "Where do you want me next?"

"Point Loma," said Flagg. "We need to lay low for a little while and let everything run its course."

CHAPTER 42

"I see a laser!" screamed Owen.

Nathan twisted in his seat, matching Quinn's urgent question. "Where?"

"Way behind us! I think it's a van."

"Keep your head down," said Keira, pulling her son lower in his seat.

The jeep accelerated past an SUV, Quinn quickly changing lanes to put the SUV between the jeep and the laser.

"What did that do for us?" asked Quinn.

"Nothing. The laser's back on us."

"I don't see anything out of place back there," said Keira.

"They're following us from a distance. They've been there all along. Owen, can you tell if it's a semiactive pulse laser?" asked Quinn.

"I don't know what that is!"

"Does the laser pulse in quick bursts, or is it like a steady line to us?"

"Looks like a steady line," said Owen.

"What does that mean?" asked Nathan.

"It means they're marking us with a rifle-mounted laser illuminator—for something or someone else. Ready your weapons and watch any vehicles that come close to us. Keira, you take our left and back.

Nathan has the right side and directly ahead. They might be handing us off to another team."

Nathan lifted the MP-20 from the foot well.

"Easy!" said Quinn, pushing the weapon below window level. "We don't want to tip our hand. Just have them ready."

"You said something or someone. What's the *something*?" asked Keira.

"They might be illuminating us for another weapons platform."

"In nonmilitary terms, please."

"They might be identifying us for a drone strike or roadside-launched guided missile."

"This can't be for real," said Keira.

Nathan reflexively leaned his head toward the window and pointlessly stared at the night sky. "What can we do?" he said.

"Drive like hell and hope they're not using a guided missile."

"What about hiding under an overpass?" asked Nathan.

"That would be a very temporary fix. We're better off moving—and maneuvering," he said. "Hang on."

Nathan turned to look at his family, scared out of his mind that a high explosive warhead could rip into the car at any moment, making this the last time he ever saw them, then reluctantly resumed watching for threats in front of them as Quinn weaved in and out of traffic.

CHAPTER 43

Sergeant Richard Lopez frowned at the navigation screen in the center of his virtual cockpit array. Traffic surveillance drone E-685 was two hundred feet left of its preset surveillance route and steadily drifting south. He turned his attention to the wide parabolic monitor above the nav screen, watching the drone's nose-mounted camera feed. Interstate 5 appeared on the left, moving toward the center—before the image disappeared. *More glitches?*

He turned his head and searched for Lieutenant Kelm while keeping a loose eye on the drone's flight path. Kelm, the North County District shift supervisor, sat in his command-and-control booth at the far end of the darkened room, switching between drone feeds. Lopez pressed a button on his command screen to connect with the lieutenant.

"What's up, Lopez?" asked Kelm.

"TSD echo-six-eight-five wandered off course, and I just lost its camera feed. Request permission to take positive control," said Lopez.

"Permission granted. Stand by to copy your onetime authorization code."

"Ready to copy," said Lopez, writing the ten-digit alphanumeric code on an electronic pad as the lieutenant recited it.

"I'll get technical support to reboot the navigation program," said Kelm. "This is the sixth time division has experienced the same problem in the past three days. A full nav reboot seems to fix the glitch. The camera thing is new."

"Six times in three days? That's a lot of glitches."

"And that's highly classified information, like everything you see or hear in drone land. Division is investigating," said Kelm. "Confirm when you have positive control. You'll control the drone for about five minutes once we start the reboot. I recommend heading out over the Pacific. Not much you can bang into out there."

"Copy that," said Lopez. "Stand by for positive control confirmation."

Lopez knew the procedure cold, but was required by division regulations to follow the laminated card hanging from the privacy screen separating his virtual cockpit from the rest. He started by typing the code into his command interface, and ended the procedure by flipping a green toggle switch.

With the checklist complete, Lopez lightly gripped the sensitive control stick and gently tilted it to the right to turn the drone west, toward the Pacific Ocean less than a mile away. The drone didn't respond. The drone's flight path remained fixed on a southeasterly course. *Shit.* He'd screwed up the procedure. Served him right for pretending to follow the checklist. Now he'd have to ask his lieutenant for another onetime code. He pressed the "Communications" button.

"Lieutenant?" asked Lopez. "I think I botched the checklist. I need another code."

"I'm showing you with positive control of the drone."

"The drone's not responding to stick input."

"Great," said Kelm. "Just what we need. More glitches. I'll give you another—"

Lopez glanced at the lower left screen, checking the drone's vitals and instrument readings. One thousand four hundred feet—and climbing! A quick glance at the rightmost screen showed a three-dimensional display of the drone's flight. It was pointed skyward at a seventy-two-degree angle relative to the ground.

"Sir, the drone is climbing rapidly," said Lopez.

"Are you sure?"

"Instrument readings confirm a full-speed climb."

"Shit," said Kelm. "Copy this down. Self-destruct authorization code five-eight-seven-hotel-zulu-niner-one-one-four-echo. Enter the code and stand by to destroy traffic-surveillance drone echo-six-eight-five."

"Roger," said Lopez, repeating the code."

"Correct. I'm calling this in as a hijack."

Jesus. A hijack? Kelm must know more than he's saying. Classifying a drone as a hijack was serious business. The department would scramble a Strikefire-armed helicopter to follow the drone. Lopez typed the code and flipped open the red toggle-switch protector, glancing over his shoulder. Several pairs of eyes watched him closely from nearby cockpit cubicles.

He checked the drone's altimeter, watching the altitude climb to two thousand feet and stall. Instead of leveling off at the new altitude, the drone pointed nose down and started to dive in a slow turn. *Holy shit!*

"It's diving!" he yelled, forgetting about protocol.

His headset answered. "Sergeant Richard Lopez, this is Lieutenant Harrison Kelm. Destroy traffic-surveillance drone echo-six-eight-five."

"This is Sergeant Richard Lopez, destroying echo-six-eight-five," he said, flipping the self-destruct switch.

The instrument display showed a continued dive, which would be consistent with a destroyed drone—if it wasn't still turning.

"Lopez. Destroy the drone right now," said Kelm.

He flipped the switch back and forth. "It's not responding!"

Kelm sprinted across the flight control room, lurching over Lopez's shoulders a few seconds later.

"What the hell is it doing?" asked Kelm.

"It's diving straight for the interstate," muttered Lopez.

CHAPTER 44

"Like shooting fish in a barrel," muttered Flagg, succumbing to cliché.

Despite the driver's wild attempts to shake the van's laser, the jeep had no chance to evade the missile.

The drone operator cut in on the loudspeaker. "Strikefire is independently locked onto the target."

"Fire the missile and circle back for possible reengagement," said Flagg.

"Copy. Firing Strikefire in three, two . . ."

The drone's nose-camera feed lined up on the front of the jeep, when the screen went green, displaying "LINK FAILED."

What the hell?

"What's going on with the drone feed?" asked Flagg. "I'm getting a green screen with the words *link failed.*"

"Stand by," said the drone operator curtly.

Stand by? He didn't want to hear *stand by.* He wanted to see a fireball erupt on Interstate 5, erasing the only known material witness who could cast serious doubt on the California Liberation Movement's complicity in the reactor sabotage. A little digging in the right place at the Pentagon could link the stealth boats to the Sentinel Group. This was taking too long.

"Did you launch the Strikefire?" asked Flagg.

"Sir, we've lost the signal," said the operator.

"As in permanently?" asked Flagg, grinding his teeth.

"Nothing is transmitting. I've only seen this with lightning strikes or a catastrophic high-impact crash. We're reviewing the data tape for any indication of a critical failure."

"Report immediately if you discover something," said Flagg, dialing Leeds.

"I missed the fireball," said Leeds.

"There was no fireball. I think we lost the drone."

"What?"

"I need you back on the highway," said Flagg. "You may get your wish to finish this yourself."

"I'm on La Costa headed to State Route 11," said Leeds. "I can't turn around and catch them at this point, no matter how fast we go. The jeep is a few miles from the Camp Pendleton exit at this point. What the hell happened?"

"We're investigating," said Flagg. "I want you on the 5, anyway. He might fuck up and go for the Pulgas Gate or the San Onofre gate at the northern end of the base. His battalion is stationed up north."

"He won't screw that up," said Leeds. "And that's a long stretch of road between gates, with nothing in between. If we're losing stealth drones, we might want to consider getting our assets under cover until we figure out what happened."

Flagg knew Leeds was right, but he still wanted to press the attack. His opportunity to deliver decisive results, well ahead of schedule, was evaporating. Chances like this were rare in an operation where public perception and political support factored just as importantly as striking targeted blows to the opposition, but required months of carefully staged events and circumstances. Shooting a lieutenant governor or trashing a nuclear reactor was easy. Swaying the public took time and money—the result often never guaranteed.

He'd let impatience get the better of him, putting too much stock in framing Fisher. He should have ordered Leeds to blow the guy's head off with a shotgun the same afternoon he spoke with the police. Problem solved. Instead, Flagg had been lured by the big score, a mistake he'd sworn he'd never make again. He'd amassed a considerable track record of big successes at Cerberus observing that rule.

"I agree," Flagg said reluctantly. "Pull everyone back and regroup. I want your tech team to walk Maclean through the process of disabling the tracker on Fisher's car. We need to make that vehicle disappear until we decide where it should reappear, hopefully containing a freshly decomposing Fisher family."

"I'll take care of it immediately," said Leeds.

"When you get back, we'll figure out the best way to slip some of our people onto Camp Pendleton."

"That won't be difficult," said Leeds. "We have a fat portfolio of counterfeit IDs. We'll send as many as feasible in the morning, when all of the Marines living off base report for duty. They'll comb the base hotels, campgrounds, officers' quarters, restaurants, and commissaries. The Fishers left in a hurry, with nothing more than the clothes on their backs. They'll need to buy replacement clothing, backpacks, toiletries, food—and everything on Pendleton is closed right now. I just checked. We'll have our people watching all of the major stores on base when they open. We might get lucky."

CHAPTER 45

Nathan tightened his grip on the jeep's roll-bar grab handle as Quinn rock-eted between two cars directly in front of them, lightly scraping one of them.

"I don't see the laser anymore!" said Owen.

"You can slow down now," Nathan told Quinn.

"Not yet!" said Quinn, swerving the jeep two lanes to the left.

"Damn it! You're going to get us killed!" yelled Keira.

"I'm not slowing down until I know we're safe from a possible missile strike!"

"How the hell will you know that? You'll have to drive like this until we get to Camp Pendleton. We'll get pulled over by the police before we get there."

"That might work to our advantage," said Quinn. "They wouldn't hit us with a missile with the police chasing us."

"I'm not slowing down until we reach Pendleton."

A brilliant orange fireball appeared in the distance ahead of them, seeming to rise in the middle of the interstate. A second explosion erupted to the right of the first, followed a few seconds later by two tightly spaced booms. The jeep slowed as brake lights raced toward them, but it wasn't going to be enough.

"Quinn!" yelled Nathan.

"Hold on!"

The jeep swerved right as Keira and Owen yelled, narrowly avoiding a stopped sedan and screeching to a halt on the paved shoulder of the road.

"That was awesome!" yelled Owen.

"No, it wasn't," said Keira.

Nathan started to unbuckle his seat belt, assuming they were done driving along the freeway, when the jeep suddenly launched forward. For a second he thought they'd been rear-ended, but the jeep continued to accelerate.

"What are you doing?"

"Getting us past this mess," said Quinn.

"Shouldn't we be driving away from the explosions?" asked Nathan.

"We can't get off the interstate here on foot or in the jeep," Quinn said, nodding at the reinforced antipedestrian fence several yards beyond the shoulder. "And we can't go back—for a number of reasons."

Nathan looked beyond Owen's and Keira's silhouettes at the mass of headlights stacking up behind them—any one of which could be their pursuer's van.

"Be careful. You won't be the only one with this idea."

Quinn was forced to take the jeep onto the evenly sloped dirt embankment beyond the car-packed shoulder as they approached the source of the flames. Fire leaped dozens of feet into the air in the southbound lanes, illuminating the inside of the jeep. Keira held the MP-20 just below the window, staring intently at the line of cars passing down their left side. Owen peered through the headrest supports, keeping his laser vigil. Nathan shifted his attention to the wreckage on the other side of the interstate.

At first glance, he thought a small, private airplane had crashed landed into traffic. The flames were spread over a fifty-yard section of the freeway, mostly confined to the southbound lanes. A few small fires burned in the median and northbound passing lane. Through the slowed traffic on his side of the highway, he counted at least four cars burning furiously around the highest tower of flame, which was centered on a warped gray fuselage. Part of a wing extended skyward, partially enveloped by the raging fire. He'd never seen anything like it.

"What is that?"

"Looks like part of an airplane," said Keira.

"It's not an airplane," stated Quinn. "Not in the traditional sense."

The jeep sped forward, passing directly parallel to the burning wreckage. He was right. The only recognizable piece inside the inferno looked definitely military. Sleek and angled. Stealthy.

"Drone?" asked Nathan.

"Sure as hell looks like it," muttered Quinn.

Owen turned in response to their conversation. "Holy shhh—. That looks like part of a Raptor drone."

"That was my guess," said Quinn.

"How could Owen know that?" asked Keira.

Nathan and Quinn answered at the same time for Owen. "Call of Duty."

"You can control those in the game," said Nathan's son.

"What happened to it?" asked Keira.

Nathan wondered the same thing. They'd seen an equally large explosion to the right of the first, possibly east of the interstate, but he couldn't locate a second fire amid the bright glow of the burning drone. Was it possible they got lucky and the drone sent to kill them had collided with a commercial aircraft or another drone? Statistically, the chances were slim that this had been an accident, but he had no better explanation.

"I don't know, but we got a lucky break. Pendleton is just a few minutes up the road. Keep your guard up until we get on base. I don't think we have to worry about drones, but you never know what they might throw at us. I think we're good, though."

Nathan leaned his head against the headrest and took a deep breath. Good for how long?

CHAPTER 46

Flagg rubbed his chin, trying to make sense of what had happened. An incoming satellite call from the Ramona airfield interrupted his thoughts.

"What do you have?"

"Something," said the drone operator. "The Raptor's top-facing proximity sensor fired right before we lost the link. It's possible that the drone collided with another aerial object, maybe a civilian aircraft or a privately operated drone."

"Or a surface-to-air missile?"

"Not likely," said the operator. "SAMs typically chase engine exhaust or independently lock onto some kind of reflected signal, arriving from a lower altitude. Air-to-air missile, maybe."

"I hope not," said Flagg, remembering something else. "Do we have any additional information on the hillside observers?"

"I can patch you through to the security head," said the operator. "They just arrived at the observation post."

"Do it," said Flagg.

A few seconds later, a gruff voice filled the room. "This is Kestler."

"Mr. Kestler, this is Mason Flagg," he said. "What can you tell me about our uninvited guests?"

"They're dead," said Kestler, pausing long enough to spark several murderous thoughts in Flagg's mind. He didn't give a single shit if they were dead or alive. He needed data. "And they have a satellite antenna. Looks intact. The woman died clutching some electronics gear. A thermal scope and some kind of data terminal. We'll bag that once we wipe her guts off the gear. I got a second meat smear about fifty yards down the hill, where the gully widens. Not much left of that one."

"Is the data terminal still functional?"

"Hold on," said Kestler. He issued orders to his team.

Flagg waited in silence for close to a minute before Kestler spoke again.

"It's functional," said Kestler. "But no one here knows how to operate it. Looks like an old piece of gear."

"What does the screen say? I assume the screen works," said Flagg.

"It says 'transmission progress one hundred percent,'" said Kestler. "Had to wipe away a big chunk of her stomach to read that."

Well, congratulations.

"Bag up everything and bring it back to the airfield," said Flagg, disconnecting the call before the idiot could respond.

His next call went to the field operative in charge of the airfield.

"Mr. Powers?" asked Flagg. "Evacuate the facility immediately. I want everything gone within the hour. Assume any unscheduled vehicles arriving at the facility to be hostile. Understood?"

"Understood," said Powers.

Flagg stared at the green screen displayed on the array in front of him. "LINK FAILED." How? He hoped to have the answer in a few hours, after his technicians figured out what the hillside team had transmitted before they were obliterated by airfield security.

CHAPTER 47

Quinn read the green sign as it raced by on the right of the interstate. **Exit 54B. Camp Pendleton. Next Exit.**

"Time to hide the contraband."

"Can't they sniff it at the gate?" asked Nathan.

"They occasionally run the dogs between the cars or do a few random searches during the morning rush, but it's primarily a deterrent. Unlike the great state of California, the military still respects the Constitution."

"Maybe California will create its own constitution," said Nathan.

"Don't say that," said Quinn. "I'd be willing to bet all of this is related to this secession nonsense."

"A lot of people believe in their cause," said Keira.

"Based on what I saw tonight, a lot of people are going to die because of their cause," said Quinn.

"This wasn't the California Liberation Movement," said Keira.

"Really?" asked Quinn. "They killed a congresswoman ready to side with the One Nation Coalition, and they killed the lieutenant governor. McDaid unabashedly supported One Nation. You don't assassinate your most powerful, politically connected allies. Typically."

"My dad said the boats were linked to Cerberus, which is Sentinel. They fall directly into the One Nation camp," said Nathan. "The secessionists have every reason to keep us alive, if we can link the boats to the reactor sabotage."

"It doesn't matter. Someone powerful is trying to kill you and the rest of us," said Quinn, slowing for the off-ramp. "Hand your rifle to Keira. Make sure you engage the safety. Stuff the weapons as deep as possible under the camping gear. Nothing showing. They'll probably shine a flashlight in the back while I sign your names into the visitor log."

"You going to use our real names?" asked Nathan, carefully handing the MP-20 to his wife.

"It won't matter," said Quinn. "My name has to go on the log—with three guests. I can change your names to Moe, Larry, and Curly and I don't think it will fool anyone."

"It won't take them long to find us on Pendleton," said Nathan.

"Honey," Keira whispered, motioning not so subtly toward Owen.

"I understand what's going on, Mom," said Owen. "We have to be careful wherever we go from now on."

"They won't find you where I'm taking you," said Quinn. "Ever been up North Range Road, Nathan?"

"I can't remember," said Nathan.

"It's tucked behind the Whiskey Impact area in the northeastern corner of Pendleton."

"By Case Springs?" asked Nathan. "Shouldn't we avoid known recreation areas?"

"This isn't a recreation area," said Quinn, laughing. "It's a little more rustic."

"Great."

Quinn eased the car onto Harbor Drive, approaching a red stoplight within sight of the main gate.

"Last check through the car," he said, tucking the pistol he'd taken off one of the operatives under his seat.

"Is it a good idea to have a pistol sliding around like that?" asked Nathan.

"I have a holster rigged to the bottom of the seat," said Quinn. "It's secure."

Nathan moved his legs and checked the passenger foot well. "Looks clear."

"Same back here," said Keira.

"All right," said Quinn. "I have to take us into the parking lot and into the Base Access building to fill out the visitor paperwork. All you need are your IDs."

"That's not going to work," said Keira.

"What's wrong?" asked Quinn, scanning the side windows.

"Shit," said Nathan. "She doesn't have her purse. We had to get out of there fast."

"Forget it." Quinn looked at Nathan. "Do you have your wallet?"

"Yeah," he said, nodding emphatically.

Quinn drove through the empty intersection toward the gate.

"Then here's what we need to do," said Quinn, addressing both of them. "Your son will have to accompany us into the building. They can run Nathan's driver's license through the DMV system and verify all of your identities, but that taps into a state-run computer database. The state will know where you are."

"I'm still in San Diego County," said Nathan.

"True," said Quinn. "But if the police have questions about anything that went down in your neighborhood, they'll know where to find you."

"What do you think happened to our house?" asked Keira.

"They probably turned the place inside out," said Nathan.

Quinn thought about this as he pulled into the parking lot and steered toward the visitor's parking lot. "I don't think they had the time," he said. "Not after the van crashed. They would have sanitized the scene and exfiltrated as quickly as possible."

"Sanitized. Exfiltrated," muttered Keira. "It all sounds so quaint."

"Game faces, everyone," said Quinn. "If anyone asks, I'm taking you to my house in the San Luis Rey housing area. We're hanging out tonight and heading up to San Clemente beach tomorrow to take surfing lessons."

"Sounds better than the North Range Road camping trip," said Nathan.

"When all of this blows over," said Quinn, nodding at Owen, "I'll take you surfing for real."

"Really?" asked Owen.

"Cross my heart, sir," said Quinn, reaching back to give him a fist bump. "I'll even drive down to pick you up, so you don't waste all of your precious out-of-sector time, or whatever the state calls it."

"I'd gladly drive up myself if it meant all of this disappeared," said Nathan.

He shared a doubtful look with Quinn before they got out of the car to register the Fisher family as visitors to Camp Pendleton.

CHAPTER 48

The jeep finally came to a stop, after a mercilessly bumpy dirt-road drive through the pitch-black hills of Camp Pendleton. Keira checked her watch. It was 11:24 p.m. It had taken Quinn over an hour to navigate them to this spot, and she wasn't sure they'd arrived at their final destination.

"I think we're here," said Quinn, raising the night-vision goggles strapped to his head.

"You *think* we're here?" she said.

"In all honesty, I usually make this trip during the day. With a lance corporal driving."

"And you can't turn on your headlights for five seconds?" asked Nathan.

"I'd rather not. The brake lights are bad enough out here," said Quinn. "I think we're at the intersection of North Range and Talega Road."

"Are you sure we're still on North Range?" asked Keira.

"Is she going to kick my ass all night?" asked Quinn.

"Probably," said Nathan.

"Great," said Quinn, lowering his goggles in place and rolling down his window to study the landscape.

She smiled in the dark. If Nathan had sided with Quinn, she would have punched the back of his head. She was still pissed at him for concealing the most important aspect of his morning fiasco at the beach.

Police involvement was frightening enough. The San Diego County Police Department, particularly its Special Activities Group, didn't have an impressive track record of observing citizen rights, but stealth boats picking up divers? At a beach adjacent to a sabotaged nuclear plant? What was Nate thinking? She wanted to hit the back of his head anyway.

Quinn rolled the window up. "This has to be Talega. We'll head up that hill, on a slightly less improved road, for about fifteen minutes or so, before we start looking for a suitable campsite."

"I presume 'less improved' translates into 'ass-breaking'?" said Keira.

"You presume correctly."

Thirty-two harrowing minutes later, their trip along a narrow gravel road ended on a ridgeline overlooking a vast sea of dark hills and ravines. Sporadic lighting dotted the horizon to their left. Behind the jeep, she saw nothing but flat, endless hues of night.

"There's a maneuver trail along the top of this ridgeline, passable by tactical vehicles, so you should stay clear of the ridge. I'll drive you about a hundred yards down the trail and get you situated. You'll find a bunch of deep draws, which would be perfect for hiding."

"I remember a lot of that from basic land-navigation courses in ROTC," said her husband.

"You'll know what I mean when you see it. Even in the dark."

"You're just going to point us in the right direction and take off?" asked Nathan.

"You'll be fine," said Quinn. "You've been camping, right?"

"Yeah," said Nathan. "We've been camping."

Quinn drove them a little farther on what appeared to be a trail wider than either of the roads they took to arrive on the ridgeline. Keira eased her sleeping son to the seat and joined her husband and Quinn at the back of the jeep.

"I can't believe he's asleep," she said.

"It's late, and stress plays weird tricks on the body. I've had Marines fall asleep during choppy fifteen-minute helicopter rides to a mountain raid. The little guy did well tonight. You all did well."

She nodded, feeling as exhausted as her son. "Let's get this over with."

She examined the vehicle's contents and was instantly reminded that Nathan had ditched Owen's bug-out bag during their desperate escape from the house. Her husband had done the right thing under the circumstances—lightening the load so Owen could keep up.

"David," she said, "can I ask you to buy Owen some new clothes tomorrow? Maybe a few items to keep him busy. We had to leave his backpack behind. We can give you money."

"That's fine. Write down the sizes of what you want me to buy. Don't worry about the money," said Quinn. "I won't be able to bring the stuff back until after dark, though."

"That's fine. Thank you. It'll mean a lot to him."

"No worries." Quinn pulled an overstuffed camouflaged rucksack out of the jeep and dropped it on the ground behind the jeep. "This should be everything you need to stay warm and dry. You'll also find a few squashed rolls of toilet paper in there somewhere."

He dragged two tan five-gallon plastic jerricans to the edge of the compartment and reached deeper into the back to grab a cardboard box held tightly together with plastic strapping. He pulled the box into the overhead light. MEAL, READY TO EAT, INDIVIDUAL.

"And this should be everything you need to eat and drink," said Quinn. "Twelve delicious MREs and ten gallons of plastic-flavored water. There's drink powder in the MREs to help with that. I'd eat two a day, just in case something happens and I can't get back tomorrow night."

"What if you can't get back at all?" asked Nathan.

"If you don't see me within forty-eight hours, assume I'm out of the picture altogether. Walk in a westerly direction along the ridgeline trail. One way or the other, you'll run into Camp San Mateo in about seven miles. Just keep working your way west. Insert the battery in your phone and call the police or something."

Then what? If Quinn didn't return, they might be better off trying to live off the land. They'd have a better chance of survival. She stared into the night behind them, trying to make sense of the ground outside of the jeep's dome-light radius. At least they had flashlights.

"Any way you'd be willing to part with the night-vision goggles?" she asked, figuring she'd give it a try.

"Not if you want me to see me again—alive," said Quinn. "I wouldn't get very far. You'd probably hear the crash from here."

"How are we supposed to set up the tent in the dark?" she said.

"We have flashlights," said Nathan.

She shook her head. "Help me out a little, honey."

"Sorry," mumbled Nathan.

Quinn stared at them with his hands on his hips. "There is no tent."

"What?" she said, half expecting him to say he was kidding.

"You've got two waterproof bivy sacks, which are like thin shells. Also, an all-weather sleeping system that consists of a light sleeping bag and a cold-weather bag. Plenty to share."

"We're sleeping on the open ground?" she said. "Is that even safe? Didn't your dad mention rattlesnakes and tarantulas out here?"

"Shhh," said her husband, pointing toward Owen. "I don't remember him saying that was a big problem in the field."

Quinn smiled and said, "Well, it is. Kind of."

"Nice," she said. "Happy sleeping."

"We sleep in the open all the time, rain or shine. Just keep the bivy sack zipped up tightly so nothing can get in," said Quinn, chuckling.

"Looks like one of us doesn't get one of the bivy things," said Keira.

"I wonder who that'll be?" asked Nathan.

"Everyone will be fine," Quinn said. "If it makes you feel any better, there's an old poncho in there somewhere that can be rigged up as a shelter, if you have some cord."

"We do, actually," said Nathan. "Each backpack has a thirty-foot length of cord. I remember my dad showing me how to make a poncho shelter."

"Well, there you go. Sounds like you *sort of* know what you're doing."

"*Sort of* is the key term," said Keira, surprised by Nate's sudden confidence in his survival craft.

"We can handle it," said Nathan, poking his head into the back of the jeep. "Owen, you ready for a little camping trip?"

"He's more or less passed out," said Keira. "Which should make hiking into one of your draws or spurs a real treat in the dark."

"You can sleep on the flat ground off the ridgeline trail," Quinn said. "Just make sure you hide yourself in one of the draws at first light. You'll get some Marines from San Mateo running up here for morning PT."

"Fourteen miles?" asked Keira. They'd stopped at his battalion headquarters in San Mateo to pick up the MREs and water. She couldn't imagine anyone jogging this far and then jogging back.

"It's not an everyday run. I take my Marines on a gut check through these hills a few times a month," said Quinn. "If things get ridiculous with Cerberus, I can schedule some kind of field operation and park a platoon around you."

"Things haven't gotten ridiculous yet?" asked Keira.

Quinn didn't respond right away. "I don't know. Somehow I doubt it."

She helped Nathan drag the gear to a flattened grassy area fifty feet away from the road, near the mouth of a deep draw. The narrow, downward sloping gulley should be the perfect place for them to hide in the morning. When they were finished, Nathan lifted their son out of the jeep and stood next to her, waiting for Quinn to finish rearranging the back of the jeep. The Marine shut the jeep's back hatch and handed Keira one of the MP-20s and two spare magazines.

"Just in case," said Quinn.

"Thank you," she said. "For all of this. Make sure you pass that along to Alison."

They'd met his wife, Alison, at the Main Side Exchange parking lot before driving to the north side of the base. She looked rattled and decidedly unsure of Quinn's passengers. Moments before, she'd received an emergency report through her vehicle's state broadcast system about an explosion south of Carlsbad, near the interstate. They'd seen the same report on the jeep's HUD, wondering if it was somehow connected to the night's insanity.

"Don't thank me yet," said Quinn. "We have a long way to go. I'll let your parents know that you're tucked away safe and sound."

"Drive safe," said her husband.

"Don't worry," said Quinn, lifting the second MP-20 off the front seat. "I will."

The night swallowed the jeep, leaving only the crackle of its tires and an intermittent red brake light.

"Are you still mad at me?" asked Nathan, holding their son's limp, sleeping body in his arms.

"Of course I am, but I still love you the same. Let's get Owen zipped up inside one of those bivy sacks," she said, digging through her backpack for a flashlight. "I distinctly remember your dad telling stories about tarantulas."

"He hated those things."

"I'm not exactly a big fan of them either."

"Then don't point your flashlight at the ground," he said, right before she was about to activate the light.

She hesitated for a second, then pressed the button anyway. The compact flashlight's LED bulb illuminated a wide swath of the ground, exposing no creepy crawlies—for now.

Chapter 49

Chris Riggs loaded the last black-nylon duffel bag into the Range Rover and closed the hatch. Standing in the dark behind the vehicle, he contemplated the dark shape of Jon and Leah Fisher's two-story, post-and-beam house. He wanted to burn it to the ground, but Leeds had been specific about what he wanted them to do.

Search the property and seize all computers, data storage devices, papers, receipts, address books—even refrigerator magnets. Anything that could reveal where the elder Fisher might hide. An obscure campground they'd visited. A nearby relative. Favorite getaway hotels. The possibilities were unlimited, and they didn't have the manpower to scour all of Idaho and its surrounding states. They needed solid clues.

He had one more piece of bad news to deliver before leaving. Maybe it would change Leeds's mind about the house. He really wanted to leave this place in ashes, and maybe start a bigger fire. Maybe burn the rest of Idaho down. He used his satphone to connect with Leeds.

"Talk to me, Riggs," said Leeds.

"I didn't find a note saying, 'Feed the fish, we'll be at the Ketchum Inn,' but we filled both Range Rovers. We'll find something."

"I have a group of techs and another team en route to help process what you recovered," said Leeds. "I want a preliminary search plan by midmorning."

He was relieved Leeds didn't say early morning. They wouldn't be finished off-loading the SUVs into the hotel rooms until at least three a.m. Now for the bad news.

"I found something unexpected in the house," said Riggs.

"Why doesn't that surprise me?" asked Leeds. "What are we looking at?"

"Jon Fisher had IR motion detectors installed in the house, but not at the entrances, where you might expect them," said Riggs. "I found one inside his basement workshop, and two more deeper inside the house on the ground level. As far as I could tell, they were hardwired to the home satcom router, which was fully operational."

"Clever."

"Yeah. We removed our countermeasure gear after clearing the entry points," said Riggs. "Wherever he's hiding, he knows we've been here. I think we should burn the place down."

"You always think that," said Leeds. "No, I'll send the tech team out to see if they can somehow ping Fisher with the system. Maybe he logs into a site to check, or gets notifications sent to a phone. It's worth a look. I'd prefer the house be there in the morning."

"I thought you might say that," said Riggs. "Hence the call. We're putting the final touches on our own motion-sensor array. I plan to drive out of here in a few minutes."

"Perfect. Send me the connection data for the array before you leave. Flagg wants everything to flow through the operations center."

What else is new? Flagg had a reputation for micromanaging the shit out of his operations.

PART IV

CHAPTER 50

Supervisory Detective Anna Reeves directed her flashlight at the ground several feet ahead of her and followed a narrow taped-off path through the backyard of 2647 Pallux Way. The flimsy yellow tape led her toward a cluster of forensics investigators pointing at a dark stain on a wide bed of river pebbles toward the back wall of the property. An excessively bright work light positioned at the end of the chute, facing the detectives, cast long shadows on the tall stucco wall behind them.

"What's up?" asked Reeves, squeezing past the tripod-mounted light.

"Good thing they held everyone back until forensics—and the lights—arrived," said Tim Jackson, the county's lead forensics investigator. "Initial flashlight sweeps missed this gem."

"We do what we can not to contaminate your crime scenes," said Reeves.

"Did you hear that?" asked Jackson, motioning with his hand toward the other investigators. "Detective Reeves respects what we do. There's still hope for the department."

"I was just being polite," she said, winking at them. "Trying to avoid another lecture."

"Aww, man. Had to go and burst my bubble—right in front of my colleagues. Brutal," he said, kneeling in the squishy pebble bed next to the dark-maroon stain.

She took a knee next to him. "I see you found a blood stain. Great investigative work."

"You're on a roll this morning," said Jackson, aiming a laser pointer at the beach ball–size stain.

The pointer's green dot circled the stain, stopping on a small blood-glistened rock on the edge of the stain. No bigger than the tip of a thumb, it stood out among the smaller, smoother pebble layer.

"Want to guess what that is?" asked Jackson.

"A rock with blood on it?"

"To the untrained police detective's eye, yes," said Jackson. "But to the expert forensics investigator, who has spent years—"

"It's way too early for this," said Reeves. "Just tell me."

"Piece of brain lobe."

"Way too early for that, too," she said. "Theory?"

"My very educated guess is that the stain came from a head wound."

"Not exactly a controversial theory," said Reeves.

"I'm just getting started," said Jackson. "We're looking at a head wound, likely produced by a projectile. Blunt-force weapons or something like an ax would leave blood everywhere—along with a lot more brain. Someone dropped right here and bled from a localized head wound. Bullet hole."

"Interesting," she said, standing up to examine the stucco boundary wall. "No splatter or spray on the wall?"

"None that we could find."

"The rest of the yard?" Reeves added, sweeping her flashlight in an arc from the wall to the house.

"This is the only visible concentration," said Jackson, standing up next to her and pointing at the house. "If our victim was hit from this general direction, we'd have some spray on the wall—and possibly some kind of bullet impact."

"If it was a through-and-through."

"Rattlers usually make a neat hole in one side and bounce around inside the skull, lodging in the brain," said Jackson. "A through-and-through almost always leaves some gray matter behind. Usually cracks open the skull on the opposite side. A nice luminol spray-down while it's still dark will tell us if we have any aerosolized blood patterns. We could determine the direction of gunfire."

"Do it," she said. "The whole scene isn't making much sense to me yet. There's no sign of struggle inside the house, besides the broken door leading from the garage. One of their vehicles is missing, last tracked heading south on Interstate 805. Exited at Imperial Avenue and parked at the Home Depot a few blocks down before it went dark."

"He removed the tracking module?" asked Jackson.

"We don't know," she said, shrugging. "We can't find the vehicle."

"I noticed a purse on the kitchen table," said Jackson. "Looked like one of those lady wallets still inside. Someone left in a hurry?"

"My purse follows me everywhere," she said, confirming his theory. "Any shell casings?"

"None. I found very little physical evidence beyond this wonderfully perplexing bloodstain, six spent M18 smoke grenades scattered on Pallux Way, and a child-size backpack filled with survival gear on Summerdale," he said, pointing past the backyard wall.

"That's another mystery," said Reeves. "If Fisher fled with his family in the car, why is one of their bug-out bags one street over?"

"Bug bag?" asked Jackson.

"Bug-out bag. It's a portable emergency kit that preppers keep ready at all times in case they have to leave their house without warning. Clothes, food, supplies for twenty-four to forty-eight hours. They sold a lot of them in San Diego after the 2023 wildfires."

"I didn't see any more *bug-out bags* in the house," said Jackson. "And they left a ton of survival gear behind. The car in the garage is mostly packed with personal stuff."

"It feels like they had been planning to leave for a while, but something happened to expedite their timeline," said Reeves.

Jackson pointed at the bloodstain. "I'd say your theory is sound."

"Detective Reeves?" announced someone from the house. "You need to see this."

"Care to join me?" she said to Jackson.

"Why not?" he said. "The scene can't get any weirder."

A few moments later, Jackson was muttering to himself as they stared into an open refrigerator. Two phones sat at the bottom of a full pitcher of water. She glanced at Jackson, who nodded with a sly smile.

"Someone was worried about eavesdropping," said Jackson.

Why would Nathan Fisher, mild-mannered water department engineer, sink his phones? This was something they saw with narcos suddenly tipped off about police surveillance. None of this added up. Bloodstain with brain chunk in the backyard. Crashed van that a dozen neighbors saw, but the police can't find. Reports of masked men running through the street with guns. Smoke grenades. Strange buzzing noises. All somehow connected to a man she'd questioned less than twenty-four hours ago in connection to the reactor shutdown.

"Detective Reeves?" asked one of Jackson's investigators from the bedroom hallway.

"Yes?"

"We found a box of pistol ammunition hidden in a clothing drawer in the master bedroom: 9mm jacketed hollow points. Sixteen rounds remaining in a box of fifty."

"I'll be right there," she said, glancing at Jackson.

"This guy is starting to sound like some kind of anarchist," said Jackson.

She shook her head. He was definitely sounding less and less like a county water engineer by the minute.

CHAPTER 51

Nathan Fisher's eyelids fluttered at the sound of chirping birds. For a few brief moments, his mind vacillated between the conscious and unconscious world, unaware that he was sleeping on the hard ground next to a jeep trail, miles from the nearest building. All at once the reality of their situation slapped him awake, his eyes opening wide, as his body snapped upright in the bivy bag. The waterproof shell arrested his involuntary reaction, knocking him back to the gravel. He lay on his back for a few breaths before unzipping the thin bag far enough to slip into the chilly morning air.

He peered north, still seeing very little of Camp Pendleton's terrain in the darkness. The view west, toward the Pacific Ocean, yielded a few scattered lights, but little more. He didn't know what to expect when the sun rose. He remembered that the base sprawled for miles, with Marine units stationed in distant camps connected by a few main roads. The northern part of the base was sparsely populated, from what he recalled. Even after the sun rose over the base, they might not see anything of consequence from their vantage point on the hill.

A thin blue ribbon peeked between the hills to the east. The birds had woken him earlier than necessary. A quick look at his watch confirmed it: 5:15 a.m. The sun wouldn't break the horizon for another thirty to forty minutes, and they wouldn't be in danger of discovery by any of Camp San Mateo's Marines for at least another hour after that.

He considered lying back down and trying to go back to sleep, but he didn't trust his wristwatch alarm to wake him.

Sleep hadn't come easy after they'd settled in for the night. The last time he remembered checking his watch had been around three thirty. His wife had finally fallen asleep, after several unverified tarantula sightings. He supposed it didn't matter. Once it was light enough outside to walk safely, they could relocate their makeshift camp into one of the nearby draws and sleep all day. They had little else to do while they waited for Quinn to show up tomorrow night besides eat and sleep—and drink coffee.

Keira's backpack contained a one-pound propane bottle and a single-burner propane stove that screwed to the top of the bottle. They could heat water in the stainless-steel canteen cup from Quinn's rucksack to make the instant coffee found in every MRE. His father had praised MRE coffee, but the man drank instant coffee spooned out of a red plastic can. Nathan expected it to taste vile, but at the same time, he couldn't wait to make a cup.

"What time is it?" his wife murmured.

"Still too early," he said. "Sun won't be up for another forty minutes."

"Shit," she said, burying her head inside the heavy sleeping bag. "Wake me up when it's time to move."

"I can give you another hour. Six fifteen," he said. "I don't know how long it will take to find a good hiding spot, and I'm thinking about making some coffee before we relocate."

"That sounds nice," she said, shifting in the sleeping bag. "Are you going back to sleep?"

"Probably not," he said. "I might make that coffee now and start looking for our temporary home when the sun comes up. We can let Owen sleep as long as possible."

"I'll join you," she said, unzipping her sleeping bag.

"I promise not to drink all of the coffee," he said. "Get some more sleep. We had a long night."

She laughed quietly. "Sorry I kept you up with the false alarms."

"I couldn't sleep, anyway," he said, kneeling next to her pack.

Keira sat up in her bag. "This is going to be a long day, isn't it?"

"Sleep will be a big part of our day," said Nathan, yawning.

"Owen doesn't nap," she said, nodding at the camouflage bivy sack between them.

"Yeah," he said, finding the propane bottle. "We have a long day ahead of us."

Keira put an arm around Owen's hidden form and nestled against him. Nathan wondered how much they could tell an eleven-year-old about the full situation they faced. Owen knew that someone nasty and well equipped was chasing them, but they'd been intentionally nebulous about who and why. Incredibly enough, his son hadn't asked last night. He'd marched forward, happy to play his role without asking questions. He couldn't imagine this temporary lack of curiosity holding much longer. They needed to be prepared with answers. Nathan leaned toward telling Owen everything, but he'd defer to Keira's judgment.

"He'll be all right," said Nathan, feeling like it was the right thing to say, even if it was a cliché.

"I hope so," said Keira. "I'm tempted to take David up on the offer to hide him with another family on base. I think he might be safer that way."

"I don't want him out of our sight," said Nathan.

"I don't either," she whispered, lying next to Nathan. "But he's not safe with us. Tarantulas weren't the only things keeping me awake last night. I couldn't stop thinking about how this whole thing unfolded."

"I should have told you about what I saw at the beach," said Nathan. "I don't know what I was thinking. I really don't. I never meant to put us in danger. I thought this would all blow over."

"Actually, your head-in-the-sand approach may be the only reason we're alive right now."

"I feel like I'm being set up for a smackdown," he said, picking up the bottle and stove. "How about you deliver it over breakfast and some coffee? Grab two of the MREs. We can watch the sunrise. Give us a little privacy, too."

"Got it," she said, pulling two plastic pouches out of the box Quinn had given them. "Does it matter which ones I pick?"

"Not really," said Nathan. "They're all pretty gross. My dad used to have MRE night at home, until my mom put an end to it."

"Sounds like a blast," she said sarcastically.

"Actually, it was pretty cool," he said. "For a while."

They sat on the western slope of a small spur and set up the stove. Nathan dragged one of the five-gallon water cans over and filled the canteen cup to the brim. He lit the stove with matches from one of the MRE packs and balanced the stainless-steel cup on the stovetop. The contraption looked like it would tip over if he breathed too hard.

"The water should be ready in a few minutes," he said, putting an arm around her and pulling her close. "So what was the crazy theory you had about how I saved us?"

"I'm still mad at you," she said, leaning her head into his shoulder. "But I really do think your patented wait-and-see attitude kept us alive."

"Smackdown coming up," he said.

"Seriously. Think about it. Quinn arriving when he did is the only reason we're alive."

"He certainly saved us from something horrific," said Nathan.

"Right. If he'd shown up in the afternoon, or the day before, he would have dropped off the phones and we would have never seen him again. We would have driven off oblivious to Cerberus and probably been killed on the road."

"Quite possibly," he said.

"Every scenario, except for Quinn showing up when he did last night, kills us," said Keira.

"What if I had told the police about the boats when they questioned me?"

"They would have promised to look into it and sent you on your way with the same geo-restriction," she said. "And Cerberus would have known that you saw their boats. They probably would have snatched us out of the house that night."

"I could have listened to you when I got back from the beach and left for my parents' house that same morning, ditching work."

"And nobody would have found the bodies at your parents' house for a few weeks," she said. "We were dead as soon as you arrived at the beach, which wasn't your fault. Bad luck. Bad timing. Whatever. Somehow the world wasn't ready to give us up."

"This is starting to sound very philosophical," said Nathan.

"Call it what you will. Quinn could have showed up earlier, but he didn't want to sit in traffic to deliver the phones. He didn't want to bring them at all, but his dad insisted. He was pretty honest about that. He begrudgingly arrived at our house moments before we were attacked."

"Or his arrival sparked the attack," said Nathan.

"Cerberus had plans to grab us last night," she said. "One way or the other, they would have paid us a visit. I think we left at the only moment we could have escaped and survived, thanks to Quinn—and you."

She was probably right, but he was too tired to think about the deeper meaning of life at the moment. Keira worked the opposite way. The more exhausted she became, the closer to a spiritual guru she sounded. Right now, he just wanted to drink some bad coffee and watch a sunset without thinking. They had the whole day to explore the cosmos.

"Water's ready," he said. "First cup is yours."

"We can share," said Keira, handing him one of the MREs.

A few minutes later, they cautiously sipped the questionable liquid from the awkwardly designed canteen cup. The distant strip of visible horizon had brightened, the wispy, scattered clouds immediately above it betraying hints of orange. He held Keira tight with one arm and held the canteen cup with the other. For a brief, fading moment, he forgot about last night. Nathan was alone with this wife, enjoying a gorgeous sunrise in a pristinely quiet, natural environment—the kind of thing they talked about doing just about every week, never putting in the effort to make it happen. He stifled a laugh.

"What?" she said.

"Now you have me waxing all philosophical over here," he said, sipping the coffee and grimacing.

"It's pretty gross," she said.

"Disgustingly good."

She took the cup from him and wrapped both hands around it, staring ahead silently.

"What's really going to happen to us?" she asked.

"Nothing bad. Someone or something is looking out for us," he said.

She turned her head and kissed the side of his mouth. "Thank you for saying that."

What choice did he have? They'd been dropped off seven miles from the nearest human with a case of MREs, ten gallons of water, a few sleeping bags, and a machine gun. They had no way to contact anyone or figure out what was going on beyond this ridgeline. Their fate was most definitely in someone else's hands right now.

CHAPTER 52

Nick Leeds stood inside the closed vestibule, waiting for the door to buzz. He checked his watch: 6:20. Flagg would be surprised to see him this early. They had adjourned from the last operations briefing at 2:15, after scouring the police channels for news related to their operation. Police units had been called out to Nathan Fisher's neighborhood but hadn't entered the residence. No surprise there. All 911 calls from the Fishers' neighbors focused on the van crash and the smoke. A few reported seeing armed men around the van, but with the van missing, it didn't elevate to the level of a critical municipal threat. Police would have knocked on doors and taken statements, alert for signs of duress, but without obvious damage to the front of a residence or signs of forced entry, they wouldn't investigate any further. The real fun would start when the police ran a list of current residents, connecting the dots between Nathan Fisher and the police department's visit to the San Diego Water Reclamation Authority corporate office in Poway.

The door buzzed, and Leeds pushed it inward, immediately seeing the faces of two men displayed on two of the parabolic screens. He recognized one of them. Jon Fisher. Nathan's father. The other had a similar haircut but didn't elicit a memory. The smell of espresso coffee filled his nose before he stepped inside the room.

Flagg swiveled in his chair. "Care to guess how these two men are connected?"

"Jon Fisher had a brother stolen by gypsies at birth?" asked Leeds, heading straight for the coffeemaker.

"You're still on my shit list," said Flagg.

"Who isn't?" asked Leeds, turning to face the screens. "What did you find?"

"While you were sleeping, I made an interesting discovery." Flagg touched the computer screen in front of him, and the two pictures on the screen expanded, showing torso-up images of the men wearing formal Marine Corps uniforms with an American flag draped in the background.

"Who's the light bird?" asked Leeds.

"Allow me to introduce you to then–Lieutenant Colonel Stuart Quinn, Sergeant Major Jon Fisher's commanding officer at First Radio Battalion from early 2019 to late 2020, currently working in an undisclosed capacity at the Defense Intelligence Agency."

"That's not good," said Leeds.

"An appropriate response, given Quinn senior's background," said Flagg. "I've called in a few favors at that agency to get a better picture of what we're dealing with. He retired from the Marine Corps in '26, after a twenty-two-year career as a Marine intelligence officer, with a secondary Military Occupational Specialty in counterinsurgency/human source intelligence."

"Like father, like son," said Leeds. "This could be a big problem on more than one level."

"This retired colonel might be in a position to learn enough about Cerberus to connect some dangerous dots," said Flagg. "Which is why we need to take Nathan Fisher out of the equation immediately. The younger Quinn, too. He saw enough last night to cast some serious doubt on the story we concocted to frame Fisher. Without Quinn, Fisher's story about the boats will sound like the desperate ramblings of a cop killer with nefarious ties to the California Liberation Movement."

"What about Fisher's parents? Same orders?"

"It's too late to back up on that one," said Flagg. "If they know we paid the house a visit in Idaho, there's no way they'll write their son off as a quasi-terrorist cop killer. They're more dangerous alive than dead, so the orders stand."

"Should we start looking for Stuart Quinn?"

"I already started that ball rolling," said Flagg. "You have enough to worry about between here and Idaho. I have a different group working on it."

Leeds wasn't sure if that signaled a loss of confidence in him, or if Flagg was starting to get nervous about the entire operation. Deep inside Leeds, a dangerous voice begged to be released from its tightly guarded cage. A voice that would love nothing more than to point out how none of this would be a problem right now if Flagg had popped Fisher on the way home from work two days ago—like Leeds had suggested. Instead, he took a sip of coffee and nodded, approaching the screens.

"I have eight operatives filtering into Camp Pendleton over the next two hours," said Leeds. "Two will locate and watch Captain Quinn. The rest will comb the commissaries, exchanges, and other base services for the Fisher family and Quinn's wife. She never returned to their house last night. I assume she's aware of the Fishers at this point."

"I don't want our operatives wasting any time when they find them," said Flagg. "The Fishers are to be terminated with extreme prejudice. Alison Quinn, too, if she's with the Fishers. If she's alone, capture and interrogate—then terminate."

"Copy that," said Leeds. "Any news on the Raptor?"

"It wasn't an accident," said Flagg. "San Diego County PD lost a traffic-surveillance drone in the same area at the same time. Twenty-three houses a few blocks east of the I-5 in Encinitas burned to the ground last night."

"From two drones crashing?" asked Leeds. "Sounds like a commercial airliner went down."

"I wish we had one to drop on the site right now," said Flagg. "Investigators are not going to like what they find."

"Doesn't the Raptor disintegrate to prevent recovery by the enemy?"

"That was the problem," said Flagg. "The self-destruct system relies on a thermite reaction built into the drone's frame, which literally burns the aircraft apart. Unfortunately, thermite burns incredibly hot for a long time, and its designers clearly didn't consider the impact of a thermite shower over a crowded suburb.

"Normally, I wouldn't be worried about this," Flagg went on, "beyond the obvious implications of explaining the loss of a twenty-million-dollar asset to the board of directors. But a CLM surveillance team managed to transmit video of the drone launch before airfield security dropped Javelin missiles on their heads. The video itself can't implicate One Nation or Sentinel, but the airfield land purchase represents a risk. We sanitized the field and burned the hangar down, with the woman's body inside. If CLM directs the police or the feds to the site, they'll have to explain why a known CLM operative was found in the hangar."

"She's a known CLM operative?" asked Leeds.

"She is now," said Flagg. "We've added her to the public list of supporters."

"Anything else before I head up to Pendleton?" asked Leeds.

"The cops have been all over the Fisher property since about four-thirty. Initial reports filed by the lead detective are sketchy at best. I don't think they have any idea what happened there. They did manage to find the bullets, despite the confusion."

"I would hope so," said Leeds. "It's not like I buried them in the backyard."

"They also found the Fishers' personal phones," said Flagg. "At the bottom of a pitcher of water, in the refrigerator."

"Clever." He hadn't been able to locate the phones during his abrupt visit to the house.

"Too clever," said Flagg. "Be careful with Quinn. You're operating on his home turf up there."

CHAPTER 53

Jon Fisher drove east into the foothills of the Lolo National Forest. Asphalt had yielded to hard-packed dirt a few miles back, starting his mileage countdown. The turnoff on Forest Service Road 1308 toward his friends' survivalist compound was precisely 3.9 miles from the last patch of asphalt. Scott Gleason would meet him at the end of the service road and guide him the rest of the way. Reaching the compound required navigating a series of forested jeep trails to reach a gentle valley cut by a little-known creek.

Scott, a retired Marine first sergeant and unabashed survivalist, had established the small homesteading compound six years before with the help of Gary Hicks, a retired gunnery sergeant, who'd spent the last several years of his service in various jobs at the Marine Corps Mountain Warfare Center in Bridgeport, California. With Gary's help, they'd turned the purchase into a self-sustaining, off-the-grid community.

It was the first place Jon had considered when Stuart Quinn told him to "go dark." Not only was the compound isolated and well hidden, it was heavily defended. Scott guessed that the eleven households scattered throughout the property could bring more than two hundred firearms to its defense—far more than the twenty-six residents could possibly use. He'd even hinted that one of the households had a functional 50-caliber heavy machine gun in its arsenal. Another reason he'd feel safe leaving his wife here while he linked up with Stuart to figure out how they could help their sons.

A swollen, fast-moving creek peeked through the trees lining the road on the right, giving them a glimpse of the freshwater source that made this remote patch work of hills and gullies viable for off-the-grid living. As the hillside closed around them, he knew without looking at the odometer that they were getting close to the end of Forest Service Road 1308. A glint of sunlight off metal in the distance confirmed his instinct. Scott's tan Jeep Wrangler blocked the dirt road where it narrowed to a trail between the tightly spaced trees.

"We're here," Jon said, nudging his wife.

Leah stirred in the front seat but didn't answer. No surprise after their six-hour midnight run out of Idaho, followed by the few hours of shut-eye she was able to get while reclining as far back as the 4Runner's front passenger seat allowed. Jon wasn't feeling so great either. Close to a decade had passed since he'd last pulled a near all-nighter on guard duty.

He'd finally passed out in the driver's seat after two uneventful hours in the darkest recesses of the Food Mart parking lot at the turnoff to Old US Route 93. The sun gave him about an hour of uneven sleep before appearing between the peaks to the east and exposing his vehicle to the locals. He'd called Scott after grabbing coffee and some snacks at a nearby Conoco station.

He slowed the 4Runner now, stopping it far enough in front of the jeep to give Scott room to pull a U-turn. Scott hopped down from the jeep, his behemoth frame crushing the gravel beneath him. His friend stood six three, and easily weighed 240 pounds. Thick muscles stretched his dark-blue polo T-shirt and threatened to rip his pant thighs. To this day, Jon scarcely believed this man had spent years mountaineering. He appeared to be the antithesis of today's compact, agile alpinist. Of course, when you're nearly strong enough to move mountains, you had a distinct advantage over the rest.

Jon met him between the two vehicles, grasping Scott's hand in a near death grip. The obligatory man-hug was crushing, popping a few tight joints in his back.

"Jesus, Scott. You look strong enough to lift boulders."

"And you ain't lookin' so pencil-pushy no more," replied Scott, nodding at the 4Runner. "Leah got you shovelin' snow or something?"

"That's the least of it," said Jon. "Leah's still crashed out. Long night."

"You shoulda rang when you got in," said Scott. "I'd uh come down to get ya."

"I didn't want to bother you that late," said Jon. "Among other reasons."

Scott stared past the 4Runner, examining the long stretch of road behind it. "I appreciate your concern for operational security," he said, patting his friend on the shoulder with a slightly pained look. "But I have to be honest with you, Jon."

"I wouldn't expect anything else," said Jon, knowing what Scott was about to say.

"My guess is that this ain't a social visit," said Scott. "Sounds serious."

"Well, I'm not going to bullshit you. My son got wrapped up in something nasty down in California. Not his fault, but it's coming down on him hard. Possibly coming down on all of us. Remember Lieutenant Colonel Stuart Quinn?"

"Shit yeah," said Scott. "I kicked your whole battalion's ass for two weeks in Bridgeport. The two of you made a good fuckin' team. One of the best sergeant-major–commanding-officer combos I recall down there. What's he got to do with this mess?"

"His son is a captain with two-four in Pendleton. Got wrapped up in this trying to help my son. Quinn senior works for the DIA in a very hush-hush capacity. He did some digging, and here we are."

"That bad?"

"Quite possibly," said Jon. "We're not taking any chances. I'm mainly looking to stash Leah somewhere safe while I try to sort this out."

"Given the circumstances, I have to tell the others. My vote is obviously a big fuckin' hell yeah, bring it on, but it has to be a group decision. Sorry about that."

"No apology needed. I don't want to put anyone in danger. There's plenty of places to go. I thought of yours first because of you and Kim," said Jon. "And that fifty-cal you mentioned might have weighed into my decision a little."

"Ha! I bet it did!" said Scott. "But don't mention that when we get into the valley. That's supposed to be secret. We'll get you fed and rested before we bring it up with the rest of the crew."

"Sounds like a plan. Thank you."

"Don't mention it," said Scott. "Worst-case scenario, they say no and I let you use our apartment in Missoula. It's not much, but it's enough to keep Kim from revolting out here. She gets her sushi fix once a month, and I get another hunting season."

"Sounds like a reasonable compromise."

"It's very reasonable. Half the folks up here keep a place in Missoula. Some even stay there during the worst of the winter," said Scott. "Before we drive in, I need you to cough up your phones—anything that transmits or receives."

"We left the phones at home. I have a DTCS secure satphone, compliments of Stuart Quinn," said Jon. "It's not traceable."

"Everything's traceable for the right price or with the right connections."

"True, I suppose," said Jon. "How can I check for messages? I need to get in touch with Quinn and my son at some point."

"Let's see what the verdict is first. Then we'll figure that out. Maybe drive you to Missoula and have you make some calls?"

"Sounds good. I also have a laptop computer that I can use through the satphone. Other than that, we're riding pretty low tech for gear."

"Cellular or wireless capable?"

"Wireless, but I have that disabled."

"Remove the battery, if possible," said Scott. "If not, the bag I brought in the jeep will keep the wireless signal contained. They can fly over and turn that shit on if they want to. Not much they can't do these days. What about the 4Runner? You hooked into automatic roadside assistance?"

"No. They use stuff like that to track you in California and a few other states. Didn't want any of those systems onboard."

"All right. Let's get the phone and the computer in the bag, and we'll head in. Kim's excited to see y'all. She's got a whole griddle packed with bacon, eggs, toast . . . you name it. Hope you're hungry."

"Starving," said Jon. "Had some coffee and beef jerky at the Conoco, and yes, I paid with cash."

"Read my mind. Can't be too paranoid."

Apparently not.

CHAPTER 54

David Quinn checked his rearview mirror again, observing the sporadic traffic following him on Basilone Road. The car behind him displayed red DOD tags in the bottom left-hand corner of its windshield, indicating that the car was registered to an enlisted Marine or sailor. With a single occupant, though, the gray sedan didn't hold his attention. He took a sip of hot coffee from a black USMC travel mug and nestled it back into the cup holder, eyeing his phone. Still nothing from his dad.

He'd expected to hear something from either his father or Nathan's by now, but the two of them had gone dark. Nathan's dad had sounded like he was a few minutes from heading north when they'd last spoken, but oddly stopped taking calls for the rest of the evening. His own father had done the same. David hoped their silence had something to do with the vulnerabilities inherent in cellular communications.

If Cerberus had the capability to turn Nathan's cell phone into a transmitter, as his dad suspected, it was entirely reasonable to suspect they could tap into the cell towers serving Camp Pendleton and work some surveillance magic. One particularly effective trick, which Quinn's unit had employed in Kabul, was to comb tower traffic with sophisticated voice-recognition software. When the software registered a confirmed voice hit, they dug a little deeper into the signal and extracted the call's digital footprint, including the phone number. His father knew that trick better than anyone else. He'd helped to pioneer the tactic in 2019 during the second war in Afghanistan. David needed to find another way to call his father, which might be possible where he was headed.

Driving to the opposite side of the base was the last thing he wanted to do under the circumstances, but he could stop by his father's old unit in the same area and see if the good legacy his father left behind in First Radio Battalion might score him a few minutes on an encrypted satphone.

Failing that, he could buy a few commercial satphones with cash at the Marine Corps Exchange. The registry process and call-plan selection for these phones were handled directly via satellite connection by the manufacturer, with the required Federal Communications Commission information sent in a massive data packet detailing countrywide purchases at 11:59 p.m. PST each day. Cerberus would not learn that he was a new satphone owner until midnight on the day he activated each phone, at which point he could assume the phone was tapped. Of course, if Cerberus continually voice-filtered every call entering each regional ground station, which he had to assume, they could unravel his trick posthaste. He'd have to limit the calls to two minutes or less.

A few minutes later, his phone buzzed. The screen indicated it was one of the burners he'd given to his wife. *Shit.* He'd told her to only use it in an absolute emergency. Cerberus would be tracking and actively pinging every prepaid phone purchased by Corporal Cerda yesterday afternoon. By inserting the battery, she'd likely given up her location. He tightened his grip on the steering wheel, ready to turn the car around at the next safe opportunity.

Alison was holed up in one of his barracks rooms back at Camp San Mateo. He could be back at the camp in twenty minutes.

David pressed the screen, accepting the call. "Make it quick and watch what you say. Thirty seconds."

"Did you see the news?"

"No. I've been in meetings, and I'm driving to Las Pulgas. Are you in immediate danger right now?"

"No, but you need to hear this."

"Before you say another word, grab your bag and start heading to the backup location. Toss this phone as soon as we hang up. What's going on?" he said.

"Nathan Quinn is the subject of a statewide manhunt," said Alison. "According to the police, he's a suspect in the murder of a police detective. How well do you know him?"

"I sort of knew him in high school. Last night was the first time I saw him in more than ten years."

"You're already risking enough here. More than enough," she said. "I'm walking out of the door, by the way."

"Good. Take in your surroundings. Do like I said."

"I know," she replied. "I think you should strongly consider cutting ties with this guy. Hiding a fugitive cop killer will not end well."

"I highly doubt Nathan Fisher killed a police officer."

"Are you willing to bet everything on that?" she said. "Lose everything?"

"I already crossed that line when I delivered the phones," said Quinn. "Take the battery out and toss the phone. Love you."

"Love you more."

He kept his phone on, planning to ditch it at Camp Las Pulgas, halfway between San Mateo and his real destination at the other end of the base.

David thought about what she'd said. Either Fisher was a cop killer, and Quinn was the victim of an elaborate con, or Cerberus had framed Fisher, making it infinitely more difficult for both Nathan and him.

With Nathan's name plastered on every police blotter from here to the border, he had little chance of escaping California. Every mode of travel short of hiring a boat to land him on a Mexican beach was out of the question. And leaving Camp Pendleton might not be an option, shortly, when local authorities learned that Fisher entered the base last night. As they had in the past when dealing with fugitives, San Diego County PD would petition the base for search authority, which the Marine Corps would refuse—igniting a standoff outside the gates.

The thought of it made him uneasy. He'd have to explain why he'd brought Fisher on base last night and what he did with him. David had no idea what he might say to investigators. Hopefully, he'd have a few more hours to come up with a story. Until then, he had to balance his attention between his job as Captain Quinn and his responsibilities as a husband and son. By the end of the day, he suspected he'd face a difficult choice between those duties.

CHAPTER 55

Leeds sat in a government-registered SUV parked in front of the Surfside Coffee shop next to the barracks building where they traced Alison Quinn's call. She'd disappeared again quickly, suggesting she was in the same barracks quad. They couldn't be sure, and it really didn't matter. Unless she screwed up and took a walk outside, or made another call, they'd never find her. The Cluster B San Mateo barracks quad was composed of four buildings, each with four levels—representing more than four hundred rooms assigned to Second Battalion, Fourth Marines. She could be in any of them, locked away safely, and he had only four men, plus himself, to watch the building.

He considered recalling the group assigned to watch Quinn, but dismissed the idea. Quinn had kept his cell phone activated on purpose and was almost certainly up to no good. He wanted to keep as close an eye on the counterinsurgency-trained Marine as possible. Quinn had already delivered one very costly surprise. Leeds wasn't about to let him spring another on this operation. He wouldn't be surprised if Flagg was on the verge of "relieving" him, which didn't mean he'd get to enjoy his Cayman Islands townhome with a golden parachute package. More like he'd be thrown out of a jet over the Cayman Islands without a parachute.

He dialed Flagg's number, wishing he could report that Alison Quinn was sedated in the trunk.

"Any luck?" asked Flagg.

"Negative. She disappeared before we arrived at the barracks."

"You weren't already at the barracks?"

"We're split between twenty barracks buildings. The first guy arrived within two minutes. She's close. I suspect in the same cluster of buildings."

"She vanished in two minutes, evading your people?" asked Flagg.

"If you want to give me forty guys," said Leeds, "I can watch every side of every building at once."

"I'll pretend I didn't hear that," said Flagg. "What about her car?"

"I have over a thousand cars parked in San Mateo alone. We'll focus on the Cluster B parking lot, but who knows where the fuck she parked it. Knowing Quinn, it's parked at a different camp."

"This Quinn guy is really starting to piss me off."

"Quinn is going about his day like nothing has happened," said Leeds. "What if he drove Fisher off the base at two in the morning and stayed here to keep us distracted?"

"We should only be so lucky."

"Did I sleep through a meeting? How would that be lucky?"

"You didn't see the news?" asked Flagg. "The San Diego County Police Department, in conjunction with the state police, have issued an all-points bulletin for the arrest of Nathan Fisher, a key suspect in the murder investigation of Detective Emma Peck, who was discovered deceased in her apartment after failing to report for her shift. Someone leaked this shocking development to the media, which has resulted in Mr. Fisher's face appearing on every television news channel and Internet media site alongside the words *cop killer*. If Fisher is anywhere outside of Camp Pendleton, I suspect his time on the run can be measured in hours."

"If he's cornered, the police might do our work for us," said Leeds. "Especially if the Special Activities Group gets there first."

"I certainly hope so," said Flagg. "But we're getting ahead of ourselves. My bet is that he's hiding somewhere on Camp Pendleton. Possibly in the same barracks building as Quinn's wife, or very close by. Stay loose. If the Fishers make the same mistake and call Captain Quinn, I don't want any near misses. Be ready to move as soon as I call with the location."

"Would it make sense to take my other team off Quinn to give me more flexibility here?"

"No. This Quinn character has something up his sleeve. I want him watched from a distance at all times. Hold on," said Flagg. "I just received word that his phone has stopped moving in Las Pulgas. Make sure your men stay back. The transcript from his phone call indicated this was his destination."

"Copy that," said Leeds. "I'll call you back in a few minutes with an update."

Flagg disconnected the call without answering.

Leeds immediately contacted the team trailing Quinn. "I just received word that Quinn stopped in Las Pulgas."

"Yeah," said the operative. "He pulled off on Brown Street and headed for the center of the camp. We're catching up to his location."

"Don't let him out of your sight."

"We're reacquiring," said the operative. "Car surveillance is a little tricky on base."

"You have to watch his ass closely," said Leeds. "He's craftier than you think. I'll stay on the line until you reacquire."

"Copy that, sir. Turning onto A Street. Looks like he's headed for the barracks. Is it possible he stashed the family here?"

"Very unlikely," said Leeds. "He left his phone on for a reason."

But why would he leave it on? A panicky idea gripped Leeds.

"Keep him in sight," he said, "but maintain a safe distance. If anything feels off, get out of there."

"Ambush?" asked the operative.

"Not the kind of ambush you're thinking. He could have set something up with base security or even his own Marines."

"Rules of engagement?"

"Same: do not under any circumstances engage base personnel."

"Copy," the operative said. "Looks like he parked at the barracks. We'll pick a distant spot and observe."

"All right. I'll stay on."

Less than a minute later, the operative was back on the line.

"Sir, I don't know about this. The tracking data sent to us by tech support says the phone is still in the jeep, but I don't see Quinn."

"Did you see him walk to the barracks building?"

"Negative. He wasn't parked long enough out of our sight to make it to the building."

"And he wasn't in the jeep when you drove up?" asked Leeds.

"I can't be sure," said the operative. "We didn't enter the lot. I didn't want to get trapped between the barracks buildings if Quinn had something planned."

"Shit. Did you see any other vehicles driving in the lot when you arrived?"

"I don't think so," said the operative. "Wait. We did have one car. A red sedan, but that was driven by a woman. A Marine."

"Goddamn it," said Leeds. "The Quinns' second car is a red Toyota sedan. How the fuck did you let that get by you?"

"I know they drive a red Toyota, but—but it wasn't Quinn. The driver was a female Marine."

"How could you know that if you weren't in the parking lot?"

"I could see long blonde hair from the road. And the Marine Corps utility cover."

"Women in the Marine Corps wear long hair in a fastened bun. Fuck. He swapped cars," said Leeds. "Which way did the car go?"

"Back toward Brown Road," he said. "I don't think it was—shit. I can't believe that. Sorry, sir. We'll reacquire."

"Don't bother. Return to San Mateo," said Leeds. "He could be headed in any of three directions right now, and he has one hell of a head start. I'll be in touch."

Leeds stared at his phone for a few seconds, shaking his head. Like Flagg said, this Quinn guy was really starting to piss him off.

CHAPTER 56

Supervisory Detective Anna Reeves stood at the back of the small conference room inside the Base Access building next to the Main Gate, shifting uncomfortably on her feet. She'd played little part in the meeting, despite her assignment as lead investigator. Deputy Chief Harris and Captain Gutierrez ran the real show. And what a shitty show it had been up to this point. Twenty-four minutes into the meeting, it didn't appear that they were making any headway with the two Marines sent to represent Camp Pendleton's commanding general.

Colonel Larry Banta, commanding officer of the base's Security and Emergency Services Battalion, shook his head, clasping his hands together on the table. "Chief, I think we've reached an impasse. You know I can't allow county law-enforcement personnel on base in an investigative capacity. Even in a liaison capacity."

"Can't or won't?" pressed Harris.

"Both," said Banta. "Lieutenant Colonel Westin has the resources necessary to handle this."

"Let's be honest here," said Harris. "Your Provost Marshall's Office is not equipped to conduct a full-scale fugitive search."

Lieutenant Colonel Westin leaned forward, forming a snarky smile. "I'm confident we can handle it—without your interference."

"You guys are unbelievable," Harris said. "We're talking about a cop killer here. Isn't there a way we can work something out? I'm asking as a professional courtesy. I have to bring something back to the chief."

Banta leaned in. "San Diego County PD will not be admitted to the base, under any circumstance or guise, regardless of whatever threat you hoped to imply. I don't see the need to discuss this any further. I spoke with the base commander immediately prior to this meeting, and he concurs with my decision."

"The chief won't be happy with this," said Harris.

"That's your problem, not mine," said Banta.

Deputy Chief Harris stifled a laugh. "We'll see about that. The chief doesn't have a lot of confidence in the Provost Marshall's Office."

"So much for his professional courtesy spiel," said Lieutenant Colonel Westin to the room at large.

Harris continued. "He asked Captain Gutierrez here to investigate the feasibility of establishing police checkpoints outside of your gates."

"Very feasible," said Gutierrez, speaking his first words of the meeting.

"You know," added Harris, "to make sure Fisher and his accomplice don't slip through your fingers. Can't be too thorough when you're dealing with cop killers."

Reeves couldn't believe what she'd heard. Did Harris just threaten to blockade Camp Pendleton?

"That would be highly inadvisable," said Harris. "I assume you understand the impact of blocking Camp Pendleton traffic on family members?"

"I understand it would be very impactful," said Harris. "And so does the chief. It would go a long way toward avoiding this kind of mess if you'd release the name of the Marine who let Nathan Fisher onto the base last night."

"I can't release that name without permission from the base commander," said Banta.

"And I presume he didn't authorize that release."

"Correct," said Banta. "The individual in question will be questioned by our Criminal Investigative Division, and if the base commander, along with the individual's direct unit commander, deem it appropriate, he or she will be remanded into your custody—as usual. We have a long history of cooperating with local, state, and federal authorities in criminal investigative matters."

"This doesn't feel like cooperation," said Harris. "I'm sure the chief will agree. I imagine he might take a really close look at Gutierrez's feasibility study."

"Very feasible," repeated Gutierrez.

"There it is," said Westin. "A fascinating two-word deep dive into the situation."

"Two words, two hundred pages," said Harris. "The result will be the same."

The Marine major stood suddenly. "Gentlemen, I need to move on to another appointment," she said, reaching her hand across the table.

This is odd, thought Reeves. The major shook the two senior police officers' hands and exited the room with her briefcase.

When the door shut, Colonel Banta leaned across the table toward Deputy Chief Harris. Reeves couldn't wait to hear what he had to say to Harris. She'd always thought the deputy chief was an asshole.

"Now that the lawyer is out of the room," said Banta in a quiet, measured voice, "we're going to do everything in our power to nab this guy, which is considerable in a closed military setting. We'll turn over Mr. Fisher without question, within minutes of taking him into custody, *and* if we determine that the individual who granted him access to the base was involved in the murder of your detective, the same deal applies.

"But hear this," continued the colonel. "If you decide to blockade the gates, you better bring something heavier than those flimsy ATAVs. Five members in the standard Marine infantry squad carry weapons capable of punching a hole straight through the ATAV's upgraded armor kit."

"Is that a threat?" asked Harris.

"No. Just an interesting fact," said Banta. "Here's another fact. The base commander takes threats to the safety and security of the families living off base just as seriously as direct threats to the service members. Make sure Chief Summers understands that."

"I'll be sure to pass it along."

When the meeting adjourned, Harris cornered Reeves in the parking lot while Gutierrez distracted her detectives.

"This wouldn't be an issue if you'd done your fucking job right in the first place," said Harris.

"Excuse me?" she said. "Fisher's case data was independently reviewed by detectives and run through the Virtual Investigative Division. They found no anomalies to suggest he was lying about his purpose at the beach. We knew that going into his interview. And it's not like he hopped a flight a few hours later. He stuck around for close to forty-eight hours. He checked out."

"Apparently, he didn't."

"I don't know."

"What?" asked Harris.

"Never mind, sir," said Reeves. "I need to get back to my team."

"No. What were you about to say? You don't think he killed Peck?" asked Harris, pointing a stubby finger at her. "I know what you've been whispering to your people around the crime scene. Quit with the fucking conspiracy theories and stick to the evidence. Fisher killed Peck. I don't expect you to suggest otherwise. That's his lawyer's job."

He was right about the evidence. They had more than enough to arrest Fisher for the murder of Detective Peck. Further analysis of his electronic profile suggested they could enhance the charges under state terrorism prosecution guidelines. Despite the evidence, something didn't add up for Reeves. The scene at Fisher's house generated more questions than answers. Questions that had left the best forensics people in the county utterly baffled. She had a duty to dig deeper, but for now—play the game.

"Understood, sir," said Reeves, knowing better than to say another word.

"You better understand," said Harris. "I'm half tempted to find another supervisory detective to run the case. One more aligned with department priorities."

"My priorities are aligned, sir."

"I hope so," he said. "Because the chief isn't going to sit on his hands with a cop killer on the loose."

She nodded, enduring one of his miserably long stares. When he disappeared into the backseat of an unmarked SUV, she let out a long sigh of relief. His departing statement signaled trouble. Harris would take this personally and blow the situation out of proportion back at headquarters. By tonight, San Diego County police leadership would embark on some kind of ego-saving, self-destructive operation guaranteed to embarrass the department in the long run. She couldn't wait.

CHAPTER 57

David Quinn took a deep breath inside the automatic door vestibule at the Marine Exchange and stepped forward, activating the outer sliding door. He strode through the wide opening, pushing a shopping cart in front of him as he scanned the parking lot. There was no sign of the silver sedan occupied by two Marines in dire need of haircuts among the hundred or so cars jammed into the lot. He'd left them behind a few hours ago at Las Pulgas, along with the jeep he needed to retrieve. All part of the plan.

His cart bumped along, jostling the electronics and assorted items he had purchased for the Fishers. Besides a few rugged outfits, water-proof boots, and a handheld virtual gamer for the son, he'd bought a two-person tent. Keira Fisher hadn't looked too thrilled by the prospect of sleeping on the ground after he'd childishly reinforced her concern about snakes and tarantulas. Fully assembled, the two-person tent would be small enough to hide in one of the draws, and if they kept it zipped tight at all times, the chance of waking up with a tarantula on top of them was minimal.

He'd probably phrase that differently when he gave them the tent.

When Quinn arrived at his car, he pretended to drop his keys. On the ground, he looked under the cars next to him for shoes or odd shadows. Satisfied that nobody was hiding behind a nearby vehicle to ambush him, he opened the backseat of the red Toyota and emptied the shopping cart. The satphones went in the front seat. He'd drive to a less congested area and activate one of them, placing a call to his dad. If that didn't work, he'd try Nathan's father.

His attempts to score an encrypted satphone had fallen flat at First Radio Battalion. He'd managed to sweet-talk his way into their operations shack for about twenty minutes, but he never came across any satphones. He'd been tempted to borrow a phone, but couldn't shake the very real threat of voice-recognition software picking up the call. Now he knew exactly how an Afghan insurgent must have felt trying to coordinate attacks: every call was a risk, every turn a possible end to your day.

Halfway out of the parking lot, he spotted a dark-green Jeep Cherokee with two occupants pulling out of a space two rows over from where he'd been parked. Cerberus would have more than one team on Camp Pendleton looking for them, and the Base Exchange was a logical place for a stakeout. Not a problem. He could work with this as long as they didn't try to grab him in broad daylight. He could deal with that, too, but it would pretty much put an end to the sneaking around on base. Gunfights tended to attract attention.

Quinn drove his car north out of Mainside, opting to take a longer, more open route back to San Mateo. The half-mile, 120-degree turn on Vandegrift Road just south of Lake O'Neil would be ideal for flushing out a tail. The turn was too long for traditional car-surveillance techniques. The following car would be forced to make a difficult choice. Stay out of sight but fall more than a half mile behind, or follow at a regular interval, alerting the target. His money was on the first tactic. He'd already identified one of their surveillance teams, and that crew had followed him at a safe distance, suggesting a passive surveillance stance.

Passive surveillance made the most sense given the situation. They knew he was armed and capable, rendering a successful kidnapping unlikely. Killing him wasn't an option either, since they needed him to find Fisher. They would follow at a safe distance and hope he led them to Fisher. At the same time, they would search for his wife. If they captured Alison, they could leverage her against him—and it would work. Forced to choose between his wife and the Fishers? He didn't want to think about it. Hopefully, he'd have some good news waiting for him back at Fox Company area. News that would take his wife out of the equation temporarily and allow him to focus on the men posing as Marines on his base.

A few minutes later, his car rounded the long, shallow turn on Vandegrift Road. Quinn watched the road across the open field to his left, waiting to see what approach they would take. It was also possible he wasn't being followed, and the two Marines he'd seen in the parking lot had extended their lunch break to shop in the exchange. He kept driving on Vandegrift, coming to the point where the road disappeared behind a low rise. The green Jeep Cherokee appeared on the road across the field moments before he lost sight of them. They were following him at a very safe distance, hoping to avoid obvious detection. That made his life easier—for now.

CHAPTER 58

Nathan Fisher stumbled over a thick, protruding root, grinding his left knee into the hard ground a few feet from their makeshift shelter. He'd quit counting the number of times he'd fallen at this point. He was exhausted, and his legs refused to adjust to the uneven ground. At this point, he simply accepted the fact that he would land on his knees every time he left the shelter. That way, if he managed to return from a bathroom trip without falling, he could consider it a major accomplishment.

He was probably being too hard on himself, but looking up from the fall to see no sympathy on Keira's face did little to validate that theory. She'd woken up in a decent enough mood, given the circumstances, but that literally went downhill shortly after sunrise, when they decided to move into the draw to hide for the day.

The gully turned out to be steeper than it looked, especially when approached farther down the ridge. He'd mistakenly assumed they'd be doing themselves a favor by heading directly into the deep gully from the side, avoiding a longer trek down the densely vegetated middle. The trip had been quicker—no doubt about that—but he would have gladly traded a barely controlled, rapid fall for a longer, more measured descent. He had several bloody scratches and a few bone-deep bruises to support that conclusion.

The first forty-pound jerrican of water broke free of his grip and slid halfway down the side of the draw as soon as they started descending its steep walls. Instead of listening to his wife's on-the-spot advice about slowing down, he embraced the can's sudden tumble with a stark lack of logic. Without thinking, he grabbed the second can out of her hand and tossed it into the draw, then jumped down after it. Maybe it was the coffee. Maybe he'd seen too many extreme-sports clips with guys throwing caution to the wind. Maybe he was just too fucking tired to make a good decision. Whatever the combination of stupid reasons, it turned out to be a severely bad call on his part.

He stayed on his feet long enough for Keira to follow with Owen, probably seeing it as her duty to tend to the inevitable injury his hasty descent promised. By the time his bruised body skidded to a rest at the bottom of the draw, she and Owen had made it halfway down. They both fell and slid into a thick stand of bushes shortly after that, scratching their faces and generally guaranteeing she wouldn't talk to him for the rest of the morning.

All she could do was point at one of the five-gallon cans, which had come to a stop behind a tree trunk halfway down the side of the draw. It took him close to twenty minutes to claw his way up to jar it loose, and when it toppled down the hill, it nearly bowled over their son, who was holding a compress bandage against his hand from a persistently bleeding scratch.

He thought the morning couldn't get any worse until the first Marines started to arrive, and not the occasional jogger Quinn had led them to expect. Diesel engines roared above them all morning at random intervals. The spur they had chosen off the main ridgeline had been wide enough to accommodate vehicles, a fact they should have recognized by the tire tracks in the dirt running along the ridge. Voices could be heard over the vehicles, and occasionally they caught a glint of sunlight reflecting off a tactical vehicle's ballistic glass. Instead of a quiet camping experience, they'd spent most of the day cowering in fear underneath a hastily tied camouflage shelter, jumping at every noise above them.

"I'm not sure we can do this for too long," said Keira, rubbing her face.

Already? They'd barely crossed the twelve-hour point—half of that spent asleep.

"I don't think we have a choice," said Nathan, sliding under the tarp next to Owen, who was now sandwiched between the two of them.

He wrapped an arm around them.

"I bet David gets everything squared away by tonight," said Nathan, pressing his head into Owen's. "We'll be fine, buddy."

His son nodded and grabbed his hand. Keira reached over and took both of their hands.

"It will be fine," she said. "If David doesn't show up tonight, I think we turn ourselves in to the first group of Marines on the trail. Maybe we're better off in Marine custody, or whatever they have. They could get ahold of your dad, and he could figure out how to help us."

Nathan met her gaze over the top of Owen's matted hair. "I don't know," he said. "It's a gamble. We could get lucky with a sympathetic Marine, or we could end up being escorted right out of the front gate by security with no means of transportation or a way to call anyone without—"

"I'm sure they'd let us borrow a phone to call a taxi," she said. "We have enough cash to get to LA."

"Then what?"

"I don't know, but I do know we can't camp out on base indefinitely. Not drinking MRE coffee," she said, offering a faint smile.

"You aren't kidding," said Nathan. "What do you think, Owen? Can you hang out here eating MREs for a little while longer?"

"I'm fine, Dad. This isn't so bad."

"Better than school?" asked Nathan.

Owen shook his head. "I wish I was sitting in class right now."

"Me, too," said Nathan.

"You'd rather be sitting in class?" asked Keira.

Owen laughed. "I think he meant me, Mom."

"Hopefully, we'll have you back in school before they let you out for summer break," said Nathan.

"I don't think that's going to happen," said Owen. "This feels kind of permanent."

"Staying out here? This isn't permanent."

"But we can't go back to our house," he said.

Keira wiped her moist eyes with the back of her hand. He felt the same deep hopelessness that he knew his wife and Owen were feeling. Their lives would never be the same. Above them, a diesel engine rumbled, getting louder until a tactical vehicle raced passed them on the trail leading to North Range Road.

"Maybe we should move to another spot tonight," said Nathan. "Somewhere a little less busy. I think we might be able to see the ocean from the northern side, across the main trail."

"We can't go anywhere until David shows up. He won't know where to look for us," said Keira. "And, sweetie, we'll find a new house—in a state where you can take a thirty-minute shower or own a pool."

"I don't want a new house," said Owen.

"Neither do we," said Keira. "But sometimes things work out for the best."

Nathan appreciated that she didn't blame him for their predicament, especially in front of Owen. Actually, her philosophical approach to the entire situation was starting to make more sense to him. Their fate was sealed when he drove into the beach community at Del Mar. Maybe everything did work out for the best, and this was the best they could expect for now.

CHAPTER 59

David Quinn pulled his Jeep Wrangler out of the barracks parking lot at Camp Las Pulgas in search of his new friends. He couldn't spot the green Jeep Cherokee that had followed him out of Mainside. He suspected Cerberus had attached a tracking device to the Wrangler after he gave the first team the slip. Now that he was back in the jeep, they could back off.

He accelerated onto Basilone Road, continuing the trip toward San Mateo. A minute into the ride, Quinn gripped the newly activated satphone lying on the passenger seat and pressed "Send." He'd already preprogrammed his father's number. The phone rang several times before his dad answered.

"Aurelio's Pizza," said his father. "Pickup or delivery?"

"I wouldn't eat that shitty pizza if it was free."

"Good to hear your voice, David," said his father. "Sorry I went dark. I saw you called a few times, but I had to solidify my vanishing act. Sounds like you're in a car?"

"I'm on Pendleton," he said. "Trying to do my job as Captain Quinn while managing the rest of this shit."

"Has this vehicle been out of your sight?"

"Yes. I swapped cars this morning, just to throw them off a bit. I have a few new friends on base."

"Of course you do," said his dad. "I need you to pull over and step out of the car before you say another word. You have to assume you're being tracked and that they've bugged your vehicle."

"Copy that," said Quinn, slowing the jeep immediately. He pulled onto the shoulder of the road and hopped out. "I'm good now," he said, taking a few steps into the scrub beyond the packed dirt.

"The police issued a warrant for Nathan's arrest. Have you seen that?"

"Alison called me with the news. The cop-killer thing has to be bullshit."

"I agree," said his dad, "but either way, expect a real shit storm on base if they figure out you brought Fisher onboard."

"It won't take them long to connect those dots. The wife didn't have ID, so Base Access had to run a DMV check."

"Shit. The provost is probably all over your battalion by now. I'll make a few calls and see what I can do. If you have to return to battalion, keep a low profile."

"I need to head back there right now," said Quinn. "I have a few things cooking up."

"Drive around a little, if possible. Give me a little time to work my contacts. How are Nathan and his family holding up?"

"They were fine when I left them last night. I have them stashed somewhere safe."

"How safe?"

"The only thing they have to worry about are rattlesnakes and tarantulas."

"Good call. I'll pass that along to his dad. I wish I had more to tell you right now, but this Cerberus group is wrapped tight. I have a few people digging deeper. People I trust—though I'm not so sure who I can completely trust at this point. The secession issue is a high-stakes game that Sentinel and their cronies can't afford to lose. They'll stop at nothing to remove any impediment to whatever their sick endgame might be. You're one of those impediments now," said his dad. "I'm sorry you got dragged into this."

"I'm not," said Quinn. "Nathan and his family would be dead by now if I hadn't stumbled into the middle of this. I plan to see this through to the end, wherever that leads."

"I wish Nathan's parents could hear you say that. They got lucky with you."

"Nathan isn't exactly helpless," said Quinn. "He's a bit of a soup sandwich in general, but he held his own last night. First time firing an MP-20, he put close to thirty rounds into an area the size of a beach ball. Punched his rounds right through an armored wind-shield and took out the driver. I have Marines that can't fire their rifles that well."

"Can I let you in on a little secret?"

"Do I have a choice?"

"Of course not," replied his dad. "Nathan Fisher shot a two forty-eight during an unofficial qualifying round during his senior year in high school. I was there. Best I've ever fired was a two forty-five."

"Two thirty-six for me," said Quinn. "Going on nine years."

"You need to do something about that problem."

Quinn laughed. "If I get out of this without going to Leavenworth, I'll make that my career goal."

"We're coming up on two minutes," said his dad. "How many phones did you buy?"

"I maxed out one of my credit cards. Figured there was no reason to limit myself to cash. They know where to find me."

"Keep the calls under a minute next time," said his dad. "If they catch a whiff of this one, they'll intensify their filter efforts at the ground stations. I'll talk to you sometime tomorrow unless anything drastic changes on your end. Good to go?"

"Good to go, Dad. Be careful."

"Back at you."

Quinn powered down the satphone, folded the antenna, and slipped it into his cargo pocket. Unlike cellular phones, a satphone would not receive calls without a deployed antenna. It required a direct connection with a satellite, which was initiated by the user. Of course, the next time he used the phone, his new friends might be listening, but he still had a few uses for the phone that didn't require sharing sensitive information. It would especially come in handy with the provost marshal crawling around Second Battalion.

He glanced south on Basilone Road without seeing any cars. The Cerberus team had stopped following him, which confirmed that his jeep was being tracked. To the north, a pair of tan, armored, light-tactical vehicles approached, spiking his heart rate. *Shit. Provost security?* As he walked briskly back to his jeep, the AL-TACs approached close enough for him to see the battalion markings: "1/1." First Battalion, First Marines out of Camp Horno, a few miles down the road. He reached his jeep as they sped past, kicking up dust from the road.

He took his father's advice and stayed away from his battalion area for an additional twenty minutes, driving past San Mateo and stopping in one of the San Onofre housing areas to gather his thoughts. First things first. He needed to figure out if it was at all safe to head back to San Mateo. He dialed Staff Sergeant Emilio Cantrell's phone.

"Cantrell," the Marine answered.

"Staff Sergeant, this is Captain Quinn," he said. "Don't say my name or act like I'm on the phone—and assume we're not the only ones on the line."

"The platoon shack is clear of unwanted guests," said Cantrell. "What'chu get yourself into, Captain?"

"It's all good, Staff Sergeant. I promise. I'm on the right side of this."

"I never doubted you weren't, sir," said Cantrell. "Figured something was up with that little mission you gave me."

While Quinn was on the other side of the base, Cantrell had run a countersurveillance operation targeting the Cluster B barracks in San Mateo. Quinn billed it as a practice mission, but made sure Cantrell understood there was more to it than met the eye, and that his Marines needed to stay clear of any identified targets.

"So it went well?" asked Quinn.

"I'd say so."

"Good. Because I have another mission for you. I'll give you the details when I get back," said Quinn. "This one builds on the last one, and if you did your job right, it should be a piece of cake."

"Aww, shit," said Cantrell. "This is gonna be good."

"This one might get a little hairy, but I hear you like 'em like that, Staff Sergeant."

"Captain's on a roll!" said Cantrell. "Wait till I tell my wife. She'll tear your arm out and beat you over the head with it."

"I wasn't talking about your wife," said Quinn. "But if the shoe fits . . ."

"All right. I give up, sir," said Cantrell. "Company area is clear. I'd stay away from battalion HQ, and your office—obviously."

"See you in about five," said Quinn. "Pop open the back door for me. And thank you, Staff Sergeant. The weirdest shit ever went down last night. I need someone to cover my back until I get it squared away."

"We got your back, Captain."

"I can't tell you how much that means to me right now."

Quinn disconnected the call, then rubbed his face and yawned. He was running on fumes, with no rest in sight.

CHAPTER 60

Quinn parked his jeep on the far side of the Cluster A barracks and walked through the barracks' open quad area to reach Second Battalion's working area. At two-thirty in the afternoon, the quad was a ghost town. The sparse, concrete-paved area would start to come alive around four, when Marines began to trickle in from each of the regiment's four battalions. By five, the space would be mobbed. Music from dozens of radios competing with the chaotic nonsense that occupied bored twentysomething Marines living too close together. The place could also get a little rough, routinely producing black eyes, nasty scrapes, and the occasional fracture for the corpsman to examine in the morning.

He crossed a service road beyond the barracks, emptying into one of the battalion's back parking lots. The headquarters building was well out of sight, on the other side of the sprawling collection of one-story structures housing the day-to-day garrison activities of Second Battalion, Fourth Marines. Quinn stopped a few rows into the lot, studying the vehicles near the long redbrick building. He had to be careful. The provost marshal had savvy career investigators at his disposal. This wasn't the first time they'd dealt with sly Marines trying to protect their own.

The back door to the Enhanced Counterinsurgency Platoon's shack opened far enough to expose Cantrell's smiling black face. He nodded once and gave him a thumbs-up. Quinn pulled the brim of his utility cover down a bit and jogged for the door, hoping to remain undetected. Cantrell opened it wide when he arrived, locking it after him.

"Cloak-and-dagger shit," said Cantrell. "Love it."

"Real-life shit," said Quinn, clasping his hand. "Thank you. Seriously. You got the photos?"

"I got the whole operation charted out, with high-res photos," said Cantrell, motioning for him to check out the desk.

Quinn walked over to the broad, metal-constructed government behemoth and examined Cantrell's sketch. He'd created a top-down view of the Cluster B barracks, with each of the surveillance targets' locations marked and labeled to correspond with a data sheet. Pictures of the targets had been paper-clipped to each sheet, underneath a brief vehicle and personnel description.

"Who helped you draw this?"

"Drew it myself," said Cantrell. "Was about to break out the crayons."

"Might have looked better," he said, popping his shoulder with the back of his fist. "This is perfect. Only four targets?"

"Four that we found."

"And you still have eyes on each one?"

"Nobody canceled the op, as far as I knew," said Cantrell, winking.

"Perfect. Here's the straight scoop, Staff Sergeant," said Quinn. "A friend of mine got mixed up in something nasty. Let's call it a case of mistaken identity. I helped him out, and now I have the same problem as my friend. That's all I'm going to say, for your safety."

"Don't worry about me."

"I am worried about you, and everyone involved in the op. This is serious shit. The surveillance targets you've been watching are very serious shit."

"NCIS?" asked Cantrell.

Quinn shook his head. "They're very bad news. That's all I'm going to say. They're watching Cluster B barracks because I hid my wife in one of the empty rooms last night. She panicked and called me this morning, alerting them to her location. She immediately moved to a backup location in the same building, and has been hiding there all day. That's how serious this is."

"They were gonna fuck up your wife?"

"Or worse."

"We gotta take these clowns down," said the staff sergeant. "The platoon can do it quiet like."

"No way," said Quinn. "We're talking trained professionals."

"And we're not?"

"I have complete faith in the platoon's abilities, but pitting one group of professional killing machines against another is a recipe for disaster," said Quinn. "This is my fight."

"Your fight is our fight. *Semper fi.*"

"You're starting to sound like a broken record," replied Quinn. "Here's what you can do for me. I need you to handpick a team to extract my wife from her barracks room."

"Where is she located?"

"Building two, facing south," said Quinn, pointing at the building on his sketch.

"Looks like we'll have to take this car out of the equation."

"I have a less hazardous way to get them out of the way," said Quinn.

"That doesn't sound like much fun, sir." His platoon sergeant sounded sincerely bummed.

"It'll be fun in a safe, standoff distance kind of way."

"In other words, no fun at all."

"That's right, Staff Sergeant," said Quinn. "Daddy's not letting the kids ride bikes without helmets today."

"Now, that's crazy talk, sir," said Cantrell. "Base police will give your ass a ticket for riding without a helmet."

"Smart-ass. Put together your extraction team and find a spare uniform. Size small. I want her looking like any other female Marine on base. Don't forget to put her hair in a bun when you move her out of the barracks."

"How about we make her look like one of the guys?" asked Cantrell. "We could shave her head and pencil in a nice lance corporal mustache."

Quinn grinned. "You'll want to put the battalion aid station on standby to receive Marines with severe testicle damage before you try to shave that head."

"Female Marine sounds good to me," said the staff sergeant. "Where we taking her?"

"I haven't figured that out yet."

CHAPTER 61

Nick Leeds watched the door that had swallowed David Quinn forty minutes earlier. Base security had arrived in force an hour before Quinn's arrival, sweeping through the battalion areas escorted by senior Marines from the battalion. Plainclothes investigators, most likely assigned to the provost marshal's criminal investigation division, entered the headquarters building at the same time, and as far as he could tell, hadn't departed. If base security detained Quinn, Leeds's job would get complicated.

Extracting Quinn from the provost marshal's custody was not an option, and without Quinn, they had little chance of finding Fisher—without a serious slip in communications security protocol. Based on the group's comsec discipline to this point, Leeds had no intention of waiting for them to make a mistake. It could be a long wait.

They still had a decent chance of finding Quinn's wife, but he wasn't sure that would bring them any closer to their objective. He doubted Quinn would have told her much about Fisher. The good captain played this game too well for that, and he was too smart to think they would spare his wife if she shared information. Leeds had to give the captain credit. The Marine was in way over his head, but he was holding up well—for now.

If passive surveillance efforts didn't yield results by tomorrow morning, Leeds would seriously consider more active measures. Flagg wanted results, and the longer this dragged out, the more pressure he'd expect his boss would apply. Shit rolled downhill, and Flagg was no doubt feeling the pressure himself.

Three tan AL-TAC vehicles appeared at the far corner of the building, on the narrow service road connecting the back of the battalion area to one of the main roads dissecting the camp. The squat, heavily armored tactical vehicles picked up speed, heading toward the door used by Quinn. Leeds shifted his binoculars, examining the fast-moving convoy. A compact light bar ran across the top of the vehicles, identifying them as base security. They were coming for Quinn. *Shit.*

A second convoy followed the first around the corner, giving him doubts about that assessment. Six vehicles converging on one door seemed like overkill. When both convoys raced past Quinn's door and screeched into a hard left on Fourth Street, he knew exactly what was happening. They were headed straight for the Cluster B barracks.

"Quinn, you son of a bitch," he muttered, triggering his communications rig. "All units, this is Leeds. We've been made. Abandon your vehicles immediately and do your best to blend. Move to pickup points."

"This is Delta," said one of the operatives situated on the northwest side of the barracks. "Too late for E and E. Two unmarked sedans just blocked me in."

"Copy that," said Leeds. "Do not attempt to engage or escape. Let them take you into custody."

"Fuck," hissed another voice. "Charlie team reports the same problem. Damn it!"

"Stay calm and cooperate," said Leeds, watching the AL-TACs bear down on the parking lot south of the barracks. "Alpha and Bravo, you have about ten seconds to clear out of the parking lot. Head west."

"Already on the move," replied one of his operatives. "Shit. Two Growlers with mounted MGs just blocked the western exit. Do we have time to evade east?"

Leeds lowered the binoculars and shook his head. The east exit would be blocked in seconds. "Negative. Alpha and Bravo, stand down where you are. I have six AL-TACs inbound from the east in a few seconds."

"Roger that," said the operative. "Here they come."

"All units, gas your comms and hang tight. We'll send a legal representative to get you out of this within the hour," said Leeds. "Echo, you still clear?" He'd positioned Echo team in the parking lot serving the small cluster of restaurants at the eastern end of Camp San Mateo.

"This is Echo. We're good so far. You want us to hit the road?"

"Affirmative. Head to Camp San Onofre. Switch to secondary encrypted network and wait for instructions."

"We're on the move," said the team leader. "Switching to secondary network."

Leeds put his SUV in reverse and backed out of the parking space, half expecting to see the opposite ends of the lot blocked by tactical vehicles. Seeing nothing headed in his direction, he slipped out of the parking lot and made his way to San Mateo Drive, turning west. He'd drive to the northernmost base gate a few miles away and leave Camp Pendleton. Flagg would certainly drop him from the operation if he were taken into custody.

Tactical operatives could be swapped back and forth from other jobs, but his position wasn't easily replaced. Not to mention the fact that his job was too high profile to risk apprehension. A Cerberus legal team would have him back on the streets within a few hours, but his cover would be burned. He'd end up in a low-visibility operations position at corporate headquarters—if he were lucky. Given the series of bumps he'd experienced over the past forty-eight hours, he wasn't willing to test that luck.

CHAPTER 62

Quinn pressed the headset against his ear, straining to hear what Cantrell was saying to his team. They had moved into position at his wife's barracks building, ahead of the provost marshal's deployment to the parking lots. Once the Cerberus surveillance teams had been cornered by base security, Cantrell's crew would head for the third floor and wait for him to contact his wife. Alison Quinn had instructions to shoot anyone accessing the room without advance warning from David.

"Captain, the surveillance team visible from your wife's room just took off. Hold on," said Cantrell. "They stopped in the middle of the parking lot. Looks like our guys parked the Growlers on the west end just in time. Base security has it under control. We're heading up."

"Any sign of resistance from the surveillance teams?"

"Not that I can see," said Cantrell. "The guy in the passenger seat of the gray SUV has his hands on the dashboard. Looks like a clean bust to me."

He figured the Cerberus teams wouldn't put up a fight against base security. The entire base would go into complete lockdown if that happened, completely undermining their mission. It might still go into lockdown if the men are armed, though he somehow doubted they were carrying firearms. Any weapons they planned to use, if they found Fisher, would be stashed out of sight somewhere nearby. This group didn't make mistakes, from what he could tell.

"Good deal. I'm calling Alison now," he said, picking up the office phone and dialing her backup burner phone.

"Major Woody," she answered.

"Sorry, I was trying to reach Private Parts," he replied, completing the ridiculous code.

"Get me out of this room, honey," she said. "I can't take it anymore."

"I have four Marines headed to your room right now. Do exactly what they say. I'll meet you a little later."

"What about the people watching me?"

"I just took care of the surveillance teams," he said. "Base security should be hauling them off."

"So we're good?"

"We're good," said Quinn. "We identified all of the teams watching your building. That phone call this morning drew them right to you."

"Where am I going?"

"I can't answer that on the phone, but you'll be safe there, as long as you don't use your phone again."

"When will you be here?"

"I can't answer that either," he said. "You'll be fine. The Marines headed to your room will give you the details. You'll recognize one of them right away. Do exactly what they say. Love you."

"Love you, too," she said, replacing the handset.

He'd be able to talk to her in a few minutes over the encrypted squad radio network transmitted into his headset. Until then, he needed to grab a few controlled items from the company supply clerk. He tucked the squad Motorola radio and wireless headset into one of his cargo pockets and opened the door leading into the platoon area. Lieutenant Colonel Smith stood squarely in his way, and he didn't look surprised to see Quinn.

"Did I catch you at a bad time?" asked his commanding officer, staring at him impassively.

"No, sir," replied Quinn, a bit stunned to think of a different reply.

"Good, because we've had quite an afternoon here," said Smith, stepping into the room.

Quinn backed out of his way, wondering if he might be better off running for the back door. His tenure on base was rapidly coming to an end, either in the provost marshal's brig or at the end of a Cerberus gun barrel. He didn't feel like he had much to lose. Smith closed the door and locked it, which struck Quinn as odd, and kept him from bolting into the parking lot. He searched for words but came up empty.

"What's going on?" asked Smith. "And don't bullshit me. I just spent a good part of my already busy afternoon talking about you with CID investigators, followed by a bizarre call from God himself singing your praise."

"Sir?"

"Major General Nichols and I spoke at length about you—or rather, I listened to my commanding general speak about you. Apparently, your father served with the general back in the day and left a lasting impression on him. An impression I have been asked to extend to you. So tell me what's happening, and spare no details. You already have your get-out-of-jail-free card—from me."

Quinn explained everything, from agreeing to run a few burner phones down to Nathan Fisher to using Cantrell's platoon to identify the surveillance teams looking for his wife. Lieutenant Colonel Smith's battle-scarred face betrayed little while Quinn told the story, and even less when he finished.

"The general does not want to get involved in the conspiracy aspect of this," said Smith. "We have enough problems as it is with the secession issue. Maybe this Fisher guy is telling the truth, maybe not. That's not for First Marine Division to decide. Fisher and his family have to go. Sounds harsh, and maybe it is, but you brought him to the wrong place."

"Fisher has nowhere else to go," said Quinn. "Everyone is looking for him now. They'll kill him on the outside."

"Sounds like they'll kill him on the inside, too, quite possibly taking a few of my Marines down with him. I can't have that," said Smith. "If there's any speck of truth to what your dad told the commanding general, and I suspect there is, this group isn't going to slink back on base tomorrow and resume passive surveillance techniques. You know how this works."

"I do, sir. That's why I can't abandon them. He has an eleven-year-old son. They'll kill him, too. And his wife. And my wife. They'll kill us all," said Quinn. "I don't see any way out of this."

"NCIS?" asked Smith, showing the faintest look of concern. "The FBI?"

"They won't believe Fisher, or me, at face value," said Quinn. "And I'm sure they won't be willing to spirit us away to some top-secret, secure location. Even if they did—we wouldn't be safe."

"You're sounding paranoid."

"So far, that's been the key to survival against this Cerberus thing," said Quinn. "Our only chance is to go off the grid completely."

"Then what?"

"I don't know, sir, but it'll give us time to come up with a better plan than this," said Quinn. "Bringing Fisher to Pendleton was my best option at the time."

Smith rubbed his face before shaking his head slowly. "Do you really think this is the end of the line for you? Even if I delivered Fisher to the provost marshal right now and we buried the fact that you brought him on base?"

"I can't picture any scenario in which Cerberus leaves me alone, Colonel. So yes, I think this is the end of the line for me." Quinn glanced at his watch. "Maybe I can get off base with Fisher during the after-work rush today. Any chance you might be interested in trading your car for my wife's Jeep Wrangler? It comes gently used, with a free tracking device."

Smith cracked a thin smile. "I have a better idea. Well, General Nichols had a better idea," said Smith. "He thinks a small group from Second Battalion, Fourth Marines, should arrive in Yuma a few days ahead of the division liaison team. To make sure everything is in order—logistically. I'm putting you in charge of this."

"Sir, I don't think—when does this leave?" asked Quinn, hoping he wasn't misreading what Smith had said.

"Tomorrow night. You pick the time—*and the team*," said Smith, emphasizing the last part.

"What type of vehicles, sir? And how many?"

"Four AL-TACs," said Smith. "Full turret configuration. It gets a little dicey on the stretch of Interstate 8 between El Centro and Yuma. A number of regular convoys have been harassed by heavily armed banditos. The Mexican border is a few miles away for most of that stretch. The state police and the Border Patrol have stopped patrolling the area at night, so nobody travels between El Centro and Yuma after dark. You'll have the road to yourself."

"We'll be careful," said Quinn. "Thank you, sir. You didn't have to do this."

"Don't thank me. Thank your dad," said Smith. "And yes, I did have to do this. You did the right thing for that family. I'm doing the right thing for you."

Quinn stared at him, cocking his head. "This wasn't the general's idea?" he said.

"Doesn't matter," said Smith. "I have his full faith and confidence. Like you have mine. Get this Fisher character and his family to safety, and do the same for you and Alison. I'm authorizing open-ended emergency leave for you. You're on your own when you reach Yuma."

"Copy that, sir. What about CID?"

"We'll keep the motor transport compound gate shut during the day, in response to whatever is going on outside right now. You'll have some advance notice if CID returns to sniff around. Lots of nooks and crannies to conceal a Marine captain in that repair garage. I suggest you stay there until the convoy is ready to roll."

Smith reached behind his back and produced a satphone. Quinn recognized the device immediately. *Beautiful.*

"General Nichols said you could use one of these," said Smith, handing over a DTCS-encrypted satphone and charger. "This is the military satellite version. Dumbed down for grunts, so you should be able to work it without the instruction manual."

Quinn was speechless.

"What's your next move?" asked Smith.

"I'd rather not say, sir. It doesn't directly involve any of the Marines, but I don't think you'd approve."

"Be careful," said the colonel. "You have your ticket out."

"Always careful."

"Uh-huh," said Smith, unlocking the door and disappearing.

Quinn pulled the radio out of his pocket and fastened the headset, immediately hearing his wife's voice.

"David, where the hell are you?" she said.

He activated the voice-activated transmit feature, turning the wireless headset into a hands-free system. "I'm back in the platoon area. Where are you?"

"Headed to the Motor T cage with one of your staff sergeants. Base security had those assholes in handcuffs," said Alison. "So we're good now?"

"We can't stay here. They'll keep coming after us."

"Stay here on base, or stay here in California?"

"Both," said Quinn. "I figured out how to get us out of the state without anyone knowing, but I need to hide you until tomorrow night."

"I'm not spending another night trapped in one of these rooms."

"I have something different in mind," said Quinn. "I'm going to drop you off with Fisher and his family."

"I'll take my chances at the barracks."

"That's not an option anymore," he said. "Not after your close call today. You can rough it for a night."

"I'm not worried about roughing it. I'm worried about Fisher," she said. "The police say he might be linked to a second murder."

"They probably found one of the operatives' bodies at the house. Maybe Cerberus didn't clean up all of their dead."

"No. Not at his house. Something about an engineer that works at the Del Mar Triad Station. They think it might be related to the reactor shutdown."

"That's ridiculous," said Quinn. "Sorry, honey, but I guarantee he's been framed. He saw something they didn't want him to see."

"When will I see you?"

"In a few hours," said Quinn. "I'll bring you pizza."

"Extra cheese, please."

"I like pepperoni," said Cantrell over the radio net.

"Good, Staff Sergeant, because I need you to pick it up," said Quinn. "It's not safe for me to drive around."

"How the hell is that you bringing the pizza?"

"It was my idea," said Quinn.

"You're paying," replied Cantrell.

"Least I can do, Staff Sergeant," said Quinn. "Honey, I'll see you in a few hours. Love you."

"Love you more," she said. "Be careful."

Quinn smirked. Why was everyone telling him to be careful?

Chapter 63

Raef Gamussen tore into a steaming slice of pepperoni pizza, wolfing down the cardboard-tasting chunks like he'd never tasted anything better. He hadn't eaten since early morning, having grabbed a bagel with his partner on the way to Camp Pendleton. He barely chewed, nearly choking on the pieces, until a long sip of Diet Coke eased their journey. Raef and his partner, Max, clutched pizza boxes in the front seat of the cramped mini-SUV, constantly scanning their surroundings.

They'd moved from parking lot to parking lot in San Onofre, trying not to linger in one place too long. Word of the security problem at San Mateo would have undoubtedly spread to the other camps. The less attention they attracted, the better. Now that it was dark, they were pushing their luck on base. They couldn't sit in the SUV much longer without drawing second looks. They probably shouldn't be eating in the vehicle. The Marines probably had some regulation against it, and it gave the impression they didn't live in the barracks. Raef didn't care at the moment.

"Echo, this is Control," he heard through his headset. "Radio check."

About time! They'd been sitting on their asses without word from Leeds for close to four hours.

"This is Echo. Clear signal."

"Quinn might be headed in your direction," said Leeds. "I need you to gear up and stand by for possible interdiction. He's headed east on San Mateo Boulevard. His jeep has been sitting in the motor-pool area for the past two hours."

"Do you have eyes on the jeep?" asked Raef.

"Negative. I'm cross-referencing satellite imagery with his tracker location. The motor pool is fenced off from the rest of the battalion areas, so it's arguably a more secure area. We think he was waiting there for the sun to go down before making a move. He might be headed for a rendezvous with the primary target."

Raef dropped the greasy pizza slice in the box on his lap and wiped his hands on the sides of his uniform trousers. "Two birds with one stone," he said.

"That would be a nice break for us," said Leeds. "Be very cautious around the weapons cache. We still don't know the extent to which our operation has been compromised. I'm pretty sure it was confined to the barracks-surveillance operation, but we can't be sure. Getting caught red-handed with weapons will negatively impact our ability to secure your release."

"Copy that. We'll scan the area with thermal gear before accessing the cache. Is the rest of the team out of custody?"

"Legal got them released about forty minutes ago. They'll be out of California by midnight," said Leeds. "Looks like Quinn's definitely headed in your direction. ETA eight minutes."

"Shit. We're on the move," said Raef, tossing his pizza box in the backseat.

Max threw his pizza box out of the driver's window and started the vehicle.

"No need to rush," said Leeds. "I don't want you following him closely. Let the tracking device do its job. I'll guide you to your target, if the situation looks favorable."

"Copy that. Will advise when we're ready," said Raef, turning to his partner. "Weapons cache. ASAP."

Less than a minute later, his partner eased the SUV into a parking space on the other side of the camp and turned off the headlights. Raef reached into the backseat and removed a pair of night-vision goggles from a small duffel bag behind the driver's seat and strapped them to his head, activating the device. The dark parking lot turned to day, but that wasn't enough. He switched to thermal imaging and let the goggles adjust to the ambient temperature. A few moments later, he stepped out of the vehicle and panned 360 degrees through the parking lot, looking for hot spots. Several recently driven cars beamed white on the gray-scale image, but he didn't see any human forms. He studied the face of the closest barracks building, looking for anything out of place.

"I think we're good," he said, leaning into the car window.

The two operatives walked one row over and approached the back of a small sedan. Each surveillance team had brought two cars onto base this morning, one to use for surveillance and pursuit, the other to carry tactical gear. Each cache vehicle contained enough gear to fully equip three teams for a diverse array of missions. Spread evenly around the base, the caches provided a relatively quick way to exploit a targeting opportunity, without driving around with weapons for hours on end—running the risk of a random vehicle stop.

Raef placed his right hand under the trunk latch, pressing four fingers against a biometric scanner programmed to read every team leader's right handprints. Three simultaneously matched fingerprints opened the cache. Silently, the trunk lifted a few inches. Raef lifted the trunk, exposing the contents.

A dark-red light bathed the customized equipment rack. Three tricked-out compact assault rifles sat next to a trio of similarly equipped submachine guns. Either choice would be suitable for close-quarters battle in and around buildings, but the rifle would give them a fuller range of shooting-situation options. Raef pulled one of the loaded rifles from the rack and handed it to Max, who placed it against the bumper—just in case they were under surveillance. The two of them had agreed earlier that they had no intention of going to jail, or being "reassigned" within Cerberus. Too many operatives disappeared after failed ops.

Once the second rifle had been removed, they wasted no time donning specialized ballistic vests designed to mimic standard-issue Marine equipment. The Cerberus version looked the same and provided the same protection against bullets and projectiles, but was lighter and more flexible. They loaded the pouches on their vests with spare rifle magazines and attached suppressors to the rifles.

"That should do it," he said. "Unless you think we need the sniper rifle."

"Couldn't hurt," said Max.

Raef yanked the SRS-A3 sniper rifle out of the trunk, grabbing the black equipment box labeled SRS. The plastic case contained four twenty-round magazines and a suppressor. The sniper rifle extended their range and accuracy far beyond the FN 2200s or the MP-20 Quinn was suspected to carry.

They returned to the mini-SUV and arranged the weapons in the backseat, covering them with blankets from the vehicle's rear compartment. Raef walked to the back of the vehicle and searched the parking lot again, detecting no observers. He smashed the brake lights with the butt of his rifle, making sure that the bulbs inside the broken plastic light housings had shattered. Max tossed the second set of night-vision goggles on the dashboard before settling in behind the wheel.

"Control, this is Echo," said Raef. "We're geared up and ready."

"Copy," said Leeds. "Quinn passed your area a few minutes ago, headed east on Basilone Road. Give it another minute and head out. I don't want to spook him with headlights."

"Starting the clock. We opted to bring the sniper rifle, so keep that in mind as an option."

"Good thinking. If feasible, I recommend taking down Quinn with the sniper rifle before moving against the rest of the group. He's the primary threat."

"Copy that," said Raef.

Leeds contacted him a few minutes later as they drove through the next camp.

"Echo, this is Control. Quinn has gone off-road about two miles ahead of you. Looks like he's heading into one of the training areas. I'll guide you to the turnoff. Satellite imagery shows nothing but jeep trails."

"Copy that."

"If he stops before you reach the turnoff, I might have you set up an ambush and wait for him to return to Basilone Road. He'll hear you on the trail if he's with Fisher," said Leeds. "I can send you in with thermals to find the rest of them."

"Sounds easy enough."

"Don't get your hopes up. Quinn has proven to be crafty."

Leeds directed them to the turnoff on a well-traveled dirt road, informing him that Quinn was still on the move. Raef switched the vehicle into four-wheel drive and lowered his night-vision goggles, driving as fast as he dared without headlights. His goal was to close as much of the distance between the jeep and his own vehicle before Quinn reached Fisher. Fifteen grueling minutes later, Leeds radioed.

"Quinn just turned off the main trail, headed northwest. Satellite imagery and base maps show him headed up a winding jeep trail. I have you point seven miles behind him. I'll have you continue to the point where he turned, then travel the rest on foot. Looks like he stashed Fisher on the ridgeline to your left."

"Copy. How far to the top of the ridgeline from the stopping point?"

"The road snakes back and forth for a quarter of a mile, but it looks relatively steep. He's moving very slowly up that road," said Leeds. "You should be able to reach the turnoff before he gets to the top. Nothing I can do about the climb, though. Sorry."

"That's why we get paid the big bucks," said Raef.

Mid-six-figure income—after bonuses. The trick was staying alive long enough to enjoy it. Quinn was the kind of target that could put a permanent dent in your retirement plan, so he planned to approach this carefully. He continued toward the turnoff, ready to stop when Leeds told him. With Quinn's jeep straining to climb the ridgeline access trail, they should arrive undetected. They'd leapfrog up the access trail, covering each other until they reached the top.

When the odometer indicated they'd traveled a half mile, Leeds's voice filled his headset.

"He's almost to the top," said Leeds. "Start slowing down. You should be able to coast to the turn. Look for an intersection. You might be able to see Quinn's brake lights from your position."

Raef didn't want to take his eyes off the road. "Max, you got anything up there?"

Max leaned forward, his head craned upward facing the ridgeline. "Not yet. Switching to thermal. Should see his exhaust."

He eased off the gas, letting the vehicle slow. A few seconds later, Max pointed toward the ridge.

"I got him," said Max. "Almost cresting the ridge."

"You should be able to see the intersection," said Leeds.

Raef stared down the road, spotting the opening between the thick scrub and stubby trees. "I'm stopping," he said, pressing the brakes and coming to a stop a few feet from the turnoff.

A window shattered behind him, followed by three loud snaps. He instinctively leaned to the right and reached behind the front passenger seat for one of the rifles. Before he could reach the rifle, a bullet sliced through the headrest and grazed the left side of his head, puncturing the windshield. A second armor-piercing bullet passed effortlessly through the top of the seat, penetrating his neck and continuing into the dashboard. He never felt the third bullet, though he witnessed the carnage it wreaked on his body. The windshield turned dark red. Then, it all went black.

CHAPTER 64

David Quinn walked toward the vehicle, keeping the MP-20 aimed toward the backseat area. The backseat appeared empty as he closed the distance to the mini-SUV. He opened the rear driver's-side door and pulled the gray blankets back, exposing their small arsenal. *This will come in handy,* he thought.

A quick examination of the front seat confirmed what he strongly suspected: the two passengers were dead. Quinn's first three shots had struck the passenger in the head, leaving no doubts after the bullets left the barrel. The driver had ducked at the wrong moment, earning a momentary reprieve, but Quinn's immediate follow-up shots had been decisive, judging by the amount of blood covering the dashboard and windshield. He activated his communications link.

"Targets eliminated," he said. "Work your way back down. Be careful."

"I'm turning around at the top," replied his wife. "How many followed us?"

He peered down the hard-packed trail toward Basilone Road. "One vehicle. Two occupants."

"I'll be down in a few minutes," she said. "Driving with these goggles is harder than it looks."

"You're seeing the same daylight image, with a moderate image flattening. You can't completely trust your depth perception wearing them. Take it slow. I'll tidy up down here. Made a bit of a mess."

"I don't want to hear about it or see it when I get down there."

"You really don't," he said, opening the front door and pulling the driver's limp body out of the car. The man's corpse hit the dirt with a thud, rolling into a contorted supine position.

Not a corpse yet, he noted. Blood pumped weakly from one of the holes in his neck. A carotid hit. The other hole neatly exited his Adam's apple.

Quinn stripped the rifle magazines from the driver's vest, contemplating the earpiece hanging out of the man's mangled ear. After stuffing the magazines in his cargo pockets, he tore the bloody earpiece away and placed it up to his ear.

"This is Control," said a gravelly voice. "Send a status report immediately. If you can't talk, click the 'Distress' button twice."

He desperately wanted to respond. To scream at the voice, or utter something dark and ominous—like a movie line. Instead, he dropped the earpiece and reached into the car to pop the trunk. The less these assholes know, the better. Let them come and investigate.

I got a little surprise for you . . .

Quinn dragged the body to the back of the mini-SUV and heaved it into the back, repeating the process with the dead operative seated on the passenger side. The armor-piercing bullets didn't behave like standard rounds. The tungsten carbide penetrator and its full-metal-jacket exterior didn't warp in the face of soft-target penetration, including bone. The three tightly spaced bullets had created six small holes, essentially evacuating the man's skull. Fortunately, the contents of his head formed a wide cone of small-particle gore on the road next to the SUV, leaving little mess in the car. He still had to stash the vehicle where no Marines would stumble across it.

With the bodies stowed in the trunk, Quinn removed the weapons and stacked them on the side of the road. He covered the driver's seat with the blankets to avoid saturating his uniform with blood, and carefully slid a small duffel bag in the backseat. He found a suitable hiding spot a few hundred yards down the road, gently driving the vehicle through thick bushes. Good enough. Now to arrange a little surprise.

CHAPTER 65

Nathan Fisher stood at the top of the winding dirt road leading to the ridgeline, cupping both of his ears. He was convinced he'd heard a vehicle on North Range Road below them.

"I don't think you should be standing in the open," said Keira.

"I can't hear it from there."

They'd moved their sleeping gear to the ridgeline trail after dark so they didn't have to slog their way out of the draw when Quinn arrived. *If* Quinn arrived. His wife had been against the idea until she spotted two tarantulas within five minutes. If her flashlight didn't give away their location, her screaming would. Fortunately, they were alone. The last Marine vehicle zipped through over five hours ago.

"What if it's not Quinn?"

"If it's not Quinn, we'll hide," he replied, peering into the murk below.

"That won't do us any good if they know we're here. They could be watching you with night vision."

Or scoping him with a 50-caliber sniper rifle. She was right. He couldn't even identify the road from here in the darkness. He was at a distinct disadvantage in the open. Nathan trotted toward her dark shape, holding the MP-20 against his chest to keep it from bouncing in the sling.

"Shit," she whispered urgently. "Now I hear it."

He stopped and crouched, listening intently. The sound of an engine barely carried across the trail. Someone was gently revving an engine, urging a vehicle up the steep ascent.

"Take Owen and our gear into the draw behind you," he said, gripping the rifle and turning it toward the access road.

"What do we do then?"

"Stay out of sight, and whatever you do, keep your head down," said Nathan. "I'll be across the road."

"Are you crazy?"

"If this goes bad on us, I'll draw them away."

She kissed him quickly and disappeared with Owen, dragging the sleeping bags behind her. When Nathan was sure she was out of sight, he crossed the road and lay down in a shallow rut, squinting over the MP-20. The engine sounds intensified, confusing him. For a moment he thought the noises were coming from the opposite direction. He'd started to shift in the ditch when a dark shape appeared at the top of the access road. Nathan pressed the rifle into his shoulder and centered the subdued green-sight reticle on the moving silhouette.

The vehicle stopped suddenly, its headlight beams flashing twice. He heard a voice.

"Nathan! Hold your fire! It's me! Quinn!"

It sounded like Quinn, but he wasn't sure enough to risk his family's safety. He stayed low and kept the rifle aimed at the vehicle.

"Seriously, Nathan. It's David Quinn," the voice stated, flashing the lights again. "I see you on the ground over there. My wife's in the car."

"Nathan," she called, "it's Alison. We have a way to get everyone off base."

He didn't know her voice well enough to trust what she said. He'd have to figure out a way to verify their identity.

"When did you and I first meet?" yelled Nathan.

"San Clemente High School, 2019," said the male voice. "My dad told me that you shot a two forty-eight on the rifle range that year. I'm jealous. Best I've done is a two thirty-six, after a lot of practice."

It had to be Quinn. He rose to one knee and waved them forward, keeping the rifle aimed in their direction, just in case. When the vehicle got closer, he could tell it was a jeep. Thank God. Nathan stood and lowered his weapon as the jeep pulled even with him. The interior lights illuminated the vehicle's interior, revealing Quinn and his wife.

"Dude, I could see you from the bottom of the hill," said Quinn through the passenger window. "Your best weapon is cover and conceal-ment, with an emphasis on concealment. We need to work on that."

"It's good to see you, too," said Nathan. "I assume everything went all right on base today?"

"Not at all. Not by any stretch of the imagination," said Quinn. "But we have a way out. Where's your wife and son?"

"In the draw on the other side," said Nathan. "Why is Alison here?"

"She's staying with you until we all leave tomorrow night," said Quinn, turning off the jeep.

"Nice to meet you again," said Nathan, reaching his hand inside the jeep to shake her hand.

She took his hand reluctantly, barely squeezing. Quinn's wife clearly wasn't thrilled about staying with them. He could understand that. Nathan had turned their life upside down, too. He met Quinn on the other side.

"What happened today?" asked Nathan.

"Long story short? Cerberus had their people all over the base—"

"And you drove right up here?"

"Relax, Nathan," said Quinn. "I took care of the problem. I had my counterinsurgency platoon sweep the jeep for tracking devices. They found one tracker, which I just left with the last group following me. They're dead. The rest of the teams were rounded up by base security earlier in the afternoon. It's been a weird day."

"Sorry," said Nathan, relaxing. "It's been a long day up here, too. This trail is a lot busier than you led us to believe."

"I didn't realize First Combat Engineering Battalion was training new drivers this week. Can you manage at this location for one more day?"

"Yeah," said Nathan. "We'll move to the other side of the ridgeline. The spurs don't look wide enough to hold one of those tactical vehicles."

"Good deal," said Quinn. "I brought a tent and some clothes for your son. Also a few satphones. I'll show you how to register them. Keep them for emergency use only. It's not safe to use them more than once, or for more than a minute."

"Have you talked to your dad, or my dad?"

"I did," said Quinn. "Your parents are tucked away in a survivalist compound in Montana. He wasn't very specific about the location."

"I've heard him mention the place. Somewhere near Missoula."

"He was planning on driving in this direction, but I told him to stay put and wait for my dad to arrive. They're in regular contact. Once they link up, we'll figure out how to head north."

"How did you talk to them?"

"I acquired an encrypted satphone. Same kind our parents are using," said Quinn.

"Can I call them?"

"The group hiding your parents will not allow them to use the satphone at the compound. They have to drive out of the camp with their sponsor to make a call. I'll let him know we spoke," said Quinn, looking past Nathan. "I think your wife is on her way over."

"Nathan?" whispered Keira. "What's going on? Where are we going tomorrow night?"

"She heard that?" asked Quinn.

"She hears everything," said Nathan.

"We tend to listen better than you guys," added Alison. "Can we move this along? I'm ready to pass out. It's been a long day."

"These two will get along just fine," said Quinn, heading to the back of the jeep.

Keira joined them. "Seriously. Where are we going?"

Quinn opened the jeep's rear gate. "I've been put in charge of a small convoy headed to the Yuma air station tomorrow night. Probably leave about one in the morning, like the regularly scheduled supply runs. I have room for four extra passengers."

"That's good news," said Nathan.

"Thank God," muttered Keira.

"You can thank my dad. He somehow convinced First Marine Division's commanding general that we weren't crazy. My battalion CO went along with it. We got really lucky with that. Things were deteriorating rapidly for me on base. The provost marshal's office is out in force looking for me."

"Because of me," said Nathan. "Sorry about all of the trouble. Seriously."

"No trouble," said Quinn, putting a firm hand on his shoulder. "Seriously. I'm glad I got involved. These people are murderers and thugs. I joined the corps to stomp on dickheads like that. I should be thanking you."

"I appreciate you saying that, but I still feel bad dragging you into this. We have a long road ahead of us."

"I'm always up for a road trip," said Quinn. "Especially when they involve tricked-out, full-ordnance armored vehicles."

CHAPTER 66

Leeds drove past the entrance to the dirt road for the third time, not wanting to take his vehicle off-road in front of witnesses. A government-plated vehicle turning into one of the base's training areas wasn't unusual, but in light of the unusual security measures implemented at the base gates in response to yesterday's surveillance debacle, he didn't want to take any chances. He'd turn around at Las Pulgas and make another pass, hoping the stretch of road was empty when he reached the entrance.

The two operatives accompanying him fidgeted anxiously. He could understand why. Exactly 4.3 miles down that same dirt road, at precisely 9:23 p.m., Echo team had inexplicably stopped responding to radio calls. Even more disturbing: Quinn's tracking signal merged with Echo team's location at 9:32 p.m. Neither signal had moved since. They had no idea what to expect at the site, though he was fairly certain they'd find bodies. The question was *whose* bodies.

He had little doubt that Raef and Max had been killed. But Quinn, too? He could only hope, even if it made his job finding the other targets more difficult. Quinn had proven himself resourceful and unpredictable. A bad combination of traits in an adversary. Finding his body would be a welcome sight.

"I think we should pick up a few weapons from the Las Pulgas cache," said the operative in the backseat.

"Too risky," said Leeds.

Neither operative said another word until he pulled into the Las Pulgas camp to turn around on Basilone Road.

"Just one rifle," he heard from the backseat. "I'd feel a lot better going into this with a way to get out."

"Not in broad daylight," said Leeds. "All it takes is one alert Marine to shut us down, and from what I've seen, they're all pretty goddamn alert. We do a quick check at the site and get the hell out. If this is too much for you, I can let you off right here. I'll be glad to pick you up on my way out."

"It's fine," said Howard. "Just a little crazy doing this without weapons."

"Get used to it," said Leeds. "We operate in a lot of places like that. This is a risky job in more ways than one."

"Yes, sir."

Leeds pulled onto Basilone Road, headed away from the road, slowing after they'd driven close to two miles. He'd keep making passes until the road was clear.

"I have the turn coming up. Looks clear ahead," said Leeds. "How does it look heading south?"

"Clear," announced Howard.

Leeds eased the SUV off the road, turning gently onto the dirt path headed into the training area. His stomach tightened as the vehicle plunged between the dry scrub and stunted trees lining the worn jeep trail. They could very well be driving into an ambush. As they rapidly approached the GPS point tracked by the navigation system visible on the vehicle's windshield HUD, tension inside the cabin intensified.

"Should be right up ahead," said Leeds. "A few hundred yards past the intersection."

"This is a bad idea," said the operative seated next to him.

Leeds slowed the SUV to a crawl, peering into the bushes on the right side of the trail, then caught a glimpse of the dark-blue mini-SUV through the bushes, spotting a broken taillight. "There it is," he said, pointing diagonally across the windshield. A longer look revealed a bloodstained windshield. He stopped the vehicle.

"Any sign of the jeep?" asked Leeds. "It should be right here."

"None," said the passenger, leaning forward in his seat. "This is not good."

"Let's get the fuck out of here," said Howard.

"Find Gamussen and Tremont," said Leeds. "I'll turn us around."

"Jesus," said Howard. "I think we can assume they're dead."

Leeds turned in his seat. "The jeep's gone. Quinn's gone. Our targets are gone. The area is secure. You'll probably find Quinn's tracker sitting on the dashboard, or stuffed in one of their mouths. Get out and find the bodies. I don't need base security running DNA on these guys."

The two contract soldiers begrudgingly exited, crossing the trail behind the SUV. Leeds had pulled forward and cut right, preparing to execute a three-point turn, when the passenger-side windows imploded, showering him with safety glass. A deafening crack followed, rocking the SUV. Leeds threw the transmission into park and crawled out of the door, scrambling into the bushes behind his vehicle.

Clumps of dirt and loose gravel pelted Leeds from above, intensifying the confusion created by the thick cloud of dust that had swallowed the road. He lay still, trying to make sense of what had happened. Over the ringing in his ears, he heard one of the men groaning. No gunfire yet. There wouldn't be any gunfire, if his guess was correct.

After several seconds, Leeds crouched and moved cautiously through the thinning dust toward the dying sounds. The explosion had cleared most of the vegetation around Echo team's vehicle, which stood intact on four flattened tires. He quickly glanced at his own SUV's tires, finding them miraculously undamaged. The same couldn't be said about the rest of the vehicle.

The passenger side was peppered with small holes, from front to back. A few jagged pieces of glass hung stubbornly from the windows.

The driver's-side and rear windows hadn't fared much better. Only the windshield remained intact, showing a few cracks. Quinn had left them a shrapnel-laced gift, probably triggered by a trip wire hidden several feet behind Echo team's car. He needed to get out of here immediately.

"Leeds," croaked a familiar voice, "I need help."

A lump crawled slowly toward the road.

"I need a medic right away," said Howard, pulling himself partway onto the trail. "I'm bleeding out."

Leeds reached along his right ankle, freeing a short two-edged knife from a hidden sheath. He walked up to the dying operative, who struggled to extend a hand for help. In an instant, Leeds dropped a knee between the man's shoulders, pushing his face into the road and sinking the blade into the top of his neck. The man's arm instantly fell slack, his spinal cord severed above the C1 vertebrae. Howard hadn't felt a thing, which was the only mercy Leeds could offer in the situation.

Leeds stood and took in the scene. No way he could load up four bodies, or whatever was left of them. He'd need every second possible to get off base safely, if that was even possible at this point.

CHAPTER 67

Mason Flagg sat in the backseat of an armored SUV, waiting at a stoplight. His phone buzzed in his suit pocket; the digital screen built into the back of the seat in front of him indicated it was Nick Leeds. He debated whether to answer. He wasn't sure he could stomach another setback. Not today. Reluctantly, he pressed the screen, accepting the call.

"Please tell me you found Quinn dead."

"I wish I could."

"How the hell does an infantry Marine outsmart and outgun tier-one special operators at every fucking turn?" asked Flagg, pounding the armrest.

"Somehow, we grossly underestimated him," said Leeds. "The first night wasn't luck. He knew exactly what he was doing."

"And he had help doing it! I have people digging into his background, and they can't seem to make a connection to any organization outside of the Marine Corps. If I didn't want to kill him so badly, I'd offer him a job."

"You might want to consider making that offer sooner than later," said Leeds. "I have more bad news to report."

Flagg closed his eyes and took a deep breath, trying to imagine how it could get worse. *One of the operatives is missing? That would certainly take it to the next level.* Leeds was losing control of this. Yesterday was bad enough, and even though this wasn't really Leeds's fault, Flagg had to hold him accountable. Quinn was the kind of wild card that popped up from time to time, but Leeds had always effectively handled those situations. Maybe the operation needed a fresh leadership perspective.

"What happened?" asked Flagg.

"Quinn rigged the site with some kind of IED. The two new operatives with me were killed in the blast."

"Did you recover their bodies?"

"I didn't have time," said Leeds. "The blast shredded the SUV. I barely managed to swap it for one of the cache vehicles."

"Should I be worried about you trying to get off base?" asked Flagg. "San Diego County PD has set up checkpoints outside of each gate. They're conducting random searches for now, to put pressure on the base commander."

"I saw them setting up this morning. I'm going to park at the museum just inside the San Luis Rey gate and take a cab to Oceanside. I'll arrange a pickup from there," said Leeds. "I honestly don't know what to say. This is a first for me."

"Likewise," said Flagg. "I was starting to seriously question your handling of this, but you've run a textbook operation. With Quinn in the way, we have to come up with an entirely different approach. I'll press headquarters to authorize the next level of surveillance. This cat-and-mouse approach isn't working. Assemble every operative available in California. I'm through fucking around."

"What will you tell the board tonight?" asked Leeds.

"Hopefully, I'll be able to report that this security risk has been contained. Everything is moving along nicely outside of Camp Pendleton."

"I'm worried about the fallout from the base. Enough has gone down to raise some serious questions."

"Let them sniff the rotten air. It adds to the confusion. Give me enough time and I'll pin the surveillance stunt and the explosion on the CLM," said Flagg. "Time is running out for Quinn and Fisher. Rumor has it that the police plans to issue a one hundred percent vehicle-search order at three p.m. for Camp Pendleton. We'll pinpoint their location and deploy the stealth helicopters."

"I'd love to see that happen," said Leeds.

"Don't worry," said Flagg. "You'll have front-row seats."

CHAPTER 68

Alison Quinn walked by their tent with a roll of toilet paper as she headed downhill. Keira lay still in the tent, watching her through the screen. *She's up to something,* she thought. When Alison had disappeared into the draw, she elbowed Nathan.

"What?" he whispered.

"She's at it again," she said quietly.

"Who? Alison?"

"Yes," she said. "She's going to the bathroom again."

"So what?" asked Nathan. "They brought extra toilet paper, and nobody is bothering us on this side."

"That's too many times."

"You're not exactly one to talk."

"Even for me, that's not normal," said Keira. "She's not drinking enough water to be going to the bathroom every forty minutes or so."

"Maybe she's drinking a lot of water in her tent?"

"She's not," said Keira. "I've been watching her."

Nathan sat up. "What's going on?"

"I don't know," she said. "I just think it's odd."

He shrugged and gave her that look.

"Trust me, she's up to something. I know it. I can tell."

"Then do something about it."

She sat up next to him, peering through the screen. "Like what?"

"I don't know. Follow her. Pretend you have to go to the bathroom, too," he said, retrieving a large Ziploc bag with two flattened toilet paper rolls from the corner of the tent. He opened the bag and handed her a roll. "You'll drive yourself crazy all day if you don't."

She stared at him for a few seconds before snatching the roll from her hands. "I'm telling you," said Keira. "I may not catch her, but I'm telling you."

"Fine," he said, smiling. "Let me know what you find."

"What are you going to do?" she asked, kneeling in front of the screen.

"Stay here with Owen and wait for you to come back. It would look even weirder if we both showed up with toilet paper rolls."

"That's not what I meant. What if she's up to something like drugs or worse?"

"What could be worse?"

"I don't know," said Keira.

"You should get going," said Nathan. "She'll finish up by the time you get there. Unless she's doing some serious business out there. Don't blame me if you see something you can't unsee."

"She didn't bring a shovel."

"Some soldiers don't bury their dead."

"That's disgusting," she said.

"Just preparing you for the worst."

"Thanks. I'll be right back," said Keira, unzipping the tent and stepping into the cool, dry air.

She walked heel-to-toe over the hard ground, trying her best to avoid placing the thick soles of her hiking boots on anything that might snap. Ducking under larger tree branches and pressing between the thick brush, Keira managed to get close enough to watch Alison, before a dead branch betrayed her presence.

Alison had been sitting on the ground, mostly concealed by a thick brownish-green bush. Keira could see the top of her shoulders and head. She was hunched over, facing down. For a moment, Keira flushed with embarrassment—it truly looked like Alison was engaged in private business. But then the branch snapped and Alison quickly stood up, fumbling with the toilet paper roll grasped between her hands. Keira's eyes darted to the toilet paper, convinced she saw something stuffed inside the cardboard roll.

"Sorry," said Keira, meeting her eyes. "I didn't hear you walk past the tent. Sort of spaced out walking down here. I'll go back. Sorry about that."

"That's fine," said Alison, shifting the roll into her right hand and tucking it into one of her cargo pockets. "I thought I had to go, but it was sort of a false alarm. I pee a lot when I'm nervous, or at least I think I have to pee a lot."

Keira wished she'd left her own roll back in the tent. She could have asked to borrow Alison's, putting Quinn's wife in an awkward position. There was nothing left to do, except act normal.

"Me, too," said Keira. "I've tried to hold back on the water, but I don't want to get dehydrated. It's kind of a losing battle."

"I've been drinking as much as possible," said Alison. "David always stresses how important it is to stay hydrated in the field. I'm paying the price."

And lying. She's definitely hiding something. Could it be a phone? Keira hadn't heard her talking, but maybe she hadn't been as quiet as she thought sneaking down the draw. *Jesus.* She could get all of them killed.

"Well, it breaks up the routine," said Keira. "Look at it that way. This is pretty much the grand total of my entertainment for the day."

They shared a strained laugh.

"I'll get out of your way," said Alison. "See you up top."

"Yep," said Keira, continuing down the draw until Alison disappeared.

She crouched behind a dense bush and waited a few minutes before heading toward the tent. At the campsite, she nodded at Alison and ducked into the tent, nestling next to her husband.

"Well?" whispered Nathan. "Is she smoking meth?"

"Worse," she whispered. "I think she's using some kind of mobile device."

Nathan tensed and turned to face her. "Really? Did you see her talking on one?"

"No. But she wasn't out there to go to the bathroom, and I swear I saw something stuffed inside her toilet roll. She was pretty flustered," said Keira. "If she's using a mobile device, we could be in serious trouble."

Nathan sat up. "Maybe we should spend the rest of the day outside of the tent so we can keep a better eye on her."

"We need to do more than that."

"Unless you plan on confronting her, there's not much we can do besides keep a close eye on her," he said, grabbing the MP-20. "I'll work my way to the top of the draw so nobody can sneak up on us. You'll be her new bathroom buddy."

"This is crazy," she said. "We're letting a little social anxiety get in the way of our safety."

"What are you saying? What do you suggest?"

"Why don't you say something to her?"

"If she had a phone stashed in the toilet paper roll, I guarantee she moved it," said Nathan. "I'm not about to shake her down at gunpoint. Her husband is the only reason we're alive."

Owen stirred on the other side of Keira. Their son had long ago given up trying to keep himself busy. Like the rest of them, he slept most of the day.

"What's going on?" asked Owen.

Keira held her index finger to her lips and whispered, "Nothing to worry about, sweetie."

"Everything's fine, buddy," added Nathan.

"I heard you talking about Alison's phone," whispered Owen.

"Well, we don't know if she has one," said Keira.

"She has one," said Owen. "I saw her texting with it before you woke up."

"Are you sure?" asked Nathan.

"Pretty sure," he said. "I peeked out of the back of the tent. She was looking at something that glowed. It was still a little dark."

"Why didn't you say something?" asked Keira.

"What do you mean?" asked Owen. "What's the big deal?"

"Nothing, sweetie," said Keira. "We don't get any mobile reception up here, so I thought it was a strange that she could use a device. It's not a big deal."

"Then why was Dad talking about shaking her down at gunpoint?"

"Your father was joking. We're all kind of desperate to make a call, but our phones don't work."

"What about the satphones?" pressed Owen.

"Those are for emergencies, and they're really expensive to use," she said.

"Then why don't you ask to borrow hers?" asked her son. "She seems like a friendly person."

He'd been a lot easier to lie to when he was little. Now he was a little logic-driven machine. Smirking at Nathan, Keira said, "I think that's a great idea, Owen."

CHAPTER 69

Quinn stood next to one of the AL-TAC vehicles assigned to tonight's convoy, overseeing the final inspection by one of the motor transport section's staff sergeants. Motor transport had pulled four AL-TACs out of the battalion's "used car lot" early in the morning, working feverishly to prepare the vehicles for a 1300-hour appointment with regiment to receive an upgraded electronic countermeasures package. The installation took two to three hours, followed immediately by the ammunition onload, which had to be inspected by the battalion commanding officer.

Quinn's involvement in the day's preparation had been limited to the motor transport garage, where the bay doors remained closed to keep him hidden from view. Every function related to the launch of the convoy would be handled by members of the Enhanced Counterinsurgency Platoon, spearheaded by Second Lieutenant Zachary Karr—under the watchful eye of Staff Sergeant Cantrell.

ECI platoon had been the logical choice to run the convoy for several reasons, the most important being that most of ECI already knew about Quinn's unusual predicament. The fewer Marines involved, the better—for everyone. The last thing the battalion commander or Quinn needed was a visit by base security, with actionable intelligence. He'd lay low and let his Marines run the show, keeping his fingers crossed that the provost marshal had bigger things to worry about than the increasingly elusive Captain Quinn. Things like dead bodies and explosions.

The improvised explosive device he'd rigged behind Cerberus team's SUV had detonated during the midmorning, putting the base under indefinite lockdown. Cantrell's Marines had created a simple pressure-cooker bomb filled with black powder and ball bearings—a painfully simple task that every counterinsurgency-trained Marine learns during ECI specialty school. Quinn had taken a huge risk leaving the IED unattended. Anyone could have stumbled across the SUV. He'd attached the trigger wire to the trunk, figuring only another Cerberus team would get that curious. Still a gamble, but apparently worth the risk.

Responding security teams found two men dead behind the Echo-team vehicle—one with a curious stab wound to the back of the neck. They also discovered a shrapnel-riddled, government-contractor-registered SUV in a parking lot at Las Pulgas. Needless to say, the base was in full lockdown at the moment, which suited Quinn fine. Nobody gets in, nobody gets out—except for regularly scheduled convoys to Marine Corps Air Station Yuma. By this time tomorrow, he'd be two-hundred-plus miles away, with nobody the wiser.

His satphone chirped from a shelf on the other side of the garage. Since the phone couldn't be used inside, his Marines had run a cable from the phone's network port to a compact communications array located outside the back of the garage. The phone was only as portable as the length of the cable, which extended no farther than the opposite side of the garage. Quinn walked between tactical vehicles and retrieved the phone, following the cable into a small office. He didn't recognize the satellite number, though he could tell that the call did not originate from another DTSC phone, but from a commercial satellite network. He pressed the phone's screen, accepting the call.

"Aurelio's Pizza," said Quinn.

"Shitty pizza," said his wife. "I have a problem."

"What's going on?" asked Quinn. "Make it quick. Your phone is on the clock."

"I'll make this as quick as possible. Your new friend, a.k.a. Nathan Fisher, insists I have a mobile device. He's demanding to search my stuff. Our stuff. What the hell is up with this guy?"

Shit. Trouble from the absolute last source he would have expected.

"He's been through a lot. I'm sure he's just being a little paranoid," said Quinn. "Let me talk to him."

"He's not the only one who's been ripped out of his house and summarily banished from life," she said. "We're all equally screwed here."

"I know. I know. We just need to keep it together until we get to Yuma."

"It was a bad idea putting me out here with them," said Alison. "They watch me go to the bathroom. The kid spies on me. It's really weird, David."

"We only have a few more hours to go. You have to make it work. I can't drive out and pick you up. I'm kind of trapped myself. Let me talk to Nathan."

"Fine," said Alison. "Make sure he backs the fuck off or I'll walk to San Mateo. I'm not joking."

A few seconds later, Nathan's voice came through.

"David, I'm sorry, but my wife and son swear she's hiding something. They think she's texting. I understand the temptation, and I apologize for shaking her down, but this is my family's safety at stake."

"Nathan, she understands the stakes. Trust me on that. I guarantee you she doesn't have a phone. She had one burner device left when my Marines extracted her from the barracks, and she happily gave that to me. She knows exactly what happens when you use a phone. They almost nabbed her at the barracks after she called me."

"Can you talk her into letting us search her stuff?" asked Nathan, lowering his voice to continue. "Look. I don't know what my wife thinks she saw, or my son. I just know that Keira isn't going to let this go. Alison's not the only one who suggested we walk out of here. If your wife's not hiding anything, I can't see why she'd be opposed to letting us take a look. I know it's intrusive, but I think it's important."

"She'll never talk to me again."

"If she's using a device, you run that same risk. I guarantee they can get people on base if they want to. We've only seen the tip of the iceberg. Base security can't monitor the entire base perimeter at once."

"Can you back off this? Just until tonight?"

"What if they come for us before tonight?"

"I can have four armored vehicles up there in five minutes," said Quinn, stretching the truth. While he could undoubtedly deploy the vehicles immediately at any point this afternoon, he wouldn't have ammunition until much later in the day.

"I hope we can last five minutes," said Nathan. "I'll take the heat on this one."

"Thank you, Nathan," said Quinn. "Let me talk to Alison. We're cutting it close on the phone."

"Hold on."

"Thank you," said Alison when she came back on. "I appreciate not being thrown under the bus, but if they want to search my stuff that bad, they can help themselves."

He wanted to scream at her. Why the hell hadn't she just let them look, then? It took him a moment to reach the point where he could respond rationally.

"All right. Thank you," he said, pausing again. "Once it's dark, I'll take them on a test run through your area. We'll pick you up and bring you back to the garage for dinner. Play nice until then."

"I love you," she said. "I'll be good. They seem like nice people. I just got a little frazzled."

"Under the circumstances, I think you're holding up just fine," said Quinn. "I love you, too. I'm signing off."

"See you later."

Quinn disconnected the call and stepped into the garage. The staff sergeant and his handpicked team of mechanics stood together behind the four vehicles.

"Captain," said the staff sergeant, "you got four squared-away AL-TACs."

He headed in their direction. "Thank you, Staff Sergeant. I appreciate your help—and discretion."

"Not a problem, sir. Sounds like we're supporting a good cause," he said. "We'll be here until you step off for Yuma."

Quinn nodded, forcing back his emotions. Every Marine in the battalion was like a close relative or friend. Eager to help, with no questions asked, and nothing expected in return. He'd miss this. For a brief moment he resented Fisher for taking this away, before remembering the bigger picture.

Nathan's father had faithfully served with Quinn's dad years ago, supporting his command and even saving his life—more than once. Nathan was part of that family, too, and Quinn was doing exactly what was expected of him as a Marine. Faithfully serving the family, or the Marine Corps motto, *Semper fidelis*.

CHAPTER 70

Mason Flagg entered the elaborately decorated elevator, wishing he'd received the good news about an hour earlier. He could have ordered the jet to return to San Diego and avoided this hastily assembled inquisition. Flagg despised these face-to-face meetings, both astonished and angry that some people still felt the necessity. Of course, if the operation had recovered smoothly after Almeda's assassination, none of them would feel compelled to "drive home the importance of the mission's success" with a personal gathering. He had himself to blame for this waste of time and money. He hoped it would go quickly. Given the news that had just arrived, he expected to be back in the air within ninety minutes.

His escort pressed the button labeled "Upper" and stepped out, leaving him alone in the elevator.

"They're expecting you," said the thick-necked man as the door closed. "You'll see them gathered in front of the fieldstone fireplace."

Flagg barely acknowledged him. He found it odd that the Cerberus executive committee allowed their clients to run security at these gatherings. Their clients paid hundreds of millions of dollars for Cerberus to field small armies around the world, but they didn't feel comfortable employing the same operatives to protect them for a few hours in Aspen, Colorado.

He turned and checked his appearance in the elevator's mirrored wall. A dark-gray suit with black turtleneck was standard dress for a meeting like this. Functional, yet formal enough without the tie to project a professional, stylish appearance. The only thing missing was his pistol. He hadn't bothered to bring it, knowing that Burridge's security team wouldn't let him leave the airport with a weapon. In fact, he'd traveled alone tonight because they refused to let Cerberus executive security guards off the jet.

Flagg hardly felt the elevator move, the motion so smooth, and he could barely tell whether the trip had started or ended. When the doors didn't open within the next few seconds, he assumed the car had just left the garage level, transporting him to his destination. The digital elevator display instantly changed to "UPPER," and the door smoothly slid open, revealing a world beyond the reach of nearly every person on the planet.

Elegant woodwork, inlaid granite, and intricately carved marble covered every surface, horizontal and vertical, easily making this the most richly appointed room he'd ever seen. The furnishings matched the exquisite setting, completing the scene, but nothing could match what he saw beyond the floor-to-cathedral-ceiling windows. Aspen Mountain, still snowcapped in June, stood magnificent in the fading light of the evening. The majestic mountain and the surrounding peaks reflected a deep-blue color rarely seen outside the Rockies. For a brief moment, Flagg stood motionless, thoroughly impressed by what money could buy. He let go of the thought and stepped onto the wide pine-planked floor, ready to go to war.

"Mason!" called Saul Prichard, his immediate boss at Cerberus. "We're over here."

Flagg nodded and headed in Prichard's direction, taking in the crowd gathered with drinks around chairs and couches facing a massive two-sided fireplace. A crackling fire blazed from one end of the hearth to the other. The fireplace looked large enough to accommodate a spit-cooked buffalo—or eight of the wealthiest men and women in the United States.

Prichard wasn't one of their number. He was merely a midlevel executive who served as a liaison between the operation leader (OL) and the company's clients. Executive liaisons were typically sourced from the operational leader ranks. Flagg had twice turned down a promotion headed for this position, preferring to stay in the field. Prichard was a glorified politician, balancing the unrealistic expectations of their clients with the reality of field operations. He spent most of his time babysitting.

Gary Silva stood next to Prichard, raising a martini glass in salute of Flagg's arrival. Silva represented Sentinel Group, Cerberus International's parent company and a significant contributor to the One Nation Coalition. He was harmless enough, his role at meetings like this confined mainly to stressing the "importance" of meeting client expectations. Like these meetings themselves, Silva essentially served no purpose that Flagg could discern.

The usual suspects were all in place. In fact, every last one of them had flown in for the meeting, which didn't bode well for his early departure. Tyler Wegman, fifth-term congressman from Kansas, and Nancy Mailer, fourth-term senator from Colorado, sat together on one of the couches facing away from the view. He'd have to work hard to get out of here on schedule with this self-important duo sipping free booze. There was nothing worse or more time-consuming than enduring the prattle of people who thought they mattered.

Graduating upward in the hierarchy, he glanced toward Jack Bernal, head of Cal Farms United, the agricultural aggregate that controlled a sizable chunk of California's produce and livestock business. Jack's influence would be crucial in the upcoming fight to keep California in the union. Without a unified agricultural business front in California, secessionists would have a hard time selling state self-sufficiency to the public. The state could produce enough food to feed itself, but not without CFU's support.

Next came Alexei Petrov. The Russian oligarch turned Texan had bought AgraTex Industries in 2017, singlehandedly triggering the New Dust Bowl a few years later. Years of corrupt water-rights mismanagement had already drained the southern Ogallala Aquifer to the point of collapse by the time Petrov arrived. The Russian wasted no time in tipping the scale by purchasing thousands of acres located above the aquifer in northern Texas, and pumping it dry to irrigate his poorly timed investment. With the Rio Grande already running at critically low levels, drought-racked fields outside of Petrov's domain in the south and central areas dried up within a few seasons. Massive dust storms swept across most of Texas, spreading to Oklahoma as the southern basin of Ogallala Aquifer quit giving water.

Even after initiating this major ecological disaster, Petrov still hadn't finished wrecking the American landscape. Questionable land purchases in northern Kansas and eastern Colorado put him in a position to expand AgraTex north, putting a severe strain on the northern basin of the Ogallala Aquifer. Facing stiffer water-management policies in the states served by the aquifer, he conspired with state politicians and landowners across the Southwest to divert water from the Colorado River to his beleaguered agricultural investments, ultimately triggering the "water wars" that would turn Arizona, Utah, New Mexico, and large swaths of western Colorado into an area collectively known as "The Wasteland."

Most Americans were blissfully unaware that a reckless Russian oil baron had caused more damage to the United States in the 1920s than the entire Soviet Empire during the Cold War. Ironically, Petrov's petro-billions couldn't buy into the Texas oil cartel, which was ruthlessly controlled by John Peralta, CEO of the American Energy Institute.

Peralta stood to lose the most if California cut economic ties to the union and took the final steps toward energy independence. That independence would be partially financed by significant tax increases levied against the petroleum industry in the state, accompanied by burdensome regulations. With a significant slice of AEI's business portfolio invested in the California petroleum industry, AEI stood to lose billions of dollars every year to the changes suggested by secessionist politicians. Ethan Burridge, the majority stake owner of AEI, wasn't about to let his California billions slip away. Burridge had worked everyone in the room to pool financial resources and broker the deal to unleash Cerberus on the secession crisis.

"Thank you for coming on short notice," said Burridge, motioning toward a mahogany bar tended by one of his security officers. "Can I get you something to drink?"

"I'll have sparkling water with lime, please," said Flagg. "I need to remain clearheaded. I just received encouraging news from one of my sources."

"I would hope so," said Petrov. "I'm growing tired of bad news."

Flagg ignored Petrov altogether, staying focused on Burridge. "Primary and secondary targets will be terminated tonight," said Flagg. "Intelligence sources have uncovered a very unique opportunity."

"We've heard this before," said Petrov. "How many times?"

He shot a nasty look at Petrov, then shifted it to Peralta when he piled on with "Too many times." The American Energy Institute CEO avoided his glare, but the goddamn Russian stood his ground, staring at him defiantly.

"I've dealt with worse than the likes of you before," said Petrov, who then waved his tumbler of vodka at the group as a whole. "I'm not even sure why we continue to deal with these people," he said, nodding at Flagg. "I told you this could be outsourced to a better group."

"Like the one you sent to kill Almeda?" asked Flagg. "My people made short work of those amateurs."

"They got the job done," said Petrov, stiffening.

Prichard locked eyes with Flagg and subtly shook his head.

"That's right," said Petrov. "Listen to your masters."

Burridge laughed. "Jesus, Alexei."

"What?" asked the Russian, slamming down the rest of his drink.

"Flagg's people killed Almeda. Not yours. He cleaned up your mess," said Burridge, pointing at Flagg.

"It doesn't matter," Flagg said. "What's done is done. Almeda's assassination unexpectedly escalated the timeline, and we've experienced a few glitches getting the operation back on track."

"A few?" asked Petrov.

"A few very unnecessary glitches, thanks to you," Flagg snapped. "But I don't get paid to dwell on mistakes. I get paid to fix them."

"*Paid* is the key term here," said Petrov. "We pay you. You work for us. Keep that in mind."

"Can we move on?" asked Senator Mailer.

"You're not paying for this," Petrov said. "I am. And I don't like it when my investments underperform."

"You should have thought of that before buying AgraTex—at the height of the worst drought in US history," said Congressman Wegman, eliciting nervous laughter from the rest.

"All right. That's enough," said Burridge. "We're all appreciably nervous about the past few days. What are you doing to iron this out, Mason? Sounds like we may have dragged you out here at the wrong time."

Flagg nodded, accepting his drink from the stocky, shoulder-holster-equipped bartender.

"Highly classified Department of Defense server message traffic between Second Battalion, Fourth Marines commanding officer and First Marine Division indicate that a convoy will leave Camp Pendleton later tonight, headed for Marine Corps Air Station Yuma. The convoy was added to the First Division schedule last night, outside of the regular convoy pattern. The convoy manifest lists Captain David Quinn as the commander, along with twenty-four members of the Enhanced Counterinsurgency Platoon assigned to Quinn's infantry company.

"Every aspect of this convoy's deployment is unusual. The timing. Quinn's assignment. From what we can tell, he should be restricted to base, answering the provost marshal's questions about Fisher," said Flagg. "And this is the only way off base for either of them. San Diego County PD has effectively blockaded Camp Pendleton from the outside, and base security has locked it down from the inside."

Flagg took a long sip of the sparking water.

"Quinn could not have ducked the Provost Marshall's Office this long without support from his battalion commander. We strongly suspect that the convoy was scheduled on Quinn's behalf, and that all of the targets will be onboard."

"What kind of convoy are we talking about?" asked Prichard.

"Four AL-TAC armored vehicles," said Flagg. "Standard armament profiles. Interstate 8 is considered a high-risk transit area due to its proximity to the border. With the right combination of weapons, we can take the convoy down."

Gary Silva shook his head. "Shit. That's a whole different ball game."

"What's the downside to letting them reach Yuma and pursuing them outside of California?" asked Peralta.

"They could disappear after Yuma," said Flagg, "and reappear at an inopportune time—in the wrong hands. We know the CLM is aware of Fisher. They undoubtedly hijacked a police drone to protect him. His testimony about what he saw at the Del Mar beach could be used against us. CLM has proven highly adept at using the media to their advantage. In their hands, Fisher could set One Nation's timetable back significantly."

"Harboring a cop killer could turn the public against them," said Bernal.

"I don't think so," said Burridge. "The California public never heard a big-industry conspiracy theory they didn't like, and the CLM has been working that fertile ground for the better part of the past decade. I think we need to put this Fisher thing to rest once and for all. We'll have all of the primary targets in one place. After that, we mop up the parents and consider any additional liabilities. I want this operation back on track."

"You better be sure they're in those vehicles," said Senator Mailer. "Wiping out a Marine convoy is a big deal."

Flagg grinned. "The secessionists will stop at nothing to liberate California from the oppressive federal government. Why should they let the deaths of a few federal enforcers get in the way? Have you heard some of the more radical CLM activists speak about the military occupation of the state? I'm confident we can spin the convoy attack against them."

"First, you have to take out the convoy," said Petrov. "Of that, I am not so confident."

Flagg ignored the comment, nodding at Burridge. "Mr. Burridge, if you don't mind, I'd like to fly back to San Diego immediately. I'd prefer to coordinate this in person."

"I agree," said Burridge. "Let's get you back to the airport."

Saul Prichard followed Burridge and Flagg to the elevator. Burridge stopped them when they were out of earshot of the group.

"Are you sure this will work?" asked Burridge. "Four armored vehicles sounds like a challenge to me. I'm half tempted to let them get to Yuma and have you pursue them outside of the state. The wastelands can be an unforgiving place."

"That's completely up to you, Mr. Burridge," said Flagg, glancing at Prichard, who nodded in agreement. "My primary concern is that we don't know what's waiting for them in Yuma. There's something else I didn't want to bring up with the group, especially around Petrov."

"Don't worry about Petrov," said Burridge. "If the guy wasn't so easy to coax money out of, he would have preceded the governor."

"This discovery carries a risk to Petrov's livelihood, which makes me very worried about him."

"What did you find?" asked Burridge.

"Nathan Fisher received two degrees from UC Davis. A bachelor's degree in civil engineering, followed by a master's in water-resource management."

"We already know he's a water-reclamation engineer, specializing in toilet-to-tap systems," said Pritchard.

"But that wasn't his primary focus in school. He wrote his master's thesis on the Colorado River crisis, specifically on how to solve the water-rights controversy sparked by our Russian friend. The paper's conclusion is particularly radical, focusing heavily on the need for the Bureau of Reclamation to either convince the upper-basin states to let more water flow through the dams or seize control of the dams by force."

Burridge's eyebrows lifted. "Pretty hawkish attitude for a mild-mannered water engineer."

Flagg shrugged. "There was no denying the strategic importance of those dams, even for a pacifist grad student. Fisher spent three summers interning at various dams, pumping plants and aqueduct points along the river, studying some highly classified infrastructure systems. I read the entire seventy-page document on the flight, and Fisher displays a disturbingly deep knowledge of these systems. If I were running CLM's operations, I'd be keen to enlist his aid, or bargain for it by guaranteeing his safety."

"Enlist his aid for what, exactly?" asked Burridge.

"To help them restore previously agreed-upon water-flow levels to Southern California. That's been one of CLM's primary goals from the beginning. Combining the current level of water production from the state's desalination plants with long-developed water-conservation habits would leave California with an abundance of water if historic Colorado River flows were restored."

"Good luck to them with that," said Burridge. "I still don't see how Fisher's knowledge of the system would help them, beyond serving as a technical consultant to lobbying efforts, which we all know would go nowhere."

"Exactly. Negotiations and lobbying are pointless at this stage in the game. The Bureau of Reclamation hasn't lifted a finger since the upper basin turned off the water, and the politicians that matter are all comfortably in Petrov's pockets. But there's another way to restore the water flow. Concrete and steel bend to a different kind of pressure than politicians."

Burridge considered his last sentence for several moments.

"They wouldn't dare," said Burridge.

"Maybe. Maybe not. But if I was drawing up plans to bring the Colorado River back to California by less than peaceful means, and wanted to maximize my resources, I'd want Fisher on my team to identify which dams strategically packed the biggest punch. Trust me, you don't want this guy falling into CLM hands."

"Very well. We'll take out the convoy," said Burridge. "And keep this aspect of your assessment out of the reports. I don't need Petrov running his own personal war outside of the council. Losing control of the Colorado River water will hit him hard."

"You can be assured of my discretion. The road ends tonight for Fisher and Quinn."

This earned appreciative grunts from Burridge and Pritchard, and would've served as a perfect exit line if the damn elevator wasn't so slow. Flagg filled the time by shaking each of their hands in turn, before at last stepping onto the elevator and repeatedly pressing the garage-level button. He had far more important things to do.

PART V

CHAPTER 71

Nathan Fisher stood next to his AL-TAC, encased in full combat gear. He checked his watch and waited for Quinn to finish talking to the vehicle commanders. The small huddle broke apart quietly a few moments later, each leader returning to his assigned vehicle. Quinn jogged toward Nathan, stopping a few feet away.

"How are Owen and Keira doing?" asked Quinn.

"Owen looks like he may be having too much fun. He wants to sit in the turret."

"He can check out the turret when we get to Yuma, if he's still awake. You have a good kid on your hands. I see a future Marine in the making."

"Please don't say that in front of my wife."

Quinn laughed. "I won't. She looks about as happy as Alison right now."

"Keira will feel better once we're out of California. I don't know about your wife."

"This wasn't how she saw the week ending."

"None of us did. Has your dad reached my parents?"

"Not yet. He made a few stops along the way to pick up some friends. They'll link up either late tomorrow or the next day. He has a call scheduled with your dad for nine a.m. Eight a.m. our time. We can send your dad a digital message right before the call and let him know to call my satphone as soon as they finish. Sorry I haven't been able to make a call happen sooner. The survivalist compound hiding them has strict rules about communications. Someone has to drive them to Missoula to make calls."

"As long as they're safe, I'm happy. I hate to think I dragged them into this mess," said Nathan.

"We all came along willingly. Except my wife," said Quinn, grinning. "Speaking of disgruntled wives, we probably shouldn't hold this show up any longer."

"Thanks again for all of this," said Nathan.

"Don't thank me until we get there."

Nathan stepped onto the metal running board under his door and grabbed an internal handle, lifting his heavy ballistic-armor-sheathed body into the rear passenger seat. Once situated in the oversize harness-equipped chair, he pulled the door shut, sealing his family inside the AL-TAC. The armored door's internal mechanism clicked, followed by a faint hiss.

"What was that?" asked Nathan, holding on to the door handle.

David Quinn turned his head in the front seat ahead of him and leaned to the left so he could see Nathan. "The vehicle automatically achieves positive pressure when all of the doors and hatches are shut. Protection against any type of biological or chemical attack. Works wonders if we hit a skunk. You won't smell a thing."

"Great."

"Ready to go dark?" asked Quinn.

"Hold on. I need to snap in to the harness."

After securing the final harness point, Nathan twisted far enough in the constrained seat to take in the cramped rear-troop compartment behind him. Two seats were bolted to each side of the vehicle, facing the tight center aisle. Keira and Owen, wearing head-conforming ballistic helmets, sat across from each other in the seats nearest him, strapped into full-vest harnesses. Alison Quinn was locked into the seat beyond Keira, looking at the empty station next to Owen.

"You guys okay?" he said.

"How long is the trip?" asked Keira.

"Two and a half hours. Roughly."

"I'm feeling a little claustrophobic," she said.

Quinn's voice echoed inside his helmet. "The harness system takes some getting used to. The vests are attached to the vehicle's gyroscopic impact and maneuver mitigation system—GIMMS, for short—which will keep your body comfortably in one place should the vehicle make any drastic maneuvers. Not that I'm expecting any. If you slam your helmet back, GIMMS will stabilize your head as well, so if you get sleepy and your head flies back, don't panic if the seat holds your head in place."

"How do you get your head loose?" asked Keira.

"Raise either hand and pull the red handle directly above you," said Quinn. "This deactivates GIMMS for two seconds. Pull down on the handle three times consecutively to deactivate the system."

"Why would you need to do that?" asked Nathan.

"In case the vehicle is disabled and you need to get out," said Quinn. "Not that we'll have to worry about that. Ready to kill the lights?"

"Do you have to turn them off?" asked Keira.

"We'll use red lights until we get to El Centro. Beyond that, we run tactical. The cabin goes pitch-black. Night vision only. Each of your helmets has built-in night-vision capability. Pull down on the goggles built into the front of your helmet and you'll be in business. Any more questions before we step off?"

Nathan reached back, grabbed one of Owen's hands, and pulled it toward the center of the compartment, where Keira grasped them with both of *her* hands. She shook her head.

"This is crazy," she said.

"This is awesome," said Owen.

"Crazy awesome," Nathan agreed, turning his head to nod at Quinn. "Let's do this."

"Roger that," said Quinn, and the vehicle's cabin went pitch-black.

Gradually, the subdued red-lighting system illuminated the cabin. In the new red glow, Nathan scanned his surroundings. To his immediate left, a pair of legs dangled from a restrictive-looking mechanical harness that held Corporal Reading in the AL-TAC's armored turret. Just beyond the corporal's legs, Sergeant Graves pressed one of several dimly illuminated touch screens imbedded into the back of the driver's seat. Quinn had explained that Graves monitored and controlled the AL-TAC's sophisticated electronics systems and sensors from that console. In the driver's seat in front of Graves, Private First Class Artigas popped an energy drink can, taking a long sip.

"Fueled up and ready to go, sir," said Artigas, draining the rest of the can.

"Raider, this is Raider actual," said Quinn. "Stand by to roll."

Nathan heard the words, but they didn't come through his helmet's headset. Quinn must have switched to a different communications net to talk to the other vehicles.

"Raider One-One, lead the way," said Quinn.

Moments later, the vehicle lurched forward, jarring the family's hands apart. He turned forward in his seat and watched them follow a set of red taillights. Nathan glanced through the narrow ballistic window set into the door next to him, seeing several Marines give them the thumbs-up as they pulled away. The vehicle picked up speed, passing through the motor-pool gate and continuing toward San Mateo Boulevard.

He'd listened to Quinn's departure briefing an hour ago, taking in as many details of their trip as he could absorb. The convoy would avoid the San Diego County PD blockade by exiting Camp Pendleton through Naval Weapons Station Fallbrook, directly east of the base. The ammunition depot was off-limits to Camp Pendleton traffic, so the police didn't set up a checkpoint beyond its infrequently traveled gate. Their convoy would travel a circuitous route through the Marine Corps base, connecting with Ammunition Road, which would take them straight through the weapons station. Once in the town of Fallbrook, they would wind south through the sleeping community until they reached Route 76.

Quinn still hadn't decided if they would follow Route 76 southeast through the burned-out mountain regions bordering the Anza-Borrego Desert, or take Interstate 15 straight to Interstate 8. The mountain route was decidedly low profile, but most of the area had been permanently abandoned after two decades of continual fires, and the seventy-five-mile stretch of two-lane road hadn't been properly maintained for years. While they would undoubtedly avoid detection, they ran the risk of hitting an impassable section and having to divert back toward the coast.

Interstate 15 was the quickest and most reliable option, but traveling any appreciable distance on the interstate was bound to attract law-enforcement attention. While the San Diego County PD had no legal authority to stop them, current tensions at Camp Pendleton created an unpredictable environment. Even if the police decided not to interfere, the convoy's location and route would be broadcast on unencrypted channels for anyone to hear.

"David," said Nathan, "have you given any more thought to the route?"

"I'm leaning toward Interstate 15. We can turn east on Route 52 toward Santee and cut through the eastern basin cities. We'll be motoring east on Interstate 8 before Cerberus can mount a response. The mountain route would add another hour to the trip, and there's no guarantee we'll get through."

"What if Cerberus has people stationed east of San Diego?" asked Nathan.

"Then we get to put these babies to the test. My money is on the unstoppable AL-TAC," said Quinn, high-fiving the driver.

"Amen," said the sergeant next to him.

"You really believe that, Sergeant Graves?" asked Nathan.

"Hell yeah," said Graves. "I did two tours in the sandbox riding around in these beauties. They're virtually unstoppable."

"He's right," said Quinn. "The V-hull bottom is designed to deflect IED blasts detonating directly beneath the vehicle, but that's only in the unlikely event an IED gets past our electronic countermeasure system. ECMS transmits on nearly every radio frequency conceivable to pre-detonate roadside bombs, plus it sends a minor electromagnetic pulse wave every five seconds in a sixty-degree arc forward of the vehicle. The EMP generates enough juice in ground wires to set off nearby explosives. We obviously can't activate ECMS until we get out in the boonies."

"Why?" asked Nathan's son.

"Because we'd open every garage door and turn on every television within a city block," said Quinn.

"That's cool," said Owen.

"I agree with you, young man," said Quinn, "but the EMP tends to mess with delicate circuits. We'd also do a lot of damage."

"Oh. I guess that wouldn't be good."

"Not unless you're traveling through enemy territory, then who gives a shit," said Sergeant Graves.

"Ooh rah to that," said the gunner, lowering a hand down to catch a hand slap.

"Watch the language, gents," said Quinn.

"It's fine," said Keira. "Not every day your son gets to ride in the Batmobile. A little colorful language adds to the experience."

Quinn turned to look at Keira, who shrugged and winked at him.

"This is better than the Batmobile," said Owen.

"Amen to that, little dude," said Sergeant Graves, reaching back to give him a high five. "Captain Quinn hasn't seen half of what this thing can do. Last time we were in Khost, the tali-rats threw like ten RPGs at us at once. This thing ate 'em up like it was nothing."

"I shit myself on that one," said the gunner. "Released my harness and dropped it into Corporal Hickam's lap."

Graves laughed. "That's right! I thought the two of you might get married after that."

Everyone laughed, except for Nathan. "What do you mean by 'ate 'em up'?"

"That's actually classified information," said Quinn. "Sorry."

"But everyone was all right?" asked Nathan.

"Trust me. You're safe inside this vehicle. Very safe," said Quinn. "At three point three million dollars a pop, they're guaranteed to keep Marines safe from anything the haji can throw at us."

Quinn's words did little to ease Nathan's concerns. They weren't dealing with Afghani insurgents on horseback. Far from it. As the ten-ton vehicle accelerated smoothly out of San Mateo, Nathan struggled to push these uncertain thoughts out of his head.

CHAPTER 72

Nick Leeds fidgeted on the ground, unable to find a comfortable prone position in the observation post. With his elbows grinding the rocky surface, he raised his upper body high enough to peer through the tripod-mounted scope. The synthetic daylight image seen through the eyepiece was overlaid with mapping graphics, showing the precise location of the road and all the terrain features. It also gave him information about their arriving target. It was moving at a speed of seventy-three miles per hour, 1.2 miles away and closing.

A series of Night Raven drones had tracked the convoy since it had emerged from the El Centro city limits. Observers in the city notified the Raven teams, which had been spaced ten miles apart along the forty-three-mile stretch separating El Centro from the ambush point. The final handoff had occurred three minutes ago to a drone hand-launched by Leeds twenty minutes before. The drone, currently under the control of Dan Vega, would fly a circular pattern above the ambush zone, giving him a bird's-eye view to coordinate the final stages of the attack.

If all went well with this high-tech ambush, coordination of a close ground assault would not be necessary. He could only hope. The technical specifications provided for the armored light tactical vehicle had been sparse on details surrounding the platform's countermeasure system. Anecdotal evidence from Afghanistan pointed to the distinct possibility that the missiles might not be enough. He had prepared a string of lower-tech options to take out the convoy, if the missiles failed.

"Leeds, this is Kline," said his lead tactical operator. "I just ran a final diagnostic check on the charges. We're looking good."

"And the men in the holes?"

"They're not happy."

"I didn't think they would be," said Leeds. "That's why I didn't mention that part of the plan until we arrived."

"I'm showing thirty-four seconds," said Kline. "I'll be in touch when this is over."

"Happy hunting."

"I'll be happy when we're out of here."

Leeds felt the same way. His team was severely exposed on the desolate stretch of land. Even though he had every advantage in this fight—surprise, high ground, concealed positions—he felt vulnerable and isolated lying on the small rocky bluff overlooking the interstate a few hundred yards away. It wouldn't take much to bleed his force into this dry landscape. Fortunately for him, the convoy didn't have air support. Once he locked the Marines into place within the kill zone, nothing could save them.

"Leeds, this is Vega. The convoy is twenty seconds from Javelin engagement range. Recommend that the missile teams start searching for targets."

The Javelin missiles had an effective range of 2.5 kilometers, but the system operators could lock either passively or actively onto IR signatures well outside of that range. He wanted the high-explosive antitank missiles to simultaneously hit the convoy at the edge of the kill zone, in case the vehicles survived. If the missiles failed, all the vehicles would be in position for the next round of surprises.

"Copy that," said Leeds. "Missile teams. Do not fire early, and do not actively lock onto your target until you're ready to fire. The transition from passive to active lock takes a fraction of a second if you've properly boxed the target. Once you've fired the first missile, ready a second launch tube and stand by for targeting instructions."

By the time the four teams responded, they were seconds away from launching. Through his scope, the first darkened shape appeared in the distance. Everything was on autopilot at this point—he hoped.

Chapter 73

Quinn's eyelids slowly drifted together, the vehicle's vibrations luring him to sleep, when he could least afford the lapse of situational awareness. They still had fifteen miles to go until the convoy emerged from Interstate 8's high-risk border area, where the interstate's closest point of approach would bring them within two thousand feet of the US/Mexico border. A few miles ahead, he would be able to look south and see the wall, supported by fifty-foot metal pylons, which closed the state of California to its southern neighbor.

Despite the towering wall's forbidding appearance, it did little to deter the desert bandits who crossed over to hijack the few travelers foolish enough to ignore the posted warnings, or in some cases to launch large-scale raids against El Centro landowners. They represented little threat to his convoy, but even a blind squirrel finds a nut once in a while, or whatever his dad used to say. Quinn forced his eyes open, taking a deep breath.

"How you doing, Artigas?" he said to the driver.

"Better than you, sir."

He stifled a laugh. "Yeah. Been a long few days."

"I got a few extra energy drinks if you're interested," said the driver, reaching between the seat and the door.

"I'll take you up on that."

The vehicle decelerated rapidly, pulling him against his vest harness.

"Watch it, Artigas," said Quinn, thinking the driver had mistakenly shifted his foot onto the brake while grabbing the drink.

"It's not me, sir!"

Sergeant Graves yelled at Quinn from the backseat. "ECMS is taking evasive maneuvers!"

"From what?" asked Quinn, as the vehicle accelerated dangerously fast toward the back of the Raider One-One.

"Booster plumes detected by Infrared. Tracking four fast-moving UV signatures. High arcs," said Graves. "Shit. Javelin profile. Impact in one-one seconds."

"What do I do, Sergeant?" asked the driver.

"Nothing," said Graves. "ECMS is in control."

"What's going on?" asked Nathan, sounding like he'd just awakened out of a deep sleep.

"Nothing to worry about—yet!" said Quinn, more or less telling the truth.

Nothing any of them did in the next few seconds would make a difference. Their lives were in ECMS's hands for now. Quinn stared through the windshield, searching for the missiles. His vehicle-integrated, night-vision helmet helped him track the inbound threat, placing a faint green icon over each rising missile.

"This doesn't sound like a 'no worry' situation!" yelled Nathan.

Explosive shudders rocked the vehicle.

"Smoke screen out!" said Graves.

"Quinn, what the hell is happening?" screamed Nathan, hitting the back of his chair.

"We're under attack," said Quinn, watching Raider One-One's countermeasures system kick into overdrive.

Externally mounted canisters fired projectiles forward of the lead armored vehicle, which burst into a cloud of burning red phosphorus particles. The vehicle disappeared into the dense cloud, which swallowed Quinn's vehicle moments later, blocking his view. Canisters continued to detonate, their IR-obscuring smoke drifting rapidly across the convoy. Meanwhile, the vehicles' computers communicated, coordinating the superheated smoke screen to best shield them from the Javelin missiles' infrared seekers. Each seeker had locked onto a specific infrared signature, forcing ECMS to pull every trick out of its high-tech hat to confuse the seekers.

"Five seconds!" yelled Graves.

His view through the windshield disappeared again, followed by the sound of water slapping the ballistic glass. When the cloud passed, the lead vehicle reappeared, spraying a high-pressure shield of water as a last-ditch effort to hide itself from the inbound missile. Quinn knew that each AL-TAC carried enough water to cover itself in a thick, cool mist for three seconds.

A short, deafening buzz-saw sound reverberated through the cabin as the vehicle's final countermeasure fired hundreds of steel pellets in the direction of the incoming missile—with the hope of prematurely detonating its warhead.

"Brace for impact! Slam your heads back!" Quinn said, before jamming his helmet into the headrest and activating GIMMS.

When his view through all the windows disappeared, blocked by his own vehicle's water spray, he tensed for the inevitable.

"Impact!" yelled Graves.

CHAPTER 74

Leeds moved a few feet to the right of the scope overlooking the highway a few hundred yards away and lowered his night-vision device. He needed a wider field of view to control the battle that would ensue if even one of the Javelin missiles failed to strike its target, and judging by the incredible countermeasures display unveiled over the past several seconds, this seemed likely. This fight would extend well into the kill zone directly ahead of him.

He caught a blur from the top of his field of view, followed by complete chaos on the road. The missiles appeared to detonate simultaneously throughout the convoy, but it was instantly clear that the attack would not be a complete success. Two of the explosions occurred far too high in the air to be effective against the reinforced armor. That was the first confirmation that this wouldn't be as easy as he'd hoped.

The second was when the lead vehicle flipped into the air and landed on its side, the victim of a very near miss. He knew from the vehicle specifications that the occupants of this AL-TAC would undoubtedly survive. Worse than that, it would come to a stop far outside the ground ambush zone. He'd have to send people out to engage the survivors.

When the smoke and dust from the explosions cleared, the situation unfolded as he expected. The second and third AL-TACs sped into the kill zone, leaving the toppled vehicle behind. The convoy's last

AL-TAC drifted across the open highway median, burning fiercely from a direct hit. He could have used a few more of those.

Leeds turned his attention to the two dark shapes speeding east on the interstate, watching them pass marking posts dug into the side of the road by his team.

"Demo team. Stand by. Passing first marker. Passing second. Blow the road," he said, ducking below the edge of the overhang.

The ground rumbled beneath him, followed by the simultaneous arrival of a crunching blast that knocked the tripod-mounted scope on top of him. For a second, he thought he had miscalculated the effects of the explosive charges set in the highway. He peeked cautiously over the top of the flat ledge, fearful of pavement fragments. His effort was rewarded when both of the Marine vehicles hit the jagged four-foot-deep, eight-foot-wide trench spanning the eastbound interstate lanes and crashed to a stop. One of the AL-TACs almost tipped over from the momentum, rising slowly and dropping sideways along the broken pavement.

He could barely ask for better. Shaken from the demolition charges, he passed what he thought would be the final combat order of the night.

"Missile teams. Reacquire the disabled vehicles and fire your last missiles. Put two on the vehicle outside of the primary kill zone. All ground units hold back. Do not approach until second salvo of missiles has hit."

CHAPTER 75

Nathan had no real concept of what had happened. One second he was asleep, the next, the Marines were yelling. Before he could get an answer out of them, the vehicle shook so hard he was convinced it would flip. Quinn started barking orders, and Nathan could have sworn he heard the turret gunner scream, "One-one is flipped!" Nathan didn't understand everything the Marine said, but he knew that "one-one" was the lead vehicle in the convoy.

A few chaotic seconds later, their own AL-TAC shook violently and decelerated hard enough for the tires to screech. He'd started to reach back for Owen, when Sergeant Graves yelled "Impact!" Out of instinct, he retracted his arm and pressed it against his chest. Time seemed to stop after that. His body lurched forward in the seat, immediately and gently arrested by GIMMS, which let the entire harness ease forward to counter the vehicle's sudden movement.

When GIMMS pulled him back into the seat, Nathan thought their ordeal was over. But before he could try to reach back into the rear compartment again, he slammed forward hard enough to knock the wind out of him. All he could hear was Owen screaming, as the back of the vehicle rose into the air like an out-of-control roller-coaster ride and crashed onto its left side. GIMMS miraculously held him in place as the driver's-side chassis buckled from the drop, shattering the ballistic glass next to Sergeant Graves.

The vehicle rocked for a moment before coming to a halt on its side. Everything mercifully and unexpectedly quieted, which felt like a huge relief, until he realized Owen wasn't screaming. Nobody was screaming. Nobody was making a sound in the dark cabin.

Nathan tried to call out to his family but couldn't form the words, his lungs unable to expel air. He clawed behind his seat, trying to grab one of them, but the harness kept him locked in place. In a blind panic, he ripped at his harness connection points, shaking desperately to get free and reach his wife and son.

"Nathan," he heard, the words sounding muffled. "Nathan. Use your night vision."

That's right! He'd almost forgotten. Nathan patted his helmet, finding the top of the goggles built into it. He pulled downward, sliding them in place over his face. When night transformed into day, David Quinn's face appeared several inches in front of him.

"I'm going to release you from GIMMS. Sergeant Graves is going to ease you down. We flipped onto our side and need to get out of this vehicle, like, ten seconds ago. Do exactly what we say. Don't think. Just do," said Quinn, pulling the handle above Nathan's head three times.

Graves manhandled him out of the seat, letting him fall gently against the rear driver's-side door. He craned his head to look into the rear compartment. His wife was out of her seat, getting ready to pull on Owen's emergency-release handle.

"Careful!" Nathan yelled. "He'll fall right on top of you!"

Keira pulled the handle, releasing their son into Alison's arms. Together, they pulled Owen toward the vehicle's rear hatch, following Quinn. Everything was happening too quickly. Nathan pulled himself up and started to climb through the seats to reach them, but a pair of strong hands held him in place.

"It's quicker this way. They'll be fine," said Graves, pulling him upright until they were standing next to each other, looking up at the undamaged passenger-side door.

"Where are we going?" asked Nathan.

"Anywhere but here," said Graves, sliding the door latch and pushing upward.

The armored door swung open, and Corporal Reading reached in to grab his hand. Reading pulled Nathan out of the vibrating truck and helped him slide into the wide, uneven ditch blasted into the pavement. Owen, Keira, and Alison crouched in front of him, keeping their heads below the surface of the broken asphalt.

Quinn pushed him toward the driver, who was crouched beyond the others. "All of you, follow Corporal Artigas once he goes. We need to get away from the AL-TAC."

"Why ain't they shooting?" hissed the gunner somewhere behind Nathan.

"Because they're going for the easy kill," said Graves. "More missiles."

"Artigas, Graves, Reading," said Quinn. "Pop your IR smoke and spread out."

A distant detonation turned Quinn's head.

"Hurry the fuck up with the smoke," said Quinn, rolling a cylindrical canister underneath the AL-TAC and crouching next to the group. "When I say run, all of you are going to sprint after Artigas to the end of this ditch. Flatten yourself to the bottom, and don't look up until I grab you. Whatever you do, don't poke your head aboveground. Use this mess to your advantage."

Nathan hugged his family as the trench filled with a thick, acrid chemical smoke.

"Go!" said Quinn, pushing Nathan after Artigas and the others into the chemical fog.

He held his breath and quickly overtook Owen and Keira, grabbing his son under the armpits and pulling him against his chest. "I have Owen! Go!" he said to Keira, who tore herself away from Owen and scrambled after Alison and Artigas.

Nathan followed, shielding the side of Owen's head from the sharp chunks of asphalt. Several feet into their journey, the smoke completely obscured his vision. They stumbled a few more seconds, until Keira's hands grabbed them and pulled them down. A swoosh passed overhead, followed by an explosion from the direction of the AL-TAC. Oddly, the blast didn't pack the punch he expected.

"Alison! Nathan!" yelled Quinn, appearing, breathless, behind them. "One of the Javelins missed! We got a second chance. I want you to stay put and stay down. We have a ten-ton piece of armor protecting our back. Most of One-Three's Marines survived, too. They'll hold the other side. I'm taking my Marines back to the vehicle."

"What? Why the hell would you do that?" yelled Alison.

"We can cover you better from the AL-TAC, and I need to use the satcom system to call the air station. They'll send a rapid-response team."

"What the hell are we supposed to do here?" asked Nathan, clutching his son.

"Hold the line," said Quinn, unslinging his service rifle. "I believe you know how to work one of these."

"Barrett M470?" asked Nathan.

"A3 model. Full auto if you want it," said Quinn. "Grab my ammo."

Alison pushed her way through, nearly knocking Nathan over. "You need to stay right here," she said to her husband. "He can't protect us."

"He has to," said Quinn, handing him the rifle. "I have to work on the bigger picture."

A swoosh, followed by a ground-shaking explosion, covered them in chunks of asphalt.

"Captain, we got rockets," yelled one of the Marines. "Unguided shit!"

Quinn quickly kissed his wife and grabbed Nathan. "You're my eyes and ears over here—stay low and report any ground movement. Keep your helmets on."

The Marine captain disappeared into the thinning smoke screen, leaving them alone. Another swoosh passed overhead, detonating with a metal thunk against what Nathan assumed was the AL-TAC. He searched through swirling fog for Quinn, who'd sprinted in that direction. *Shit! If Quinn was dead, they were all dead.*

"I'm fine!" yelled Quinn. "Keep your goddamn head down. You look like a turtle!"

Nathan ducked below the highway, moments before a powerful bullet tore a chunk out of the broken asphalt next to his head. Snaps and cracks passed close overhead as their unseen enemy zeroed in on his position. He wasn't sure how he could hold the line when he had no intention of sticking his head up again.

CHAPTER 76

Leeds studied the scene from a few hundred yards away, careful not to expose too much of his body. The surviving Marines had their hands full with his sharpshooters, but he didn't want to tempt fate. He was well within range of their rifles. From his vantage point in the observation post, he could tell that Captain Quinn had made the best of a bad situation. A few well-placed, infrared-obscuring smoke grenades had sent a $120,000 missile chasing tumbleweeds, leaving the Marines with an intact armored vehicle.

He needed to end this quickly. If Quinn managed to contact Yuma, the night would get extremely complicated. He had several handheld surface-to-air missile systems at his disposal, but shooting down Marine MV-22 Ospreys was something Flagg desperately wanted to avoid. Taking down the convoy would stir up enough controversy—and back-channel trouble.

"Kline," said Leeds, "time to wake up the men you have in median. Next round of smoke grenades, send them in. Start at the northern end of the demolition line. I think that's where Fisher and the rest of the civilians are hiding."

"Copy that. I'll need you to guide them in. I can't see past the tactical vehicle, and the Marines have me locked down."

"I can do that," said Leeds. "What's your progress with the stragglers from the lead vehicle?"

"Snipers report four Marines KIA," said Kline. "Never seen anything like it. Nothing but scrub grass and a few road signs between here and there—and they kept trying."

"Don't get weepy-eyed," said Leeds. "Raven feed shows three more hiding out behind their vehicle. Leave one fifty-cal sniper covering them, and turn the rest loose on the kill zone. We need to wrap this up in the next few minutes."

"Understood," said Kline. "I'm contacting the ground team now."

Leeds pulled the spotting scope in front of him and settled his view on the median west of the demolished section of highway. Eight men crawled out of concealed holes, keeping low in the sandy depression between the eastbound and westbound lanes.

"Kline. I see all eight of your men. Their target is forty feet east. Demolition charges blasted pavement all the way to the median, so they should be able to toss a few grenades and clean up with small arms."

Planting one of Kline's teams in the median had been a stroke of genius. Without them, they would've faced a protracted long-range fight and the prospect of sending their own people down from each side, across open ground. Now the whole thing would be over in a few minutes.

The team squirmed closer, the Marines oblivious to their presence. When Kline's team had closed to within thirty feet, the Marines threw another round of smoke grenades toward the western edge of the perimeter, letting the smoke drift east to give them a short reprieve from Leeds's snipers.

"Kline," said Leeds, "halt your team until the smoke clears."

"Team halted," said Kline. "I'm going to ready an assault team to move against the Marines holding the southern side of the intact tactical vehicle."

"Sounds like a plan," said Leeds. "I'll let you know when the smoke clears."

CHAPTER 77

Nathan crouched over his son and wife, protecting them from the sharp fragments kicked loose by the ricochets striking the chunks of highway piled around them. He popped his head up again to make sure the flat ground beyond the westbound lanes was still clear of shooters. From what he could tell, all the gunfire came from the ledges and low hills a few hundred yards beyond the highway's shoulder.

He glanced to the left, seeing another billowy cloud of smoke drifting toward him. Thank God. The volume of gunfire slackened significantly for a minute or two, while the smoke screen obscured accurate fire. Satisfied that the northern flank was secure, Nathan was dropping his head back into the trench when he detected movement in his peripheral vision.

He kneeled on the ground next to his family, not sure what to do. If he looked again, before the smoke arrived, a sniper might drill him through the forehead. Corporal Artigas had taken a large-caliber bullet to the head firing the vehicle's heavy machine gun from the front passenger door. Nathan had been relieved to hear the vehicle's big gun pounding away at the hillside. When he glanced toward the vehicle to see the gun in action, the corporal's headless body dropped into the vehicle. He was pretty sure it was headless. The body had fallen like a rock. Quinn appeared in the same spot a few moments later, pulling the machine gun through the open door. A second bullet struck the door inches from the captain's head, closing the door on top of him.

A dense blanket of chemical smoke poured into the ditch, rolling east down the highway. Whatever Nathan had seen out there was close. Too close. He had to do something before the smoke screen cleared. Nathan crouched low and whispered to Keira, "There's something out there. Really close. I'm gonna hop out and take a look while I can."

Bullets hissed overhead, causing him to duck. Maybe he should yell for Quinn.

"Are you crazy?" asked Keira. "Let the Marines deal with this."

"I don't think there's too many of them left," he said, pressing Alison's shoulder. "David's fine. I just saw him."

Alison didn't respond. She stayed crouched against the side of the ditch with her back to the rest of them.

"I'll be right back," he said, rising a few inches.

Keira yanked him down again and pulled his face to within inches of hers. Her eyes blazed. "You move *fast* and stay low." Both of them were shaking and breathless; when they kissed, their teeth knocked together. "I love you," she said. "Don't do anything stupid. Just check and get back in here."

Nathan tasted blood from their kiss. He bent down and kissed Owen's head. "Keep your mom safe, buddy."

His son grabbed his arm. "Don't leave us."

"I'm not leaving, buddy," he said. "You'll see."

Having no real plan, Nathan flipped the selector switch to semiautomatic and crawled over the craggy asphalt onto the median. He lay on the rough gravel, peering into the corrosive smoke, his visibility reduced to a few feet beyond the M470 rifle barrel. The screen drifted quickly by. He didn't want to move, but staying in place wouldn't help the situation. *Shit.* He really had no idea what to do, besides aim the rifle in the general direction of the movement he'd thought he'd seen. What if he didn't see anything? He'd be stuck out here when the smoke screen dissipated. Easy pickings for the same sniper who'd taken Artigas's head off. He had to do something, and slithering back into the hole wasn't an option. Not anymore.

Nathan thought of Owen and Keira for a moment, accepting the fact that he might never see them again. With that heavy thought weighing him down, he managed to move his left arm forward along the gravel, followed by his right arm. Before he realized it, he was low-crawling toward the westbound lanes. When his rifle barrel touched the side of the highway, he crawled parallel to the upraised road, his body shielded from the northern hills, and aimed the rifle toward the eastbound lanes—waiting for the smoke to clear.

Dark human shapes slowly materialized along the edge of the east-bound lanes, aiming rifles toward the exploded section of highway hiding his family and Alison. The commando closest to the ditch leaned on his side and cocked his elbow back to grab something underneath him. Nathan centered the M470's green ballistic reticle on the side of the man's head and slowly applied pressure to the trigger, but the man moved—rolled onto his back and put his hands together, then separated them quickly. Despite the remaining smoke, Nathan knew exactly what the man had done. He found the man's head again, and the rifle bucked into his shoulder; the man's head snapped backward against the ground—the grenade rolling off his chest.

Nathan shifted his aim to the last man in the group and squeezed off a single 6.8mm bullet before the grenade detonated. The blast tore into the closest operatives, showering the line with shrapnel and shoving Nathan against the raised highway bed. Two men farther down the line, and out of immediate blast range, rose to their knees and scanned the area directly behind them. Nathan fired twice at each of their heads, seeing them drop instantly.

He worked his rifle back and forth over the group until nothing moved. A cylindrical canister skidded across the highway toward him, from the direction of the Marines. *Why the hell would—*

A deafening crack pounded his face into the gravel.

CHAPTER 78

David Quinn threw the smoke grenade, jumped down from the AL-TAC, and sprinted in Nathan's direction. Fisher had done something incredibly brave but hopelessly reckless—and now he was just lying there waiting to be killed. A loud snap passed next to Quinn's head, dropping him into a crouch as he ran into the fresh cloud of billowing smoke, bullets chipping away at the pavement by his feet. The volume of gunfire increased when he disappeared into the fog, the gunners situated in the hillsides desperate to hit something. With ricochets smacking the ground and near misses zipping to his sides, Quinn knew it was only a matter of time before he was hit. Reaching the edge of the eastbound highway lanes, he threw himself to the ground next to the dead bodies, yelling for Nathan.

"Don't shoot. It's me!" he bellowed, crawling frantically in Fisher's direction.

A bullet struck Quinn's helmet, knocking his head forward.

Jesus! Where the hell are you, Fisher?

"Nathan! Answer me!" Quinn yelled, a sharp pain creasing his left shoulder. "Damn it, Fisher!"

"I'm here!" said a voice to his left. "I think I'm hit."

He scrambled toward the voice, bumping into Nathan, who hadn't moved from the prone position tucked against the highway.

"We're exposed here," said Quinn. "Let's go."

"I can't move."

"Where are you hit?"

"I think in the head."

You think? Quinn ran his hands over the outside of Nathan's helmet, finding it intact. If a bullet had penetrated the ballistic layering, the entire helmet would be cracked.

"Nathan, I can't find anything wrong with your helmet. Did you get hit anywhere else?"

If Fisher was paralyzed, they were in trouble. He couldn't carry or drag him back to the ditch quickly enough to stay ahead of the snipers—and he'd thrown the last smoke grenade to protect Fisher. The screen currently protecting them from aimed fire wouldn't cover the entire return trip.

"I think one of the bigger calibers hit my helmet," said Nathan. "I saw what it did to Artigas."

What? Quinn slapped Nathan's leg as hard as he could.

"Hey! What the fuck?" yelled Nathan.

Nathan wasn't paralyzed. Quinn grabbed the back of Nathan's tactical vest with his free hand and pulled him up, trying to get him on his feet.

"We can't stay here. The smoke is thinning," he said, tugging against Nathan's unwilling mass. "The next bullet will find its mark."

With Fisher finally up, they ran through the thinning smoke, breaking into the open fifteen feet away from the protective ditch. Quinn caught a glimpse of two helmets protruding above the pavement where Alison should be, before he was knocked backward by a hammer blow to his chest. He slammed into Nathan, who grabbed him under both arms and kept him from falling to the road. Bullets snapped past them and chipped the asphalt as Nathan pulled him toward the ditch.

Chapter 79

Keira peeked beyond the edge of the jagged, asphalt-chunked ditch, searching for her husband through the smoke. An explosion had rocked the side of the road a minute ago, throwing gravel and chunks of pavement into the trench. The sounds of nearby gunfire, mixed with screaming and groaning, resonated from the median—until everything went momentarily silent. She'd popped her head up in time to see Quinn barrel across the highway lanes and disappear into a new smoke screen. The shooting intensified a few seconds later, followed by yelling. A bullet struck the pavement inches from her face, stinging her cheeks with tiny asphalt fragments. She ducked and grabbed Alison.

"David is out there with Nathan," said Keira. "I don't know what they're doing."

"Damn it, I knew your husband would get him killed," said Alison, raising her head to see.

"Careful," said Keira, her warning emphasized by an overhead crack that caused them both to duck.

"Where is he?" asked Alison, lifting her head again. "There!"

Keira pulled herself high enough to see two figures emerge from the smoke. Quinn had a hand on Nathan's vest, pulling him toward their ditch. They ran a few feet before Quinn stumbled backward into Nathan, stopping their momentum. Her husband grabbed Quinn under the armpits, keeping him upright and tugging the Marine slowly toward Keira and Alison.

Without thinking, Keira started to pull herself out of the trench, but Alison yanked her back.

"Stay with Owen," said Alison, scrambling over the broken chunks of highway.

Keira launched forward, angry with Alison for stopping her, oblivious to the woman's gesture. By the time Keira reached the edge, Quinn's wife had traveled most of the distance to their husbands. Alison had just extended a hand to help Nathan when a dark softball-size hole punched squarely through her back, tossing her forward like a rag doll. Her body skidded across broken asphalt face-first, grinding to a lifeless halt several feet past Nathan.

Nathan dropped to a knee, still holding on to Quinn. Her husband contemplated Alison's body for a moment, before standing up and continuing to pull a staggering Quinn toward the ditch. Keira glanced down at Owen, who looked up at her.

"Stay here no matter what happens!" she yelled.

As soon as he nodded, she sprang out of the gulley, hell-bent on making sure nobody else died tonight. She reached Quinn and pulled one of his arms around her shoulder. Nathan adjusted his grip, and they ran with Quinn for the longest few seconds of her life before piling into a ditch. Keira slammed the front of her helmet against a protruding chunk of road, the impact jerking her head backward, and everything went dark—but she was still conscious.

"I can't see!" she screamed. "I can't see!"

Keira tried to stand, but a strong pair of hands held her down.

"Stay down!" said Nathan, working on her helmet.

The sheer darkness yielded to a shadowy, monochromatic, deep-orange glow that outlined the uneven edges of their refuge.

"Your night vision is busted," said Nathan.

"We have to get Alison," she said desperately.

"Our only job is to protect Owen."

She started to crawl toward her son, who crouched at the end of the twisted gulley, looking like he might risk a peek over the lip of the asphalt.

"Stay down, Owen!" she yelled, as a gloved hand grabbed her arm.

"Where's Alison?" groaned Quinn.

Keira didn't know what to say, or how to say it. Even under the brutally matter-of-fact circumstances of combat, she had no idea how to tell Quinn that his wife had been killed. She stared at the barely discernible silhouette of his face.

"She's gone, David," said Nathan, crouching next to them. "She ran out to help. She's gone."

Quinn struggled to stand.

"Hold him down!" said Nathan, wrestling to keep Quinn in place.

Keira took an elbow to the face but kept struggling to hold Quinn down as bullets struck the warped edges of the trench.

"David!" she screamed at him. "She's gone."

Quinn released a broken, animal howl, thrashing against them, and then finally sagged to rest at the bottom of the ditch.

Footsteps crunched on the broken ground of the trench behind them, causing her husband to spin with his rifle. The outline of a combat helmet was superimposed against the yellow-orange glow of the vehicle burning behind the overturned AL-TAC.

"Watch where you're pointing that," hissed Sergeant Graves, pushing past Nathan. "Captain. We're in a bad way back here. I can't hear you on the squad radio."

Nathan began to speak for Quinn, but the Marine spoke for himself, his voice ravaged. "I took a hit out there. Couldn't hear you after that," he said, trying to get up. "Help me grab Alison."

Sergeant Graves put a hand on each of Quinn's shoulders and held him down, kneeling in front of him.

"Alison is dead. She died very bravely—and very instantly," said Graves. "I need you focused here, sir. Staff Sergeant Cantrell's team popped their last smoke, and they're starting to take hits. Raider One-One reports possible enemy reinforcements. Parachutists."

"What?" asked Quinn. "Parachutists?"

"That's what they're fuckin' saying. I just got the report. They landed close," said Graves, flinching from a nearby bullet impact. "Those fifty-cals are doing some damage. We need to find another position or we won't be around by the time Yuma puts a bird in the air."

"This is it," said Quinn. "Without smoke, we can't leave the highway."

"Then I guess we make the best of it," said Graves. "I need you back at the vehicle, Captain. The M240 doesn't shoot by itself—and I think these two can hold the northern flank."

"I'm coming," said Quinn, turning his head in Alison's direction.

"David," said Keira, grabbing him by the elbow. "Don't."

"We'll get her later," he whispered, rubbing his face. "If there is a later."

Keira and Nathan crawled several feet to the end of the ditch, sandwiching Owen in between them as a burst of gunfire swept across them.

"Daddy's back, sweetie," she said. "We're both back."

"Where's Alison?" asked Owen, trying to raise his head to look.

Keira forcefully held him in place. "I want you hugging the bottom of this ditch."

Nathan crouched next to them. "She's not coming back, Owen. Listen to your mother."

"She left her phone behind," said Owen.

"What do you mean?" asked Keira.

Owen twisted between them, opening his hand. "She dropped this when she left."

"Can I see it, buddy?" asked Nathan, taking it after he nodded.

Keira couldn't see the device very well in the dark-orange light, but she knew it was something she'd never seen before. It appeared half as wide as a typical mobile device.

"What is that?" she said.

"I have no idea," said Nathan, pressing a few of the buttons.

The device's screen activated, glowing dark green. A compact, backlit keyboard illuminated below the screen.

"I told you she had a phone," said Keira.

"This isn't a phone. It looks like military-grade equipment," he said, touching the stubby, foldable antenna. "Satellite communications."

A text message scrolled across the screen.

```
Friendly units on the ground south of
interstate. Assembling for attack. Advise
captain.
```

"What is this?" asked Keira.

"I don't know," said Nathan, typing with his thumbs.

"What are you doing?" she asked, reading the screen as he typed.

```
Alison KIA. Who is this?
```

A few seconds passed before a response appeared.

```
Identify yourself.
```
Nathan started to type.

"I don't think that's a good idea," said Keira. "We don't know who that is."

"Only one way to find out," he said, pressing "Send."

```
Nathan Fisher. Who is this?
```

The answer arrived instantly.

```
CLM. Get this to Captain Quinn ASAP.
```

"How is that possible?" asked Keira.

"I'm not sure," said Nathan. "But I need to find Quinn right away."

Chapter 80

Back in the AL-TAC, Quinn took the radio handset from Sergeant Graves and stared at it, still in a daze from witnessing Alison's lifeless body sprawled on the highway during their scramble to the vehicle.

"Captain!" said Graves. "Talk to One-One! They're getting panicky!"

Quinn nodded, slipping the handset under his helmet and pushing it against his ear.

"Raider One-One, this is Raider Actual. Send your report again. What are you seeing?"

A panicky voice filled his ear. "Didn't Graves tell you? I got a platoon-size group moving toward the hill from the south. They dropped in about a kilometer back."

"Dropped in? By parachute?" asked Quinn, convinced Graves had misheard the radio transmission.

"Yes! By parachute! I already passed this information. They glided in out of nowhere using square rigs. Never saw them until they started hitting the ground."

Quinn did the math. They couldn't hold on against a reinforced enemy. His Marines were pinned down from multiple directions, unable to put their weapons to effective use without sustaining casualties. Nathan's wild card, surprising the enemy as they advanced from their hiding places in the median, had bought them a little more time, but the writing had always been on the wall. Now it flashed bright neon. They would all die here when this new paratrooper platoon arrived. There was no question in his mind about that. The quick reaction force from Yuma would find nothing but death here.

"Raider One-One," said Quinn. "I'm ordering you to head southwest. Use the vehicle to cover your withdrawal and get into the hills. Get as far away as possible. They won't have time to pursue you."

"Captain, we're not going anywhere. We can still put some fire down on these fuckers."

"Who am I talking to?"

"Corporal Cerda."

"Cerda, are you the senior Marine present at your position?"

"Affirmative. Lieutenant Karr and Staff Sergeant Jax were killed in the last attempt to move our position forward."

"Then it is your responsibility to see that the Marines under your charge survive this. You're too far away to make a difference here. I need you to make a difference *there*. You have to clear the area. Yuma's quick-reaction force is still twenty minutes out. I'm giving you a direct order to withdraw," said Quinn. "Someone has to survive this."

He heard an excited voice in the background through the handset.

"Corporal Cerda. Did you copy my last?" asked Quinn.

"Captain. I need to confirm something. Stand by," said Cerda.

What the hell? This isn't a committee decision. The level of gunfire outside the AL-TAC intensified, immediately followed by a maelstrom of metallic clangs against the armored hull of their makeshift command center. *This might be the end.* Quinn poked his head out the door above him—coming face-to-face with Nathan Fisher. Without thinking, he let go of the handset and grabbed Nathan's vest at the front collar and pulled him headfirst through the door. Nathan bounced off the turret-harness mechanism and landed on his back against the broken driver's-side window.

Quinn kneeled next to him. "Are you out of your mind?" he yelled. "You're supposed to stay with your family!"

"You need to see this," groaned Nathan, digging through one of his cargo pockets.

He didn't have time for this. Quinn turned and searched for the radio handset, finding it in Sergeant Graves's hand.

"Quinn!" Nathan barked. "Alison had some kind of satellite communications device. You have to read this."

Quinn took the radio handset from Graves and looked down at Nathan, who held a familiar device in his hand. It resembled the plaintext, secure satellite communications devices they'd distributed to informants in Afghanistan. Why would Alison have one of these?

"I think she left this with my son on purpose," said Nathan, stretching his arm further. "They're here."

"Who's here?" muttered Quinn, hesitating to take the satellite communicator.

"California Liberation Movement," said Nathan. "I think Alison was working with them."

Quinn grabbed the device, activating the screen and reading the first few lines on the screen. *Jesus. How did Alison get caught up in this?* He scrolled through several more lines, then looked at Nathan. "Are you absolutely positive this is Alison's?"

"Owen said she left it behind, when she—" Nathan didn't continue.

Quinn nodded slowly, raising the radio handset to his ear. "Cerda. Are you still there?"

"Affirmative. Did you copy my last?" asked Cerda. "You dropped out on me, sir."

"Negative. Send it again."

"The platoon halted about a hundred yards from the hill," said Cerda. "I think they left a few behind to cover their approach, but I can't find them."

"Copy your last," said Quinn. "Disregard my previous order. I want you to stay in place. I think these are friendlies. Stay frosty until we know for sure."

He gave the handset to Graves. "Only one way to find out."

Quinn held the device in both hands and started typing.

CHAPTER 81

Kline placed his rifle sight's two-hundred-yard reticle mark at the left edge of the pavement hunk and began to apply pressure to the trigger, waiting for a hint of movement before firing. There it was. The powerful SCAR-H battle rifle kicked into his shoulder, knocking the sight picture askew. He didn't need to see the impact to know that his bullet had found its target. The Marines below fired fully automatic bursts to cover the withdrawal of their downed comrade.

That was the fourth hit his team had registered in the past two minutes. This would be over shortly, despite the unfortunate setback in the median. Without looking, he issued a hand signal to the assault-team leader twenty yards away. His signal redeployed them along the crest of the hill directly east, where they would pour concentrated gunfire into the Marines from a new angle. He decided against using them in a direct-action attack after his median team was annihilated. They'd lost enough tactical team operators tonight. He'd send them down when the odds were squarely stacked in their favor.

"Sierra-One," said Kline, designating the message for his sniper squad. "Alpha-Three is moving into position farther east. Look for Marines repositioning when they open fire."

A few seconds passed before he received a response. "This is Sierra One-Three. Copy."

"This is Sierra One-Five," he heard, followed by silence.

What the hell was wrong with their gear now? This was supposed to be top-of-the-line, battle-tested gear.

"Sierra One-Five, this is Kline," he said. "Say again, over."

"This is Sierra One-Three," said a panicked voice. "One-Five is down. I think a few of the Marines got behind us."

"Negative," barked Kline. "We've been watching them from the start."

"I'm taking suppressed fire from—"

While Kline waited for the sniper to finish the report, gunfire rippled across the hillside directly east. *Damn it.* He hadn't given the order yet. When he looked east along the hill, he saw Alpha Three firing south—in the wrong direction.

"Alpha Three, check your fire. Disregard Sierra One-Three's report. Concentrate your fire on the highway."

"Negative! Negative! This is Trenker. I'm taking effective fire from the south. I can't see it," said the team leader, who was crouched next to a small boulder on the south face of the hill.

While Kline watched, the sand exploded around the smooth rock, enveloping the operative. When the fine cloud dissipated a few seconds later, the team leader lay on his back, trying to push his way behind the boulder. A burst of gunfire stitched the sand, catching the operative across the chest. *Shit.*

Kline reacted instinctively, launching his body across the crest of the hill and rolling several feet down the northern face. At least he knew what he was up against on this side. He came up from the roll with his rifle pointing toward the Marines below. Flashes erupted from the highway, the bullets not far behind.

CHAPTER 82

From his position on the northern ridgeline, Leeds peered beyond the highway, momentarily forgetting about the convoy. He couldn't be sure what was happening to the south. None of the reports made sense, and Kline had stopped transmitting. His operatives situated in the low hills south of the interstate had straddled the crest of the hill, firing in both directions to little effect. A few had tumbled down the north face. The Marines had finally put the M240 into action, firing at Kline's operatives from a protected position on the opposite side of the overturned AL-TAC. Snipers on Leeds's hill didn't have a visual on the machine gun.

"Vega. What's happening over there?" asked Leeds.

He'd sent the Night Raven toward Kline's position as soon as Alpha Three confirmed an enemy attack from the south.

"Thermals show eighteen heat signatures moving up the southern face of the hill in three groups of six," said Vega. "I have an undetermined number of snipers hidden about two hundred yards due south of the hill. I don't know how they got this close without being detected."

"How many men do we have alive on that hill? Can you find Kline?"

"It's hard to differentiate. They're all on the ground."

"Just try! Look for muzzle flashes. Movement. I need to know if this is over."

"Stand by," said Vega.

Stand by? This could be over before he finishes counting. Shit! Leeds glanced at the four-wheel drive, custom-built Sportsmobile van at the bottom of the hill behind him, wondering how long it would take for him to boogie down the uneven hillside. He was a good two hundred yards from the van and the rest of the assault group's desert-capable vehicles.

Vega's voice crackled over the radio. "I see four active shooters in a consolidated position to the east. Possibly the remains of Alpha-Three. I can't identify Kline," said Vega. "Hold on—shit! I have a group of hostiles cresting the western side of the hill."

Bullets snapped overhead before Leeds could respond, forcing him to lie flat. He slithered feetfirst down the rock behind him as the sand around his abandoned spotting scope exploded skyward. The operatives hidden in positions around him fired back on full automatic, turning the hillside into a staccato free-fire zone.

"This is most definitely over. I'm ordering a full withdrawal. Put the Night Raven in a high-altitude circle over the kill zone," said Leeds. "Shut everything down except for the Raven feed. We need pictures of everything and everyone on the ground. I have no idea who we're dealing with here."

"We'll have to bring the bird in pretty low for that," said Vega.

"As long as we get clear pictures, I don't care what happens to the Raven," said Leeds, activating the tactical net. "Maclean. Kline has been overrun. Keep your team in place on the hill long enough to give us some breathing room. Don't linger. Use the ATVs to catch up."

"I got it, sir," said Maclean. "Where the hell did they come from? I thought Kline cleared the area south of his position."

"He did. Very carefully," said Leeds. "See you a few miles due north. We'll stop and load up the ATVs if we have the time."

Leeds started down the hill with the surviving snipers, taking it slow enough to stay in control of his descent. He reached the bottom of the hill out of breath, pausing for a moment and turning toward the hill. The rapid automatic fire from the Marines' M240 machine gun dominated the battle, burst after burst echoing down the hill. One of Maclean's operators flew backward and rolled halfway down the hill before sliding to a stop in the sand. Leeds was losing too many people.

"Maclean. Pull your team back."

"We can hold a little longer!"

"You can't hold them off with that two forty in action," said Leeds. "Load up and get out of there."

He didn't wait to see if Maclean listened. Leeds dropped the scope and sprinted for the van. He reached the oversize all-terrain van as a few of the other vehicles skidded out in the desert sand. Glancing around at their fleet of eight vehicles, he wasn't sure they'd have enough people left to drive all the SUVs away from the site.

The van door facing the hill swung open and Vega appeared, extending a hand down to Leeds. "I split the Javelin teams between the vehicles when I saw how many you had coming off the hill," he said.

Leeds could barely talk from the sprint. "Let's go."

Vega pulled him inside as the van lurched forward, knocking them both to the metal deck. Lying on his back, he glanced out of the sliding door. Three ATVs raced down the hill after them, and for a split second, Leeds wasn't sure if the ATVs were friend or foe.

"Who is that?" Leeds asked, pointing at the hill.

Vega slid the door shut. "Maclean."

Leeds glanced at the technicians seated at their stations. They stared at their screens, pretending not to see him. He pulled himself into the front passenger seat and took several long, deep breaths.

"You know where you're going?" Leeds asked the driver.

"Heading to the first evasion waypoint."

Leeds glanced at the windshield HUD, making sure they were headed north. "Vega," he said, "I want to know if we're being followed."

"I'm watching closely," said his lead tech. "Looks like foot mobiles only at this point, and Maclean took all of the ATVs. I don't see any way they can catch up with us."

"This group is full of surprises," said Leeds, thinking about something Flagg had said: *Fisher has more than one guardian angel watching his back.* He wasn't exaggerating. More like an army of guardian angels.

Leeds opened one of the pouches on his vest and removed an encrypted satphone. There was no point in delaying the inevitable. Flagg needed to know. He pressed Flagg's contact icon.

"Yes?" asked Flagg.

"It didn't work."

A long silence passed before Flagg spoke.

"How bad is it?"

"Bad. I'm headed north to the first evasion waypoint with all of the vehicles and approximately twenty personnel," said Leeds, not adding, *out of the sixty-one I dragged into the desert.*

"I see," said Flagg. "Continue to follow the waypoints. Observers in Yuma report a flight of three Ospreys readying for immediate departure. You need to be pretty damn close to Route 78 by the time they reach the ambush area."

"We'll make it."

"Part of me hopes you don't make it, but most of me hopes you do—just to see the look on your face when you hear what *we* have to do to make this right," said Flagg, disconnecting the call.

Leeds didn't like the sound of that at all. It almost made him wish he wouldn't make it, too.

CHAPTER 83

Quinn kneeled on the rubble-strewn pavement, holding his wife's body in his arms. He pressed his forehead into her matted hair, crying silently against the side of her face. He didn't want to believe she was gone. It felt like she'd fallen asleep and he was carrying her to bed. He wanted that to be true so desperately.

"Captain Quinn, I need you to make a decision," said a serious-looking, bearded Hispanic man wearing a black-and-tan-checked shemagh around his neck. "We can take your wife with us so you can bury her properly. Sorry to push you, but I can't be here when your Ospreys arrive."

Quinn turned to look at Staff Sergeant Cantrell and Sergeant Graves, who stood behind him, waiting for him to answer the man. He knew what he wanted to say, and where he wanted to go, but he still had a duty to protect the Marines assigned to what little was left of the convoy. How many Marines were dead because he was protecting Fisher?

He'd failed to protect Alison, who gave her life trying to protect him. All the lives lost, including the one that meant most to him in all the world. All of them gone, and all of them on him. He glanced at Nathan's son loaded in the back of one of the dune buggies idling on the highway. Another life. On him.

"Sir?" asked Cantrell. "You still with us?"

"What?" asked Quinn, squinting and blinking his eyes to clear his tears. "Yeah. Sorry. I'm here. Still here."

Cantrell crouched behind him, putting a hand on his shoulder. "Go with them, Captain. Air support is twenty minutes out. We got this."

"I don't want to leave you guys," said Quinn. "Not after I got you into this."

"Sir," said Cantrell, looking him straight in the eyes, "this is what we do. What we did here is no different than what we do overseas. Just different bad guys."

"Gentlemen," pressed the Hispanic man, who Quinn assumed to be this mystery group's commander.

"Go with these guys," said Cantrell. "Take Alison with you. You won't get a moment of peace with her if you come back with us. You'll be lucky if they don't lock you up as soon as we arrive in Yuma. Seriously, sir. I think you can find some closure with these people. A little payback for all of us. I get the impression this won't be the last time they tangle with the people responsible for this ambush."

"I don't know."

"We're good here, sir," said Graves. "Poncho Villa's crew swept the area for us."

"I'm just as American as you," snapped the Hispanic-looking soldier. "Whatever was left of the ambush group fled north across the sand. Probably hit the Coachella Canal Road a few miles north of here and eventually connect with Route 78."

"Set up observation posts on both hills," said Quinn.

"We got it," said Cantrell. "The natives are looking restless. You better get out of here."

Quinn nodded. "All right. I'll go with you, but I'm not making any promises about getting involved in your fight."

"I'm not asking you for anything," said the man. "You've given enough."

He knew better than to believe that. They'd recruited his wife for a reason, and it likely had something to do with him.

"What do I call you?" asked Quinn.

The man grinned. "Jose—until I know I can trust you."

"I don't think we'll be spending that much time together."

"Maybe," said Jose, his face darkening. "Maybe not."

CHAPTER 84

Sand pelted Nathan's face below his night-vision goggles as the dune buggy tore through the sand toward the border. He reached next to him to check his son's harness strap again, paranoid that the constant jostling might have loosened it. They sat side by side behind Keira and the driver, in raised metal bucket seats bolted to the buggy's sparse chassis, their only protection from the outside elements provided by steel caging mounted to the squat-roll bar frame. Not exactly a design that inspired confidence. He tugged on the strap, which didn't budge. Owen wasn't going anywhere.

"Hold on!" yelled the driver.

Before he could think to respond, the buggy launched over the bank of a dry gulley. Free of the tires' vibrations against the ground, they sailed peacefully through the air for a few seconds, before slamming to the hard-packed sand on the far side. His wife screamed and clutched the bars in front of her as the buggy picked up speed again, spitting sand skyward in thick plumes behind them.

"Do it again!" yelled his son.

"No! No! Do not do that again!" yelled his wife.

The driver gave her a thumbs-up, but Nathan wasn't sure what that meant. A couple of seconds later, he found out. They hit a small dune, catapulting the buggy into the air again. His wife didn't scream this time, even when the vehicle landed on its left tires first, jerking the buggy right.

"Woo hoo!" screamed Owen, as the vehicle settled into the sand and took off again at breakneck speed.

Keira took her left hand off the bar directly in front of her seat long enough to give Owen a shaky thumbs-up.

The driver eased into a turn to avoid a long, narrow hill, which could have been mistaken for a sand dune from a distance. When they passed the smooth, boulder-strewn rise, the landscape opened onto a flat, sandy area pockmarked with dark-green splotches.

Not vegetation. Some kind of billowing, synthetic fabric.

The rest of the dune buggies and ATVs in the convoy spread out and approached the area slowly. As their buggy decelerated, Nathan reached for the rifle strapped to the back of Keira's seat, ready to release the quick mounts keeping it in place. This was his life now. Grabbing for a rifle at the first hint of abnormal.

"You don't need that," said the driver. "We won't be here long."

The vehicles stopped, and a few dozen soldiers jumped to the sand from the other vehicles, running toward the billowing green shapes. Parachutes. Nathan had wondered how so many soldiers had reached the highway so quietly.

Within a few minutes, most of the men were headed back carrying overstuffed parachute bags. Four of the soldiers arrived at Nathan's dune buggy, dropping the heavy bags in the sand behind the vehicle. They went to work immediately, barking orders in Spanish as they strapped the bags inside the wide gear tray attached to the buggy's rear bumper frame.

He studied them carefully, convinced they were different from the small group that didn't stray far from "Jose." The differences were subtle, but potentially important. His family's safety was in Jose's hands for now, and Nathan sensed that something was off with these new men.

He'd studied Spanish from elementary school through his senior year in college, and these men spoke a rapid, fluent Spanish that he barely understood. They didn't use school-taught *español*. They spoke an authentic, idiomatic version among themselves that made Jose's quick-paced Spanish sound hopelessly Americano.

That wasn't the only difference. Jose's crew carried themselves like the kind of independent special-forces operators you might see on a TV news segment, trekking through the Taliban-controlled hills of Afghanistan. Competent and alert, but marching to a less structured though no less effective beat. These men, though, reminded Nathan of Marines. They moved with the practiced efficiency of a rigorously drilled, cohesive unit. And they carried the same essential gear, without variation. Same rifles, same night-vision goggles. Same boots. Same tactical vests. All gear he didn't recognize, especially the rifles.

They didn't directly belong to Jose's special-operations group. He was willing to bet on it.

When the four men sprinted away, he leaned forward and whispered in Keira's ear. *"Fuerzas especiales—Mexicanos."*

"Probablemente," replied Keira.

"I speak Spanish," said the driver. "And this is not a Mexican Special Forces troop."

"Then what is it?" asked Nathan.

"It's *not* a Mexican Special Forces troop, or any unit affiliated with the Mexican government."

"Right," muttered Nathan.

It made sense in a big-picture kind of way. The Mexican government stood to gain from California's secession. They would be able to approach the new California government on an even economic footing with the rest of the states, unburdened by federal trade restrictions. This was bigger news than the Sentinel connection. The parachute landing, if discovered, could ignite a border conflict, drawing everyone's attention away from the real enemy—the One Nation Coalition.

"Tighten those harnesses," said the driver. "The ride gets a little rough up ahead."

"That wasn't rough before?" asked Keira.

"It gets worse."

"Where are we going?" asked Nathan.

"You haven't figured it out yet?" he said.

"We didn't bring passports," said Nathan.

"I left mine at home, too," said the driver, gunning the engine.

They sped ahead of the other vehicles, picking up speed as they crossed the open area. From his seat, Nathan could see the dimly lit navigation console aimed toward the driver, who maneuvered the buggy to keep the course arrow matched to the track arrow, taking them to the next waypoint. They were headed almost due south. Unless the border wall had been breached, Nathan wasn't sure how they would get through. As promised, the buggy bounced over nasty terrain for a few minutes, before the desert opened wide—revealing the border wall in the distance. The buggy slowed as it approached, but not as much as he expected given their rate of closure with the towering structure.

Several ATVs and buggies passed them as their driver slowed, merging into a single column ahead of them. The wall continued to approach at a crazily rapid pace, as if none of the drivers could see it. Another buggy zipped past, chasing the line, distracting Nathan from the looming disaster ahead. When he turned his head forward again, half of the line had disappeared. Vehicles disappeared one by one, the barren landscape in front of the wall methodically swallowing them.

Their buggy slowed at the last possible moment before dropping below the surface of the desert on a steep decline. The ramp ended abruptly, jolting them against their harnesses, as the ride leveled. Keira turned her head toward the center of the buggy, most likely squeezing her eyes shut. He felt like doing the same. At forty miles per hour, the tunnel redefined claustrophobia. The timber-reinforced walls and ceiling seemed close enough to touch, and the tunnel ahead didn't look wide enough to pass through.

Nathan closed his eyes and held Owen's hand, reminding himself how lucky he was to still have his family. A ghastly image flashed through his head, and he squeezed Owen's hand tighter. Luck had nothing to do with it: a lot of good people died to give him this, and he wouldn't forget that.

He suspected the CLM wouldn't let him forget it either.

They had taken a serious risk mounting this rescue operation, committing extensive resources to a gamble that could have backfired in any number of ways. He couldn't help think that the CLM had higher expectations of him than just giving his testimony regarding the stealth boats near the Del Mar nuclear desalination plant. The information contained in his master's thesis had barely scratched the surface of what he'd learned about the intricacies and vulnerabilities of the Colorado River water-distribution system.

If they wanted his help analyzing the dams and associated infrastructure, he'd have to carefully weigh the implications of his decision against the safety of his family. Family came first, no matter how much he'd like to deliver a toppling blow to the One Nation psychopaths responsible for attacking his family and killing Quinn's Marines—not to mention Alison Quinn. Nathan had a tough choice ahead of him.

A bump knocked him against the top of his harness, and he opened his eyes in time to see a spray-painted plywood sign zip past them.

"What did that say?" he yelled.

"Bienvenidos a Mexico!" replied the driver.

Acknowledgments

In no particular order—maybe. Always a conspiracy lurking in my words.

To my readers: Obviously, I wouldn't be here without you.

To the Thomas & Mercer team: I couldn't have put *Fractured State* in better hands!

A special thank-you to my editor, Kjersti Egerdahl, for guiding me gently through the Thomas & Mercer experience. She took my "slightly" different ending in stride! It has been a pleasure, and I look forward to writing more books under her guidance.

Thanks to David Downing for an insightful, humorous, and most important, productive developmental edit. Ivan Kenneally for an incredible copyedit. I accept your changes—all of them! Jacque Ben-Zekry and Sarah Shaw for creating a wonderful family environment for Thomas & Mercer authors. They're always there for me. Finally, Alan Turkus. I wish him the best with his new career. Thank you for keeping our conversation alive!

Thanks, also, to an incredible author-support group: Russell Blake—I'm drinking margaritas (or straight tequila) with you one of these days, and the first round is on me. Joseph Souza—miss our coffee meet-ups. R. E. McDermott—fellow swabbie and one of the funniest guys I know. Murray McDonald—longtime friend who taught me everything I know about guns and scotch. I meant to say gun control and scotch. Randy Powers for feeding me an endless stream of Internet articles covering the drought in California and our natural-resource challenges. Tom Abraham for our fun conversations about all things writing. Bobby Akart for his unwavering support—look who's flying like an eagle now! Sean Fitzgerald—his contributions are classified. The Pine Cones Writers Den, an extraordinary collection of writers in Maine . . . miss you all. Theresa Ragan, who has been an inspiration and a fantastic friend. And finally, Blake Crouch—I wish you the continued smashing success you've worked so hard to achieve . . . thank you! This list is really just the tip of the iceberg.

Last, but certainly not least, thank you to my wife, Kosia. None of this would be possible without your tireless support, endless ideas, and dead-on critique.

ABOUT THE AUTHOR

 Steven Konkoly graduated from the United States Naval Academy in 1993, receiving a bachelor of science degree in English literature. He served the next eight years on active duty in various US Navy and Marine Corps units, traveling the world extensively as a naval officer. His travels spanned the globe, including a two-year tour of duty in Japan, which brought him to more than twenty countries throughout Asia and the Middle East.

From enforcing United Nations sanctions against Iraq as a maritime boarding officer in the Arabian Gulf, to directing aircraft bombing runs and naval gunfire strikes as a forward air controller (FAC) assigned to a specialized Marine Corps unit, Steven's "in-house" experience with a wide range of regular and elite military units brings a unique authenticity to his thrillers.

Steven lives with his family in central Indiana, where he still wakes up at "zero dark thirty" to write for most of the day. When off duty, he spends as much time as possible outdoors or traveling with his family—and dog.

You can contact Steven directly by e-mail (stevekonkoly@stribling-media.com) or through his blog (www.stevenkonkoly.com).